SUNSET OVER CHERBOURG

(The adventures of Jamie on the *Alabama*)

by
Harry McLeish

"SUNSET OVER CHERBOURG" is based upon the factual history of the *Alabama* and its exploits in the American Civil War. However, except where historical facts exist relating to people, events, places and artefacts, this is a fictional work about fictional people and any resemblance to any person, living or dead, is purely coincidental.

First published 2001 by Countyvise Limited,
14 Appin Road, Birkenhead, Merseyside, CH41 9HH

Copyright © 2001 Harry McLeish

The right of Harry McLeish to be identified as the author of this work has been asserted by him in accordance with the Copyright, Design and Patents Act 1988.

British Library Cataloguing in Publication Data.
A Catalogue record for this book is available from the British Library.

ISBN 1 901231 24 0

Acknowledgements

There are many people to thank.

This book is dedicated to those friends who have helped me in preparing this great adventure story merging fictional characters (too numerous to mention) with historical fact.

Thanks to friends who have read and corrected this manuscript - Bill McFarland, of Beaverton, Oregon, Kate Skinner, my nephew Alan Francis, Marc Jaffee, of Brooklyn, New York, Brian Leeson, Steve Riordan, Frank Weighill and the late Ray Dunbobbin (ex. Brookside) along with others who have given valuable advice, particularly Bill McMath for his help and support in publishing this book.

Thanks to my many friends in Cammell Laird (where the "Alabama" (vessel No. 290) was built in No. 4 dock), Probus and Rotary Clubs, Amateur Operatic Societies, the Merseyside Submariners Old Comrades Association and Old Bootelians. John and Jean Emmerson of the publishers, Countyvise, have always given advice, guidance (for a first time author) friendship and encouragement.

Finally my especial thanks to my wife Sheila, for her patience and helpful co-operation.

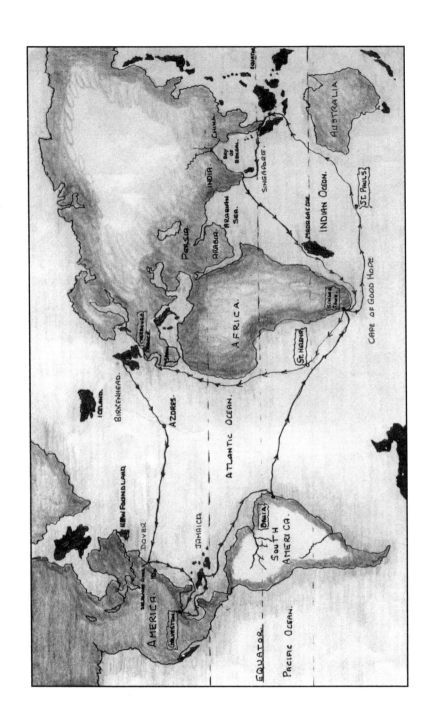

Chapter 1

Following the morning service, the harmonious tones of the pipe organ in the Toxteth Presbyterian Church echoed a voluntary through the porchway and could be heard by the congregation gathering in groups outside, greeting each other on this cold January morning in 1862.

The well-dressed Mr. Freeman puffed contentedly on his pipe, addressed the tall, well-built Jamie MacPherson, who was standing with his wife and daughters:

"Welcome home, Jamie," he said, shaking hands with the wavy haired, brown-eyed young man. "How was your last Transatlantic sea voyage?"

"The sea was rough," Jamie answered in his soft Scottish brogue, "what you would of course expect this time of the year. It was Christmas and I certainly missed the New Year Hogmanay, which did not please the family. However I have an extended leave, which we will enjoy together, as I've brought gifts for Matilda and Victoria and a teddy bear for young Anne," and with a chuckle and a smile he added: "I'm sure we will enjoy a late Festive season."

He paused to wrap his scarf around his neck before proceeding.

"How are things in the port? I've missed the home news these last months sailing the Atlantic. Incidentally, the news is grim over there - the Civil War is now eighteen months old, with heavy casualties on both sides, so I was glad when I left America."

Mr. Freeman re-lit his pipe before replying.

"There's a lot of gossip around the port. We don't seem to be getting the cotton, iron and grain from America - I suppose it's because of the blockade on the Southern ports! Even in the shipyard across the river, where I work," he paused looking intently at Jamie, "there's intrigue and gossip about the building of a mystery ship - she hasn't even got a name! Only the current yard number 290. She is being built for an American gentleman named Mr. James Bulloch. I'm in charge of fitting and testing a new type of engine in this 213-foot long wooden schooner."

"That sounds interesting," butted in the eager Jamie, "Please tell me more."

'The engines are direct-acting, twin horizontal, which turn a shaft, fitted to a propeller at the stem, and which can be hoisted out of the water when not in use."

"That is totally different from my last steamship," Jamie reflected. "which had the popular side paddles, but I did visit a similar steel ship on the River Clyde last year and I was puzzled how such a long shaft could turn the propeller. Quite ingenious, this future design!"

"I tell you what, Jamie, you seem to be interested and you seem to have a lot of sea-going experience, I'm looking for a fourth engineer at the shipyard and you're just the engineer to fill the vacancy." He paused to light his pipe.

"It sounds a good proposition, Mr. Freeman."

"The money will be less of course, but think about it and talk it over with your wife."

Matilda, who had been listening intently to their conversation, quickly intervened:

"As far as I'm concerned, Jamie, I would accept the job as I'm sure the girls and myself would love to have you working from home."

'Well...' pondered Jamie, 'here's a chance to start a new life in this progressive shipyard in Birkenhead.' "Yes, I will accept your kind offer."

"Good, I'm very pleased. You'll enjoy working with my engineering team in this rapidly developing shipyard - it's called the Birkenhead Iron Works, and Mr. Jonathan Laird is the Managing Director." Freeman consulted his diary.

"I will expect you on Tuesday 3rd February. Report to my office at 5-30, and, in the meantime, Matilda, Jamie, enjoy yourselves and have a good seasonal holiday.'

Mr. Freeman doffed his top hat and bade them a cheery good-bye. On the way home from the chapel in Oldham Street to their home in Fairview, which was situated about half a mile from the docks, Jamie and his wife chattered away very excitedly about the new turn in their lives.

"How are you going to travel to the shipyard by 5.30 every morning?" asked Matilda. Jamie pondered for a while about this question.

They had arrived at their beautiful furnished white washed cottage, which commanded a fine view of the River Mersey. The weather was bleak and snow was threatened. Jamie pointed across the river."There's the shipyard, and there"- pointing -"is the ferry, which conveys passengers, horses and carriages across the river from St Nicholas Church, just nearby. I would be working long hours, just like when I served my apprenticeship on the Clyde. When I was a 15-year-old youth I began at 5.30 in the morning and finished late. Mind you I was in lodgings in Greenock, within five minutes of the shipyard." Jamie paused, thinking that might be the best idea, lodge near the yard and come home at week-ends, then perhaps I could work longer hours and earn more money.'

Matilda remarked "On the other hand you could get up at about 4 o'clock and arrive home here about 8 o'clock in the evening and after a wash and a meal it would be time for bed. That's not much of a life - I think we will look for lodgings in Birkenhead."

So that was settled! The family continued enjoying their holiday which included a trip sailing on the River Mersey.

They had a breezy day trip on the ferry, sailing to Birkenhead. The children had an exciting time, running around the dock in and out of the carriages and then pausing to stroke and fondle the horses. Jamie pointed out to the interested Matilda the numerous ships in the river. "There," indicating, - "a barque - a brig - and look at the fine lines of that Yankee clipper! and there's the paddle steamer with its long funnel, sailing on the return journey to Liverpool.

Leaving the ferry, hand in hand, the happy family wandered into Birkenhead, visiting various houses until Jamie found lodgings in 23 Cleveland Street, near Hamilton Square, which was about fifteen minutes from the iron works.

Jamie rose early at 5 o'clock on the 3rd February in his   lodging. Mrs. Isa Gillies, the widowed Scottish landlady, brought him a bowl of hot water for washing and shaving. It was cold. He drew the curtains aside and wiped the misty window with his hand. The street looked lovely and white, the snow was falling lightly and he shivered and quickly dressed, putting on his thick warm trousers and a heavy woollen Jersey over his shirt. He applied shaving soap, strapped his open razor and nearly cut himself when Mrs. Gillies shouted up "Jamie you are going to be late, your porridge is on the table."

He hurried down, added milk and salt to the porridge and then gulped a mug of tea, wrapped a thick scarf around his neck, donned his heavy short black coat and cotton cap and grabbed his luncheon sandwiches. He said cheerio and thanked the buxom Mrs.Gillies, who looked at him with a smile and wished him good luck on his first day in the shipyard.

He dashed down the street, not wanting to be late on his first day, and bumped into another young man coming out of a doorway.

3

He apologized and they hurried along, chatting away, mainly about the weather and then about the shipyard into Hamilton Square.

"Mr. Jonathan Laird, the shipyard boss, lives over there in number 63." His companion pointed. "By the way, my name's Alex MacKenzie."

His deep bass voice indicated that he came from far north of the Border, 'Too far' thought Jamie, who could hardly understand the Gaelic-accented English. "I'm Jamie, I was born on a farm near Aughtergaven in Perthshire. I served my apprenticeship on the Clyde and this is my first day at the shipyard."

They hurried through the old Priory churchyard of St Mary's and entered the shipyard by the Monks Ferry entrance.

Jamie found Mr. Freeman's office after being instructed by Alex. He knocked timidly on the door and hearing 'Come in,' took off his cap and positioned himself in front of the Chief Engineer's desk. "Glad to see you, my boy." He was about twelve years older than Jamie and about the same height, "And glad to see that you are warmly wrapped up, wearing strong boots for you'll need them. Take care when you descend the steep slippery steps of number four dock." He paused to light his pipe, "I would like you to meet the other engineers. Report to Mr. Eric Knowles - he's in charge. You'll find him working on the staging on the stern end."

"Thank you, Mr. Freeman," Jamie replaced his cap and was about to depart, when Mr. Freeman addressed him again. "I'm sure you will be interested in fitting this new type of propeller, it's been especially designed in the drawing office, by Mr. Frank Weighill our Chief Designer. It can be lifted out of the water and housed in a specially designed compartment. He is very experienced in this type of work and I would like, sometime in the future, for you to get together with Weighill, as I'm sure you might have some ideas to pass on from your past experiences in your sea-going life." He stood up. "Best of luck, Jamie and I'm pleased you are part of my team."

Jamie quietly closed the door, left the office and walked down the ramp known as Monks Ferry.

He paused at the head of number four dock and viewed with awe the bow of vessel number 290 and was amazed to find it was built (so a passing lad said) of the finest English oak and not steel. Jamie walked along the quay wall on the port side of this 213 foot long, well-shaped ship, viewing its fine lines, and approached the top of the steep icy stairway. He cautiously grabbed the right-hand rail and carefully, step by step, slowly descended all 215 stone steps (so he counted) to the wet, muddy bottom of the dock.

'That was steep and dangerous. It's cold and damp at the bottom of this dock.' He shivered and noticed - 'Ah, there's a brazier, I'll join the lads for a warm.'

It was gloomy and smoky but the brazier glowed red with the heat. Four men were warming their hands and chattering away. Jamie joined them and listened to their conversation which concerned an explorer named MacGregor Laird, who apparently was the brother of the present owner, Jonathan. A big brawny man approached and tossed some wood on to the fire. Sparks flew and he laughad loudly. He sounded Irish! "That will warm you up. Hi there stranger, I'm James Brennan."

"Hi there, I'm Jamie MacPherson, a Celt like yourself, but born in Perthshire."

"Meet the rest of the lads, - we'll all be working together."
Jamie shook hands with Samuel Williams and in his lilting Welsh accent he in turn introduced Jamie to Jack Winters. "Now he's an interesting mate to get well in with Jamie. His father is the ticket collector at the Adelphi Theatre and usually has a few tickets over. I'm sure he'll pass some your way!" They all laughed, 'I might hold him to that,' thought Jamie. What a friendly lot of mates. 'Time to look up Mr. Eric Knowles and begin earning my living.'

Jamie walked through the mud and slush underneath the sheath-covered bottom of the ship and watched the carpenters fitting the Swedish manufactured copper sheathing to the bottom of the hull. He came to the stern end and looked up at the staging where four men were working, fitting the propeller. "Mr. Knowles," called up Jamie. A well-built man in his early fifties, a large spanner in his hand, looked down. "I've been expecting you. Make your way up the ladder, take your time and be careful - it's very slippy." "I'm Jamie MacPherson." He shook hands with the firm-gripped Eric. "Yes, you're just in time to assist in hoisting up this new propeller into position. I must first explain, it is fitted into these steel guides and is hauled up by rope."

5

"Alex, will you help Jamie to haul up the propeller". Jamie was agreeably surprised to recognise his early morning companion. They spat on their hands, took a firm hold on the rope and began hauling up the propeller with the help of a block and tackle. It was eventually housed in a safe position in a compartment in the hull.

Mr. Knowles then examined the guides and eased them with a file. The guides were cleaned and grease applied and the propeller was hoisted up and down several times until it worked. It reminded Jamie of the French Revolution, which he had read about in his father's books - how a guillotine was used for beheading the French political prisoners. That had been just before be was born - how horrible. "Jamie, stop day dreaming," shouted Mr. Knowles and then in a more friendly tone - "I would like to introduce Alex MacKenzie. He hails from Scotland, hundreds of miles away, you both should get on well together, being Scottish. It will be the engineer's job, in the next few days, to make sure the propeller can be hoisted up and down and safely housed when completed and then the next job will be on the main engines."

The three engineers continued working on the moveable propeller, at the same time chatting away. Jamie was interested in Alex.
"So you come from the Outer Hebrides Alex?" "Aye," rather a slow reply, in his deep Gaelic accent, "It's a God forsaken island," continued Alex, "where time has stood still. I was educated on the mainland and worked as an engineer on a fishing boat and during one trip it came to Liverpool for repair and I heard they were looking for engineers in this shipyard. Jamie, pass me that file, let's, complete this job and go home, it's been a busy day."

Jamie was able to get home at weekends to be with his family. So the weeks drifted by. In the engine room Jamie really interested himself in this new type of horizontal engine, designed to drive through a long shaft a fitted propeller, not, like a paddle steamer, fitted amidships.
'Must have a word with Mr. Weighill the chief designer about my ideas of a permanent propeller on the end of a long shaft, in a steel ship and not a wooden vessell' thought Jamie.

It was a beautiful Monday morning in May. Jamie was down on time at the shipyard working on a steel spring fitted to a valve on the main engine. He viewed out of the corner of his eye, a well-built stranger, balding, with side whiskers, dark brown penetrating eyes, looking at the gauges and the fittings. 'Very curious he seems to be,' thought Jamie, as he came round the engine. "My name is James Dunwoody Bulloch, who are you?"' remarked this tall well-dressed gentleman, facing the 28 year old young man. "I'm James MacPherson, sir, an engineer employed by Mr. Laird." Bulloch smiled, detecting a strong Scottish accent!

"I'm from Georgia in America and I'm very interested in the building of this unique ship. I hope you don't mind if I have a look around and perhaps you could explain some of the finer details of this engine room." "Certainly sir". 'Must humour this gentleman. In fact he could be a friend of Mr. Freeman or Mr. Laird,' thought Jamie. 'I wonder why an American is interested in this extra-ordinary ship? I must try and find out!'

Little did Jamie know but number 290 was no ordinary ship and Mr. Bulloch was not just a curious and interested person, he had served as an Officer in the United States Navy before joining the Merchant Marine and was in fact the owner's representative. The steamship '*North America*' had brought Bulloch from Canada, from the south via Detroit and Lake Erie. He had sailed from Montreal and arrived in Liverpool on 4th June 1861. James Bulloch would set in motion and trigger off a series of events that would bring the American Civil War right into the heart of Merseyside. Yes, he had business in Liverpool and Birkenhead across the Mersey that was to be anything else but ordinary. On his arrival in Liverpool he was to meet Charles Prioleau who worked for the cotton merchants Fraser Trenholm and Company whose offices were at 10 Rumford Place. They were linked with Charles Fraser and Company in Charleston, South Carolina (which was the first Southern State in December 1860 to secede from the Union.) There was no doubt Bulloch had something very special in mind when he visited Mr. Laird in the Birkenhead shipyard.

He did not want anything ordinary, but something outstanding and the best ship for the cause, which was of course for the Southern States. He had been specially chosen by President Jefferson Davis to order (ignoring the cost) a wooden barque, as this could be repaired anywhere in the world, whereas the repair of an iron ship was very limited and costly, and their technology was new and not every shipyard could cope with such a ship. So on 1st August 1861, the Confederate order was placed for a Merchant vessel and the contract simply named the vessel as the current yard number 290. She was built of the finest English oak with iron fastenings and her bottom was sheathed with copper to reduce fouling. This mysterious vessel shrouded in secrecy was now nearing completion and on a mild Tuesday 17th May, the carpenters lowered the two long masts into position. This enabled her to carry large fore and aft sails, which are of course so important to any steamer in an emergency and she had an added speed with her twin horizontal engines and the newly designed propeller which could be raised out of the water.

Jamie could not help but ponder as he viewed these long yellow pine masts being carefully lowered and securely wedged into their cradles in the bowels of the ship. He could picture them bending in a gale like a willow wand without breaking, and the rigging was of the best Swedish iron wire. Back in the engine room, Jamie was working on something he had experienced before. It was the apparatus for condensing the vapour of sea water, into all the fresh water the crew could drink. He had actually been the engineer-in-charge of this similar apparatus when he had previously crossed the Atlantic. The boilers were already in position and all piped up ready for firing. Jamie arranged for about eight tons of coal to be hauled up from the bunkers and gave the necessary instructions to Iain Grinham, the senior fireman, who was ably assisted by Sam Williams, Jack Winters and George Doyle, four hard-working firemen who amidst grime, sweat and coal dust succeeded in the first trials for the boilers to roar into life and for Jamie to report to Mr. Freeman that he had power on the main engines.

On the 31st May, number 290 was floating in the dock. Mr. Freeman started the main engines and the trial lasted three hours, the engines performed sweetly and satisfactorily. Alex MacKenzie's job was to examine the main coupling bearing, to see and feel that they did not overheat.

"Sir, the correct pressures are maintained on the boilers," reported Jamie.

"The bearings are cold and the shaft is running at 4-0 revolutions," replied Alex. "That is perfect" remarked Mr. Freeman, "we shall have a further trial on Monday 9th June and in the meantime Jamie and Alex, will you please log the pipes and the cylinders and if necessary ask Eric to advise you in which store to obtain the lagging. You might find him on the quay attending to the chain and anchor."

The eighteen-and-a-quarter ton chain for the anchor had been weighed by the engineer Eric Knowles, also the two-and-three quarter-ton anchor. Eric's job was to report all weights to the designer, Mr. Weighill, so he could calculate the draught markings, which to date was 10-8". The displacement of the vessel was 832 tons as compared to 690 tons at launch in the dock, that is allowing for the hull alone being 655 tons.

So with the anchor stowed in position and the chain safely housed in its locker, the dock was again flooded for the second engine trial which was to take place on Monday 9th June.

Jamie was up bright and early to make sure everything was satisfactory for the second trial. On his way to work along Cleveland Street he entered the old Priory Churchyard of St Marys. Jamie had learned from a booklet how it had been shelled and gutted by Oliver Cromwell's troops positioned on nearby Bidston Hill and how the soldiers came and murdered the Monks and looted the Priory.

Jamie continued through the churchyard, stopped and removed his cap, looking reverently at the gravestone of William Laird and his family - the founder of the Birkenhead Iron Works and father of the present owner John Laird. What a tremendous personality and drive he must have had mused Jamie to have created and built this shipyard and brought employment to the people of Merseyside. He reverently doffed his cap and entered the shipyard. Arriving at number four dock, he viewed the magnificent barque secured with ropes to bollards on the quayside, walked up the railed gangway and made his way into the engine room, there to be greeted by the other three engineers. They were awaiting Mr. Freeman to start the main engines for the second sea trials.
"Did you have an enjoyable week-end Jamie?" asked Eric. "It was very interesting. We had our usual walk around the busy docks - I always enjoy viewing ships from all over the world and listening to sailors' yarns and Matilda and the girls always like to visit the old sailor's church at the Pier Head."

"It is one of the oldest in dockland," chipped In Eric, "'and its correct name is 'Our Lady of the Sea - Saint Nicholas' and naturally it has a very strong connection with mariners who have brought various relics and archives from all over the world to adorn this magnificent old established chuch."

"Listen my friends," said Jamie to Eric and Alex, who joined them, "I heard some interesting and disturbing gossip from a seaman I met in the church. Do you remember I mentioned I met an American gentleman prowling round the engine room a week ago - Mr. James Bulloch - well, rumour has it he is a spy for the Southern cause and apparently this vessel is going to be eventually a man-of-war and what is more a Cunard Captain has been appointed named Matthew Butcher, who lives in Stanhope Street in Liverpool, and this ship is going to be his first command."

"Rubbish," retorted Alex. "You have been listening to dockland rumours."

"Furthermore," Jamie was now getting really wound up and ignoring Alex's remark, "it was said that recently the pressure was mounting on Bulloch, because there had been complaints at a very high level even to the British Government from the American Consul, Thomas Dudley in Liverpool, which they could not ignore, that this vessel is no ordinary ship and her purpose anything but peaceful. We know that this wooden barque has a designed speed of thirteen knots, that its funnel is retractable and its propeller can be lifted out of the water to make it more streamlined. We know these facts and that it's also been designed for long distance cruising - you can tell by the huge coal bunkers and look even these engines," turning with pride, Jamie concluded, "were built and tested to latest Admiralty standards."

"Now I come to think of it, " said Alex. "Do you remember how that Southern Irishman, Sean McNaught was snooping around the ship asking all kinds of questions?" "Indeed I do," remarked Eric. "I got angry one day when he butted in when I was doing a very important job and I chased him. I bet he was a spy or investigator." How true it was.

The conversation ceased when Mr. Freeman appeared.
"All is ready to start the main engines, sir," Eric remarked. "Very good, - open up the necessary valves, Alex,"
"Is steam pressure on the main engine, Jamie?"
"Yes sir," was his prompt reply.
Mr. Freeman slowly moved the starting lever, and the 300 horse power engine slowly throbbed into life.

The trial lasted three hours and the Chief Engineer was very pleased. He congratulated his team and was satisfied with the 50 revolutions obtained from the main shafting.

Following a longer third and last trial on Thursday 12th June it was decided by Jonathan Laird and Mr. Bulloch that the ship was ready for her christening and commissioning ceremony, following which would come her sea trials in open waters.

Everything that Bulloch had planned was taking place.

It would not take much to convert number 290 into a man-of-war; in fact things were taking their course in this direction, but an uneasy Bulloch decided he could no longer keep up this pretence.

Tbe British Government could no longer ignore American Consul Dudley' s complaints. Questions were being asked even in the Houses of Parliament. Rumour also had it that the United States warship the U.S.S. *'Tuscarora'* was steaming to the Mersey, intent on stopping Number 290 leaving 'one way or another.'

Tuesday 29th July was the christening day for 290. Jamie was pleased and so were his friends because they were invited to take their families for this important event in the life of the ship. Matilda and the young girls were excited. Dressed in their Sunday best frocks they proceeded from their home in Fairview, crossed the River Mersey on the ferry and made their way through Monks Ferry Gate.

Jamie, leading the way, clutching Anne and Victoria's hands, rushed up the gangway, followed by Matilda and they joined Mr. Freeman and his family on the main deck. All the children were pushed to the front for a better view, where they could see the large christening bottle poised near the main mast.

It was a magnificent sight - the excited crowd on the deck with ladies and gentlemen dressed in their finery and the vessel be-decked with flags and bunting.

Suddenly there was a hush, as marching up the gangway appeared Mr. Jonathan Laird accompanied by Mr. Bulloch with a lady dressed in sombre black (quite unbecoming, thought Jamie, in this carnival atmosphere). The procession of dignitaries was led by the smartly uniformed Mr. Matthew Butcher and the crowd parted as they made their way on the deck and the lady in black (rumour had it she was Mrs. Bulloch) took up position between the wheel and the main mast. There was a pause, then she took hold of the bottle which was secured to the mast three feet above her head by a thin rope. The crowd fell silent, watching with awe, wondering what was coming next. She exclaimed in a deep American accent. "I name this ship *Enrica* and may God bless her and all who sail in her,' and she crashed the bottle against the main mast. Mr. Bulloch and Mr. Laird both gripped the five-foot double wheel, gave it a spin around amidst a mighty cheer. Susan, Alex's daughter, presented the lady in black with a lovely bouquet of blue and white flowers to mark the occasion.

'Well that was a very unusual and different way of christening a ship," imused Jamie, having seen one previously on the River Clyde.

About one hour passed and the children where running around the deck having a good time. Groups gathered chatting and laughing. Everybody seemed in a jolly mood, the wine flowed freely, served by the ship's staff who were mostly Lairdsmen. The menfolk gathered amidships. Jamie was rather confused by what was happening. There seemed something sinister in the air especially with Mr. Bulloch on board. Mr. Freeman approached Jamie. "Find Mr. Knowles and Alex and report to the engine room. Alert the firemen to light the boilers and when there is enough pressure report to me, I'll be on the main deck with the Captain."
Jamie carried out the orders and on completion, reported up on deck to Mr. Freeman, who then reported to the Captain.
'Mr. Butcher, the engines are available, sir."
'Very good Chief Bosun, man your stations and prepare to get under way."

Mr. Bulloch took command.
'Ladies and gentlemen, I'm afraid all good things must come to a close. Thank you for coming to witness the naming of this ship. We are now going to proceed with sea trials. Jamie escorted his family to the quayside.
"I'm afraid I've got to leave you now Matilda as we are about to undock and proceed to sea. As far as we know we are going to Port Lynas in Anglesey to complete the sea trials and from there we will be ferried ashore and we will make our way home."

Jamie hugged and kissed his little girls and turning to his wife, embraced her fondly.
"Listen my dear, if we don't complete sea trials successfully I may be away a little longer, because I don't know where we are sailing to from Anglesey, but do not worry and take good care of things until I return, my love."

With a final kiss and fond farewell and a wave Jamie proceeded up the gangway, along the deck, still waving and descended into the engine room.

Once the pilot Mr. Patterson was on board and the gangway and ropes removed by the sailor gang the Captain gave the order through the engine room voice pipe.

"Start main engines and work up to four or five revolutions." The engines throbbed into life, the last rope was thrown ashore and the dock gate opened. The 'Enrico' slowly eased her way into the River Mersey amidst tumultuous cheering from the dockyard workers and their families and proceeded under steam to Seacombe.

Bulloch made an announcement that he wanted the vessel to go to the mouth of the Mersey for extra trials. A steam tug came alongside and embarked Mr. Bulloch and the dignitaries aboard and the 'Enrica' sailed slowly and gracefully down the river.

Chapter 2

By now Captain Butcher knew the plan. 'Enrica' was never to return to Merseyside. He dropped the pilot, Mr. Patterson, at the Bar Lightship and set course under sail for Moelfre Bay in Anglesey.

On Woodside landing stage next day, there was a party made up of forty-two Merseysiders, from all walks of life. Some were handpicked men; carpenters, experienced seamen, gunners, cooks, riggers; most of them ex-Royal navy reserves. Another bunch apart from the rest looked very bleary-eyed, some with damaged faces and limbs as though they had been in a brawl. Actually they had been having a quiet drink in the Paradise Tavern in Dale Street, enjoying themselves, when the tough "press gang" appeared. Fighting broke out and they finished up on Woodside Pier next day, were "escorted" on to the tug *Hercules* by Mr. Bulloch and some American naval officers, taken to Moelfre Bay and "assisted" on to the "*Enrica.*"

The ex-Cunard Captain standing on the poop deck alongside Mr. Bullock orderd the bosun to assemble the crew on deck while the ship was anchored in the bay and Mr. Bulloch addressed the men. Mr. Freeman said he would attend to the engines and ordered Mr. Knowles, Jamie and Alex on deck.

Mr. Bulloch, a short, stocky man, balding, with sideburns, stood on a raised platform and looked at the seamen.
"Gentlemen, we have reached our first rendezvous and we nearly have a full crew. Some of you, I understand, are volunteers, but most of you are shipyard workers, for whom there is still some outstanding work to complete, particularly by the carpenters. We have brought materials to finish the job and the final intention of this ship is to be a man-of-war and serve the Confederate States of America. Some of our engine trials still have to be completed and I would ask the engineers to complete the trials by our second rendezvous in the Azores. If any man does not wish to continue with us he is welcome to disembark here, in Anglesey. I will give

you a little time to think it over, but having declared this vessel as a future Confederate ship, we have heard strong rumours that the United States steamer *"Tuscarora"* is steaming from the south to try to intercept us, so try and make your minds up soon.
Thank you gentlemen."

The engineers quickly assembled to discuss the startling news!
"This is something very sudden and unexpected," said Mr. Freeman.
"Part of our contract with the owners is to complete the trials as we are still paid by the company. However if you wish to return to the shipyard you are at liberty to do so and you can now go ashore and arrangements can be made for you to be transported back to Birkenhead."
"I'm expected back from Port Lynas." remarked Eric Knowles. "However I will stay on to the Azores until the engine trials are completed."
"So will I," declared Jamie and Alex simultaneously.
"Well, we are all agreed," remarked Mr.Freeman. Let us get back to the job and prepare the engines for sailing and I'll report to the Captain."

Nobody went ashore, so next morning the 'Enrica' sailed for open waters into the Irish Sea, through the treacherous 'narrows' between Scotland and Ireland and round the Irish coastline to hove-to off the Giants Causeway.

Bulloch and Butcher suspected that the U.S.S. 'Tuscarora' was rapidly overhauling them to intercept the 'Enrica'. Bulloch transferred to a fishing vessel and 'Enrica 'headed for open waters, under full steam round the Irish coast. At the same time the 'Tuscarora' arrived at Moelfre Bay, but there was no sign of the enemy, so the Union vessel retreated south for normal duties with her navy.
Meanwhile the 'Enrica', under the command of Captain Butcher hugged the Irish coastline and when she reached the southern tip headed starboard thirty degrees for open waters, heading for the island of Terceira in the Azores.
Eric, Alex and Jamie, having time off after completing a successful engine trial (which took one week) were relaxing, leaning on the port rail, when a cry came from Anthony Malony - the fiddling Irishman up aloft.
"Land a-hoy! on the port beam."
Most of the crew rushed to the for'd port bulwarks and all eyes focused on the hazy horizon ahead in the distance. It looked

indistinct at first in the distance and then white houses could be seen dotted in the hills.

"I've never been to these islands before,' exclaimed Jamie. "Have you Eric, Alex?"

"No, my sea trips were around the Clyde in a coastal paddle steamer," said Alex in his broad Scottish accent.

"I always find it interesting and exciting visiting a place for the second time," remarked Eric. "I was in these waters about five years ago, when the ship berthed at the Azores to re-fuel and take on fresh provisions."

As the '*Enrico*' approached the harbour of Porto Prava, the rendezvous, Captain Butcher, scanning through his telescope, detected the masts of two ships in the harbour, which signified to him that Bulloch's plan had materialized.

James Bulloch's secret plan, conceived back in early August in Birkenhead had worked. Accordingly when the steamship '*Bahama*' arrived from Nassau and berthed at Woodside Ferry, on board was Captain Raphael Semmes of the Confederate Navy. A tall, lean man with deep penetrating eyes, he sported a curly, waxed moustache. He was born in Maryland in 1801 and educated as a midshipman, a studious youth who studied numerous subjects - accountancy, politics, beside seamanship and all about square rigs. He also studied Maritime and International Law and was eventually admitted to the Bar.

In 1837 Semmes had become a Lieutenant and took part in the Mexican War. He then returned to his hometown of Mobile where he was employed as a lighthouse official, eventually becoming secretary of the board, stationed in Washington.

When the Civil War was declared, he resigned from the U.S. Navy and journeyed south to the capital - Montgomery. He was given command of a mail steamer and quickly converted her into the '*Sumpter*' - a man-of-war. She became the first Confederate raider and played havoc with the Northern fleet. Finally Semmes received orders from Richmond to go to Nassau and travel to Birkenhead.

Bulloch gripped Semmes firmly by the hand as he stepped ashore for the first time on British soil.

"Have a good trip, Raphael?" "Yes, indeed," he replied in his Southern drawl. "The '*Bahama*' behaved magnificently in the bad weather and survived the storm."

Bulloch remarked. "Well, you will be pleased with your new command, the '*Enrica*'. I understand she's at present on her way to the Azores."

"Mr. Bulloch, I would like to introduce my fellow officers. One of my oldest friends, we have served together many years, Mike Kelly, who will be the First Lieutenant: Lieutenant William Armstrong from Georgia, Second Lieutenant: midshipman Joseph Hardman, whom I promoted on the '*Sumpter*', he will be the Third Lieutenant: my Fourth Lieutenant is also an American - Michael Lawson who comes from good Naval stock, an experienced and professional Naval Officer: Hornby Lowe of Florida will be the Fifth Lieutenant, a gunnery officer. Meet the junior ship's Doctor Graeme MacGregor from Liverpool and Lieutenant Murdo McKenzie of the Marines. Unfortunately, the paymaster and postmaster, Kenneth Andersen," Semmes laughed, "is in prison, but I'm sure he will be joining us later." Semmes paused, looking around the assembled officers. "I understand Mr. Joe Mills has already presented himself as he was residing in the village of Sefton. You know James", the Captain took Bulloch to one side. "I don't trust that man Andersen, at one time he worked for the enemy". "Also I nearly forgot, on the '*Enrica*'" butted in Bulloch, "we have the senior ship's Doctor Maurice Edwards who was born in Ireland, but brought up in Wales - an excellent surgeon I understand - it seems," - Bulloch smiled, "though we have quite a few Scots, Irish and some Welsh on board."

"I also understand you have nearly managed to persuade Mr. Raymond Freeman and three engineers to join us from the shipyard, on pretence that they are only on sea trials as far as the Azores. We shall see - wait till they hear about the carrot I'm going to dangle before them!"
"Well, the best of luck, Raphael, and may God go with you. By the way - how are things back home?"
"Not so good. We win some and we lose some battles. I'll tell you later."
"I forgot to mention. Some steerage officers will be joining us later this evening from Liverpool."
"Well, gentlemen", said Bulloch, addressing the assembly. "When we have wined and dined at the Royal Hotel just up the road, I will explain the rest of my plans."
So later, when they had settled down in the hotel to serious wine drinking and pipes and cigars were lit, Bulloch went into detail. He mentioned that when the '*Enrica*' was hove-to in the Azores the plan was to change her roll and name, from a merchant ship into a fighting man-of-war. This had involved buying another vessel, - the '*Agrippina*' - which was loading in London docks with coal, guns, ammunition, uniforms and supplies. When these were stored on board, she would also head for the Azores. To a man the seated Confederacy gentlemen stood up and applauded and congratulated James Bulloch, the master spy, on a job well done, and the evening

concluded with several lusty renderings of "Dixie" then they retired for the night in the hotel. In a few days time they would be in the Azores to join their new ship.

No wonder Butcher on the *'Enrica'* was looking anxiously through his telescope, at the harbour in Praya Bay. He was relieved to detect spars of two ships and as they approached, signals were passed identifying each other as the *'Bahama'* and *'Agrippina'*. 'What a relief' thought Butcher, 'that Bulloch's plans were successful.' The crew of the *'Enrica'* let out a big cheer that echoed across the harbour.

James Bulloch immediately took charge of proceedings on the leeward side of the island in calmer waters as the *'Enrica'* nestled between the *'Bahama'* and *'Agrippina'*. Both began unloading their cargoes.

Every man turned to, while Mr. Freeman remained in the engine room in case of a quick get-away.

"Eric, Alex, Jamie," shouted Mr. Freeman, above the noise and din of loading, "Look out for the main engine spare gear parts; and stow them in their correct lockers in the engine room."

"Have you any idea which ship brought the parts, Mr. Freeman?" asked Jamie.

"Yes, I'm glad you've asked, the *'Bahama'*." The engineers contacted the *'Bahama's'* crew members who located the spares and these were soon stored away in their respective lockers in the engine room.

The decks on the *'Enrica'* bustled as over one hundred men were involved, officers as well as marines, carpenters, cooks, mates - all heaved-to and soon the deck of the *'Enrica'* was strewn with guns and their carriages, shells, boxes of ammunition, barrels of gunpowder, gunners' spare gear, barrels of beef, mutton, boatswain's stores, numerous boxes, spare sails, large bales and boxes containing uniforms. In a short time everything was stowed away in correct place.

The following day, while last minute provisions such as fresh fruit, eggs, fish and fresh water, were being stowed on board, the engineers assisted the carpenters and gunners in fitting the circles of curved iron tracks for the wheels of the heavy guns as they swung round on the deck. It was an ideal job for Jamie as he had served his apprenticeship as a boilermaker. The heavily built, balding bosun, James Bellew, a Liverpool man, with his mates, Adams, George Archibald, Johnson, assisted by four marines, were working fitting side and train tackles for the broadside guns. Engineer Alex also helped in the installation of the iron fittings. Within seventy hours of the converging of the three ships the transformation was completed, '*Enrica*'s' decks were cleared and the goods stored away.

On the 23rd the '*Enrica*' steamed around the island and anchored off the old Portuguese/Moorish town of Angra on the south side of the Azores.

The American Lieutenant, Armstrong, standing at the for'd end of the ship, introduced himself in his Southern drawl, to a slim built young man about five feet nine inches tall.

"I'm Bill Armstrong, I'm from Georgia."

"Pleased to meet you, Bill". They shook hands, "I'm Joe Mills," he smiled and smoothed down his dark brown hair which was being ruffled by the slight breezes. "My mother was born in North Carolina, where I was born and raised, but my father was sea-going, and we moved to Lancashire, where I was educated. I was lodging in a suburb of Liverpool called Walton, when I heard about vessel number 290 being built in the Birkenhead Iron Works. When word got around the port that they were looking for a crew I applied and here I am," he laughed. "Well I see that's one thing we both share in common - being Lieutenants!"

Armstrong, being a military man, remarked "Not quite - you are in the Navy and I'm in the Army, though you wouldn't think so, dressed in these shabby working clothes. However like yourself I was born in Georgia, which is two states away from North Carolina! Look," he said, pointing. "What lovely scenery and what a colourful layout of this Moorish town and those beautifully different styled, white houses with their individual sharp gabled ends."

Mills was also showing interest now the ship had hoved-to and anchored. "Over there," pointing to the bright multi-tiled roofs, "every house different and the verandas adorned with lavish coloured curtains. I can't wait to go ashore to take a closer look at this old town."

The town looked quiet and peaceful, bathed in brilliant sunshine. The inhabitants must have known something strange was happening on the three ships in the harbour, especially when the crew went ashore and invaded the market and drinking taverns. Jamie and Alex stepped off the liberty boat onto the quay. They were dressed casually.

"What a lovely, picturesque old town," said Alex. "Let us find a place to eat and then we will visit the market for some fresh fruit. There's a place over there," indicating a tavern with the sign 'The King's Head'

"This could be an interesting place to have a meal," exclaimed Jamie. After a fresh lobster meal, washed down with a jug of ale, they made their way down the narrow streets with stone-bricked houses bedecked with colourful flowers and overhanging baskets. It was hot and Alex flung his thin jacket over his shoulder as the two friends eventually found the noisy and bustling market.

They loaded themselves up with fresh fruits and fish and hired a small cart. "Our mates will enjoy a good supper tonight," remarked Alex.

"What's your name, laddie?" Jamie asked of a small, black teenage youth dressed only in dirty grey shorts.

"Joseph, sir."

"How would you like to earn a £5 note?"

"What do I have to do to earn that large amount of money, sir?"

"Just loan us your cart, help us to load it with fruit, fowl, vegetables and fish and wheel it down to the quay."

"We'll help you, of course, and perhaps you would like to accompany us and look around the 'Enrica'" butted in Alex. So they returned to the ship.

Jamie and Alex were joined in the officers' mess by Mr. Freeman, Townsend, Butler, Alan Francis and Eric Knowles. After a hearty meal, prepared by Alastair Liddell and his assistant cooks, the party settled down with drinks and, smokes and discussed the recent sudden changes to their future.

On Sunday 24th August 1862 the 'Enrica', her decks scrubbed, brasses polished, flags and buntings aloft fluttering in a slight breeze and the British Union flag proudly displayed on the stern end, together with the 'Bahama' and the 'Agrippina'. sailed out from the Azores and about twelve miles out the three ships hove-to.

Captain Raphael Semmes, neatly dressed in his number one outfit, sword at his side and standing on a platform on the main deck, addressed the officers and crew of the three ships:

"Gentlemen, I have yet to enlist and sign my crew. I have realised that you have sailed thus far under the articles of agreement. These are no longer obligatory, for shortly the Liverpool-born Bosun, Mr. James Bellew will be striking the English colours and we will become a fighting man-of-war for the Confederacy of the Southern States of America."

"I have here," flourishing a piece of parchment, "a sealed and signed Declaration as a Commissioned man-of-war, signed by the President, Mr. Jefferson Davis. This fine ship has been built and paid for by good Confederacy currency and Commissioned by the

Confederate States as a ship of war and not as a privateer!"
It will become a commercial raider to strike against Union
shipping."
"I give you a choice of either signing on with me or shipping out on
the '*Bahama*' or '*Agrippina*'. If you enlist with me I promise you
double pay in gold, double grog, ample rations and plenty of action,
plus a share in any prize money if we capture an enemy."
"There will be great danger and hardship, and particularly - and I
mention this strongly - strict Naval and Military discipline." He
paused and stroked his moustache, a nervous habit.
"Think it over very carefully and discuss it amongst yourselves.
You are under no obrigation to continue sailing with me, your
contract has finished." He wiped his brow and thought - 'Gosh it's
hot, I only wish I could get out of this damned uniform.' "I'll be
back in half an hour for your answers!"
Mr. Freeman, Alex, Eric and Jamie went below decks to discuss
this important matter about their future, because they understood
they were only connected with the trials party and the contract
according to Mr. Bulloch had concluded in the Azores.

"It's certainly an interesting proposition" said Jamie, "and what
benefits if we sign articles of war with the Confederate Navy. I
know I have a wife and children to support back home, but never-
the-less I would hope to return a wealthy man."
He was getting excited over the sudden change of events -
"Yes, I'm all for signing up."
"So am I" remarked Alex.
"I'm not so sure," quietly whispered Eric. "I suppose you have to
think of the risks and dangers like the Captain said, I'm not as
young and daring as I used to be. I think I will return home to my
family and, continue my job in the Shipyard, for after all we were
expected back home before now - I thought we would be returning
from Point Lynas."

So the three friends made their decisions and Jamie hurriedly
wrote his letter home, which Eric said he would deliver.
'My dear Matilda,
I have had to make a very serious decision regarding our future.
As you are aware I originally intended coming home after the sea
trials were completed at Point Lynas, where we were going to
disembark and make our way home. The situation changed and it
was decided the engines needed adjustments and as a result
further sea trials were necessary. These have been completed
satisfactorily and the ship is now at the Azores. The Captain has

21

explained in detail that the vessel is now a fighting man-of-war serving the Confederacy of the Southern States of America.

He also explained to all the crew that we had a choice of signing on with him or shipping back home. If we enlist he has promised the crew double pay in gold, double grog, ample rations, uniform and plenty of action, plus a share in any prize money when we capture an enemy ship. What a golden opportunity to make money and perhaps become rich! So I have decided to sign on after much discussion with my friends, Mr. Freeman, Alex and Eric Knowles. Eric, being much older, has decided to return home. I know there will be certain dangers as we are going to war, however I shall take great care and return safely to the ones I love. Give my love to the girls and don't worry, my darling, everything will turn out for the best and I shall keep in touch wherever I am and you will always be in my thoughts.

All my love, your ever loving husband.

Jamie.'

The men who were staying assembled on the deck where the Captain was standing and everybody agreed and signed unanimously to the terms.

Jamie joined the officers in Semmes's cabin to sign the articles of war.

A few including Eric collected their belongings and after farewells made their way to the '*Bahama*' which was lying alongside.

Some men alighted on to the '*Enrica*' from the other two ships, including an engineer who made himself known to Mr. Freeman.

"My name is Harry Carruthers, I understand you want a replacement for Mr. Knowles?"

"Indeed I do,", responded Mr. Freeman, sizing up the sturdily built, brown wavy-haired youth. "You are more than welcome. I shall notify the Captain. In the meantime I would like you to meet your fellow engineers, Jamie and Alex."

Carruthers lived in the village of Crosby. Broad shoulders, tall, sporting a moustache. He had been educated near the docks. A bachelor, lived with his parents, his father being a surgeon in the local hospital. He had sea-going experience on a coastal paddle steamer. "I suppose you realize what you have let yourself in for, joining this ship?" said the smiling Jamie "Indeed, Mr. Knowles explained in detail when he boarded the '*Bahama*' and I couldn't wait to get aboard this vessel - and being offered a job in the engine room, especially as it was built in the Birkenhead Iron Works."

"Let's go below decks - follow me, Harry," said Alex.

22

In the officers' quarters Mr. Freeman looked at his latest recruit, Engineer Harry Carruthers; and said:

"We'll have to get you a uniform, Mr. Carruthers, befitting a fourth engineer. Now let's see!" he paused to light his pipe and weighed him up and down. He laughed. "Forty inch chest, thirty inch inside leg measurement. How am I doing?" He puffed away on his pipe. The smell was repulsive; Jamie started coughing.

"What did you say your first name was - and what is your waist line?"

"Harry, sir - waist thirty-six inches."

"Now we don't want any formalities Harry - except in public, when everybody is mister!

"Jamie, take Harry to the quartermaster and get him rigged out, also some working clothes and boots."

Carruthers returned smartly dressed, brass buttons shining, one epaulette signifying fourth engineer on his shoulders. He clutched a sword in his right hand, (which mystified him) and under his left arm he held a haversack containing his additional clothing.

"Now for a bunk. Well, you'll be with the rest of the engineers and you can have both a bunk and a hammock. You might like to sleep on deck sometime in the very hot weather. We will see you in five minutes on deck for inspection, as the Captain wishes to address the crew."

The stage was set. Captain Semmes and his officers turned out smartly dressed in their number one outfit, swords at their sides and white gloves, standing smartly to attention.

The 120 man crew, faces scrubbed, hair washed and combed, were dressed in red, green and blue shirts, dependent on their trade. Some wore hats bedecked with artificial shamrock, some men sported Scottish bonnets, with grey and brown wide trousers and brawny chests exposed. Most of the crew were from the Mersey dockland. Mr. Bulloch and Semmes had been careful in choosing the right crew.

The engineers, Mr. Freeman, Jamie, Alex and Carruthers were familiar with the direct-acting twin horizontal 300 "horse-power" engine and also the special apparatus for the fresh water supply. The sturdily built firemen, Hedgecock and his team including stokers could handle the boilers and fires.

Captain Butler, the senior gunner, Townsend, Captain of heads, and Mills, Captain of the aft guard, were especially selected ex-Royal Navy reserves, who were familiar with the thirty-two pounders, the one hundred pounders, the rifled Blakely and the pivot guns. Captain Francis manned the main deck.

Captain Murdo MacKenzie and his Marines, dressed in the Confederate grey uniforms, were standing at ease with their rifles. There were carpenters, seamen and riggers to man the main masts and lower the braces, all hard and seasoned ex-merchant servicemen, and cooks, yeomen and medical men all skilled at their jobs.

It was a colourful scene with all in different uniforms and attire. There was a slight breeze, a hazy hot sun, which beat down on this August Sunday.

A small band assembled on the main deck. Mr. Bellew, the Bosun with his mates, stood by the English colours, fluttering aloft, and Ray Ryan, a gunner, stood by the weather bow gun awaiting orders. The Captain mounted a platform by the mizzen mast to address the turn-out of smartly dressed officers and the crew assembled on the quarter deck. They heard their first loud command from the Bosun.

"Att - en - tion! - Doff hats."

Some were quite bewildered, but eventually grasped the point that the Bosun was serious. With the water lapping gently against the ship's side they stood quietly to attention as the Captain, Raphael Semmes, unrolled a scroll and read a Commission from Mr. Jefferson Davis, the President, appointing him as Captain in the Confederate Navy and, by order of Mr. Stephen Malloy, the Secretary of the Navy, directing Raphael Semmes to assume command of the vessel.

Jamie glanced aloft and noticed two small balls ascending slowly, one up the peak and the other up the main mast head. They were the ensign and pennant of the future man-of-war.

A seaman, Frank Donaldson, grasped a thin rope which controlled the pennants. The Bosun and the gunner had all eyes on the Captain, who braced himself, took a deep breath and exclaimed in a loud and clear voice: "I name this ship *Alabama*" and may God bless her and all who sail in her."

"Att - en - tion, on hats."

The Captain and all the officers saluted, the First Officer, Mike Kelly, signalled for the gun to be fired by Ryan. The pennants unfolded to the breeze and the English flag was slowly lowered by the Bosun.

He attached the Confederate flag and it was hastily raised aloft. There was a deafening cheer, hats were flung into the air and the band under the leadership of Mullard struck up the tune "Dixie," that soul stirring marching song, the National Anthem of the new-born Government of the Confederacy.

The '*Agrippina's*' Captain, Stanley Threlkeld, had assembled his crew to witness the re-naming of the latest warship to join the Confederacy Navy. Likewise on the '*Alabama's*' port beam, the '*Bahama*' lay, alongside.

Her Captain, hearing the gunfire from the '*Alabama*', ordered the '*Bahama*' gun to be fired and both crews joined in the cheering.

Then the celebrations followed. The Captain had ordered extra rum all round and the crew were quick to seize his generous offer. In the for'd quarters the firemen were in full song led by Ronald Richardson in his fine baritone voice, Donaldson on a violin. Reg Williams and Schmechel, deep basso, and Monroe with his fine profundo tenor voice were in close harmony singing Irish songs, ably supported by their messmates.

On the deck amidships the Scots, led by pipers Crichton, Unsworth and Butler, were playing reels and their countrymen were soon 'choosing' their partners for the Highland dances.

Jamie, Alex and Carruthers, having struck the main-brace, were enjoying themselves in the engineers' mess with Mr. Freeman. Once they heard the sound of the pipes on the main deck, they asked to be excused. Mr. Freeman, puffing away on his pipe, waved his arm in acknowledgement; he understood and carried on reading the newspapers given to him by the Captain of the '*Agrippina*'. On the stern end the Medical team, cooks and deck officers were chatting away, at the same time enjoying the rum and the company. Doctor MacGregor conversed with Alastair Liddell.

"What do you think of today's proceedings?"

"Well, things certainly moved very quickly, the Captain had things well organised and planned. No doubt in my mind, this vessel was a mystery from the start, being given a yard number of 290 and then christened the '*Enrica*' and now today's ceremony."

The Doctor filled up his tankard before answering:

"We certainly know our future. We are going to war and going to face a formidable enemy and some of us might not see England again," he laughed, "but it's my job to see that you are kept in good health and it's your job to see that they go into battle on a full stomach."

"I'll drink to that." They touched glasses.

Captain Semmes, sitting at his desk in his cabin, reflected on the day's events and wrote on page one in his log book:

"Sunday 24th August 1862. This day a new ship is born, the English flag was buried with the '*Enrica*'. The crew mustered and supported the change-over - every man Jack. I feel proud and pleased to have inherited such a fine ship and excellent crew. The Captains and crew of the '*Agrippina*' and '*Bahama*' ably supported the change over of the goods, provisions, weapons and materials successfully and joined in our celebrations. It's been a satisfying day for the Southern cause - and now into battle!"

He slowly closed the book, tapping his fingers on the cover, thinking, 'Into battle, we are at war. The noise and hilarity of the crew echoed into his cabin.

"Make the most of it, me hearties, God knows when we will celebrate again."

He withdrew from a drawer a chart of the local waters. He began making notes and positioned markings on the chart. He folded it up and returned it to the drawer.

He undressed and lay on his bunk. It was hot and humid, he was thinking what the morrow would bring. The tune of the pipes and the laughter and singing slowly diminished into the distance as he slumbered into a restless sleep.

The men slowly retired to their bunks or were carried and the ship settled down, with only the gentle lapping of the water heard as she lay at anchor. Jamie heaved himself out of his hammock and went up the companionway to the stern end of the ship, his favourite position to communicate with his loved ones. He gazed into the distant horizon, reflected by the moon and the twinkling stars.

'What have I let myself in for?' he thought. 'Matilda, hundreds of miles away must have her own thoughts wondering where I am this Sabbath evening! No doubt she took the girls to chapel this Sunday morning and prayed for my safety and perhaps sang that popular sailors' hymn, 'For those in peril on the sea'.

He wiped a tear away with the back of his forefinger, and looked once more into the distance and then with a sigh returned to his hammock.

Chapter 3

The '*Alabama*' left the island of Terceira the same time as the '*Bahama*', which headed back to Merseyside.

There was a fresh north by north-west wind and a rough sea, which caused the '*Alabama*' to roll heavily, much to the discomfort of the crew, especially the seamen, who climbed up the rigging, some for the first time, under the discipline of a man-of-war, manning and unfurling the heavy sails on the main, middle and mizzen masts. They experienced great difficulties and many a harsh word and snarling escaped the lips of the Bosun. James Bellew was a hard, big, six-foot man, born and bred in dockland in Liverpool, having served a harsh apprenticeship before the mast.

This ship of war of the Confederate States, was commissioned by the President, Jefferson Davis. The Northerners had already heard the news that the '*Alabama*' was on the warpath heading directly into their Atlantic shipping lanes and called her a privateer and warned all Northern ships to be aware and wary when engaging the '*Alabama*' in battle.

Jamie, leaning on the aft stern-end rail watching the wake of the '*Alabama*' as the island of Terceira receded into the distance, was lost in thought, thinking of his loved ones in Liverpool.

He was joined by a well-built Welshman, Alan Francis, who introduced himself. "I see you joined the vessel in Birkenhead Alan, how come?"

"I had just left the army after serving four years, and was having a farewell drink with some of my army friends at a tavern near St Nicholas Church, when some hardy and aggressive looking seamen came in and started drinking heavily. I didn't take much notice at first, but an argument started, followed by fighting. I had been drinking, so I thought I would join in the fight, I don't know on whose side, I don't remember much except finishing up on the Birkenhead wharf, and when I came properly to my senses, I was confronted by a Mr. Bulloch".

"Oh, I remember him well," burst out Jamie. "He was an American Naval Officer and a representative on Merseyside for the Confederate States."

"He put a proposition to me I couldn't refuse - about having an American Army commission with the rank of Captain - and the pay was excellent so here I am!"

"Well my case was quite simple really." remarked Jamie. "I more or less grew up with the '*Alabama*,' - and now I have quite an affection for the lady, particularly the engines which I have worked on from the start on board in Birkenhead, together with two of the other engineers."

Their conversation continued for a while and then they parted, Alan going up forward and Jamie returning to duty in the engine room. A few jobs had to be done and on completion, he made his way to the Engineer Officers' quarters.

Mr. Freeman, Alex and Carruthers were relaxing in the wardroom when Jamie entered after cleaning himself and joined them for an evening meal.

"I have corrected and adjusted the exhaust valves," said Jamie addressing Mr. Freeman.

"Good. By the way, gentlemen, conversing with the Captain I learned he only requires engines when docking, or manoeuvring in or out of harbour. This of course conserves our fuel, which has been worked out for only eighteen days' supply. The idea is to look to the sails, however he did suggest that we interest and familiarize ourselves with other crewmen's jobs."

The vessel was in a bad way below decks. Nobody had been berthed or messed properly according to their rank or jobs.

The First Officer, Mr. Mike Kelly, assisted by officers, William Armstrong, Mike Lawson, Hornby Lowe and Joseph Hardman, set about directing the seamen and firemen to their quarters. Riggers, cooks, gunners, carpenters, yeomen and marines were housed and the officers and Bosun berthed in wardrooms equivalent to their rank, most in the forward end of the ship either in bunks or if they preferred, hammocks.

The ship was leaking considerably above the water line mainly because of the heavy seas. Her green, unseasoned timber had been caulked in the shipyard in Birkenhead during an icy and cold winter. During the tropical heat this caused the timber to gape, so more caulking was carried out by the carpenters under the direction of the Bosun's mate, Ray Tyler.

The guns were now in place and practice took place using blank cartridges under the direction and orders of the Gunnery Officers. Captain Robert Townsend was in command of the eight-inch Blakely gun, assisted by a four-gunman team. The nine-inch Blakely came

under the command of Captain Oliver Butler, also ably assisted by four gunners.The six thirty-two pounders came under the commands of Gunners' Mates - Briggs and five gunners.
The practice was necessary and beneficial to quicken up loading and firing. An enemy ship might be sighted at any time, though Captain Semmes was astute and careful in cruising the vessel away from the regular tracks of commerce until the ship had been repaired and the crew disciplined in their various jobs.

So the '*Alabama*' and her now efficient crew, eager to engage the enemy, resolved to strike their first blow at the enemy's whale fishery grounds off the Azores.

The weather was fine and clear on the afternoon of 4th September when the '*Alabama*' sighted the Pico and Fayalin Islands. It was time to unfurl the sails and cruise in on main engines.

Captain Semmes issued an order to the First Lieutenant.
"Assemble the seamen on deck and divide them up into teams to practise furling and unfurling the sails. It's about time I saw some discipline and order on this ship."
 "Bosun," Mike Kelly shouted in a stern voice to Bellew:
"Assemble the seamen into four groups and see these instructions are carried out -
Eight seamen will be under the command of Lieutenant William Armstrong to man the main mast,"
Six will man the foremast under Lieutenant Joseph Hardman.
Four seamen - Prouse, Dorney, Joynson and Royce, will be on the flying rig, under Lieutenant Michael Lawson."
And finally Lieutenant Hornby Lowe will look to the gafftop sail and spanker, that of course is the mizzen mast, with six men.
So, crewmen, up aloft and see how quick you can rig the sails."
The rigging soon became alive as the sails were being unfurled and secured and finally the ship hove-to and anchored for the night.

 The officers relaxed in their quarters and the crew were scattered around the deck, singing or conversing into the night.

There was a light, easterly wind the next day and a ship which proved to be a whaler, the thirty-seven manned '*Ocmulgee*' showing the United States colours, hove into sight.
The '*Alabama*', flying the United States colours, came within hailing distance and closed alongside the enemy on the port beam.

There was a huge whale supported on the starboard side, partially hoisted out of the water by yard tackle. The Yankee whaling Captain, Derek Leekie, looked astonished and amazed when the 'Alabama's' Northern flag was struck by Ray Tyler, the Bosun's mate, and the Confederate flag raised. The bewildered Leekie realised he had been tricked by a perfect surprise on the part of Semmes. Some of the men on the whaler were still working on the mammal, removing its blubber. They were not aware that the 'Ocmulgee' had been boarded by Captain Alan Francis and ten armed Marines led by Sergeant Ray Ryan. Lieutenant Armstrong, accompanied by the Bosun, inspected the ship's papers.

The large sperm whale was a big strike and the whalers were busy removing the oil from a hole in the whale's head, by buckets transferred to barrels on the starboard deck of the 'Ocmulgee'. Sergeant Ryan, clutching his rifle, approached the astonished whalers, declared that they were prisoners of war and asked them to form up on the whalers' deck. The ten men joined the twenty-seven bewildered crewmen and Captain Francis read the Articles of War to the prisoners.

Captain Leekie was greeted with courtesy by Semmes and given special privileged quarters befitting his rank.

The 'Ocmulgee' was looted, but the prisoners took their personal belongings and warm bedding during the transfer from one ship to the other.

The Chief Cook, Alastair Liddell, accompanied by Dunbar and Lenny "Gillie" Fisher, boarded the enemy ship in the evening for food and transported beef, pork and cutlery, mainly for the prisoners, back to the 'Alabama'.

Captain Semmes consulted his officers and addressed them:
"I think it's too late to burn the whaler, as it will attract the attention of other whalers and scare them off. So we will hove-to alongside our prize and tell the crew they can help themselves to anything they like on board. By the way, I'm surprised there's no protection for the whalers; it was a sitting duck - our first prize!"
"Very good, sir," replied Kelly. "I'll arrange for a light on the whaler's foremast and a skeleton crew on board and in the morning we will burn her. And sir, here is your first chronometer!"
"Thank you, Mike, I'll treasure this prize."

The 'Ocmulgee' was burned next day and sank taking the whale with it. Ship's in the area must have thought it was just a passing steamer in the distance.

The following day the '*Alabama*' cruised along under full sail, the seamen having spent the night drilling, furling and unfurling the sails with much shouting and cursing from the officers in charge. By the morning they were quite proficient, when the look-out man, Riordan, in the crows-nest shouted - "Sail ho! on the port beam." When they were in telescope distance, Semmes perceived it had French colours and immediately ordered the Yankee flag to be hoisted. The two ships sailed within hailing distance of each other. Greetings were exchanged, Semmes trying out his French, but he was ably assisted by Captain Robert Townsend. They informed the French captain that they were a Northern cruiser and so amid much shouting and cheering the vessels parted, the '*Alabama*' changed course and headed north-by-north-west to the island of Flores in the Azores, shortened sail and anchored overnight. Semmes called Kelly to his cabin and informed him that he would inspect the ship and have a full turn-out of the crew in number one dress at twelve noon the next day. Mr. Freemen asked the engineers to meet him in the engine room.

"I wonder what is happening?" Jamie seemed inquisitive.

"The Captain is going to tighten up discipline, so as to make us more proficient and I understand," said Carruthers, "that we will be doing various other jobs."

"As long as I don't have to climb the rigging, I haven't a head for heights," remarked Alex.

Mr. Freemen appeared and gathered the engineers around him.

"Gentlemen, the Captain means business, he's been a bit lenient in the past, but things have changed drastically, He does not want us to be caught unawares in battle and we have to be very alert, quick to answer commands, ever mindful that the enemy is out there and can strike swiftly. It is up to us to meet force with force and win the fight. The Captain will be inspecting the engine room after the ship inspection tomorrow noon, therefore I want you to get busy. You all know the requirements - to bring the engine room and the boiler room to the usual high standard, so go to it."

On Sunday morning, Jamie, who had worked all night, was greeted by a picturesque view of the high, the most westerly rock and luxuriant growth of a verdant island in the Azores, set in semi-tropical waters, rising like an unbroken mountain over 1,000 feet. The hot climate in the summer and gale forces in the winter blended to produce beautiful shrubs and colourful flowers which littered the valleys. Strewn here and there were neat white farm holdings, making the whole peaceful scene picturesque. Jamie was within distance to inhale the fragrance of this beautiful paradise.

The crew under different commands prepared the ship for its first inspection. The white decks had been washed down and scrubbed, the brass and iron work glittered in the bright sunlight. The sails were neatly trimmed with the Confederate flag proudly flying at the peak. The Captain, neatly dressed, sword at side, pistol in holster, together with his smartly dressed armed officers, grouped on the main deck. "Assemble the crew for inspection, Mr. Kelly" commanded the Captain, "Aye, aye, sir." The First Lieutenant saluted.

The crew appeared on deck in duck frocks and black trousers, well polished shoes and straw hats. The officers in number one dress, all quickly assembled. Even the military had turned out in their grey uniforms, side arms, pistols and muskets. At the command from the first Lieutenant "Company, attention" (most experiencing this command for the first time) they snapped to order.
The First Lieutenant approached the Captain, saluted him and loudly exclaimed:
"The crew are assembled and ready for inspection, sir."
"Thank you, Mr. Kelly."
The Captain inspected the crew, pausing to have a word with the engineers, telling Mr. Freeman he would inspect the engine room in an hours time. Semmes was pleased with the turn-out and congratulated his Officers.

There was a raised platform, forward of the main wheel and the Captain stood on it and addressed the stand-easy and relaxed assembly.
"Gentlemen, I would first like to congratulate you all on this my first inspection. When you joined this ship and signed Articles giving your allegiance to the Confederate States of America I explained about this warship and what is expected of you all. I will now present to you for the first time the Articles of War. These lay down the Naval rules and regulations of the United States."

The Captain paused for a moment. 'How fragrant the air,' he thought. He then continued:
"It is quite severe in the denunciation of crime if you are found guilty by a court martial on serious offences such as mutiny, murder or treason the penalty is death by hanging, or in the case of severe military offences the firing squad, and for minor misdemeanours, flogging. You will of course have a fair trial, convened by myself and a court martial and you will be legally represented by one of the Bosun's mates - Stephen Riordan.

In the weeks we have been together, some of you have committed offences, been tried and, where necessary, confined in irons. You are now on board a ship-of-war and not a privateer, as those damned Yankees call us. Therefore from now on, discipline will be severe and if you default, you will be dealt with accordingly, but if on the other hand if you are are willing and obedient, do your duties and I'm sure you all will, because you would not be here otherwise, you will be treated with kindness and humanity. That is all I have to say, gentlemen - are there any questions?"
"Yes, sir," said Carruthers.
'There he goes,' thought Jamie, 'I wonder what's on his mind.'
"Sir, some of us are British subjects, fighting on a foreign ship, for a foreign country and a foreign cause which is not our own, and I am concerned if we are captured by the enemy."
"Have no fear," said the Captain. "You will be covered by International Law, which I have made a study of - and," with a laugh, "I will personally see nothing happens to you, have faith, Mr. Carruthers."

"Well, that is all I have to say, gentlemen," continued the Captain. "Enjoy yourselves for the rest of the day, if you want shore leave, Mr. Kelly will arrange it, for tomorrow we will be sailing to engage the enemy."
Quite a crowd gathered in the Engineers' mess for the evening meal. Mr. Freeman being the senior officer was the President of the mess, and friends were allowed to dine, by his permission. Jamie invited Alan Francis, Raymond Tyler, and Iain Grinham and they seated themselves to enjoy an evening meal especially prepared by the Officer's chef, Alastair Liddell.

Jamie enjoyed a fish course and was casually examining the upturned plate and pointed to an inscription on the back of the beautiful polished porcelain plate.
"Look at this"- it was the name Davenport.
"That plate was manufactured in the Midlands, I think a place called Stoke, who specialise in expensive crockery and the best in the country, not surprising Mr. Bulloch spared no expense in furnishing the very best for this vessel," butted in Carruthers.
"Let's have a game of cards." interposed Alex.
"Good idea," said Mr. Freeman. "Alastair, fill up our glasses and where is that tobacco you swiped off the deck the other day, Alan?"
So Mr. Freeman, Francis, Tyler, Grinham, Alex, Jamie and Carruthers settled down to serious drinking, general gossip about their future and playing cards and just after midnight the party broke up and they all retired for a good night's sleep.

Chapter 4

Lagens is a beautiful and peaceful seaside village situated on the south side of the island of Flores.

Captain Semmes guided the '*Alabama*' towards the beach, hove to and dropped anchor.

The paroled prisoners from the '*Ocmulgee*' embarked on the beach from their four whaleboats. This was beneficial to the thirty-seven prisoners as they could sell the boats and any personal possessions and use the monies until they could contact the United States Consul on the nearby island of Fayal.

The hefty Bosun's mate, Stephen Riordon, six feet in height was appointed by the Captain to climb the rigging and occupy the crow's nest in the masthead. He was especially chosen because of his big booming bass voice and it could be heard on this occasion when the '*Alabama*' lay peacefully by the beach. The prisoners had hardly left the ship, rowing briskly to the beach when the cry from aloft, "Sail ho!" echoed from the masthead.

"To your stations," roared the First Lieutenant.

The seamen, now specially trained, scrambled up the rigging and unfurled the sails on the fore and main masts.

Within a short time, with the aid of engines, the '*Alabama*' was racing towards a schooner which was hastening under full sail towards the island.

"Hoist the English flag, Mr. Kelly, it will throw the beggars off guard," ordered the Captain.

The schooner still headed for the island. Captain Semmes surmized that their Captain was suspicious and was trying to make a run under full sail, to be within shelter and safety of the well-known marine league which was about four miles distant. The '*Alabama*' quickly caught up to the small ship and Semmes sailed across the schooner's path, lowered the English flag, raised the Confederate one and ordered the Gunner's Mate, Alex Allan, and his gunner Speakman on the forward starboard thirty-two-pounder gun, to fire a shot across their bow. This was effective. She raised her

Stars and Stripe colours, brailed up her foresail and tried to make a last desperate run for it, but as Semmes had anticipated this and was wise to the wily Yankee skipper, he gave an order to the midship starboard thirty-two-pounder: "Fire a round."

Semmes watched intently through his telescope. The thirty-two-pounder shell whistled noisily only a few feet above the heads of the frightened passengers assembled between her masts. The gallant little craft unfurled her sails, lowered her colours and hoisted the white flag.
"Mr. Kelly, arrange for the Master to come aboard with his papers" Semmes added with half a laugh. "Don't forget the chronometer."

Captain Joseph Flynn climbed aboard the 'Alabama'. He approached Semmes and saluted "I'm Flynn, Master of the schooner 'Starlight', registered in Boston, where I'm bound from Fayal. These are my papers, and I understand from your First Lieutenant that you collect chronometers." He handed over the 'Starlight's' papers, chronometer and flag. "I have twelve passengers including some ladies and only eight crewmen."
"Please return to your ship, Captain Flynn, and assure the passengers that no harm will come to them and that at a convenient time you will all be shipped ashore."

The 'Alabama' hove to all night in a calm sea alongside the 'Starlight', which had a prize crew on board under the command of Lieutenant Hornby Lowe. It was too late to land the prisoners, so the following morning they were shipped ashore with their ladies to the lovely town of Santa Cruz.

Later a long-boat approached the 'Alabama'. Jamie, who was standing near the ship's side gangway, suddenly observed that it contained some uniformed dignitaries. He quickly informed the Captain and mustered some of the crew as the Governor of the Azores was piped on board with ceremony and dignity. "I'm Sir Graham Day-Barrett, Governor of the Azores, and may I introduce my daughter, Janette, some of my staff, Captain Donald Lyons of H.M Dragoons aud Lieutenant John Irlam."
"Excellency, delighted to meet you, your escort and your charming daughter, welcome aboard the 'Alabama'." Semmes was the Perfect Southern Gentleman. Smiling he continued: "Lieutenant Stewart Owens, will you personally escort Miss Janette, you both seem about the same age. Doctor MacGregor and Carruthers, will you accompany me to my wardroom and attend to the comforts of our honoured guests?"

The distinguished assembly were wined and dined with excellent service from the Captain's steward, Ramidios, who was the expert wine connoisseur.

Lieutenant Owens enjoyed the company of the Governor's daughter, Janette, who seemed very pleased to be escorted around the ship to meet the crew by such a handsome six-foot officer in white uniform."I would like you to meet Jamie, who hails from Scotland." Jamie stepped forward - "Delighted! it's such a long time since we have had such charming company on board. Where did you originate, in England?"

"Actually I was born in the Wirral, and I have always been fascinated by the *'Alabama'* because I visited it with my father during its building. It seems so strange looking around and listening to so many dialects." She adjusted her parasol, to protect herself from the sun (it was ninety degrees!). "Perhaps you would like to visit the Officers' mess and partake of some wine," suggested Michael Lawson.

"Thank you, it's most kind, this heat sometimes is most unbearable. I often wonder how we English people survive."

So a pleasant few hours were enjoyed by the officers entertaining a friendly and pretty, brown haired young lady, while in the Captain's wardroom the evening concluded after cigars, champagne and mild conversation about life on the island and in England and the war between the States. Towards midnight the *'Alabama's'* dinghy was manned by Lieutenant Lawson, Fred King the Bosun's Mate, two oarsmen and young Stewart Owens, (who by now was most engrossed with his charming companion and who vowed that if he was ever in these waters would call on her). They escorted the Governor ashore, who thanked the officer in charge for an excellent evening. Stewart helped Janette on to the quay, held her hand, kissed it and thanked her for a most enjoyable and pleasant evening and with a smart salute (and a smile, which was returned) joined the escort to row back to the *'Alabama.'*

Early next morning, leaving the island in search of the enemy, the *'Alabama'* overhauled a whaling brig, flying the Portuguese flag. The master of the brig visited the *'Alabama'* and showed his papers, which turned out to be genuine. Semmes thanked the Master - Captain Peter Carletti, and both vessels parted amicably.

In the late afternoon Semmes, flying the American colours, chased a large ship and caught her up at sunset. The Master, Captain Keith Newman, after he had been duped by the flags, went aboard the *'Alabama'*. The oil-carrying fishery vessel, the *'Ocean Rover'* had been cruising around the world for three and a half years, and when Captain Newman heard from some of the '*Alabama's*' crew how Semmes had graciously allowed the Master of the '*Ocmulgee*' and its crew safe passage in their long-boats to carry them to the Azores, he requested the same, which the tolerant Captain granted, but pointed out they were fifty miles from the islands. "That is nothing," remarked Newman, "we whalers are used to chasing the great mammals many miles in our long-boat. The thirty- six crewmen headed for the islands in four longboats fully laden with all their personal effects plus barrels of beaf and pork, even the ship's tabby cat and parrot. Jamie and his friends watched them depart and bade them a safe journey as they slowly rowed in the direction of the island paradise of the Azores.

The '*Starlight*' and '*Ocean Rover*' were manned by skeleton crews and another prize, the '*Alert*', was also captured a day later and similarly was boarded and manned by crewmen from the '*Alabama*'. The First Lieutenant, acknowledging that Jamie was showing an aptitude for seamanship, placed him in command of the '*Starlight*'. The three vessels lying about one mile apart were put to the torch. Any distant whalers must have thought that a few ships were heading for the Azores.

Jamie lost no time in seaching the '*Starlight*' for any valuables before giving the signal to burn the vessel. He discovered a secret panel in the captain's cabin, a small pouch containing pearls. He could not believe his eyes viewing these priceless gems and quickly stowed them away, thinking about his future and what benefits they would bring to his family when he returned to England.

The skeleton crews returned safely from the prize vessels, and the quarter-deck of the '*Alabama*' was strewn with clothing, boots, crockery, meats, bottles of wine and heavy oaken boxes of Virginia twist tobacco. That night the '*Alabama's*' crew certainly enjoyed themselves smoking their pipes and drinking wine amidst a merry song and dance led by Charlie Mullard on his concertina, Anton Forrest on his flute and violin playing by the wild Irishman Anthony Mahoney. Next day, while the '*Alabama*' was sailing peacefully along, special gunnery practice was ordered by the First Lieutenant who gave Jamie the firing command. A barrel was used as a marker and it was launched overboard. It was distinguished by a pole with a white flag! The eight-inch Blakely gun was under the command of Captain Robert Townsend, a quiet man who would rather study languages than gun drill. His four-man team consisted of William Wilding, George Penman, the small-of-stature Robert Anderson and Norman Gillies who enjoyed telling funny stories, but this drill was far from humorous. The huge gun was swivelled round until it pointed over the starboard side in the general direction of the floating target, which by now was a quarter of a mile away. The gun was laboriously loaded somewhat clumsily by the team and when it was ready, Jamie worked out the angle and the distance and gave the order - FIRE. The vessel rocked from the recoil, but all eyes were on the target. The shell exploded on impact in the sea about fifty yards short of the floating barrel. In the meantime, while this gun was being re-loaded the nine-inch Blakely was swivelled into position under the command of Captain Oliver Butler.

His team consisted of number one gunner Bob Mack, Norman Heritage, big John Jamieson and the bearded, deep thinking John Thornhill, who mustered to load the charge and shell down the barrel. Jamie again set the sights on the floating barrel which by now was about three quarters of a mile away. The shell exploded about eighty yards short but dead in line with the target. The First Lieutenant who was observing the slow reaction of both teams thought: 'Must certainly quicken up these lazy English louts and give them a sharp lesson.' He did not know but both teams were specially chosen to man these special guns as they had been ex-British army reservists - it was just a case of the morning after the night before - after the heavy drinking. "Captain Townsend, have the gunners lined up for inspection," snarled Lieutenant Kelly, "What the hell is up with you lot? Just look at yourselves. You - what is your name?" "Penman, sir". Six-foot Kelly looked him in the eye "You're a disgrace, look at your dress - unshaven bleary-eyed and lazy, how do you expect to do your duty?"
  George Penman straightened up, he was not going to let a Navy 'snotty nosed' officer address a gunner like that. He was just about to explode when a cry from aloft saved a nasty situation "Ship ahoy, on the port beam." Semmes was resting in his cabin as he had like the rest of the crew had a most 'enjoyable' evening the night before, but he hurriedly dressed when aroused by the Midshipmen Owens.

Dusk was approaching when Semmes arrived on the starboard rail and viewed through his night glasses a ship about two miles away. Jamie, who happened to be alongside, enjoying the balmy evening air, also peered into the distance "What do you make of that vessel, Jamie?" remarked the Captain, handing over his glasses "Unmistakably a Yankee built brig, sir, judging by its lines and it appears to be rapidly heading for the shelter and haven of the islands. No doubt the stranger must have heard of our victories in these waters," was Jamie's response.

"Change course, Bosun Bellew, ten degrees starboard. Lieutenant Kelly - man all stations, full ahead, we are about to engage the enemy. Hoist the United States colours," shouted the Captain. Jamie, who wanted to be in the action, dashed to the near starboard thirty-two-pounder and removed the canvas cover, as gunner's mates Finley MacKenzie and Jim Henderson appeared on the scene. They loaded a blank shell (as was the custom) and stood by awaiting further orders. The *'Alabama'* became suddenly alive, seamen swarming up the rigging to unfurl additional sails, gunners alert, prepared to load the weapons, Captain Vernon Callaghan on the Yankee ship, the whaler *'Weathergauge'* of Princetown, Massachusetts, telescope to his eye, was looking curiously into the distance at what appeared to be three mysterious cones of smoke (which were from the three burning ships on the horizon). He swivelled his telescope to port and watched suspiciously as this well rigged ship about one mile away was boring rapidly towards his ship.

A burst of gunfire shattered the night air, Callaghan waited for the explosion, but none came, because it was a blank shot. The rapidly approaching ship suddenly lowered its colours and hoisted the dreaded Confederate flag.

"Damn" exclaimed a puzzled Callaghan, I've been tricked by that Southern swine! It must be that Confederate raider, and as I'm no match I must yield to submission."

He decided to surrender, lowered his colours and hoisted the white flag, thinking 'Better be a live coward than a dead hero.'

 The *'Weathergauge'* was boarded by the Bosun, James Bellew, ably supported by Hughie Morris, the tough fireman, Ronald Richardson, and Kenneth Andersen - one of the paymasters, who demanded that Captain Callaghan hand over the ship's papers. These were examined and proved that she was a whaler six weeks out from Boston, bound for the whaling areas off the Azores.

Semmes decided after receiving the ship's papers, its flag and the chronometer (a prize he carefully stowed way) and a number of newspapers (applicable only to the successes of the Yankees) to place a prize crew on board in the capable hands of Lieutenant Bill Armstrong, a seasoned Officer trained in both navigation and military, ably supported by the Captain of Marines, Alan Francis, who would deal with any mutinous problems. He had under his command six marines, but they were not really necessary after all, she was just a peaceful whaling ship.

Semmes decided that the '*Weathergauge*' would hove to off the island of Corvo for the night with the some prize crew on board.

He was alerted from aloft by Riordan that a vessel on the starboard bow seemed to be running away. The Captain quickly prepared the '*Alabama*' to pursue the ship.

"Jamie, what do you observe about the vessel we are going to engage?" said the Captain after handing over his glasses. Jamie focussed the night glasses on what appeared to be a 'ghost' ship. "Sir, from the taper of the spares and the whiter-than-white canvas, which I surmise were manufactured from the Northern cotton fields, I would definitely say a Northerner, sir. "Quite correct, prepare to engage the enemy" commanded Semmes. The stranger appeared to be a ghost, with its snowy white canvas in the bright moonlight. Nevertheless Semmes went in hot pursuit, which lasted all night, as these two fast vessels were evenly matched, but the '*Alabama*' with her tall, longer masts and fore and aft sails quickly overhauled this 'so-called' Yankee ship, A blank shot was fired, she quickly heaved to and was boarded by Lieutenant Michael Lawson, Bosun's Mate, Ian Fisher and three seamen. She turned out to be a Danish ship, the barque '*Overman*' from Bangkok, Siam, bound for Hamburg. She had no need to flee, being a neutral ship, but Lieutenant Lawson, after examining her papers, congratulated the Captain on his speed and performance.

The nervous Peter Van Baylis, Captain of the '*Overman*' shook Lawson warmly by the hand and, glancing over to the '*Alabama*' agreed that his ship had all the appearances of a Northern ship, hence the hot pursuit, for which Lawson apologised. The two officers saluted each other and they all parted in a friendly manner.

The following day the '*Alabama*' rejoined the '*Weathergauge*' off Corvo. Callaghan, her Captain, and crew were put into their own boats with their provisions and directed to the safety of the shore, which was about three miles away. The '*Weathergauge*' with her skeleton crew under the command of Bosun James Bellew set sail and about twenty miles from the islands she was burned after Bellew and seamen were safely aboard the '*Alabama*'.

A couple of days later an innocent Portugese barque, homeward bound for Lisbon, was sighted, but was allowed to proceed after Lieutenant Hornby Lowe examined her papers.

Semmes decided after consultation with his senior officers to head northwest about fifty miles from Flores, ever seeking the enemy.

On the fifth day came the cry from the crow's nest by Riordan. "Sail ho!" the look-out man was becoming quite proficient in detecting various ships by their shapes and sails. It turned out to be the American brig the '*Alabama*' from New Bedford, five months out from Boston, as reported back by the boarding Officer, Lieutenant Joseph Hardman.

The '*Alabama*' had not commenced hunting the whale so Semmes decided to assisted by putting her to the torch and gave Jamie the honour and he was assisted by Richardson and Marine Schmechel. The weather was fine and pleasant, the red sun had disappeared over the horizon and the '*Alabama*' continued northwest. Jamie, leaning on the aft rail, his favourite position most evenings, dreaming about his home and family, was joined by Bosun's Mate, Ray Tyler and the assistant surgeon, Doctor Graeme MacGregor. Ray opened the conversation "I don't think you've met Doctor Graeme, Jamie, he hails from Wigan, just outside Liverpool."
"How nice to meet a fellow Lancastrian, Graeme. Naturally I heard you were on board, bunking up forward, near the surgery with Doctor Maurice Edwards.
"I take it you're from a different part of Scotland, not having my dialect?"
"Yes, I suppose it's a generation back. I might add it's rather curious how I came to be standing here with you gentlemen. I had only just qualified from my medical training and one Friday evening I was celebrating in the Water Street tavern with Alan Francis, Charlie Mullard, a school teacher, John Doig who was entertaining us with his pipes, Robert Anderson, a boilermaker from Bootle, and young Paul Harris. We were having a jolly time. The ale flowed freely. We were singing away, some tough-looking strangers entered the bar and in next to no time an argument started, fists flayed and bottles hurtled around the tavern. "It was a right battle scene," continued Graeme. "I remember hitting a chap with a chair leg, when, "Don't tell me," sniggered Jamie. "You were hit on the head by a delaying pin and lost consciousness. I've heard it from Alan - the same thing happened to him. You came to on the quayside in Birkenhead!

"Oh no, it's not quite like that, I'm not really a fighting man, I like to save life not destroy it. When I came round I helped to attend to my battered friends who were carried to an enclosed horse and cart and I was transported across the Mersey by ferry and literally dumped on the quay. I suppose you could say I was virtually a prisoner attending to the wounded and then next morning I was introduced to Mr. Bulloch who was looking for a ship's Doctor. "That's interesting," chuckled the tall Ray Tyler. "Life's full of surprises. Do you know, I was playing cricket for a team called Sefton, I had just made fifty runs and was bowled out. Returning to the pavilion I chatted to one of the spectators, Mervyn Kingston, who is incidentally a seaman on board and he talked about this mysterious vessel being built in the Birkenhead Iron Works. Having a bit of experience sailing on the river I joined this vessel in time for sea trials. Because I had a good education at the Blue coat school - you see I was orphaned when I was a youngster - Mr. Bulloch decided to encourage me to become a Bosun's Mate." "Well, Ray," said Jamie, "you've had an interesting career in your twenty-six years. Life has been quite different."

"Briefly, I worked on the engines on board this vessel in the Birkenhead Iron Works throughout its building and trials and here I am on the stern end of this foreign ship, fighting for a war that is not mine. I am beginning to wonder what is to be our destiny."

And then from the masthead, fresh news - a ship had been sighted. The moon rose brightly, the crew manned their stations, seamen climbed aloft to unfurl further topsails, the marines manned two of the thirty-two pounders and Captain Semmes trained his night glasses upon the white canvas of a fleeing vessel. It appeared from the cut of the sails and the taper of spars to be an American.

"Give her all you've got, Mr. Kelly," yelled Semmes. With her tall masts and large fore and aft sails billowing in the breeze the 'Alabama' picked up speed. The chase was now on; under no circumstances was Semmes going to be outrun by a merchant ship.

The stranger was now within range of the starboard amidship 32-pounder manned by MacKenzie and Henderson. The stillness of the night was shattered by the accustomed blank cartridge. There was no change in the stranger's speed, so a second blank was fired and she shortened sail and the vessel was brought to the wind.

"Detail a boarding party, Mr. Kelly" commanded the Captain. "Lieutenant Armstrong, Sergeant Ryan, Gow and Paul Harris, arm yourselves, man the longboat, with oarsmen Roughler and three others, you two and Billing and when you have boarded her show a light in the stranger's forward peak, if she is the enemy."

Armstrong presented himself to the Captain, Gerald O' Connor, and the Lieutenant noted from her papers that the vessel was the

'*Benjamin Tucker*' of New Bedford, eight months out, with 350 barrels of oil. Armstrong ordered the light to be raised on the peak. He thought he could hear cheering from the '*Alabama*' which by now was almost alongside.

Armstrong and his prize crew remained on board the Yankee boat overnight and next morning brought the prisoners aboard the '*Alabama*'. Tobacco, clothing, everything edible, cutlery and plates (for the prisoners' use) were transferred on to the '*Alabama*,' together with the Yankee flag.

Sergeant Ryan on his return saluted and addressed Captain Semmes "Sir, the '*Tucker's*' Captain presents you with his chronometer." "Thank you Sergeant, my compliments to Captain O'Connor, I will see him in my cabin."

"Very good, sir. I surrender my ship, Captain Semmes, and my crew, and I believe you collect chronometers - how many have you captured?"

Semmes handled the chronometer fondly and gently, admiring the techniques of its design and manufacture. He noted the firm's name in Boston and remarked:

"Actually this one is the seventh and I must admit it's quite unique and, I suppose, more up-to-date in its markings and design." Addressing his devoted steward he said: "Will you please show Captain O'Connor to his quarters and attend to his needs."

The next morning dawned with a slight mist but a smooth sea and billowing clouds sailing lazily overhead. The latitude was 40° north and longitude 350° west. The barometer stood at 30.3 inches and the thermometer at 75 and it was nearing the end of September 1862. As soon as breakfast was completed, Semmes appeared In the now clearing mist on the foredeck, bracing himself, and breathed deeply. Jamie, who was jogging around the deck, nearly bumped into him. "How are things in the engine room, Jamie?"

"Satisfactory sir, and by the way, Captain, could I have some navigation practice on the deck?"

"Certainly. Report to Mr. Kelly. I will alert him to train you up as a deck officer. I am always advising everybody to do 'other men's jobs. In fact," with a laugh, "I must, if you will show me, start the main engines!"

The rolling mist lifted from the sea and a Yankee schooner appeared about half a mile on the port beam. Semmes, who was taken unawares, yelled loudly - "Action stations!"

The Yankee made no attempt to escape - she had no time, as she was also taken completely by surprise. The port thirty-two- pounder fired a shot across her bows and within a short time the '*Alabama*' lowered a longboat under the command of Lieutenant Hardman assisted by Ben Mackay, Dennis Reeves, armed marines and the Paymaster Bill Crichton, who examined the Master's papers.

She was the '*Courser*', a whaling schooner from Province Town, Massachusetts. Russell Grindley, the six-foot handsome Captain, surrended his flag and chronometer and joined the other captured Captain, Joseph O' Connor from the '*Benjamin Tucker*', together with his crew. There was now a total of seventy-two prisoners aboard the '*Alabama*'. This was causing a problem to Semmes so he decided to proceed and land them at Flores, along with their personal belongings, and they boarded the eight whaler long-boats and rowed towards the distant islands.

The First Lieutenant decided to give the gunners some target practice sinking the '*Courser*'. The forward eight-inch smooth-bore Blakely gun under the command of Marine Captain Robert Townsend and his team Bill Wilding, George Penman, Bobbie Anderson and Norman Gillies swivelled round the huge gun to starboard and directed it below the waterline of the enemy schooner. The gun crew rammed the gunpowder and shell down the the gun's barrel. "Fire!" roared Townsend. The shell exploded successfully below the waterline amidships.
"Reload." The gunners quickly reloaded, all done within seconds.
 "Change to five degrees, same elevation and - fire, fire."
The repeated shells ripped through the '*Courser*' and with gaping holes on and below the water line the water gushed in and she began to list to port. Within a matter of minutes she turned completely upside down and, in her death throes, sank with a gurgling noise and with a massive bubbling foam, the surging waves dancing against the gently swaying '*Alabama*'.

Jamie watched with interest, noting how quickly the gunners manned and loaded the gun and, turning towards the first Lieutenant, thought that it was about time he started studying navigation.
"Hi! Jamie, the Captain has mentioned you are interested in studying navigation?" ('Must have read my mind,' thought Jamie.)
"I think we will start with the helmsman, so let us stand by the steering platform and I'll leave you in the hands of the Bosun's Mate Ian Fisher." Jamie noted how the course would be relayed via the First Lieutenant from the Captain, using his chronometer, and then an order would be issued, "north-by-north west, ten degrees."

"North-by-north-west, sir," repeated Fisher and the five-foot diameter double wheel moved slowly to the new position indicated on the compass. Day turned into night and Jamie was intrigued by the way Ian kept looking up to the stars and then there was a slight movement of the ship's wheel.

"Watch the stars, Jamie boy," said Fisher, his eyes scanning the heavens, "Let them be your guide, always watch the North Star."

'Must study the stars, that's a new subject,' thought Jamie!
Next morning there was a moderate breeze blowing from the south-west, latitude 40° and longitude 36°, when a large schooner appeared sailing parallel about three miles on the port beam. Semmes immediately altered course and gave chase.

About four hours later the vessel was boarded by the Bosun, James Bellew, assisted by armed marines. The senior Officer, Joseph Hardman, confronted the schooner's Captain, Joseph Pollard. It turned out to be a whaler, the 'Virginia', from New Bedford. Once the usual chronometer had been received, the Yankee flag, newspapers, ropes, crockery, food and the sails were transferred from the 'Virginia' to the 'Alabama' and were carried by prisoners under the watchful eyes of Gow and his fellow marines.

The 'Virginia' was burned, after the prisoners were safely boarded in their longboats with their possessions and directed towards the Azores, which were about ten miles away. The 'Alabama' proceeded north-west and Jamie watched with Adams, another Merseysider, together with several of the ship's crew.

The burning "Virginia" receded during the evening into the distance, until she finally disappeared over the horizon.

A storm was brewing as the 'Alabama' overhauled a brig and as she was flying a French flag, Semmes despatched Captain Robert Townsend, a proficient linguist, to examine the ship's papers, and since they were satisfactory, Semmes allowed her to depart in peace. Dawn had barely broken when from the masthead rang the booming bass voice of Riordan.

"Sail ho! on starboard beam."

The watchkeeper, Midshipman Stewart Owens, immediately commanded the trainee helmsman, Bill Crichton:
"Ten degrees north-by-north-west."
Owens alerted Lieutenant Armstrong.
"Man the main top gallant sail," and to Lieutenant Hardman,

"Man the fore top gallant sail." The seamen swarmed up the swaying buckling bent masts, the weather was really rough and the rain lashed down. The '*Alabama*' responded magnificently - trembling from stem to stern she met with a challenge the buffeting waves that pounded the ship, until her very timbers groaned and creaked. But the enemy ship was like a true racer and with the wind behind her, she rapidly chased and overhauled the schooner. The '*Alabama*', about half a mile away and bearing the Union Jack, fired the thirty-two-pounder port gun. Bill McMath, assisted by gunner John Kirwan, loaded another shell, realizing the first shell was well off target and fired another right across her bow.

The schooner raised her true Southern colours, eased her sails and a boarding party headed by Lieutenant Hornby Lowe, ably assisted by Marines Captain Joseph Mills, Finley, Mackay and Brian Leeson, braved the heavy swell and the fierce gale, headed into the wind and with difficulty boarded the enemy ship. Lowe had instructions from his Captain to return with the prisoners, flag and chronometer and set the ship ablaze. Captain Peter Ledwidge of the '*Elisha Dunbar*' with thirty-five crew members together with the boarding party managed to survive the hazardous return journey to the safety of the '*Alabama*'.

Another burning spectacle of the enemy whaling ship being tossed about like a cork and shrouded in a black cloud amid the crashing thunder and lightning, heavy rain and tumultuous seas, was a sight to behold to the onlookers. Captain Ledwidge, standing alongside Jamie and Rob Adams, sobbed, as his ship (now denuded of her masts) lay rolling and tossing in the rough sea. The '*Dunbar*' with her heavy rolling took in so much water that she settled in the raging sea. The fire was practically quenched as she disappeared into the ocean's depths, a victim of the passions of man and the fury of the elements.

Chapter 5

It was Sunday 2nd October 1862 and the '*Alabama*', owing to the recent severe gale which lasted six days, together with a cold north wind, had found herself drifting south to 33° latitude and was now in an unfrequented part of the ocean. The bad weather had also put an end to the whaling season and Captain Semmes seemed to have time on his hands, which he took advantage of by exercising the crew and alternating each man's duties. Because of this the performance and the discipline had improved enormously, making the ship a truly fighting disciplined man-o'-war.

The captured prisoners, who spent most of the time in chains except for three boys and two cooks and a steward, complained bitterly about their conditions, which were very uncomfortable, being partly exposed to the elements of the bad weather. The sea poured in through the guns port holes, they lay in chains soaked to the skin, but as they were in the open, Semmes ordered an old sail, captured from the '*Ocean Rover*', to be thrown over the imprisoned chained men and some were lucky to be lying on planks. The imprisoned Captain Joseph Pollard of the '*Virginia*' and Peter Ledwidge, Captain of the '*Elisha Dunbar*' lay huddled together bound in chains, clothing soaked, wondering about Semmes and his changing personality - one minute being courteous, kind and understanding and then for some unknown reason changing suddenly to a mood of bitterness, malice and revenge. Pollard remarked through chattering teeth:

"What have we done to deserve such punishment by this hard and callous creature from the South. I was just earning my living as a whaler like yourself, doing my job, but who would expect an armed raider to pounce upon us, fire across our bows until we surrendered and then to be boarded by armed men, our vessel ransacked, our ships burned, our livelihood gone and here we are lying together, trying to survive. It seems almost like a nightmare. What kind of person who calls himself an officer and a gentleman would treat us so inhumanely?"

"I experienced almost a similar situation," said Ledwidge, "But these are quite squalid conditions for us prisoners. I realise there is no room below decks, but to find ourselves nearly under water like we experienced last night, - well you would think he would have done something about it. He must be taking his revenge out on prisoners generally. From what I heard, one of his officers on his previous ship, the '*Sumpter*', was captured by the enemy, clapped in irons, had his head shaven and was tortured, and so he is retaliating and here we are in these atrocious conditions, but I must admit the sea is rough. But we are given the same food as the '*Alabama's*' crew and I suppose we must be thankful to be alive."

The stormy weather moderated. The '*Alabama*' bade farewell to the Azores and headed west towards Nova Scotia and Canada following a regular trade route.

About 150 miles from the shores of the Eastern Americas, midday on the 3rd October 1862, Riordan hailed from the crow's nest, observed two ships, one on the starboard side and the other dead ahead. Judging by the spars and hull lines Semmes thought that there was no doubt as to their identity and he had a second opinion from Jamie, who was standing nearby, both agreeing that they were Northern vessels. It was not necessary for the '*Alabama*' to alter course, as they had no colours fluttering on the stern. The three vessels closed in, with the '*Alabama*' in the middle, when suddenly she fired one shot port and the other starboard and the Bosun ran up the Confederate flag. There seemed to be a shambles and confusion on both enemy ships - no doubt both Captains realised they had been tricked and both hove to, showing the white flag. The Captain of the '*Brilliant*', Peter Robinson, looking through his telescope at the '*Alabama*', seemed very surprised and alarmed, viewing the activity aboard the Southern ship, with its manned guns, the grey uniform of the marines with muskets and side arms at the ready. Robinson decided prudently to show the white flag immediately. He did not want to go down in history as a hero with a posthumous award trying to resist this man-o-war.

A longboat was lowered from the '*Alabama*', and Robinson saw a tall well-dressed Officer, sword at side, pistol in holster, accompanied by six armed grey-uniformed marines. He certainly looked a dangerous adversary, thought the enemy Captain. Lieutenant Armstrong presented himself, saluted Peter Robinson and said rather firmly:
"I demand to see your papers."

"I am the Master of the *'Brilliant'*, my name is Robinson. The vessel is bound for London from New England, shipping wheat and grain and various fruits."

"I see from your papers its value is $90,000," remarked Armstrong. "It's a pity, as the cargo is worth more than the ship. However I have been ordered to burn the ship. You and your crew will be prisoners aboard the *'Alabama'* and I might add it will soften the Captain's heart if you present him with your chronometer as he collects these as souvenirs and yours will be the eleventh."

"I don't often plead for mercy," remarked Robinson. "but you see I am part owner of this vessel, I was present during the building of the *'Brilliant'*. It is a fine craft and this is my first command sailing to London. Please, please spare my vessel" he implored him.

Armstrong remembered his position and orders, whatever his sentimental feelings for the ill-fated Northern vessel.

"Step aboard the longboat, sir I might add that you should be grateful, you are lucky to be alive to tell the story of the *'Alabama'*."

Robinson was greeted courteously by Captain Semmes who also introduced him to Stanley Wilson, Captain of the other Yankee vessel, which turned out to be the *'Emily Farnum'* bound for Liverpool. "Gentlemen, please come to my cabin. where we will discuss your future," courteously remarked Semmes.

"I intend to release the *'Farnum'* and you are free to sail, Captain Wilson, your neutral cargo and papers are in order. I see you are bound for Liverpool, so would you be kind enough to convey two of my sick crew, Frank Donaldson and Alastair Munroe aboard your vessel? Naturally you will be paid; please accept four golden sovereigns. Also would you take any of my crew's mail for their families? I have already mentioned it to my crew and no doubt you will be inundated with correspondence. Captain Robinson, you and your crew will also board the *'Farnum'*. I understand you have received your parole papers from my First Lieutenant. I am sorry I could not spare your ship, the *'Brilliant'*, I know you are attached to her, just as I am fond of the *'Alabama'* and I know the feeling." Robinson was furious, but what could he do? He had to accept, 'What a devil', he thought, 'taking away my livelihood by burning my ship. I feel so humiliated. I can't even return home, I have to go to England. Some day our paths might cross, then I shall get my revenge."

Semmes stood up.

"Gentlemen, we are at war and I bid you goodbye and a safe journey."
Both Robinson and Wilson returned his smart salute.

The '*Alabama*' slowly drew away from the blazing '*Brilliant*'.
Captain Robinson on board the '*Farnum*' looked on with anger and
remorse, watching his future dreams slowly sinking into the great
depths of the Gulf Stream.

In the next few days the '*Alabama*' sailed into the Transatlantic
sailing lines, ever eager to engage the enemy. The only vessels
they encountered were numerous passing neutral European ships
from New York. They were boarded by Jamie, who was establishing
himself more as deck officer than an engineer, together with the
boarding party, but they were mainly shipping flour, coal, iron and
grain. Semmes acknowledged their neutrality and they passed
peacefully on their way.

On Friday 7th October, just off the American coastline, the
'*Alabama*' pursued and boarded a Northern brig which turned out
to be the '*Wave Crest*'. When her papers were examined by
Lieutenant Hornby Lowe they revealed that she was bound for
South Wales.
After being looted she was put to the torch, the crew taking to
their boats loaded with their possessions, hoping to be picked up
by another vessel in the busy shipping lanes.

The '*Alabama*' was heading due west, latitude 40°, longitude 52°,
towards the North American coast.

Just towards dusk, as the moon was penetrating through the dark
clouds, the ever-alert Riordan's booming voice - it's a wonder the
enemy ships did not hear - echoed from the top mizzen:

"Ship ahoy, about twelve miles, on the starboard bow."
All stations were immediately manned. Morgan Page Wickame,
Captain of the Lisbon-bound brigatine the '*Dunkirk*', viewed with
anxiety a burning ship in the moonlight about thirteen miles away.
He then turned his telescope to port to what appeared to be a
white ghostly vessel, sails billowing, bearing at full speed in his
direction.
Wickame decided to try and outrun what appeared to be a menacing
raider - he had heard disturbing news about a Southern man-of-
war!

Every inch of sail was unfurled and the 'Dunkirk' with her long tapering bending masts buffeted the waves and responded well with a gentle motion, but still the pursuing ship was gaining.

Aboard the 'Alabama', Semmes relaxed his crew as they steadily headed after the brigatine. Being a mild night, most of the crew had brought their hammocks and slung them on deck. Jamie was slung between Rob Adams and Ray Ryan and they chatted for a while, then the gentle swaying soon lured the shipmates to dreamland.

Just after midnight the peaceful tranquillity on this beautifully moonlit night was suddenly shattered by the firing of the starboard thirty-two pounder gun, manned by Alex Allen and Speakman.
The 'Dunkirk's' bow quivered as a shell struck her bowsprit - good aiming by the gunners. It trailed behind, still attached by ropes on the starboard side, entangled by the flying and outer jibs.
Wickame realised at once he was outweighed by a warship and quickly lowered his colours and surrendered. The boarding party under the command of Jamie, accompanied by marines, searched the ship and discovered her cargo was grain.
Jamie confronted Wickame:
"Sir, you are now a prisoner of war. Will you please accompany me and I shall present you to the Captain of the 'Alabama'."
The prisoners boarded their longboats and rowed over to the 'Alabama', where Wickame met his victor.
Next day another vessel was boarded by Captain Francis of the marines and the ship's papers proved it to be the 'Tonawanda' bound for Liverpool and the prisoners consisted of women and children.

On Sunday evening 9th October, Semmes was in a good mood after the capture of his fifteenth ship, but it proved difficult with having females on board. He did not want any trouble with his sex- starved crew, as he knew from bitter experience about seamen not having seen a human female form for months on end, so he made a decision. He boarded the 'Tonawanda' with a skeleton crew under the command of Lieutenant Joseph Hardman (an experienced and disciplined officer) together with Bosun Bellew, six seamen and Captain Francis and two marines with orders to follow the 'Alabama' , but another vessel had been sighted and Semmes ordered full sail and set off in hot pursuit.
At daybreak the 'Alabama,' and the prize ship, both flying the Yankee flag, one legitimately, drew level with the stranger and fired a blank

shot across her bow. The Captain on the 'Manchester' was taken by surprise, sailing peacefully on course from New York to Liverpool, and was even more alarmed when a party of marines boarded his vessel and Lieutenant Joe Mills demanded to see his papers.

He despatched Sergeant Ryan back to the 'Alabama' for some further instructions and he was thanked by the Southern Captain. A plan was now formulating in the mind of Semmes as to what to do with these two enemy ships, the 'Tonawanda' and 'Manchester'. The 'Alabama' was on a regular shipping route for Europe, so he could not burn them or sink them by gunfire as it would attract the enemy's attention and that was the last thing he wanted.

A boarding party was placed on board the latest prize - the 'Manchester' - under Lieutenant Joe Mills and was instructed to keep astern of the 'Alabama'. Newspapers were delivered to Semmes by Sergeant Ryan from the 'Manchester' and some were fairly recent, headed 'New York Times' one dated Monday 18th September 1862. These were distributed even in the crew's quarters.

Naturally being Northern newspapers it highlighted only the Yankee victories, but Alex and Jamie, simultaneously reading, were quick to notice the headlines regarding the battle on 20th September at Antietam in Maryland when 2,010 Yankees were killed, 9,416 wounded, 1,043 missing, giving a total of 12,469 against 25,899 Southern losses.

"I suppose," remarked Alex, "it must have been, judging by the losses a Northern victory?"

"But look at this" said Jamie, pointing to the headlines in another paper. "Harpers Ferry in Virginia, Union losses 11,783 and only 500 Confederates lost. That is certainly a decisive Southern victory and that's only twenty miles into the State of Virginia and only four days before. It's amazing how far north the thousands of greycoats have advanced."

Jamie folded the newspaper and tossed it to Carruthers and remarked:

"See what you can make of the War, I think it' s going to be a draw! Before you have a nap, let me know your results."

The following morning there was a strong breeze as the "Alabama", her sails billowing, was followed by the "Tonawanda" and the 'Manchester'. The three ships - in line - sped steadily westward towards the American coast.

Bowen, who had relieved Riordan in the crow's nest, hailed the deck: "Vessel dead ahead." He suddenly observed through his telescope a man on the stern end of the ship ahead, loading a gun barrel in its stanchion.

He shouted down:
"Vessel ahead is arming at the stern."
"Action stations," yelled Semmes.
"Marines up the rigging and when I give the order fire down on the enemy when we are within range. Captain Butler, have your men ready behind the bulwarks and I will give the order to fire when we are alongside."

Captain Wrightson on the '*Lampeter*' noticed through his telescope the rapidly approaching vessel flying the Northern flag. When it was approaching about a quarter of a mile away on the starboard beam, it was hoisted down and the Confederate flag raised. He was alarmed to see men swarming up the mast, armed with rifles "Damn, it's that bloody Southern raider, fire at will, Anderson,' he yelled to the gunner on the stern end.

He swivelled the gun round to the starboard side to engage this rapidly approaching ship and fired a shot. It fell short of the '*Alabama*'.

Semmes and his crew were taken aback that anybody could fire first, especially a merchantman, even though he had been warned by the look-out man.
 "We will close in - stand by for boarding."
The '*Alabama*' fired a warning shot and rapidly closed in alongside, bumping as they collided. Marines in the rigging swung across on ropes and infantrymen under the command of Townsend used boards to cross between the two ships. Men yelled and shouted "Up the Fed's, long live Dixie."

 There was no opposition to the attack as the soldiers swarmed over the deck. Captain Wrightson and some of his huddled, terrified crew gathered together alongside the wheelhouse, nervous, shaking, wondering what was happening. They were joined by the equally bewildered engineers as they came up from the engine room and one by one the entire crew were assembled on deck.
Wrightson was abruptly confronted by a snarling officer who presented the tip of his sword at his throat.
"Do you surrender?" shouted Townsend.
Wrightson, wide eyed, shocked, put his hands above his head, Townsend lowered his sword, realising there was no opposition.

The Captain lowered his arms and remarked:

"I surrender my ship, my crew and cargo."

Jamie pushed Townsend to one side and confronted Wrightson.

"Why did you fire at our ship?" demanded Jamie angrily.

"When I realised you were the '*Alabama*' I knew I was in danger of being attacked and so I used the only means at my disposal, a twenty-pounder gun. Unfortunately the gunner had no experience about firing the cannon, I only wish I had more guns - the sneaky way you approach a merchant vessel."

"Hold on, we are at war, mister and we are using every means to dispose of enemy shipping."

Captain Wrightson was presented to the angry and annoyed Semmes.

"How dare you fire at my ship. Put him below with his crew, in chains if need be, you buggers will be dealt with later. Mr. Townsend, organise what provisions we might require, especially enough for the captive crew. Arrange for a skeleton crew to be under Mr. Hardman. I will arrange a meeting to discuss future plans." He paused to regain his composure. "Ramidios, ask Mr. MacPherson, Butler, the Bosun and Captain Francis to come to my cabin." Within minutes there was a knock on the cabin door.

"Enter." Semmes was quite calm. "Gentlemen, be seated. We are heading for the American coast and as you know there are three captive ships following us which I intend in the future to man and use as warships for the Southern cause. Of course we will have to raid an armament to supply the necessary guns and ammunition. Think it over, if you have any ideas, tell me!"

In his hammock, slung across the aft end of his cabin, Semmes was deeply engrossed reading in the Northern newspaper about 1,200 Southern captured prisoners, imprisoned in a stockade situated near the coast at Dover, a small shipping port on the Delaware River, which is about 500 miles south of New York.

A plan was beginning to form. 'Why not free the prisoners and use them to man three ships and form a small fleet?'

He was so tired his eyes dulled, closed; the newspapers fell from his relaxed hands to the deck, and he was soon in slumber, his brain still active, thinking about his daring future battle plans.

Chapter 6

On Wednesday morning 12th October, Semmes eased himself from his hammock and sat at his desk, his mind formulating his latest plan. He searched the desk drawers and eventually found a map of the east coast of America. He started to make some notes on a pad. After half an hour his plan was complete. He exclaimed, banging the desk with his right hand: "That's it!"
He summoned his swarthy Mexican steward, Ramidios.
"Order Townsend, MacPherson, Francis and Mike Lawson to come here immediately."
The officers entered the Captain's cabin and stood smartly to attention in front of his desk.

"Be seated gentlemen. Would you like some of this fresh Virginian tobacco? Bob - Mike, I know you both smoke. Ramidios - some wine for the gentlemen."
They settled back sampling the excellent captured Spanish wine, Lawson and Bob Townsend packed their pipes and puffed away, all waiting to hear the Captain's latest news.
"Gentlemen, I have read the headline news in the New York Herald. I have a daring plan, which, if it comes off successfully, will enhance our war effort.
There are about 1,200 of our countrymen prisoners in a stockade approximately here." He indicated on the map with his finger.

"The small port of Dover, here," - pointing - "is situated on the left bank of the Delaware River and according to this newspaper the prison is about fifty-five miles north of this town. It appears to be surrounded by a dense forest, extending to the river bank."
He paused to sip his wine.
"We will camouflage our ship - the Blakely guns will be covered, giving the appearance of deck cabins and the thirty-two-pounders will be removed and concealed below decks. I want the ship to look just like an innocent Northern ship and certainly no uniforms should be worn, just casual seamen's clothing. We will sail into the Delaware river using engines." He paused to refill his glass

with white wine, took a sip and remarked, smelling the contents, "Delicious."

"My plan is to land here, in four different places." He indicated again.

"Hack our way through the undergrowth, I suggest with very sharp machetes, attack the stockade or fort on four points, and escape in four groups with the able-bodied prisoners. You will have to overcome the guards quickly and silently. Don't forget, gentlemen, surprise is the best form of attack - the knife, strangling, or the garrotte, definitely no guns, only as a last resort - too much noise. Once you have released the prisoners you will return by four different routes back to the *'Alabama'* and I hope by then to split up into three captured ships, manned of course by our own crew." Ramidios filled their glasses while the company pondered.

"Any questions or any other suggestions?"

"Perhaps it might be an idea," suggested Captain Francis, "if my group, which could be anything up to one hundred men or more, depending on how fit they are, could cross the river at the narrowest point and rendezvous over there with boats."

"That can be arranged. We can have one of the captured ships in the area."

Semmes paused to let his plan sink in to his eager audience, who were looking for some action other than just burning and sinking enemy ships.

"Jamie, I would like you to go in advance under cover of darkness and reconnoitre the land and the prison. Take the Middy - Stewart Owens - I believe he understands the terrain as he was brought up in the Everglades in Florida.

You will be casually dressed, but take a Northern uniform, you might find it handy and don't use firearms but take them by all means. You will go ashore in the longboat, manned by the Bosun. Also take Captain Butler and two seamen to man the oars. They will all be disguised for a fishing holiday. You will proceed inland and if possible you, Jamie, will penetrate the prison, contact the Southern Commander and tell him rescue is at hand and that he should be prepared to escape, say at......" He paused for a moment to consult his diary, "Eleven pm next Friday and use the pass word *'Alabama'* as they might be confronted with yourself or one of us in Yankee uniform. I don't want you to attract the attention of the enemy, otherwise our plans will have to be aborted."

He filled his empty glass. "We are a couple of days from the coastline. You will choose, prepare and train your teams, say twenty men. I hope to capture another ship tomorrow, then we will have three to man with skeleton crews together with the released prisoners. These ships will be in the close vicinity of the '*Alabama*' at all times."

On Sunday, 17th October, the '*Alabama*', flying Yankee colours, entered the two-mile entrance of the Delaware River, the casually dressed crew going about their various duties. Passing vessels acknowledged the '*Alabama*', some lowered and raised their flags. Some of the enemy crew waved. This was acknowledged and it gave Semmes and his crew confidence that they had 'passed the test' of being a Yankee ship.

They sailed fifty-five miles north of Dover, passing various ships of all sizes and anchored in the river.

Captain Semmes assembled his assault team together and addressed them:

"I will repeat the plan of attack and God help anybody who lets me down!

This afternoon Jamie and the Middy will land over there in that cove."

He indicated, pointing with his telescope.

"Bellew and his team will row you ashore and there wait under the pretence of fishing."

He paused, nervously opening and closing his telescope before continuing:

"The boat will wait twenty-four hours only and then you will all return to the '*Alabama*'. We will then discuss our next part of the campaign, which I understand, Jamie, you want to call Exercise '*Alabama*' - good - when you meet our countrymen's leader you will tell him to prepare to escape on Friday - that is the 22nd - at 11 pm. Have you got that Jamie? Remember the whole success of our operation depends on silence and timing. Good luck, Jamie, Stewart, - I hope all goes well and you return safely."

The big brawny Jim Bellew boarded the longboat together with Captain Butler, Jamie, Stewart and two seamen. Hedgecock clutched fishing rods.

They all manned the oars and started rowing for the shore. It seemed a quiet part of the river, but popular for fishing. They passed three small boats, the relaxed occupants intent on waiting for a bite. One person gave a friendly wave. Butler waved his fishing line, which he was about to cast, minus bait.

Jamie laughed.

"You haven't put bait on the hook, Ollie". He turned to Jones: "You know the game, Mick, I've seen you cast your lines over the side many times."

They all laughed; it gave the appearance they were just friends out to enjoy themselves fishing.
"Ray, why don't you show him how to fix the bait?" Jones raised his voice, to impress the local fishermen, in a loud New York Irish accent.

They rowed deeper into the cove. The vegetation thickened on the sandy bank. There were no other boats around; the only noise was the cricket and the hum of a thousand mosquitoes. "We'll pull in over there." pointed Jamie. The boat grounded and he leapt out followed by Stewart, clutching a rifle in his hand. They both had haversacks on their backs containing the dark blue Northern uniforms. Jamie addressed Bellew:
"We will see you this time tomorrow." They bade each other farewell and, with a wave, Jamie and his smaller companion were soon lost in the thick undergrowth, the only sound being the swishing of Stewart's razor-sharp machete which he had been advised to carry by Semmes. They made their way west, guided by Jamie's compass. The thick undergrowth in the forest slowed them down, but Stewart, who led the way, was used to such conditions in the Everglades and he hacked his way ahead. They paused occasionally to etch with their knives on the trees an identity, so they would know the trail back to the boat.

They travelled about four hours through the dense jungle-like undergrowth.
'A good job,' thought Jamie, 'I chose the competent Stewart to accompany me and lead the way. He seems at home in these surroundings.'

The terrain changed and they came into a clearing. The trees were sparse, the ground rose and became steeper and rocky. At the top they had a view of a plain, that stretched flat for miles into the distance.
There, about one mile away, was their objective. They lay on the ground and Jamie could see the stockade clearly through his binoculars. It was almost dusk, which suited their plans.
The wired stockade was about two acres square with guards around the outside. Huts and tents were scattered, there were grey-coated soldiers everywhere. Being October there was a bite in the air and

some men had blankets, some top grey coats and littered inside the stockade were numerous camp fires.

Jamie and Stewart lay silently in the twighlight watching the guards on this side of the stockade. The two sentries would meet in the middle, wait together for a few minutes and then separate and walk out to each corner, where they would each meet their opposite number from the other side. After a few minutes there, they would walk back to meet each other in the middle.The whole operation took approximately five minutes according to Jamie's watch. As Jamie watched the pattern evolved.

"Now here's the plan, Stewart," Jamie remarked in a low voice. "First we change into blue uniforms and when it is dark you take up your position near that tree," (pointing) "and just march up and down like the other guards. I will crawl inside the wired fencing and make contact with the senior Southern officer and inform him of our plans which will take place in two days' time. We must be very careful, silent and alert; if not, the whole plan will collapse and I'm sure Semmes will be really annoyed and angry."

An inky blackness settled around them with a few gleaming stars scattered across the velvet sky. A half-moon slowly lifted from the horizon giving a ghostly tinge to the landscape.

Jamie looked at Stewart and nodded. He felt a reassuring squeeze on his shoulder from his senior officer.

The guards left each other and walked away towards the corners of the stockade, tired now, nearing the end of their watch. Keeping low and praying that the guards did not turn around Jamie sped across an intervening space to a small patch of low bushes near the fence. He flung himself down, breathing heavily, his skin clammy with fear in spite of the cold. He lay there while the guards chatted at the far corners, then made their deliberate way back towards him. Heavy marching feet stirred the dust near Jamie's prone body. The hairs on the back of his head prickled as he held his breath and waited for the man to pounce. The feet moved slowly on and the two guards stood near Jamie, yawning and complaining of the cold. Minutes passed and the tension ached in Jamie's body. Would they never move?

After minutes which seemed like hours the two soldiers turned and walked away, backs to each other, and Jamie. Here was his chance. He ran the short distance towards the wire fence, stumbling on a loose rock, his heart jumping with fright, but the two guards did not turn. He scrambled desperately under the wire fence, kicking as his clothes caught then freed themselves.

Seconds later Jamie slid into the welcome shadow of the nearest hut. At that moment the Northern soldiers on guard reached the corners of the stockade, turned and scanned the area, but saw only stillness and shadows. Nothing to worry about. Jamie tapped gently on the window of the prisoners' hut. A face appeared. He beckoned that he wanted to enter the hut. The grey-coated soldier gestured to the door. It was silently opened and Jamie found himself facing some very curious and wary, scruffy and tattily clothed Southerners. Jamie quickly introduced himself to the senior officer, Colonel Henry Frost, a small dapper man from Georgia. He was surprised to be confronted by an officer in blue, but immediately co-operated when Jamie explained and the plans were made clear about the attack on the Northern camp:

"Four teams will be coming in from an easterly direction, but will be split up, one team to take care of the guards, of course with your assistance, once the operation has commenced. We will seize the munitions and arm your men. The able-bodied men only will accompany the four officers and their teams, through the well-marked route to the river. There will be fifteen boats available at the rendezvous, and your men will be rowed and dispersed to various ships."

"This seems incredible! I feel that I am in a dream;" said the elderly Colonel, "I've been eighteen months a prisoner in this hell hole, I can't believe it is really happening."

"It is, Colonel, and it is all going to take place in the dark next Friday evening, precisely at eleven o'clock. Synchronise your watch now, Mr. Frost, and be prepared for your release. Incidentally our password will be '*Alabama*'." Jamie wished everybody good luck and was silently escorted to the wire fence, where he scrambled underneath, there to be greeted by a vigilant Stewart.

"Now this is the most dangerous part of our mission and we will have to depend entirely on you. How would you like to stay on as a Northern soldier, Stewart? I'm sure you'll get by, for a couple of days. I will contact you first when I return and perhaps you will have the layout prepared for me. I have informed the Colonel where you will be positioned. Don't forget the password." With a laugh he continued:

"You must change your accent, by the way. Your Southern twang might give you away"

"It's all right you talking, you Scottish haggis," laughed Stewart.

They parted and Jamie back-tracked through the thick undergrowth, searching for the markings on the trees, and eventually arrived at the rendezvous point, to be greeted by Bellew and his companions.

They rowed back in silence and boarded the '*Alabama*' at daybreak.

The officers assembled in the Captain's cabin where Jamie drew a map that showed where the stockade was situated in relationship to the rest of the army buildings. Semmes listened intently as Jamie related his night's adventure and explained why and where he had left Stewart.

"Good," nodded Semmes, "and as you suggested, Jamie, you will go in first and contact him, finally reconnoitre the land, report back and having made our plans we will go in at dusk, attack and kill the enemy, show no mercy, no prisoners - release our countrymen and return to the ships.

Jamie's report continued: "Those who are left behind in the stockade - and there could be about 300 of those who are unable to escape, the weak and the wounded - they would create and improve their own camping conditions. If there are no enemy soldiers around, why not impersonate them and dress up in Northern uniforms and just continue running the camp? They could even have their own guards and officers, live comfortably and then, when they are ready make their way to the river and join or capture a boat that will take them to the South and freedom."

"Brilliant idea, Jamie, I don't know how that Scottish brain dreams up all these ideas," blurted out the excited Townsend. "Kill the enemy, by just strangling," he demonstrated, by grabbing Alex around the throat. Everybody laughed.
"Break their damn necks, or hit them on the head, then there will be no blood flying around!"

Semmes took command, "Right, you all know what to do and we will have a final briefing on Thursday afternoon before we embark on this daring adventure, and I hope it will a success. Good luck, gentlemen!
On Thursday, the 21st, the weather was calm as the '*Alabama*' steamed slowly up the Delaware River and anchored together with the three captured ships which were also in the vicinity.
The assault team had been finally briefed by Captain Semmes. It was dark when the men took to the six boats and rowed down without lights and muffled oars, keeping to the left bank of the river. Jamie in the lead boat was at the bow carefully watching the way ahead and the bank for the cove his crew had originally rowed down.
He held up his right hand and his crew stopped rowing. The boat slowly glided along and he indicated with his left hand the opening to the cove.

Bob Mack, who was on the tiller, indicated to the second boat that they were turning to port and proceeding down the cove.

Jamie waved his arm forward and the rowing continued. They rowed for about half a mile, when he indicated with his left hand that this was the place to land. They leapt ashore, pulled the boat into the bank and secured it by rope to a tree. Marine Sergeant Ray Ryan led the way, directed by Jamie and his sharp machete through the thick undergrowth. The men following also hacked a wider path, as this would be the escape routes for the released prisoners on the return journey. The undergrowth cleared and Jamie recognised the rocky hillock ahead. He signalled caution and they made their way, slowly crawling until they reached the ridge where they viewed the vast plain with the stockade and log buildings which housed the Northern Commander and his troops.

"This is the plan." Jamie went over it repeatedly and looked at his watch and then looked through his binoculars. He located Stewart marching up and down by the tree. The sun sank slowly over the western plains.

"Rest, men, and while the other teams are positioning themselves around the outside of the stockade, I shall go and contact Stewart - I showed you where he is marching up and down - and I'll be back by ten o'clock. We'll commence the attack just before eleven as arranged with Colonel Frost in the stockade."

Jamie made his way down the hill slowly and was quietly followed by Ryan. It was so dark they almost bumped into a Yankee soldier at the corner of the stockade. Ryan quickly and expertly wrapped a thin piece of cord around his neck from behind and slowly squeezed it tight until the soldier lay lifeless at his feet. He also claimed the next victim who was fifty feet away.

"Alabama, over here, over here," came a muffled voice in the pitch blackness. "Alabama, Alabama," hoarsely whispered Jamie.

"This way, Jamie."

"You stay here, Ryan, until I return."

Jamie and Stewart crawled under a prepared opening into the stockade where they were confronted by Colonel Henry Frost, the senior officer. They shook hands and men in grey clapped the two men in blue on the back.

"We are ready, those that can travel. We will be leaving the weak and the wounded behind."

"What if they took over the prison?" suggested Jamie.

"What do you mean?" asked the interested Colonel.

"Firstly, strip all the dead Yankee soldiers of their uniforms and bury the dead a distance away from the camp. Select certain officers and dress them in blue uniforms, replace all the guards and carry on just normally running the prison. You could enhance the stockade, by constructing cabins from the local woods. Make use of some of the enemy, say Doctors, by employing them in an improved hospital inside the stockade."

Jamie paused and looked at his watch. "You could live comfortably, the enemy would never suspect and as the Southerners' health improves encourage them to escape via the river."

He gestured towards the opening in the stockade.

"I must go and alert my team, because the assault will commence as arranged at eleven o'clock. You stay and assist here, Stewart, and don't forget, Colonel, once it starts, get your men out and attack the enemy, and good luck, gentlemen."

Jamie made his way back with Ryan to the top of the hillock. In a few minutes it would be eleven o'clock.

"Let's go..."

They moved down the hill silently. A final signal, then they engaged the surprised enemy. All hell seemed to have broken out as the rescue teams attacked on all sides. There was shouting and screaming of the dying, a gun went off and one of Townsend's men fell mortally wounded. Muffled blows continued as the small invading party showed no mercy during the surprise attack.

 A shrill blast on a whistle was the agreed signal by Captain Francis that everything was under control and the enemy had been overwhelmed and defeated. A loud cheer went up, the invaders warmly greeted their grey-uniformed comrades.

Lieutenant Lawson forced an entry into the armoury and distributed the weapons amongst the jubilant, excited prisoners.

Grey uniforms were replaced by blue by stripping the dead. The spared, paroled doctors and medical staff were escorted under guard to the stockade hospital.

 Near-naked Yankee bodies were piled into carts, pulled by mules and solemnly driven away from the carnage to be buried at a distance on the fringe of the forest, later to have a Christian burial, over which Jamie contacted Colonel Frost.

"Colonel, we lost one man, shot by the enemy. Would you please see that he receives a Christian burial with military honours. His name is Seaman Neville Lear, age about twenty-eight. He was born in Birkenhead and worked on the '*Alabama*' during its building and sea trials. A popular man who liked his grog, enjoyed singing

the bawdy songs. He certainly enjoyed life. May he rest in peace"
Chaos - excited and happy men running in all directions. Jamie
tried with his fellow officers to restore order, but it was achieved
by Captain Townsend, thrusting his way into the stockade with
his team of armed marines and firing shots into the air. The
silenced prisoners gathered around as Jamie stood on an upturned
barrel and addressed the men in grey:
"We have a timed schedule to meet at the river. We have to evacuate
the prison immediately and travel along marked guided paths
through the dense undergrowth. I understand you have been
divided into four groups. So will the first group of about 200 follow
Captain Butler. Then Captain Townsend with the next party,
Captain Francis following and myself last." Jamie indicated the
officers.

"Don't forget to bring your personal possessions and when you
are in the deep undergrowth, please hurry as we have to ensure
we meet the boats on time." With a wave he shouted and indicated
to Captain Butler to lead the way, ably supported by Ryan, followed
by Stewart with about fifty men, Bob Mack and Reeves taking up
the rear. So off went the first jubilant party, towards the forest
and freedom, closely followed by Townsend with 150 grey-coated
soldiers, who entered the undergrowth, following another well-
marked path. Then the final party. Jamie addressed the senior
officer:
"Good-bye, Colonel Frost, I see you have already exchanged your
grey uniform for the Yankee's blue. I must say you look smart and
judging by the exchange you must be staying behind."
"Yes, I feel it is my duty to look after my men, and after all I have
been eighteen months inside this filthy, smelly, disease ridden
stockade," he smiled. "It will be a comfortable change outside."
"I wish you well and your companions; it has been a privilege
meeting such a brave man."

They shook hands and saluted. Jamie took a final look around the
now dimly lit stockade. There was hardly anyone around and he
was satisfied the job, so far, was well done. He hastened towards
the marked trail. Mullard and Russ Tudor were just ahead.
"What happened to you?" exclaimed Jamie.
"We went to the armoury to assist in giving out the rifles to the
newly formed blue-coated guard and also to the men in the
stockade."
"Dawn is breaking , we must hurry."
They hacked their way along the well marked path to the river. It

was light, no rescue boats. They made themselves comfortable, and waited till nightfall.

Captain Semmes together with Lieutenant Kelly and a group of seamen were watching anxiously and looking into the darkness of the river for any signs of the returning boats.

"It will soon be dawn," Semmes looked at his watch. He peered into the darkness, He thought he saw a movement, but it was Kelly who first saw the crowded boat manned by Hughie Morris, Adams and Lomax and grey-coats who were rowing furiously. Then they drew alongside.

"Quickly down to the *'Tonawanda'*, unload, change crew and return." All Kelly could see were drawn haggard faces in grey uniforms or wrapped in dirty blankets.

'Ugh,' he thought, 'they must have been ill-treated'.

Another and yet another boat appeared. He issued the same orders. About two hours later the last of the returning boats had   arrived back, but still there was no sign of Jamie, only some of his team. It was now daylight.

Semmes decided the three captured ships should put to sea so as not to attract too much attention and should rendezvous at an agreed latitude and longitude. They weighed anchor and departed. He decided to wait until dusk to rescue the last of the party, knowing that Jamie would understand the situation.

At nightfall, he despatched four boats to proceed to the recognised cove and to return in the darkness to the *'Alabama'*. About six hours later the full boats returned; Jamie had come across Southerners who had lost their way.

Semmes was overjoyed to see the safe return of his popular Lieutenant as he stepped aboard the *'Alabama'*. He staggered over and saluted his Captain.

"Mission successfully accomplished, sir. There was one fatal casualty, Seaman Lear who was shot and died. Colonel Frost, who decided to stay behind with his disabled men, assured me he would give him a Christian burial."

"Thank you, Lieutenant MacPherson your mission will be entered into my log book. I will need you sometime for the details. Thank you for a job well done."

Captain Semmes looked around the deck. He addressed the Bosun:

"Get everybody below decks, Mr. Bellew, let us up anchor and prepare to sail."

Chapter 7

It was Sunday the 23rd of October 1862, the *'Alabama'*, her sails billowing in the light breeze together with the *'Tinawanda'* on her starboard beam, *'Manchester'* on the port and *'Lamplighter'* immediately astern. All four ships easing their way so as not to attract attention from the east coast of America, heading south, into the Gulf Stream, away from any of the Transatlantic sailing routes. Captain Semmes summoned his officers to his cabin to discuss the next plan of campaign.

"Ramidios - attend to the needs of the gentlemen, you will find some vintage Italian wine in my locker and I'm sure Jamie, Captain Butler and Carruthers would like some of their native brew - Scotch, do you call it?"

"Och aye," blurted the three Scots in unison.

Well, gentlemen, my immediate concern is for the safety of the women and children aboard the *'Tonawanda'* and the release of the former captured prisoners." He paused and took a swig of ale.

"I'm pleased our Northern plan in releasing the Southern soldiers was successful, thanks to you gentlemen."

He raised his tankard in a silent salute.

We now have 720 extra men to man the three captured ships - more than ample." Jamie butted in:

"Sir, how would it be if we transferred the prisoners aboard the first English ship homeward-bound we sight?"

"Jamie, you took the words right out of my mouth, that is my plan. Mr. Kelly alert the other ships and their look-out men, to keep a sharp look-out for any such vessel."

A few days later Riordan shouted from the mast head.

"Ship ahoy! - on the starboard beam."

He had sighted through his telescope a majestic looking ship flying the British flag fluttering on the aft end, about three miles ahead. The *'Alabama'* Captain viewed through his glasses and surmised that by her fine lines she must be the luxurious British paddle steamer the *'Britannia'*, crossing the Atlantic bound for Liverpool. 'Ideal,' thought Semmes, I wonder what she is doing so far south, she must be on an extensive cruise - I must try that one day, I have read about these lovely voyages in the newspapers.' "Mr. Kelly, arrange to contact the English vessel, which by its shape and size and flag, I imagine, might be the '*Britannia*'."

The flag signal was raised and both ships hoved to. Jamie called Semmes, "Dress in your number one uniform, look smart, as I know you can, and explain to her Captain the circumstances, the transfer of the women and children and the paroled prisoners." "Very good, sir."
The gig boat manned by the Bosun was lowered over the side. Hedgecock and Jones pulled away on the oars and eventually drew alongside and observed the name '*Britannia*'/Liverpool on the stern end.
Jamie and the Bosun were welcomed on board the crowded ship by the Captain.
"Lieutenant MacPherson of the '*Alabama*,' sir." Jamie saluted. Captain Semmes sends his compliments and requests if you could please accommodate on board some women, children and paroled prisoners of the American Union. Could you land them at your nearest destination."
"I'm Captain Swinnerton," replied the slim-built uniformed commanding officer. "Certainly, we can accommodate them. I'm a native of the old village of West Derby and I have found it very exciting to read about the adventures of the '*Alabama*'. I support the Southern cause, like most people in Liverpool!
He paused for a moment to address his senior officer:

"Mr. Macro, launch two longboats and proceed over to the '*Alabama*'. Give my compliments to Captain Semmes and tell him we shall be pleased to accommodate and land his passengers in Liverpool." Swinnerton paused.
"I understand by your accent you're Scottish." He thought for a minute. "Now I come to think of it we have an engineer named William MacPherson on board, a Scot like yourself, who came from Dunkeld. Could he be related?" "I will summon him from the engine room."
Mr. Macro, please ask Mr. MacPherson if he would come on deck." Jamie was speechless, all kinds of thoughts flashed through his mind. He had lost contact with his folks in Scotland, but he was pleasantly surprised when he was confronted by his bewildered and open-mouthed younger brother, Willie.
They hugged each other, both emotional, wondering what to talk about, all Jamie could say was:
"How are the folks back home? I have been away over twelve months, I have written only twice, because of lack of safe delivery

of the letters. Perhaps you heard my news. Unless Matilda has written to Dunkeld. I'm a serving officer on the '*Alabama*', a stranger on a foreign ship and fighting for a foreign cause."

He paused and gave an hysterical laugh!

"But the pay is good, Willie, that's what keeps me going. This wretched war can't go on for ever, some day I shall be returning. Will you promise me one thing. Please visit Matilda and the girls and give them a hug and kiss from me. Tell them I love them dearly and shall be returning home safely - and united some day. I must go now."

"Good luck, Jamie, and may God go with you."

They shook hands solemnly. Jamie, his eyes misty, looked into his brother's blue eyes, he looked so young and handsome. Then Jamie turned smartly and saluted the '*Britannia*'s' Captain.

He took one look at his brother, smiled, waved and descended the ship's ladder and stepped into the gig boat and returned to the '*Alabama*.'

Semmes set the '*Alabama*'s' course south-south-west. The following day he summoned the four ships to hove to and requested the presence of the three appointed Captains to his cabin aboard the '*Alabama*'.

"Gentlemen, this is our future plan. You'll be supplied with an experienced skeleton crew, men who know their jobs, who will be able to teach the greycoats all about seamanship".

He paused, handed glasses to Hardman, Mills, Armstrong and Kelly and poured some red wine from a silver decanter.

"Your health, gentlemen. Now to business. We will continue to harass, burn, and sink the enemy. We will sail down to the Indies, Martinique and rendezvous in Port Royal, keeping in mind, gentlemen, hugging the coast to sink any vessel flying the damned Yankee colours." He paused to have a sip of wine.

Mills decided to speak his mind. "We can't go and board an enemy ship. I've studied your technique about raising Northern colours, giving the enemy a false and relaxed impression as to our true identity - brilliantly worked out and it has always worked, but none of the three captured ships has any weapons, only a few soldiers with muskets. We cannot fire across their bows at close quarters which is your method."

"I thought you would raise that point," remarked Semmes with a smile. "You will have to find and raid an arsenal and obtain some thirty-two-pounders, they are ideal, and can be easily stored. And

of course other heavy guns, muskets and plenty of ammunition and powder. It is up to you individually to use your initiative."
Semmes gestured to his faithful Mexican steward.
"Have you any of those special Havana cigars? Also top up the wine glasses."
"Si, Señor," the swarthy Ramidios's English was limited, having been raised in a Catholic Mission school in Buenos Aires. "We will hug the eastern coast for a few days and then we will split up. You will furbish your vessels and burn any enemy ships. Loot, especially food, blankets, guns, ammunition, telescopes compasses, night glasses and of course - "
"Now don't tell me sir," quipped Armstrong with a grin. "Chronometers?" They all laughed, knowing the Captain's passion for the various captured instruments!

"We will rendezvous in Port Royal in January. Good luck, gentlemen, and your good health." He drained his glass. A squall blew as they headed south and the ships split up.
Late October, a ship was sighted, the *'Lafayette'*. It was looted, the crew put to their boats and the enemy ship burned.

The next month the *'Alabama'* attacked the *'Crenshaw'* with its cargo valued at $31,350 - it was burned.

Jamie was asleep in his bunk when eight bells sounded, it was his turn on watch. He yawned, stretched himself, washed in the beautiful enamel bowl and went to the officers' mess. "What are you serving up now, Alastair?"
"You will be surprised! I have kept some warm, especially for you - porridge, you will need this, it is wet and windy on top."
He placed an ample bowl in front of Jamie, to which he added salt. He finished his meal and went on deck to be greeted by the wind-lashed rain.
'What weather - good job I was warned to wear my heavy weather gear' mused Jamie, adjusting his sou'wester.
He relieved the officer of the watch, Lieutenant Armstrong.
"We are sailing south-west, longitude 30°, latitude 76°. The weather has been a bit rough, but with the rain it has slightly calmed down. Our rendezvous will be in ten days' time in Port Royal. Those are the latest orders."
"Thank you, Mr. Armstrong, goodnight." The hours drifted by and then Bowen shouted from aloft:
"Lights on the starboard beam about four miles away."
The ship's warning bell clanged and the Captain was alerted.

"Action stations," thundered the Bosun
Captain Semmes appeared, wrapping around him his heavy mackintosh. "What is it, Jamie?"
"A lighted ship, there!" - pointing in the gloom.
"Prepare for action, Mr. Kelly we will attack in the usual manner, hoist the Northern flag and when we close in give him the signal."
It was the '*Baron de Castine*'. Her papers were examined, she was bound for France with a valuable cargo. The crew were transferred, together with certain provisions and she was burned.

The Confederate raider having refurbished her provisions and coal, roamed off the American coastline. Seven more Northern ships were looted and burned. The prisoners put in open boats and directed to the mainland, which was about 400 miles off Cape Canaveral.

She steamed through the Florida Straits, hugging the coastline off Havana on her port beam and into the Gulf of Mexico.

It was Christmas Day, and all the ship's crew were relaxed. A group had assembled amidships. Charlie Mullard sitting on a bollard played on his concertina the introduction of an old English carol. The officers and crew joined in the singing of 'The first Nowell the angels did say, was to certain poor shepherds in fields as they lay.'

Jamie standing on the stern end, watching the white wake disappearing into the distance, pictured the scene 3,500 miles away, the stone-built little chapel in Oldham Street. Matilda, dressed in her blue crinoline, her curly golden hair peeping out of her green bonnet. On either side in the pew, nine-year old Anne and her younger sister the blue-eyed Victoria in their Sunday best, wearing straw hats. Under the pulpit, the crib and the Christmas decorations.
Jamie began to hum - 'Away in a manger, no crib for a bed' - when suddenly his dreams were shattered by Alex.
"I've been looking for you, we need your deep bass for 'Silent Night'.
The singing and the drinking carried on into the night and concluded with the final carol - 'Christians awake, salute the happy morn.'
Eight bells sounded as they sang 'God's highest glory was their anthem still, peace upon earth and unto men'.
'Strange', mused Jamie, who was deep in thought, 'I wonder if the Yanks are singing the same carols in their dugouts or on the high seas.'

"Merry Christmas everyone" shouted out Kelly and slowly the crew dispersed. During the night Semmes was at his desk when he realised he hadn't read the newspapers captured from the Yankee clipper - '*Parker Cooke*'. He studied the latest war news and made some notes. He then made his way to the officers' mess and placed the newspapers on the mess table. Addressing the officers who were at ease, either drinking ale or smoking he said: "I can never understand which direction this bloody war is taking. For instance at Antietam in Maryland, not sixty miles from Dover where we released our prisoners, the enemy lost 12,469 men according to the newspapers and we lost nearly twice as many. Not ten miles away, three days later, at Harpers Ferry they lost 11,783 and only 500 of our brave soldiers died. Moving hundreds of miles west to Kentucky on the 29th September at Mumfordsville, we lost 714 against 3,616 of the enemy. Two weeks later at Corinth in Mississippi we lost 14,221 against 2,359." He paused to drink some wine, offered by Jamie, who thought 'He is getting really into his stride, what next?'
"Who is winning this goddam, bloody war? They must judge each battle on how many are killed - I suppose that is the usual way. Northern papers naturally say the Union is winning and the end is in sight."
Semmes was getting really worked up: "We have so far sunk twenty-four ships and I'm bloody sure," crashing his clenched fist on the table - "we will go all out to destroy their supply ships bringing in their vital war materials. My future plans are to sail south hugging the South American coast line, that is of course after we have berthed in the Indies for repairs and to replenish our supplies, then cross the Atlantic to the Cape of Good Hope. I'm sure we will find lots of prize ships in these seas."
With a slight smile on his face, he remarked:
"Goodnight, gentlemen, and I wish you a Merry Christmas."
He was agitated and bad tempered!

The officers looked at each other, silently wondering who would be the first to speak. Jamie shrugged his shoulders, Mr Freeman puffed away on his pipe, when Edwards the surgeon rose and said goodnight. The company broke up and went to their various quarters, when came -
"Land ahoy!" from the masthead. It was the French-owned island of Martinique. Semmes searched the sandy coastline through his telescope.
"There," he pointed, to the officer of the watch. Head for that sandy cove and beach the ship. We have already discussed that,

having left Birkenhead seventeen months ago, she is beginning to creak and leak. We must repair the damaged canvas and scrape the copper plate below the water-line and she certainly needs a good coat of paint."

The *'Alabama'* grounded on the sandy beach and the repair work commenced within the hour. However naturally all work ceased midday on 31st December and the crew prepared to welcome in the New Year, eighteen hundred and sixty-three. Curious native islanders in their small flat-bottomed boats hovered around the *'Alabama'* and eagerly traded meat, vegetables, fruit, fish and turtles. The decks were scrubbed, brasses polished and bunting hoisted aloft, which seemed to be a signal for several sarong dressed young native girls to be welcomed aboard the *'Alabama'*. The weather was idyllic, four bells rang, the festival began, the laughing, dark skinned native girls mixing with the crew.

Towards dusk the dancing had commenced led by Charlie playing his concertina ably supported by flutes and the Irish fiddler. The native girls, some now stripped to the waist, performed their quick hip-gyrating, foot-stamping dances, their bouncing breasts certainly exciting the sex-starved hungry crew. Semmes, leaning on the main mast, relaxed, watching the antics, became aware that trouble was brewing. He called the Bosun over:

"Alert the First Officer and the marines - you will find them scattered around. Tell them to arm themselves with batons I can sense trouble." Sure enough as the dancing became more frenzied, Jolly Jack, drunk to the eyeballs, decided it was time to grab a dusky young maiden, then all hell broke loose. The marines, led by Captain Francis, charged in swinging their batons. Fierce fighting continued but the tough marines succeeded in restoring order. The first Lieutenant ordered the native girls to be thrown over the side. Alex was in his element, ably assisted by the younger officers, many breasts were fondled and the girls were slowly and gently heaved, some laughing, into the warm waters. They swam towards the beach, some waving, to a chorus from the ship, every eye searching in the gathering dusk in case a leg or breast was exposed as they swam slowly into the night. Order was restored when the four pipers led by Bill Crichton paraded around the deck. The deck was cleared for eight Scots led by Jamie, and Alex in his green kilt, to perform Highland jigs, strathspeys. Townsend, MacKenzie, Ian Fisher and Mackay performed the sword dance supported by the crew, who were beating time by stamping their feet and clapping to the rhythm. Jimmy Black beat time with a belaying pin on a huge pan lid. A few joined the dancers for the reels until everybody

was exhausted, then it was time for Charlie to play the crew's favourite tunes accompanied by Anton Forrest on his flute and the Irish fiddler. The cove resounded to the lusty singing of shanties and songs from the deep South. Lilting Irish songs were sung by Jim Brennan and Frank Jenkins in his rich tenor voice.
Jamie sang:
'Flow gently, sweet Afton among thy green braes;
Flow gently, I'll sing thee a song in thy praise;
My Mary's asleep by thy murmering stream,
Flow gently sweet Afton, disturb not her dream.'
('If only', dreamed Jamie, 'I was on the bank of the Afton with my beloved, just like our Rabbie and his beloved Mary.')
Eight bells clanged, louder than usual. "A happy New Year, everybody," called the Bosun and there was the sound of tankards clanging together and the tinkle of glasses as friends greeted each other. The evening concluded with the crew joining crossed hand, singing and swaying to the Bard's National Anthem - 'Auld lang syne. The Southerners, not to be outdone, sang 'Dixie', everybody joining in and then it was time to hit the bunk.

The next day being New Year was relaxing for the crew, for swimming, the clear blue warm waters being the attraction. Jamie leaning over the forward starboard side, viewed the anchor wedged in the clear coral reef thirteen fathoms deep. Small fishes in their hundreds were feeding and groping turtles in the ferns and an abundance of sponges. He took off his clothes - it was so inviting - and dived into the warm waters, soon to to be joined by a large number of the crew. Four musketeers posted around the ship were alerted in case there was a shark invasion.

The First Lieutenant arranged a race between two longboats, one manned by the engineers, versus the deck officers. Jamie having training in both jobs decided to man the engineers' tiller and Midshipman Owens the deck officers' tiller. They rowed round the 'Alabama' ten times and the deck officers won admidst rousing cheers from the men leaning over the ship's rail. Lieutenant called out:
"We shall now have a race between the gunners and seamen, the boat likewise, Jim Brennan for the seamen."
Briggs chose Mackay, McMath, Speakman, Heritage, Morris and Thornhill, who quickly manned the boat and raised their oars, ready for the off. The unpopular Brennan had difficulty raising a crew, but as news spread about the prize, which was a keg of ale, men volunteered immediately.

At the firing of a pistol by Bosun Bellew both boats' bows leaped into the crystal clear waters for the race around the ship. After the ninth lap the excitement and cheers encouraged both boats, who were neck and neck, but the seamen, who seemed to have more stamina won by a few feet amidst a deafening roar from the crowded rails. Even the captain cheered the seamen to victory; the crew revelled in competitions.

So Kelly arranged squadron swimming races. The Medics captained by Graeme MacGregor, versus carpenters with Rob Adams as their leader; bosun's mates versus firemen, cooks and stewards versus marines. All good and exciting fun which everybody enjoyed, lots of merriment (and Joe Mills taking bets on the side). By process of elimination Stephen Riordan, who had been replaced aloft by John Bowen, judged the winning squadron team by a short breadth were the cooks and stewards - rank outsiders in the betting. Joe made a fortune.

While the Captain was presenting the keg to a proud Alastair Liddell, the swimming captain, a gunshot from a ship about one mile away echoed across the cove, causing a mushroom of birds flocking into the blue skies.

Chapter 8

The officer on watch, Lieutenant Armstrong, viewing the rapidly approaching ship, suddenly realised it might be a Northern warship. "Action stations, action stations," yelled Armstrong.

"Weigh up anchor. Engine room - raise steam, lower propeller. Bosun - raise funnel - Lieutenant Lowe man the guns. Captain Townsend - marines on parade and sound general quarters."

Swiftly the '*Alabama*' was ready for action and within half an hour was steaming out to engage the schooner, which was heading straight for the Confederate raider.

They passed each other and Semmes let out a sigh of relief as he recognised his supply ship, the '*Agrippina*'. A loud cheer went up, the crew relaxed and stood down and the two vessels drew alongside each other. Greetings were exchanged and Captain Threlkeld boarded the '*Alabama*', saluted, shook hands with Semmes and they retired to his cabin for 'refreshments'.

As greetings were being exchanged between the ships' crews, a tall, slim seaman leaning on the '*Agrippina's*' taffrail waved to Jamie who waved back and beckoned him on board the '*Alabama*'. They shook hands.

"My name's Jonathan Taylor."

"Pleased to meet you, I'm Jamie MacPherson" - with a laugh - "Lieutenant, engineer, seaman, navigator, deck officer, fireman, you name it - we are taught various trades and skills on board this ship. May I escort you to my cabin for a glass of cool ale? It is very hot on deck."

They were seated comfortably, eyeing each other for several seconds. The wavy-haired, brown-eyed Jonathan finally spoke.

"We have heard about the '*Alabama's*' adventures, how it has become famous or infamous." They both laughed.

"I'll drink to that" quoth Jamie.

"Of course," continued Jonathan, "dependent on whose side you are on" - another laugh. "But you are certainly feared by the enemy. Whatever port we visit, the '*Alabama*' is named, even headline news in the newspapers."

He seemed excited and leaned forward:

"Have you any influence, Jamie? Could you get me transferred to your ship? I'm an experienced seaman and have studied navigation, in fact I studied law before I smelt the briny, and like yourself I'm a stranger on a foreign ship, fighting for a foreign cause."

"Well, that's interesting, I'll put your case before Captain Semmes. We are always looking for enthusiastic and experienced men. I'll go and see him now. Help yourself to some more wine." Jamie knocked discreetly on the Captain's cabin door. Semmes said "Enter". He was in conversation with the 'Agrippina' Captain. "What do you think, Stanley?" when he heard Jamie's request. "Would you be willing to release Taylor? Perhaps we might do an exchange? There's bound to be someone who would like to return to England to get away from this wretched war!"

"I'm sure that can be arranged, Raphael."

"Good! Jamie, that is agreed. Arrange accommodation for Taylor, indeed you could train him up for any necessary jobs and see if anybody would like to return to England. When we have unshipped all the 'Agrippina' cargo including the coal, please arrange to ballast her with coral and she will return back to Liverpool, there to be loaded with further supplies."

Semmes paused and - addressing Captain Threlkeld who appeared to be nodding off with the heat and the amount of wine he had consumed - remarked:

"Stanley, we will arrange another rendezvous for our supplies on your return from Liverpool."

Jamie returned and with a smile on his face told Jonathan the good news.

'What a likeable chap,' thought Jamie. 'I can see us becoming firm friends.'

He then inquired from the crew anybody who would like to return to Liverpool on the 'Agrippina'. Albert Royce volunteered and Jamie asked him if he would mind delivering any mail from the crew, to which he readily agreed. "Anything to get off this goddam ship!"

After refurbishing the 'Alabama' with her stores, the 'Agrippina' departed midst cheers and the raider also left, full steam ahead and sails billowing, into the Gulf of Mexico.

Semmes addressed the officers in his lounge: "The news, gentlemen, from Captain Threlkeld is that the Unionist Captain Blake is in command of five warships off Galveston. This town has been retaken by my friend General Magruder, ably assisted from the Gulf by Captain Robert Leon Smith, commander of two small river boats, which were heavily bagged on deck where good marksmen were concealed. He surprised, engaged and outwitted four heavily armed Union ships. Their fate seems mysterious, so we are sailing to investigate if these four enemy ships are still in the Galveston area."

During the early morning of 11th January 1863, the keen-eyed, well-built Riordan on the masthead shouted down that a ship about four miles away, was bearing straight for the '*Alabama*'. Jamie, being the watch keeper, ordered battle stations and summoned Mullard, the drummer, to sound the alarm.
Chief Engineer Freeman slowed the ship down to three knots. There was a gentle breeze blowing on this straight moonless night.

Captain Blake, standing on the poop deck of the Northern warship '*Hatteras*', viewed through his night glasses, with suspicion, the steamer sailing towards him about three-quarters of a mile away on the port beam. 'Lieutenant McFarland, what do you make of that vessel?" to his first officer, handing him his glasses.
"That's strange - it appears to be gathering speed. It has passed us and is turning around and coming up on our starboard beam."
The Captain and his First Lieutenant crossed amidships to the starboard side.
"I think it could be,' remarked McFarland. "Just a minute ....." - a pause - "Yes, I see guns, yes I'm sure, it could be that darned Southern raider. Oh no, it's flying British colours.
"Just to be sure, Mr. McFarland, order battle stations."
Both vessels came within hailing distance.
"Identify yourself - what is the name of your ship?"
"It is Her Majesty's ship '*Vixen*'" replied the '*Alabama*'s' First Lieutenant.
"Just to be sure we will visit you" shouted Blake through his trumpet.
He was almost about to lower the longboat, when suddenly over the '*Alabama*'s' loud hailer came her true identity.
She raised her true colours.
We are the Southern raider '*Alabama*'."
Then followed a broadside from the eight-inch Blakely gun, manned by Captain Townsend.
The shell struck the '*Hatteras*' aft of the paddle wheel just below the waterline and water poured into the engine room, causing clouds of steam from the damaged boilers. It was intermingled with the cries of the bewildered injured firemen and engineers.
On board the '*Alabama*', Captain of Marines, Alan Francis, ordered immediate firing from the fifty muskateers sheltered behind the

ship's bulwarks which raked the deck of the '*Hatteras*' inflicting heavy casualties. The Blakley gun played havoc, causing fires in the enemy warship's holds and the 100 rifled gun pounder did severe damage and the armament on the '*Alabama*' proved far superior to the enemy's guns.

Fire enveloped the '*Hatteras*' amidships, the sea roared into the engine room. Men were shouting for help, some screaming in pain. She was shrouded in black smoke.

Captain Blake knew he had lost the short battle. He was taken by surprise and overwhelmed - a hopeless situation, with no pumps available to combat the flooding. She was flooding rapidly.

He ordered the colours to be lowered.

"Mr. McFarland - flood the magazine and prepare to abandon ship. Place the wounded, yourself included, into the only available boat on the port side and head for the shore" - pointing. "In that direction, about twenty-eight miles away - and if you make contact with our fleet give them the last position of the battle."

The '*Hatteras*' was sinking rapidly. Blake ordered all hands over the side.

"Grab spars, anything that floats", he shouted above the din. 'Head for the '*Alabama*'."

The crew of the '*Alabama*' were leaning on the port bulwarks, watching by the illuminated fires on the doomed ship the throes of their enemy. With a rumbling as her boilers exploded, she seemed to be torn apart and with a loud rumble she slowly sank into the shallow waters. When she settled on the seabed, her drab pennant, wrapped around the masthead, could be seen faintly silhouetted above the water.

The turbulent raging sea became alive with the white faces of the shouting crew of the '*Hatteras*', swimming desperately towards the '*Alabama*.' The tackles creaked as Bosun Bellew immediately ordered longboats to be quickly lowered to rescue the swimmers. Ropes were thrown over the side to be grabbed by desperate hands who were hauled to safety.

The shouting of the drowning, pleading for help, could be heard in the darkness as Ray Tyler dived over the side, followed by Graeme the surgeon and Alastair the cook, another strong swimmer, and then the athletic Jonathan Taylor, all eager to take part in the rescue in the warm waters of the Gulf. Those rescued boarded the '*Alabama*', were given blankets and ushered below and given hot drinks. The longboats searched the debris and then reported back to the First Lieutenant. Three of the last survivors lay shivering, as the last boat was hoisted on board. Blake, the last to leave the doomed ship, swam towards the '*Alabama*' and being exhausted was assisted on board. He confronted Captain Semmes, who saluted the bedraggled and wet enemy Captain. Clutching his sword with his left hand, he pulled his damp peaked cap from underneath his navy jacket, punched it carefully into shape, fitted it upon his head, straightened himself, and smartly saluted Semmes.

He took his sword from its scabbard and clutching the blade with his right hand placed it across his left forearm and presented the handle to Semmes remarking:

"Sir, will you accept my sword? This is the formal surrender of myself, crew and the '*Hatteras*.' We lost the battle, I think only two of my men perished. Thank you, sir, for your help in rescuing the wounded and my crew. We are deeply grateful. War is grim, atrocities take place on both sides, but we humane seafarers seem to have a different code in battle. We have a respect and admiration for each other." Having handed over his sword, which Semmes graciously accepted, Blake stepped back and they both saluted. Semmes offered him the use of his cabin, having a spare room.

He summoned the First Lieutenant:

"Mr. Kelly, heave to, release the anchor and will you ensure the safety of the prisoners and see they are safely bunked. At day break scour the seas and search for any more survivors among the debris and flotsam."

Two boats were launched next morning, searching the area and the only evidence a battle had taken place were two masts of the '*Hatteras*', one displaying the Union pennant, which was carefully taken down and reverently folded. There didn't appear to be any survivors, until Bob Mack, the oarsman, shook Thornhill's shoulder. "Look over there, isn't that a body on that board?".

They brought the boat around and as they approached the thick board which was part of a bulkhead, being gently lapped by the sea, they saw two bodies lying face down, but one lying partly across the other with his right arm across the back clutching a handful of shirt. Obviously he had rescued one of the survivors and had pulled him onto the floating board. Bob gently turned the body over, looking for signs of life.

"Good lor'," exclaimed the shocked Thornhill as he examined the face of Alastair Liddell. "It's the cook!"

They quickly lifted the two bodies into the boat with the help of the Bosun's Mate, Alex Allan, who adjusted the oars, and began rowing quickly towards the '*Alabama*'. Big Bob turned the cook face down on the bottom of the boat and tried to revive him by pressing vigorously, using both his muscularly strong tattooed arms, working rhythmically into the small of the back, compressing the lungs. He worked strenuously on Alastair, sweat pouring down his face, but there was no sign of a trickle of water from his mouth. John Thornhill, working on the other body, was more successful as he began dribbling out water, coughing, vomiting and his eyes flickered open momentarily.

They reached the side of the '*Alabama*' and willing hands quickly lifted the two bodies out of the longboat and rushed them to the surgery, where Doctor Edwards tried to revive Alastair, but his efforts were in vain and he pronounced him dead to the anxiously gathered crew members, and reverently covered his body with a sheet.

The officers and crew were shocked with the loss of their friendly Scottish cook and baker, particularly Jamie as they shared many a joke and laugh. They had 'pulled each other's leg,' especially when discussing the ingredients of haggis.

The following day Captain Semmes ordered a full dress parade for the burial service. He instructed the First Lieutenant on the order of the service, including the pipe band, fifes and drums.
"By the way, Mr. Kelly, it is my intention to parole the prisoners. Will you assemble them on deck, make them as presentable as possible in one hour's time, including of course our crew."

"Captain Blake, officers and crew of the '*Hatteras*', by the power vested in me by our President, please raise your right hands. I hereby parole the Captain, the officers and crew of the Union warship '*Hatteras*' and you will be repatriated in the near future."

It was a sad day on Monday 13th January 1863 at 93° longitude and 27° latitude, 130 miles from Galveston as the '*Alabama*' hove to, on a bright sunny day. The crew stood to attention together with Captain Blake of the '*Hatteras*' and the paroled crew. The pipers, Bill Crichton standing amidships, Unsworth forward, and aft Gordon Forrest, commenced playing the lament, supported by Mullard and Jaffee on drums.

The sound of the pibroch echoed in the stillness on this idyllic sunny day.
"Company, at ease" commanded the First Lieutenant. "Lower the colour Mr. Riordan. Off caps."

Captain Senmes thumbed and opened the Bible and commenced reading.:

"I will lift up mine eyes unto the hills from whence cometh my help" - his voice droned on.

Jamie, standing next to Alex, could not help but ponder how much Alastair had loved talking about the hills and picturesque countryside, which at this time of the year would be covered in snow, surrounding his beloved native town of Dunblane.

"Behold He that keepeth thee will not slumber........ the Lord is thy shade upon thy right hand."

'The great safety of the godly who put their trust in God's protection - Psalm 121,' mused Jamie. He looked towards the canvas-shrouded body lying on a plank, draped halfway with the Confederate flag and the other half the St. Andrew's flag.

Semmes concluded - "The Lord shall preserve thy going out and thy coming in, from this time forth and even for evermore." He closed the Bible.

"Gentlemen," contintinued Semmes, "let us repeat together the prayer our Saviour taught us 'Our Father which art in heaven.... ,' at the conclusion of which the First Lieutenant signalled to one of the drummers, Marc Jaffee. (The medium-built dark-haired teenager had survived this sea battle by using his drum to keep himself afloat.)

He braced himself and commenced the muffled beat on the drum. Captain Semmes opened his Prayer Book. "Let us pray for our departed shipmate. They who go down to the sea in ships............."- 'He was never a fighting man' muttered Jamie - "Greater love hath no man than this, that a man lay down his life for a fellow man."

"Amen to that" muttered one of the crew of the '*Hatteras*'.

"Company - attention - on caps," ordered the first Lieutenant.

"Let Alastair Liddell's body be committed to the deep."

To the roll of the drum and the lament on the pipes, two of the pall bearers (Butler and the man Alastair had saved from drowning, Richard Henry Roberts) gently lifted one end of the board which was balanced on the ship's bulwark.

The officers saluted. The pipes and drums ceased and the bosun blew on his whistle - the highest Naval honour any seafaring man could bestow on his fellow shipmate.

The final tilt of the board, then a splash as the body entered the deep off the Texas coastline. The slight breeze which ruffled the flags on the board was the only moving epitaph to a brave man who sacrificed his life.

"Atten - tion" - Commanded the First Lieutenant.

Semmes addressed the assembly: "At ease, gentlemen, thank you for attending to pay your respects to departed merit, especially to the crew of the '*Hatteras*.' Alastair was a gentle man we held in high esteem and he will be sadly missed. Mr. Kelly, you may dismiss the company and will you see me together with the senior officers. "I'll be amidships."

The Captain strolled along the port side deck, deep in thought, almost bumped into Captain Blake and addressed him. "It was gracious of you to attend our committal service Captain."
"I deemed it an honour and felt so humble when Mr. Kelly allowed the man Mr. Liddell saved to take part, by assisting in committing his body to the deep. The young man's name is Richard Henry Roberts and also the drummer boy, Jaffee, who felt so thankful that the drum saved him from drowning."
"Thank you for those kind words - will you excuse me as I have to meet my officers."

Semmes addressed his senior officers.
"Gentlemen, we will sail to Galveston, just to satisfy myself that we are in control once more of the area, keeping in mind that we want to be in Port Royal at the end of January."

There was a fair wind as the '*Alabama*' headed north-by-north-west sailing across the Gulf of Mexico towards Galveston. "Jamie" Semmes standing amidships breathed deeply and flexed his muscles. He beckoned his First Lieutenant.
"Keep the crew alert. There could be enemy ships in this area, I learned from the Captain of the '*Hatteras*,' that Galveston has been retaken by our gallant soldiers. Would you order Captains Butler and Francis to drill their men and arrange target practices."
"Aye aye, sir." Jamie continued to pace the main deck.
The '*Alabama*' was fifty miles from Galveston when the look-out shouted down.

"Ship ahoy - dead ahead."
"Ac - tion stations," shouted Jamie.
Semmes went to the bow and viewed through his telescope the stern end of a brig.
"Increase sail, Bosun." Jamie's command saw Roughler, Leeson and six seamen scrabbling up the masts to release the main sky sail, fore sky sail and mizzen sky sail.
The ship responded well and the distance was reduced. The Southern flag replaced the Northern one. Gunner Schmechel fired the 32-pounder, but the shot fell short of the stern of the brig."

The quiet Captain Dobbs of the '*Chastelaine*' wondered if he was seeing things as the flags on the rapidly approaching ship were exchanged, and when a shot was fired he was really scared and ordered his ship to reduce sail and heave to. Carruthers accompanied by the armed Reeves and Schmechel and six marines boarded the enemy ship.

Carruthers confronted and saluted Dobbs "I'm Lieutenant Carruthers from the Confederate ship '*Alabama*' and I demand to see your papers."

Captain Dobbs pushed his way passed the members of his crew, made his way to his cabin, and with shaking hands produced the ship's papers.

"Sit down there, Captain, and pour yourself a glass of whisky, and pour one for me. I can assure you no harm will come to you or your crew if you behave yourselves and don't do anything foolish."

Carruthers examined the ship's papers. The '*Chastelaine*' was registered in Boston, her home trading port - and her cargo was sugar and rum.

'Captain Dobbs, you and your crew are now prisoners of war. Will you explain the position to your crew and arrange for everybody to leave the ship with their personal possessions in two of your longboats. Schmechel will accompany the Captain and escort them to the '*Alabama*'.

Carruthers, assisted by three marines, removed ten barrels of rum, and placed them in their boat, put the hatchet to another ten in the hold and set the ship alight.

Captain Semmes saluted Dobbs as he stepped aboard the '*Alabama*.'

Accompany me to my cabin, Captain, where we will discuss your future and you can take my word no harm will befall you or your crew while you are on my ship. Sometime in the future you will be set adrift in your longboats within easy access to the shore and safety, after you have been paroled."

The prisoners were herded below deck, the enemy's longboats were secured on the stern and and the '*Alabama*' got underway, heading into heavy seas with a strong north-easter blowing. The destination was Galveston.

Off duty in the officers' mess, Jamie was chatting with Freeman and Carruthers.

"I wonder what awaits us at Galveston?" asked Jamie.

"Hard to tell until we arrive," declared the pipe-smoking Mr Freeman. "The latest news is that Galveston has been re-captured after a bloody battle in which 600 Northerners were killed and some of the town on the outskirts is in ruins. Our Captain is curious, I don't think we will be able to contribute anything to its independence, except to land the prisoners."

"Shore leave won't be very exciting either," chipped in Carruthers.

"Unless we have the support of the Southern troops, if any of the enemy are in the area," said Jamie.

The weather was stormy when the '*Alabama*' arrived off Galveston. Semmes ordered the gig boat and, dressed in his blue uniform, went ashore with Jamie, Jacko, the Bosun and seamen at the oars. He decided to meet the Mayor and he was delighted to shake hands and renew acquaintance with one of his old friends, Captain Charles Bartlett, who was also born in Maryland, but he was ten years older than Semmes. He was tall and slim with grey curly hair. "May I introduce the acting First Lieutenant, Jamie, and Mr. Taylor. My gig is at the wharf guarded by the Bosun."

"Fancy meeting you after all these years, Raphael," remarked Bartlett. "We heard of your heroic adventures on the high seas, mainly from Northern newspapers. Galveston was captured by the enemy, but fortunately a bombardment from some ships' heavy guns scared them off and they ran," Charlie chuckled, "with their tails between their legs. It was quite exciting and a quick victory for us. We also have a small number of Northern troops on the outskirts of the town but we haven't enough troops to engage them."

Semmes related the Dover campaign, how 750 troopers had been released and should be arriving in this area in three ships. Captain Semmes smoothed his moustache, a gesture he did when he was deep in thought.

"What would you say, Charles, if my crew - we have some tough and seasoned seamen and marines - engaged the enemy on the outskirts of the town?" He gestured.

"Have you a map of the area and where are they hiding?" Jamie sensed a battle. The crew would relish a fight with the enemy after so many months at sea.

"We are here and the bluecoats are here,' pointed Bartlett. "What is left of our troops are billeted here, but they only patrol in this area." He pointed with a pencil. "The immediate danger is raiding parties and snipers."

"We'll have to put an end to all this, and wipe out these bastards," said Semmes. "If they think they can surround and cause trouble to this town with just a handful of men, they've got another think coming. Jamie, muster about fifty armed men." Semmes added with a chuckle, "and bring some riggers and seamen, mainly handy with knives and the cosh. Charles, can you get me the army's senior officers and we shall meet here, say in about one hour."Jamie immediately went to the wharf, stepped into the waiting gig and while the seamen were rowing to the *'Alabama'*, he related the future campaign to the Bosun, asking him to choose fifty tough hand-picked men including Ryan, Francis, Doyle and Hedgecock. He also alerted the other officers about future plans. Officers and men mustered, all eager for some action, and a shuttle service quickly rowed the fighting unit to Galveston's jetty.

At the meeting the garrison Captain - Joseph Sarni, a seasoned soldier with his slightly Italian drawl explained in detail about the enemy raids - how the mounted patrols would make raids, killing men and women, looting and burning buildings, mainly the farms on the outskirts of the town.

"Do they have any special route and where do the patrols start?" asked Jamie.

"There's a rock formation about here." Sarni pointed out on the map. "About fifteen miles out of town. We have sighted enemy soldiers on the highest advantage points, who can view the countryside for miles around and alert the 'Yankee troops on the other side of the hillock."

"I see.' said Semmes. He was deep in thought.

"Could you supply about twenty horses for my men. The plan I have in mind is: my cavalry will go to a point, say about here," pointing to the map, " which looks a likely patrol area - by this stream and about ten miles from their camp. You will be in charge, Captain Francis, and separate the men into groups, casually dressed. When we engage the enemy - kill, kill, kill!" - his eyes blazed, he looked wild and savage. "No bloodshed, strip them of their uniforms, like you did on the Dover raid, dress and disguise yourselves and act like Northerners, mount their horses and together with your own horses rendezvous, say here," pointing to a rocky canyon, "until nightfall."

"In the meantime," interrupted Butler, "my men will be in our usual grey uniform waiting, when you arrive at this canyon."

"Quite correct, Ollie how did you get that funny name - you bald-headed old coot?" Semmes laughed, which was a signal for everybody else. "Never mind" he chuckled.

"So in the darkness we will go in and strike the enemy and wipe them out," said Francis.

"That is the plan of campaign, gentlemen, let's sleep on it," concluded Semmes. "Mr. Bartlett - will you see that the Yankee soldiers receive a Christian burial."

"I shall arrange with the undertaker, Reggie Guest and his team to recover the bodies."

"Captain Sarni, I think it would be wise if your soldiers stayed behind to guard the town - in case anything should go wrong. I know you would be anxious to take part in the battle. After all," Semmes couldn't control himself, "you are the army and we are only the navy." Everybody cheered, chorusing "Long live the Confederates." "Up Dixieland" - and immediately burst into that song.

"So we will meet here" Semmes said, when everybody had quietened down, "outside the barracks - if you will set your watches - 7am tomorrow."

"How would you and your men like to spend the night in the barracks?" suggested Captain Sarni.

"Thank you kindly, sir," said Semmes. "We accept!"

There was a heavy mist next morning, which suited the Southern raiders as they set off to engage the enemy. The party led by Captain Francis on a fine black stallion dismounted in a gully by a swiftly flowing deep stream. They were ten miles outside the town of Galveston. The horses were hidden in the brush and Francis despatched patrols to report back any enemy movements. He also posted sentries in various strategic positions around the gully. It was reported back by Ray Ryan that blue-coated horsemen were approaching single file about a mile away.

"Ready for action, men," said the Captain."Now remember, the cosh, garrotte, silent killing, no blood on the uniforms and I hope they fit. Hey! you there - are you paying attention? What's your name?"

"Leeson, sir."

"I would like you to ride alongside me. Prepare to mount and good luck, men."

They mounted and, led by Francis, they rode towards the enemy. Jamie, riding ahead as scout, reported back that about thirty blue-coats were approaching a clearing in the trees. They quickly dismounted and leading their horses quietly spread themselves hiding in the cover of the thick undergrowth which surrounded the clearing.

The signal to attack was given by Francis with a wave of his arm. The casually dressed Southerners surprised the bewildered men from the North. The thud of a cosh, the butt of a rifle, crushing of skulls, caused shouting: the screams of the dying as the men from the '*Alabama*' fiercely combated their opponents, first dragging them from their horses. Jamie ran and leapt on the back of a Yankee horsemen and wound his arm around the throat of his enemy from behind. They both crashed to the ground, he lost his grip and the heftily built, snarling blue-coat fisted him a mighty blow on the chin, knocking him senseless into the undergrowth.

The trooper withdrew his sword and was about to thrust it into Jamie's body when Leeson hit the man a violent blow on the back of his head, which split his skull open! Leeson turned Jamie over and Jamie's eyes flicked open. He was dazed and shaken. He felt his swollen jaw and groaned. Leeson sat him up. He mumbled: "I think my jaw's broken."

"What a blow!" - rubbing his numbed chin.

"Thank goodness you're all right, sir. I feared for your life. Come on, let me help you up." Schmechel, who had seen the incident, dashed across and leapt off his horse and between the two of them they dressed Jamie in the dead Yankee's blue uniform. Schmechel laughed. "He's just about your size, sir." Jamie felt a lot better seated on the black gelding and he thanked the troopers. The battle was over, the dead men were disrobed and their bodies hidden in the undergrowth. They mounted up.

Corporal Fishwick, a wrangler, with help from McMath and Willis rounded up thirty loose horses and they left the clearings. Captain Francis, being the last out after seeing there was no evidence of a battle, thought: 'You wouldn't think an hour ago a surprise attack had taken place,' and trotted off to join the newly formed 'Northern troop'.

They rendezvoused with Captain Butler at the appointed place and bivouacked until nightfall.

Given a signal from Francis, Ryan moved quietly, arousing the sleepers with his boot. The saddled horses were tethered and guarded by Fishwick and his team.

"Check your weapons," ordered Captain Francis. "We will divide into two groups. Captain Butler, you will be second in command. Officers and sergeants, just gather around and I'll explain the plan of action." He produced a small sketch and held it for the team to see. "This ellipse represents a hillock. We are here," pointing, "and the enemy are camped on the other side, here."

"Butler, arrange for some of your men to skirmish the rocky hill, silence the guards and approach the enemy camp from the rear down the slope of the hill."

"Can I suggest something, sir?" interrupted Fishwick, a wrangler. "How about stampeding the horses through their camp, followed by a cavalry charge? The enemy no doubt will be asleep in their tents and taken unawares." Francis paused for a moment, weighing up the new situation.

"Let's get it organised. Jamie and Ryan scout ahead and report back." Off went Jamie and his companion, down the long ravine. The watery moon presented a wintry scene. A gentle breeze blew. Ryan, riding ahead, stopped and raised his arm.

"There's a soldier ahead about 100 yards. I can just about see him. Leave him to me, he's probably on guard duty. You go back and alert the troops. This ravine leads to their camp."

Jamie retreated and told Francis. The troops prepared for action. The horses were herded together for the drive by Fishwick. Ryan reported back the way ahead was clear to the enemy camp, "Is everybody assembled and ready for action?" Francis asked quietly. "Don't rush things, Fishwick, maintain quietness until near their camp, then charge and then you can make as much noise as you like when you're on top of the enemy - good luck!" Fishwick mustered the loose horses and slowly the herd entered the ravine. Francis rode on the right flank, with Leeson alongside. At the end of the ravine on a slope he noticed the tents and the camp fires of the Northern troops. Francis gave a signal and the charge commenced, slowly at first - and then gathered momentum.

The thundering horses slowly awakened the bluecoats, but they were quickly cut down by Francis and his cavalry. Butler attacked them down the slope of the hillock. It was over in an hour! Prisoners were rounded up. He summoned the wrangler: "Fishwick, thank you for your herdsmanship and you can now return to the town with Leeson and inform Captain Semmes of our victory; also tell Captain Sarni to arrange a burial party and wagons to carry the wounded to hospital.We have several casualties."

The victorious Southern soldiers led by Captain Francis returned to the barracks in Galveston. They were warmly greeted by the happy and cheering townspeople, knowing that the men from the 'Alabama' had rid them of their oppressors. Captain Semmes welcomed his crew at the army barracks and congratulated them on routing the enemy. A celebration dinner was arranged in the evening and the wine flowed freely and after a singalong ending with 'Dixie' they retired for a good night's sleep.

Chapter 9

Severe gales battered the '*Alabama*', she groaned and creaked in every beam. Part of her canvas sails were torn to ribbons, sailors dreaded the Gulf of Mexico and the crew were relieved when the Captain informed them that they would head for Port Royal, via Havana and the Cayman Islands. This he calculated would take about ten days, arriving on the 28th of January. They had a date with the three captured Union ships, manned by Southerners, in Port Royal. The "*Alabama*" arrived in Havana to replenish some of the supplies and when they arrived a few days later at the Cayman Islands the weather was really warm. The sea was calm as the ship anchored in a picturesque cove surrounded by palm and coconut trees. The crew were quite excited as Semmes had indicated a stay of a few days.

 "I wonder if the dusky maidens are hospitable,'" laughingly exclaimed Ray Ryan. 'I don't know but we shall soon find out," responded his mate Norman. "Who is the first for shore leave?" called the Bosun loudly.

He nearly got bowled over in the rush for the longboat. The native canoes had already left the beach before the anchor had struck bottom.

Lomax, Massey and Griff Williams, followed by Ray Ryan, were first on the beach. They dashed towards and embraced the smiling dark skinned young girls, some topless, with grass skirts. They clasped the hands of four young slim girls and dashed into the foliage and trees to frolic and embrace. Captain Semmes and his officers paid their respects to the local dignitaries. The sun-blest tropical island had not lost its identity, the islanders still had their chieftains and native customs.

Angelene, a young dark-skinned brown-eyed maiden, was standing outside a big log cabin watching along the beach about a hundred yards away, as the men from the anchored ship in the cove made their way along the jetty. She recognised her father amongst the dignitaries who came forward to embrace and shake hands with the visitors. She ran along the hot sands, her long black hair swept back in the slight breeze, her ample breasts, bobbing up and down, swelled in her silk dress as she rushed towards the large crowd now gathering around the smartly dressed white-uniformed men. The young girls, laughing and excited, placed garlands of flowers around the necks of these handsome young men. Angelene observed a tall well-dressed figure talking at the far end of the jetty to a sailor in a boat. She made her way along the wooden planks and looked into the boat. "Hello there," said a cultured English bass voice. She glanced shyly into the blue smiling eyes of Jonathan, who stood in front of her and saluted. "My name is Jonathan, my friends call me Jacko. I'm happy to make your acquaintance."

"I'm called Angelene," her English was slightly broken. "I was baptised by a missionary who lives in the hills." She pointed with her slender brown arm.They walked along the jetty talking and onto the silvery sands for about a mile, the sea lapping in gently as she related the history of the beautifully flowered and wooded island.

'I was born in England in a place called Birkenhead, and I was working in a lawyer's office when the call of the sea beckoned and I have been sailing twelve months. Gosh, it's hot" said Jacko, unbuckling his belt and sword. "Do you mind holding this." He took off his uniformed jacket and shirt, displaying the whiteness of his skin.

She laughed and placed her slender brown hands on his chest. "What a difference in our skins! Are all Englishmen as white as this?" He smiled and gently took her hands in his, looking for several minutes into her twinkling brown eyes. 'Gosh,' he thought, 'I haven't known her long, but I think I'm falling in love.'

"Shall we go for a swim" he suddenly blurted out. She quickly discarded her coloured dress and ran into the blue waters. He was not far behind her, having slipped off his trousers. They swam out, but Jacko was not a strong swimmer and soon got into difficulties. Angelene realised and came to his rescue, supporting him till they were in shallow waters, where they romped around laughing and shouting and splashing each other.

Twilight found the two young lovers lying on the silvery hot sands in each other's arms, on the deserted beach embracing and fondling each other.

The blackness of the night enshrouded them, they disentangled themselves laughing, and standing up in their nakedness, embraced each other warmly.

They strolled along slowly, hands holding clothes which trailed behind them, their arms around each other.

The moon was rising, causing a shimmering on the waters. They reached Angelene's cabin. They dropped their clothes, Jacko kicked open the door, lifted the smaller slim girl in his arms, took her to the bedroom and gently laid her upon the bed.

The next morning, Jacko retrieved his uniform which he found in front of the cabin and went inside and dressed except for his white jacket. Angelene was lying naked on the bed.

'Gosh, what a night! I feel drained and wobbly, I had better go for a walk - might feel better,' thought Jacko.

He was standing by the water's edge, the sea lapping gently over his bare feet. He heard a shout from Angelene asking if he wanted anything to eat. He felt ravenous and quickly devoured some fresh fruit followed by some smoked fish.

"How would you like to meet the Scottish monk up in the hills'? I could borrow some horses," suggested Angelene. "Good idea, I have ridden a horse in my youth." About an hour later, she returned riding a big brown gelding and another saddled white horse and they set off following the dusty road away from the jetty, passing white-coated houses and well kept vegetable gardens. People came from their houses to wave and talk to Jacko and the happy Angelene.

Eventually they left the well surfaced road for a dirt track. The vegetation gave way to swaying palm, coconut trees and gigantic cactus trees. They came across clearings with a cluster of homes, quite different in structure from the previous houses - more like Angelene's log cabin. They stopped to water the horses and were invited into the house of one of Angelene's relatives for cooling liquid refreshment. The vegetation changed to fields of various crops, with people working who stopped to pause and wave to the happy couple.

They climbed higher and higher, the ground becoming rocky, but no problem to the sure-footed horses, only to Jacko. Eventually it levelled off. "We are nearly there, Jacko, just past that clearing straight ahead." They hadn't spoken much, only to smile at each other.

"Here we are, you can see the white chapel through the palm trees."

The brown-robed monk was tilling the soil around his vegetable garden. It was hot, being midday. He paused for a drink of water and he was about to raise it to his lips when he shaded his eyes to see two riders approaching. He recognized one of the riders as his young parishioner, Angelene. She leapt off her horse and ran over and embraced him. "How are you, my dear? You are looking very fit and well. I see you have brought a friend."

"Yes, Father, may I introduce Jacko, a naval officer from the *'Alabama'*." Jonathan shook hands with Father Andrew. "Let us go indoors. I'm sure, Jacko, you are not used to this intense heat?" smiled the Reverend Father.

As they entered the white stone chapel with the bell in the arched belfry tower, Angelene took off her neckerchief and draped it over her head. She walked up the aisle, knelt in front of the wooden cross and prayed.

After a short silence she held out her right hand, which Jacko grasped and she eased him gently beside her. They stood up after a moment's silent prayer together, and, smiling, they looked into each other's eyes.

"The cool drinks are in here, Angelene," interrupted the Father. They entered the simple stone-built room with its old fashioned English-styled rough wooden table and chairs and made themselves comfortable.

"Please try my home-made wine - I'm sure you will enjoy it."

"It's delicious," remarked Jacko. "Did you brew it yourself?"

The aging Reverend Andrew smiled.

"I'm glad it is to your taste. I've ordered some light refreshments and also arranged rooms for you. I'm sure you will stop the night; it's not often I'm entertained by such charming company. I'm rather lonely and exclusive up here in the mountains on this craggy island." Jacko. Is it a naval nickname?"

"I don't know," said Jacko. "It is a shortened version for Jonathan, according to my friend Jamie. I was originally a seaman on the *'Agrippina'* until I transferred to the *'Alabama'*."

"Yes, I've heard all about this famous Confederate raider."

Following the meal they had a conducted tour around the ancient chapel, which according to the monk was built over a hundred years ago by the Spaniards.

"I was brought up in the Presbyterian faith in Scotland," explained the Reverend Father. "I have been on the island about ten years and I have familiarized myself with the native customs and language. Naturally, being a British Colony most of these friendly people have adopted English as their mother tongue."

"Yes," added Jacko. "That explains the British flag I saw fluttering at the end of the jetty."

"They still adhere to some of their native customs. The order of service was adopted from the Catholic faith, but slowly converting" (with a smile) "these charming people." (looking at the beautiful black-haired young girl.) "slowly - to my faith. I adopted the monk's garb from my predecessor, who was a Catholic Priest. My full official title is Reverend Andrew MacGillie Iosa. The Gaelic translation means 'Son of the servant of Jesus'."

"Are you of Scottish descent?"

"Yes. I was born near Edinburgh, where I took the subject Divinity at the local college, then ran away to sea," (with a chuckle) "and here I am on this island of paradise."

"May I show you around my part of the country? We don't need the horses, they will be well taken care of by the servants and after the walk we'll enjoy an evening meal prepared by my housekeeper."

Off they set, led by the monk with his stout rod grasped firmly in his right hand. The ground rose sharply until they came to a rise where they had a panoramic view of the cove where the 'Alabama' was anchored surrounded by numerous small trading boats.

Angelene pointed to her cabin where the surging breakers tumbled along the beach.

The trio continued on a trail through the cedar trees, shrubs and wild flowers. The monk would stop and stoop and fondly hold the exquisite and colourful flowers delicately in the palm of his hand. He named them to his companions and tenderly released them. "God planted these for you and me to behold and admire." They came to a waterfall gushing down on its way to the sea.

Jacko knelt down by a small pool of crystal clear water and scooped it into his hand and offered it to Angelene. She was grateful, for it quenched her thirst. She smiled at Jacko and she took both of his hands in hers and kissed them. He held her close and kissed her, feeling the warmth of her hot, yearning, young body nestling in his strong arms.

Father Andrew coughed on to the back of his hand, very discreetly. He exclaimed with a smile: "Let's continue along the ridge over there and we shall come to my vegetable garden." After an hour's walking they arrived back at the small chapel. The sun settled on the horizon as an orange ball of fire.

Following the evening meal the monk and his guests lounged in cane chairs on the veranda at the back of the chapel. The noise of the crickets and the hum of the mosquitoes and dragonflies filled the balmy night air as the three conversed while drinking the delicious home-made wine. "Well, I'm ready for bed, goodnight, God bless, I'll see you in the morning." The monk thought: 'They don't want me around.' The young couple nestled into each other's arms, cuddling, caressing, whispering words of love to each other, well into the night.

The following morning they enjoyed a hearty breakfast and after fond farewells, Angelene on the brown horse, bare-backed, led the way back on a different trail. Jacko kept up behind her on his sure-footed white mount. Later, as they were riding side by side along the beach with the waves gently bathing the horses' hooves, the quietness was shattered by a gun being fired three times from the '*Alabama*'.

This was an agreed signal, that all hands had to report back immediately to the vessel. It certainly altered any future plans for Jacko.

They tethered the horses to a post and went inside the sparsely furnished cabin. Jacko gently held her hands and looked into her troubled eyes. She must have guessed something was wrong.

"Listen, Angelene, the cannon fire you heard is the signal that I have to return to the ship and I'm afraid I have to leave you and sail away, goodness knows where I'll be bound for after Port Royal, but someday I'll be back and we shall continue my dearest, just where we have left off at this precious moment."

She clung to him desperately, her pleading eyes asking a hundred questions. He kissed her passionately. (What could he say?) Tears welled in her eyes; he drew away, pushing her, turning to gather his uniform together and get dressed. They strolled arm-in-arm together along the beach - not speaking, stopping and kissing. There was a bustling crowd at the jetty, men piling into the longboats. "Hi! Jacko, over here, you had better hurry, you're one of the last." called Carruthers, one of the officers in charge of the boat. "Look, my darling, I will just say au revoir, until we meet again." Angelene held him tightly in her arms, kissed him, let go and turned and ran down the jetty, not even bothering to wave goodbye.

Three days had quickly passed by for the relaxed crew; even some of the paroled prisoners had enjoyed shore leave, they even had the opportunity to settle on the island. The crew, singing shanty songs, hauled in the anchor and on her main engine the '*Alabama*' slowly left the lovely sleepy cove. The seamen climbing the mast waved farewell to many a heartbroken dusky maiden, whom they would never see again or enjoy the pleasure of holding and cuddling in their arms. Jacko stood at the aft end, shading his eyes, scrutinizing the jetty and the beach, hoping to see his beloved Angelene.

He was joined at the taffrail by Ryan.

"What's troubling you, Middy?" said Ray, laughing. "I know like me, you've romped in the foliage with one of the maidens." "I'm afraid I've more than romped." remarked the serious-looking Jacko. "I think she took me up into the hills to meet the monk with a view to getting married."

He hurriedly began to take off his boots and tunic and began to climb on the top of the taffrail, hoping to dive into the water, when Ryan, taken completely by surprise, grabbed hold of him and they both crashed to the deck.

Two or three of the crew gathered around, thinking there was a fight. Bellew, the Bosun came on the scene.

"What's all this, Ryan, striking an officer?"

"No, sir."(He did not know what to say!) "I - was......."

Jacko pushed him aside.

"No, nothing like that. It was my fault. My boots are hurting me, and I was showing Ryan my foot when a shark caught my eye in the wake and I stood on the rail to get a better view. I nearly lost my balance when Ray grabbed me and we finished up on the deck." Everybody laughed, but when the stern-looking Bosun glared at them, they quickly dispersed and went about their various jobs. Eventually Jacko was able confidentially to say: "Thanks, Ray." "Don't thank me, you've a lot to learn about life, and remember," - with a grin - "there's a girl waiting in every port!"

The weather was really fierce with heavy seas in the Tucatan Strait. The 'Alabama' took a tremendous battering. Sighting the lighthouse at Plum Point on Jamaica was a welcome sight.

"We'll try something for a change, Mr. MacPherson," with a grin, said Captain Semmes. "Hoist the French flag, give them a salvo and request a pilot; as you are well aware, we are in a neutral port. We shall try to make contact with the ships we captured, go ashore, make discreet inquiries in the town. I shall be visiting the Governor of the island, hoping he will be sympathetic and friendly towards us and discuss the landing of the paroled prisoners." He paused, to view the bustling and picturesque harbour. He continued, addressing Jamie who was the officer of the watch, "Attend to our provisions, especially extra coal, also any minor repairs to the rigging during the recent storm. Give the crew long shore leave - we'll be here about three weeks. Tomorrow will you arrange for my gig boat. I shall be visiting a British man-of-war, prior to visiting the Governor. After all we are on British territory!"

• • •

It was just on sunset when a Pilot boarded the 'Alabama'. Jamie was the officer of the watch and greeted the stocky, well-built, uniformed man. "Lieutenant MacPherson, sir," left hand on the sword hilt, he smartly saluted the Pilot.

"You're not French - Celt I think, with that strange accent. I notice you are flying my country's flag. My name is Pierre Gerhardie and I will guide you safety through this dangerous channel to a safe anchorage"

"Thank you, no, we are not French. We are American," with a grin.

"It was the only flag I could find," said Jamie with a chuckle. "This ship is the '*Alabama*'."

"Dieu, mon ami." His mouth dropped open. He gave Jamie a mischievous smile. "Ha! Ha!" and replied in broken English: "The '*Alabama*' - I feel privileged to pilot this famous vessel."

The welcome noise of the anchor rattling through the port hawse hole, supervised and watched carefully on deck by Carruthers, signified they were safely berthed.

"Bosun," commanded Jamie, "Man the longboat and escort the Pilot ashore."

"Thank you, sir, for your safe navigation - no doubt in the morning we will be inundated with visitors. Goodnight" saluting M. Gerhardie.

The watch passed uneventfully for Jamie. He viewed the twinkling lights of Port Royal as he walked around the silent deck and as the dawn was breaking he was greeted by the next Officer of the watch.

"Nothing to report Mr. Francis, by jove you get around, one minute you're firing that old cannon and next minute you're the navigation officer and now officer of the watch."

"It is not what you know, it is who you know." They both laughed.

"No doubt you are looking forward to shore leave and meeting some dusky young maiden, I never trust you Welshmen," Jamie smiled.

They saluted each other and Jamie retired to his bunk to dream of bygone years in this buccaneers' paradise, and the hidden buried treasure chests. He turned over in his sleep and smiled. 'I wonder where they are hidden - I must make some enquiries!'

Next morning Jamie was again on watch and looked on leisurely as the boats left for shore leave for crew members. They jostled and laughed amongst themselves.

'What a great crowd of chaps,' pondered Jamie. 'There goes Leeson, Lomax and Tudor, they will be round the shops looking for gifts. The Scots - Mackenzie, Mackay, Doig and Briggs off to the tavern to try the local ale. The scenery is magnificent!' His thoughts were interrupted by Captain Semmes.

"I'm going to pay my respects to that British man-o'-war, over there, I would like you to accompany me, Jamie. Dress - number one white outfit and choose four well-dressed seamen to man the longboat."

"Yes, sir!" Jamie was delighted to visit a British ship and quickly changed, returning wearing his white uniform. The hot sun gleamed on his polished buttons and sword. He carefully chose the longboat's personnel, including Taylor the midshipman, with the Bosun, Bellew, in charge. They were joined by Semmes, his moustache waxed (and he looked every inch a great Captain, noted Jamie.) As they approached the British ship, Jamie admired the fine lines of the 300-foot-long flagship. Captain Semmes, the First Lieutenant, the Midshipman, and the Bosun were piped aboard Her Majesty's ship, '*Jason*'. They were expected, having received a signal from the '*Alabama*' and a guard of honour stood smartly to attention. Semmes was warmly welcomed aboard by Commodore Dunlop, who escorted Semmes to his wardroom and left Jamie with Lieutenant Gratton. The First Lieutenant shook hands with Jamie, and Taylor.

"My name's Bill Gratton, I joined the Royal Navy as a midshipman from Her Majesty's Ship '*Conway*'. "Mine's Jamie, I joined the '*Alabama*" as an engineer in Birkenhead and that was over one long year ago. On board, everybody has to learn everybody else's job!" He laughed. "I'm now equivalent to the First Lieutenant - oh, meet the popular Jacko."

"We will drink to that," said the stockily-built Gratton. "Please follow me to the officers' quarters, to meet my team. "Do you know that once we recognized your vessel, the harbour and the town have really buzzed with curiosity to meet this famous ship and its distinguished crew!"

The overcrowded wardroom let out a cheer of welcome when Jamie and Jacko entered. "Gentlemen, let me introduce you to our distinguished guests, Jamie and Jacko from the '*Alabama*'. A loud cheer followed. "You're very welcome aboard," said Peter Miles. "By now the whole of Jamaica will know you have arrived, in fact I think the Governor is arranging a garden party and banquet in your honour and it's to be in the house of Sir David Sullivan, one of our most influential and wealthiest plantation owners on the island."

"Are you married Jamie?" chipped in the stout Gordon Abrahams. "Yes. Matilda is my wife and I have two daughters." proudly said Jamie.

"Pity! Sullivan has four charming daughters," laughed Tom O' Ryan. "But that shouldn't make any difference, he's trying to marry them off. How about you, Jacko, you seem eligible?" "Now don't talk to Jacko about young maidens, he flirted with one on the Caymans and he's still pining for his Angelene," teased Jamie. "But these four lovely young maidens don't seem to like British ship's officers," grimly added Alan Wilkie, who looked very ferocious with his black beard.

"We don't blame them when you're around, Alan," two of them chorused. Everybody laughed. Tom sniggered. "True, we mates don't stand a chance, though I must admit your uniforms look more attractive than ours and you're certainly more fearless and heroic. We are only leisurely patrolling, keeping the peace and protecting British interests."

How about some more grog, Jamie, or would you like to try some of Jack Tar's rum?" offered Peter.

"Don't mind." Jacko drank a mouthful. He opened his mouth and spluttered. He nearly choked, tears streaming from his eyes. He was not used to such strong beverages. Everybody laughed.

"You are not eligible for the British Navy, Jacko boy," remarked Gordon, smiling. Then he looked serious.

"Talking before about British rights, interests and protection, what about the Earl Russell's report - destroying British goods and materials bound for England, stored in Northern ships, and then burning the ships, you're right buccaneers!"

'What a good-humoured lot of shipmates,' thought Jamie. 'After all, what am I thinking about! We are all British, but not fighting the same war!'

"I don't know anything about the Russell report," remarked the puzzled Jamie. "We always inspect the ship's papers and then the cargo and anything that we fancy-" - tapping the side of his nose.

"Tell us more, Jamie," asked Wilkie.

"Well, our victories have been relatively easy, thanks to the genius of our Captain, with little loss of life. We have so far sunk twenty-seven unarmed enemy ships, except of course for the defeat of the '*Hatteras*', a warship whose guns and armament were similar to ours, but we struck first and severely damaged the paddle steamer by penetrating the engine room, aft of the paddles."

"Did you salvage anything interesting?"

"Mainly clothing, boots, engine equipment, food, instruments, crockery. We just helped ourselves, shipped the prisoners aboard the '*Alabama*', together with their personal equipment and then put the enemy ships to the torch."

"We did this mainly during daytime," interrupted Jacko. "as it wouldn't attract as much attention as at night."

"I must admit," interposed Jamie, "we did not usually consider which country owned the cargo. By the way, Jacko as a seaman was transferred from the '*Agrippina*', our supply and back-up ship.

He joined us about two months ago and the Captain rewarded him for his bravery in diving from the main mast to rescue survivors from the '*Hatteras*'. Jacko looked bashful. Jamie continued:
"For his gallantry Captain Semmes promoted him to Midshipman and I have been responsible for his training. Sadly we lost our cook, who also swam to rescue men, but he didn't survive. Everybody is trained in every job on board. For instance Jacko can fire a musket and cannon, climb the rigging to unfurl the sails, cook, or act as fireman, navigator or engineer."
"Ha! I was not a good cook, I hated the job," exclaimed Jacko. Everybody laughed.
"Good job I'm not on the '*Alabama*'." blurted Abrahams.
"I'm glad I trained as a dragoon," butted in Wilkie.
"Would you like some more wine, Jamie, Jacko?" Peter was poised with the decanter. "Or would you like some more rum and we also have some freshly caught lobsters?"
"Delighted." It was Jamie's turn, he took a swig of the rum. A strange expression appeared on his face as though he was going to explode, he choked and said in a whisper, "Water, water!" He soon recovered amidst roars of laughter.
"I remember the '*Conway*' in the River Mersey, anchored off Eastham," said Jamie when he was able to speak, addressing Gratton.
"That was a training ship for Merchant and Naval cadet officers," responded Gratton. "There was the older ship of the line, the '*Indefatigable*', that was for orphaned boys if I remember," continued Jamie. "You're quite right, Jamie," remarked Peter, "and once a year they had a race in longboats down the Mersey from Eastham to New Brighton and pity help the boys of the '*Indefatigable*' if they lost!" The conversation continued in the wardroom, Jamie enquiring about the latest news about the Civil War, the Royal Navy and life on the Island of Jamaica.

The Bosun of H.M.S. '*Jason*' piped a well-dressed gentleman on board. The officer of the watch saluted him:
"Sir David Sullivan, I presume?" recognising the popular islander, who tucked his silver-handled cane under his left arm and doffed his grey top hat. "I have an appointment with the First Lieutenant, William Gratton.
"This way, sir, if you please, he's conversing with some officers from the '*Alabama*'. Watch your head on this beam as you descend the ladder."
Officer of the watch knocked on the wardroom door, entered and introduced Sir David to the First Lieutenant. "What a pleasant

surprise. You know my fellow officers, but may I introduce you to Lieutenants MacPherson and Taylor, two officers from the 'Alabama'. Please be seated and I know you would like a glass of our favourite rum."

"How long will you be in the port?" Jamie enquired to Sir David.

"I understand about three weeks, sir, but God knows where we will go from this island!"

"We must arrange a banquet and dance in honour of the gallant men of the 'Alabama'. I'm sure my daughters will arrange this as they are always looking for an excuse to dine, wine and dance."

The conversation continued until Commodore Dunlop and Captain Semmes entered the wardroom.

Gratton addressed the assembly: "Gentlemen, may I introduce Captain Raphael Semmes of the 'Alabama'.

A loud cheer and clapping of hands was the response Semmes received as he entered, looking at the assembled officers.

"Gentlemen!" the 'Alabama' Captain was overwhelmed. "I did not expect such a welcome, after all there is a war on and I am on what you might describe as neutral territory; however the hospitality and friendship we have received is very gracious. There is a common bond between us, we are all men of the sea and sail the oceans of the world."

The response was a mighty cheer and then the assembly broke to converse into various groups.

"Gentlemen" Gratton clapped for order: "our visitors are leaving."

"Sir, can we land you at the wharf?" remarked Semmes. "Thank you, that is very kind of you, Captain." So the longboat landed Sir David Sullivan at the wharf and continued on to the 'Alabama'.

The crew in the next few days, between shore leave, carried out repairs to the vessel. The seamen were kept busy, while the port beckoned them with its bright lights.

Chapter 10

Ryan and Gow were working on the spanker spar, repairing a hole in the sail and discussing their future visit to the port.

The sun was tanning Ryan's muscular hairy chest. He enjoyed the ninety degree temperature. His friend Norman was the opposite - being fair skinned he wore his navy striped jersey with a wide brimmed hat. Crew members were attending to various jobs, mostly painting the tarnished woodwork.

The Bosun's whistle suddenly shattered the silence and all curious eyes turned as a tall well-built gentleman dressed in a brown suit and matching top hat, presented himself by doffing his hat to the officer of the watch. Midshipman Taylor acknowledged with a salute.

They shook hands, introduced themselves and Jacko requested the Bosun to escort him to the Captain.

"I wonder what that was all about?" remarked Norman. "What a posh outfit he was wearing - must be an important person in the port."

Captain Semmes rose from his desk. He had been writing a letter to his wife when a knock on the door revealed a tall, important-looking gentleman, who introduced himself:

"I'm James Whittle, Chief Constable and Mayor of Kingston and, I might add, Councillor for the island. Why I'm here? - as a peacemaker. This island is British with our rules and laws as laid down by the Parliament in Westminster."

He paused. 'Damn, what is he getting at? I can't get a word in' thought Semmes.)

"Apart from the English descendants the island is cosmopolitan. Spaniards, French, Mexicans, you name them, we've got them, they all live on this 4,450 square mile, British island, the largest in the West Indies - not harmoniously I may add at times, and I have to keep the peace with my police force - and to officiate. I only have fifty men. Fighting breaks out occasionally. We have some North American patriots and sympathisers. They even have an Ambassador resident in Kingston."

'I'd better soften up this guy, he seems quite an aggressive character'. mused Semmes. "Excuse me, Mr. Whittle, may I offer you a drink? - tobacco?"

"No thanks, I'm here on official business."

The Chief Constable was beginning to rattle his sabre.

"I don't want any trouble between your crew and the resident North American sympathisers. Don't bring your bloody war to this peaceful island."

"All my crew will be given shore leave in the next three weeks and I can assure you they will behave like Southern Gentlemen, or I will want to know the reason why." Pointing a finger at Whittle (Semmes was getting fed up and bored with this meeting) he retorted:

"If they break the law, I will deal with them, not you. Is that understood?"

"Good!" Whittle smiled and added:

"The pleasant news I have" (reaching into his pocket and bringing out an envelope) "is that Sir David Sullivan asked me to deliver this letter to you, an invitation to his garden party, and I can assure you, sir, it will be the best party on the island."

"Thank you, Mr. Whittle, I shall send a formal reply," and with a smile asked: "Now can I offer you a drink?" ('Bit of a bastard' thought Semmes.)

"Yes, I shall enjoy it now that I have completed my business."

The Captain went to the wine cupboard smiling ('Wish I had some poison.') "It is my duty to visit every ship to impress on the crew that this is a law-abiding community."

"That's reasonable," replied Semmes They drank each other's health, at the same time weighing each other up eye to eye.

"Delicious," said the Chief of Police, raising his glass. "However I must be going, thank you for your hospitality."

"Ramidios," Semmes called his steward, "summon the Bosun to escort Mr. Whittle off the ship." Semmes was a bit abrupt. "Perhaps we shall meet again, Mr. Whittle. There is one thing, we understand each other - you have a community to protect and I have a ship to run. Good day, sir!"

After Whittle had hurriedly departed the Captain opened the envelope containing the invitation, which was for Friday 23rd January - three days away. He summoned his officers, informing them of the arrangements:

"Gentlemen, we have received an invitation in three days' time to attend a banquet and dance, organised by one of the most influential men on the island. It would appear it is in our honour. Carriages will be available on the wharf at 10 am to convey us to Sir David Sullivan's country mansion, which is about fifteen miles inland from the port."

"What about his four daughters?" remarked Carruthers, when the young officers were discussing the invitation in the mess. "You can have them all," said Alex, laughing. "You are the only eligible bachelor amongst us, except for Jacko, but he left his heart in the Caymans and young Owens." They all laughed and Jacko flung a book at Alex, which missed and hit Mr. Freeman on his right leg. He was quietly minding his own business puffing on his pipe and reading a Northern newspaper. He looked annoyed, but realised it was only a joke and tossed the book back. The young officers rolled dice for the duty watch on the 23rd. Jamie was unlucky and lost the toss. There was hilarity and jokingly Carruthers said: "Serves you right - but hard luck!"

Mr. Freeman interrupted the merriment: "Jamie, I'll be a sport - I'll do your watch. I don't want to attend any garden parties and I've forgotten how to dance. You can do me a small favour though. Can you bring me back some of that fine Virginian tobacco?"

"That's very kind of you, Mr. Freeman."

"Hey! how about a reminder, let's have a few dancing lessons, especially for the two middies?"

They moved the heavy wooden tables to one side and chose their partners. "I'll go and get Mullard and his concertina," volunteered Mr. Freeman. "while you sort out your partners."

So the officers practised the correct approach to their partners: "Now don't forget to introduce yourselves correctly and don't forget to wear clean white gloves, which will of course match your white uniforms," instructed Doctor Graeme

"You just practice the steps slowly at first," said Mullard, "particularly the waltz - that will be a great favourite."

"May I have the pleasure of this dance, Miss?" said Jamie, approaching young Owens. Jacko partnered Carruthers. There were many mistakes, but they had a lot of fun until eight bells, when Alex and the young Midshipman Stewart went on watch.

• • •

Calderstones Gardens, the Sullivan mansions, were situated in a lush valley. Orange, coconut, and banana trees abounded and palm trees swayed gently in the breeze.

In this colourful setting on the morning of the 23rd, a large green marquee had been erected on the banks of a rumbling stream and stewards were busy decorating the tables to receive the exotic meat, fish and fruit dishes. Wine waiters bustled setting up various bowls on the laced tables. The sun shone, the setting was perfect for this show of the year. It was the dream arrangement of the four Sullivan daughters.

The four sisters chatted away. Their ages ranged from seventeen to twenty-five years. The conversation was naturally about the young heroic officers of the '*Alabama*'.

"I wonder if I should wear this light green dress with a red silk scarf around my neck," and trying on a straw blue bonnet.

"How does this look?" said the brown-eyed, dark-haired Kate.

"No, the straw hat does not suit your dark fringed short hairstyle," remarked Gaynor, the eldest of the plantation owner's daughters. "I would not wear a hat, Kate, your hairstyle suits your tanned complexion. I have to wear a hat because I have pimples and my skin is blotchy. I have to use lots of make-up and eye shadow, whereas you have a beautiful and natural skin." Gaynor took hold of the neckerchief.

"Yes, just let me adjust your silk scarf and I will loan you my golden toggle which our grandmother gave me for my twenty-first birthday."

She slipped the toggle between the ends of the red scarf and eased it gently over Kate's swelling breasts. She looked - admiring Kate's slim figure.

'Gosh, I only wish I had been endowed with Kate's figure - being much taller I have very small breasts which I have to pad, and men quickly go off me when they realise I wear padding!' Kate hugged her elder sister.

"Thank you for helping me, it's more than Alyson would do."

She thought: 'Poor Gaynor, being the eldest, has flirted with numerous elegant and rich bachelors, but has never settled down.' Kate smiled at Gaynor, grasping her by the shoulders.

"Never mind, don't worry, I'll look after you when these tear-away sailors arrive and they will certainly be looking for a good time, having been at sea for a long period. I'll find you a tall handsome man."

The other two sisters, Alyson and young Janette, were helping each other with the choice of dresses. The long-haired Janette, aged seventeen, was tall for her age, having matured gracefully and, being an athletic tomboy, was competent at riding a horse, swimming, running, or diving off a cliff into the sea.

Alyson was just the opposite. She was three years older, brown curly hair with light brown eyes, shy and elegant. She felt she was responsible for her younger sister.

"This blue dress will suit you. I would not wear a hat unless you go outdoors to protect you from the sun!"

'It suited her,' thought the serious-minded Alyson. 'After all she's too young and not the marrying kind like me, she is just a flirt.'

Friday morning, nine o'clock, Captain Semmes standing amidships inspected the officers and crew to see if they came up to his standards for shore leave: the officers in white duck suits, golden buttons gleaming, with gold epaulettes on their shoulders, black caps and polished swords at their sides, the crew dressed in striped shirts and baggy trousers with wide brimmed ribbon boater hats. Semmes raised himself on to the wheel mounting and addressed the assembly:

"I want you all to behave yourselves like gentlemen of our beloved Confederate Navy. We have a good battle record which is appreciated on this neutral island of Jamaica."

He paused to adjust his stance.

"I visited a British ship the other day and they are certainly in support of our war effort and we will expect a good welcome when we go ashore. The officers will be attending a garden party and you men will no doubt be visiting the local taverns to partake of the local beverages and I suppose entertain the local wenches. If any man gets drunk and disgraces our flag, he will be strung from the yard arm." Pointing upwards, he stamped his foot, glaring at the men. He felt arrogant, bad-tempered and shouted: "Is that quite clear, do I make myself understood? We had a visit from the Chief Constable of the island - a nasty customer, and, I may add, a strict disciplinarian. We don't want any trouble with him, so take care and look after each other, that is our tradition and" - with a grin - "enjoy yourselves - have a good time and" - with a chuckle "if you can, keep sober."

There was a cheer from the deck, the crew raising their hats.

Numerous sized boats and tenders were along the wharf as the longboats approached. The quay swarmed with all classes of people, the wealthy well-dressed, rubbing shoulders with the wharf wenches, labourers, seaman, beggars, urchins, policemen, shopkeepers - all thronging, eager for a look at the rapidly approaching longboats as they eased their way to the stone steps of the wharf.

Bellew, the Bosun, led the way to the top of the stone steps, followed by Semmes. Policemen ushered people aside to make way for the Captain and his party to be presented to the Deputy Governor of Jamaica, Sir Michael Kennedy K.B.E.,K.V.C.O., who was elegantly dressed in his dark blue uniform with his left hand on his sword at his side.

"I'm Sir Michael Kennedy." He doffed his white plumed hat, acknowledging the Captain's salute. They shook hands.
"I'm deputising for our Governor, who has returned to England on some important political issues in Parliament. May I welcome you and your crew? The hospitality of our island awaits you. The carriages are - over there," - pointing, "to escort you to Sir David Sullivan's residence, where I shall be attending later."
"Thank you, Sir Michael."
A resounding cheer echoed from the bystanders on the wharf as Semmes and his officers stepped into the carriages and wended their way through the cheering and merry crowds into the town, passing taverns, warehouses and a white church surrounded by palm trees.

Travelling out of the town, the coaches climbed on to high ground, palm trees, which gave way to vegetation, fields of sugar cane and shrub pine, until it cleared into a sweeping valley of banana and orange trees. The carriage with the white harnessed horse leading the way entered the ornamental iron gates leading to a palm covered driveway and approached the stately mansion.

The front of the mansion was bedecked with tables and chairs, covered with multi-flowered overhead awnings. The seated company rose when the carriages arrived and Captain Semmes approached Sir David Sullivan, whom he saluted. They shook hands and Semmes presented his nine officers.
"May I present my daughters," said Sullivan proudly, "and not forgetting of course my principal guests."
Sir David led the way into the coolness of his mansion.
'What a lovely panelled room,' thought Alex. 'I must have a closer look at those paintings, I don't like the look of that pirate, he looks grim and ugly - he reminds me of the bosun.'
'What lovely daughters,' thought Doctor MacGregor. 'I fancy that tall girl.'
'I wonder which one I will be dancing with? Perhaps that brown curly-haired young wench with the big bust, cor!' thought Jacko.
"Gentlemen,'" after everybody had been introduced, "my servants will escort you to your rooms and when you have restored yourselves to your personal comforts, please join us in the green marquee for refreshments. My daughters will escort you."

Kate was the first to arrive at the long self-service table, richly adorned with a variety of food. Somebody touched her arm. It was Carruthers.

"Excuse me, Kate, would you like a plate and napkins?"
"Thank you. That salmon looks delicious. Would you like some?"
"Yes please. It's some time since I tasted salmon. Also could you serve me some of those large prawns and pieces of lobsters?"
With full dishes they left the marquee for a canopied table down by the stream, gossiping generally until they were seated.
"What kind of wine would you like, Henry?" He was taken aback - he was used to being called Carruthers, 'I'll kill that Jacko bloke. He must have told her!'
"White if I may - Spanish preferably."
The sun shining, colourful scented flowers, a rumbling stream, a beautiful and attractive young lady, 'What a romantic setting' thought our Henry.
The luncheon finished, Kate suggested a walk around the estate. They set off chatting about their background, - in a merry mood, walking hand in hand on the path alongside the stream.
'What a handsome chap, and how smart he looks in that white uniform.' She glanced at him shyly. 'Three inches taller? Slim, a brown moustache - I suppose that will tickle when he kisses me! Curly brown hair, brown eyes and Scottish descent'. She paused and smiled.
He laughed "Please call me Carruthers, Kate" he smiled.
"As you wish. How old are you Carruthers?"
"Twenty-five - I have not got your scholastic education, which I admire - I'm an engineer - fighting a war and God knows how it will end. I have no future!"
"I'm your friend, Carruthers. I like you. Look over there - those thoroughbred black and white horses. Father breeds them. All the family ride. Do you?"
"Yes, we had stables near our home in Liverpool.
"Perhaps we will ride together - tomorrow."
"I'll look forward to that, Kate. I'm really enjoying your company and you look so lovely. Your short hair style."
"Yes, I only had it cut yesterday, by my younger sister Alyson."
"Those twinkling humorous brown eyes." he continued. He held her close in his strong arms, could feel the thrill of her young eager exciting body pressing close. They gazed into each others eyes lovingly and he gave her a long passionate kiss. They continued walking, pausing to embrace and kiss.

"We'll have to return to the house. The dance is commencing at eight and I have to bath and change for the evening." Arms around each other, chatting away they returned to the mansion and Kate led him to a shaded part of the trestled flowered verandah, where they sat opposite each other in cane chairs.

Carruthers gently held Kate's hands and looking into her smiling eyes remarked: - "Will you reserve a dance for me tonight, Kate? - I'm not a very good dancer, we only practised on board the other day and I only learned the waltz."

Kate laughed - "I'll arrange that every other dance will be a waltz and I'll dance them all with you, especially the last one!"

He kissed her hand, "Thank you for a lovely day so far. Until tonight, my dear."

They entered the house, through the brass-handled oak door.

"The officers have a spacious bedroom at the top of the stairs and also the large room opposite." With a smile Kate said:

"Look forward to seeing you tonight, Mr.Carruthers."

He laughed and held her hand. "I'll see you to your room." She opened the bedroom door and he kissed her on the lips.

Jamie, Alex and Jacko were enjoying themselves at the banquet, chatting and eating delicious and tasty food and wine, entirely different from on board the ship.

Fans in the roof of the marquee, pulled rhythmically by ropes, manipulated by a small black boy, wafted a pleasant breeze.

MacGregor, sitting on his own away from the crowd, cradling a glass of wine, was approached by a tall slim young lady.

"Excuse me, you seem all alone, would you like my company?"

"I would appreciate it very much, I'm afraid I was daydreaming."

"What is that you're drinking? Perhaps you would like some of our special Jamaican rum?"

He stood up, noting he was slightly taller than this slender blond-haired lady.

He offered her his hand. "Thank you, my name is MacGregor and I'm from the '*Alabama*'.

'What a firm grip!' she thought and she chuckled, "I guessed that, judging by your uniform. It looks a lot smarter than the drab British naval uniform. Surely you have a Christian name? Mine is Gaynor."

"Yes, Graeme, but my friends call me Mac."

She was teasing him, with a merry lilt in her voice, when she commented, "That's a good old Celtic name. You are not related to that Scottish brigand, I have read about, who stole from the rich to give to the poor - Rob Roy MacGregor?"

"It's rather strange you mention his name. The '*Alabama*' was built in Birkenhead." She interrupted him, "Now this seems to be an interesting story. Will you excuse me, I must get you the rum I promised." She returned with a tray, two bottles (one of wine) and two glasses. She offered him a drink, which he accepted with thanks and took a sip of rum. "Delicious. May I continue? Rob Roy would just roam the Highlands, round up some sheep and cattle, drive them many miles away, and leave them on some poor crofter's land and disappear into the night supported by his brigands as you call them." They both laughed.

"The shipyard where the '*Alabama*' was built was called the Birkenhead Iron Works and owned by a Scot - John Laird. He had a brother named Robert MacGregor Laird. Their forefathers were related to the famous outlaw. It's strange that Robert - a former shipowner - is in Africa as an explorer and looking for riverboat orders. I don't know if you have heard of the Scottish missionary - Doctor David Livingstone?"

Gaynor answered him: "I've read about him. Didn't he visit Birkenhead in 1858, stay with Mr. Laird and actually viewed the plans on the drawing board of his famous ship named after his wife - the '*Ma Robert*'? You must have some more rum." She chuckled. "This is very interesting. How did they get the '*Ma Robert*' to the Livingstone settlement in Africa?"

"John Laird had a wonderful foresight and technique. He arranged after the engine trials in the dock, for the thirteen-foot-long steel boat to be dismantled on the quay, the rivets burned out, the plates, engines, propeller and relevant parts boxed up and shipped to North Africa on the steamship '*Pearl*'. "Then came the tedious and laborious job of transporting the parts across the desert by camel to the settlement of Lairdstown." Gaynor leaned forward in her chair, really engrossed by the interesting story.

"What happened on this long journey when the large camel train arrived at the settlement?"

"Well, Laird's men who accompanied the camels across the desert, on arrival on the banks of the Niger river, assembled the boat and tested it, then they returned across the desert to a west coast port and embarked on a ship bound for Birkenhead."

"Goodness me, men from the Mersey area must be tough, skilful and dedicated. What does the light red badge signify on your epaulettes?"

"Oh! didn't I mention, I'm a Doctor. I did my studying and training in Edinburgh."

Gaynor brushed the long hair with her hand from her face to behind her right ear. "I was educated in Kingston at a private school, specialising in Spanish, French and Latin."

"Wish I had learned Latin and possibly Greek. It would have helped me in my medical studies."

"Let us enjoy the sunshine, Mac, and I'll show you our colourful gardens."

As they were leaving the marquee, Graeme, smiling, stooped down and spoke to the seated young negro lad who controlled the fan by rhythmically pulling on a rope, which kept the air cool in the marquee.

"What is your name, boy?" pressing a gold coin into his hand.

"Samuel, sir." He opened his mouth wide and gasped. "Thank you, sir."

"What are you going to do today, Samuel?"

"After midday, when I have finished here, I'll be going down to the beach. I enjoy swimming with my friends."

"Good idea, I might join you. Swimming is a very healthy exercise, keep it up, Sam. By the way, how would you and your friends like to visit the '*Alabama*'."

Samuel's eyes widened, he was speechless and all he could say was: "Thank you, sir, thank you." Gaynor and Graeme made their way through the sweet-scented gardens. She paused, explaining the various names of the flowers. He was enthralled by her knowledge and they chatted away to each other, walked hand in hand up the stone stairs leading to the mansion doors and into the large hallway.

'I'm going for a rest now, Mac, I'll reserve dances for you this evening and until....then." She paused and faced him.

"It's been a delight meeting you, Gaynor. I'm sure our friendship will continue, but," - smiling he continued, "wait till you meet some of my friends, I might lose you."

She smiled, showing her lovely white teeth: "We'll see."

"How did you go on, Mac, with that luscious blond?" Alex, sprawled on a couch, chuckled. "And you, Henry? Ha! Ha!" - to Carruthers. "Young Kate, now she's a cracker."

The nine officers settled down, resting, before they changed for the evening ball.

Sir David Sullivan, in his longtailed evening dress, welcomed his guests within the entrance of the baronial hall. The orchestra were tuning up in the minstrels' gallery.

The 150 guests arranged themselves on chairs around ornamented flowered tables which surrounded the dance floor. Young negro youths, dressed in white shirts and shorts served drinks to the assembly. Michael, the conductor, raised his baton and the eight-piece orchestra quietly commenced with a Viennese waltz.

There was a hush, as all eyes turned to the polished mahogany staircase as Captain Semmes, dressed in his white uniform, bow tie, gold epaulettes and polished buttons, looking immaculate, descended the stairway, accompanied by his nine officers. Semmes seemed nervous and uneasy, viewing the crowded ballroom.

Sir David welcomed them at the foot of the stairway and took Semmes to one side, guided him to a table, to introduce him to some of his distinguished guests, including the Chief Constable. Townsend, Butler, Francis, Jacko and the young Midshipman, Owens, made their way to a bar in the anti-room where they were offered drinks served by a smartly dressed young negro boy. Jamie and Alex intermingled with the guests, renewing their acquaintances with the officers of the British warship, '*Jason*'. MacGregor quickly located Gaynor.

Carruthers found Kate, who introduced him to some of her friends. "Lieutenant Carruthers, I would like you to meet Judge and Mrs. Sheridan and their daughter-in-law, Cheryl."

"Delighted, it's my pleasure." He shook hands with the Judge and bowed to his wife and Cheryl. "I'm afraid you will not have the pleasure of meeting my son, Roland. He's a geologist." The Judge laughed. "He's the other side of the island looking for some pirates' buried treasure."

"I suppose," Carruthers said with a grin, "these buried wooden chests still attract visitors to the island? I wouldn't mind treasure hunting. How about it, Kate? We will visit the waterfront tavern and talk to the old sea dogs. It will be good fun."

"There's no need to go to all that trouble, Henry," chipped in the Judge. "You must meet our Roland and do some digging with him. He's very knowledgeable about Jamaica and the surrounding islands."

The Master of Ceremonies, Arnold Martin, took command. "Sir David Sullivan and honoured guests, let me introduce you to Maestro Hoyland and his orchestra. Will you please take your partners for the first dance, which will be a waltz."

Most of the ladies' dance cards had already been marked, so the ballroom was soon occupied by the partners dancing the rhythmical steps of the waltz.

Jamie was chatting with Judge Sheridan, his daughter-in-law Cheryl and the Chief Constable.

"You mentioned earlier, Mr. Whittle, that you joined the police force in Liverpool, having been a Captain in the army. "Quite correct, in fact I was born in Hale, which is a very small village near the banks of the upper River Mersey."

Jamie remarked, "I'm a Liverpudlian by adoption, I was born in Aughtergaven in Perthshire."

Whittle chuckled. "That figures, with that accent!"

"'And you, Judge Sheridan, are you from Liverpool?"

"Indeed my wife and I lived in Childwall, where our only son Roland was born, but he was educated in Manchester University studying geology. I moved to Liverpool from London after studying at the Bar and graduating after I practised law to be a Judge at the Supreme Court, but now I'm only part-time."

A young negro youth approached with glasses of wine on a tray.

"Thank you," said Jamie, accepting a glass from Whittle after he had served Cheryl.

"Judge?" offering him a drink.

"No thanks, I see my wife approaching. She does not approve of my drinking habits. However I promised her the first dance. I understand, Whittle, that you have marked her card for the next dance?" he laughed and said: "Good luck." He paused and addressed Jamie: "Do you dance, Jamie?"

"Well, I try, being brought up on a farm I prefer cows, sheep and horses to dancing a Valeta."

"Now look here young man, please show me how good you are?"

"I can only do my best, sir. Cheryl, may I have the pleasure of this dance?"

And off they went to join the the other dancers to the strains of the Blue Danube waltz.

They chatted away about life on the island.

'What a charming lady,' thought Jamie. 'Glad I'm a bit taller, though she's nice and slim, blue eyes....the scent from her brown-hair! She must have washed it in lavender oil or something - I hope she doesn't use engine oil!' He chuckled.

He held her close and she snuggled in.

'Must be sex-starved,' thought Cheryl.

She gripped his raised left gloved hand firmly and looked into his hazel eyes. She thought: 'I wonder what he's like in bed.'

She smiled and her blue eyes twinkled. Strangely he was thinking the same thing - "Must be careful, she has a husband on the island digging somewhere, fancy leaving this lovely creature with me! I don't want any trouble.'

The first dance ended amidst applause and clapping from the crowded ballroom.

The officers from the British warship, wearing their dark blue uniform were enjoying themselves, intermingling with the society ladies and partaking of the refrehments and wines. They discussed amongst themselves how the 'Alabama' officers dominated the scene and were the centre of attraction, especially with Sullivan's charming daughters. Well, they would soon be sailing away to their bloody war and the island would return to normal.

The dancing continued, the young Midshipman Owens tried dancing with Sir David's younger daughter, Janette, but he was having problems with the rhythm. Jacko, who was enjoying a glass of champagne, noticed his predicament and approached the dancing couple. "Excuse me, may I cut in?" Owens looked relieved and disappeared through the dancers and sought solace in the bar, joining Townsend and Francis.

Jacko found Janette very easy to address and they were soon enjoying the pleasure of each other's company until the end of the dance.

"Take your partners for the Lancers," announced the Master of Ceremonies. "But for your guidance there will be a demonstration performed by four couples. It is a square dance."

The popular dance ended amidst loud applause.

"Come on, Henry." Kate took Carruthers' hand, "I know this dance, let's make a team with my sisters. It will be great fun. We have practised this dance and it is very popular on the island."

Gaynor and Graeme, Alyson and Alex, were joined by Janette and Jacko and the old English army dance commenced. Mistakes were made but it caused a lot of merriment and laughter.

After the dance, Alyson invited Alex on to the verandah. She eyed this Scot with suspicion. He was like a cart horse and clumsy in his dancing, very dour, in fact she was wondering if he ever smiled, but he was smartly dressed and behaved in a gentlemanly manner. They received a glass of wine from the negro servant and stepped out into the moonlit night. The crickets and mosquitoes were singing away amidst the sweet-scented flowers. 'A complete setting for romance,' thought Alyson. Alex had other ideas, thinking of his loved ones in Liverpool. She approached him, looked into his dark stern eyes, she took his glass, went close to him then clasped her hands around his neck and gave him a soft gentle kiss, which took him completely by surprise.

'Gosh,' thought Alex, 'she's a quick worker,' but he enjoyed her approach and responded by holding her firmly around the waist. They kissed and cuddled for a while until Alyson decided to return to the dance, in time to hear the announcement of the Quadrilles, another of the sisters' favourite square dances.

The following dance was a waltz and Gaynor seized Graeme and led him to the dance floor. The orchestra struck a Strauss tune and they held each other close, cheek to cheek. He could feel the warmth of her young eager rhythmical body as she held him firmly. 'Now this is real romance,' thought Mac. "What a figure and those long legs! 'They twirled and Graeme suddenly noticed in the corner of the ballroom a black youth clutching the curtain tightly with both hands.

'No, it can't be,' he thought. 'Yes, it is - the young negro youth, Sam.' He broke off the dance, Gaynor holding on to his arm, as he approached the bedraggled young lad. He was nervous and shaking."What's the matter, Sam, you look very distressed."

"Sir, I was swimming down by the beach with my friends at dusk and a longboat suddenly appeared" a pause as he wiped tears from his watery eyes - "washed up by the - surging waves and grounded - on the beach"

The Doctor lifted the boy in his arms, carried him to an anteroom and gently laid him on a couch. Gaynor offered Sam a glass of water and he seemed to be slowly recovering from the shock.

"Go on, Sam," continued Graeme offering him a handkerchief.

"The boat had a name on it - Lam - Lamp - and there were two bodies lying on the bottom of the boat."

Chapter 11

Jamie, being the senior officer, knelt in front of Sam and gently put questions to the boy:
"Do you feel better, Sam?" The boy nodded. "Now let's start again. You say that just at dusk a huge wave carried a boat on to the sandy beach. You and your friends observed two bodies slumped in the bottom.You saw a name on the bow end - Lam- something or other?"
"Excuse me, was it a lamp? - like this?" said Alex, who had joined the group and held up a lamp.
"Yes," whispered Sam.
Alex put a light to the wick.
Sam sat up, pointed and exclaimed "Light!"
"Lamp - lamp - light," muttered Jamie.
"Lamplighter" shouted Alex.
Jamie jumped to his feet.
"Look, we must get organised and investigate immediately. Kate, will you see that Sam is given a hot bath, change of clothing, some food and prepare him for a journey. Likewise later, I'm sure you'll look after the other two lads. Gaynor, can you organise a horse and a big buggy and, say, two saddled horses. Janette" (who had joined the group with Jacko) "will you obtain some blankets and medical supplies - and two oars."
Jamie's mind was racing ahead.
He wanted to keep this serious problem away from the public.
"Also about twenty-five foot of rope and a loaded rifle. We don't know what to expect."
He paused, viewing the group around him.
"Now this is the plan. It looks as though the captured Northern ships, which you may recall had skeleton crews on board, must have run into those hurricanes in the Gulf. Some men must have taken to the boats and one of these has been washed up on the beach with two bodies in it. I will lead the way, directed by Sam on horseback. You, Graeme and Carruthers, will ride the buggy with Gaynor. Bring some medical equipment," and (with a laugh) "some liquid revival. Alex, Jacko, you will be on horseback and see if you

can muster up Francis and Butler, no doubt in the bar, to ride in the buggy." He paused, thinking quickly:
"We will meet discreetly at the stables. I'll go and alert the Captain. Owens, get Townsend and stand by here until we return. I want this operation to be kept secret until we find the facts."
He looked sternly around the company.
"Is that understood? Good - go to it. - Ladies, thank you." A barn dance was in full swing, gentlemen honouring their partners and then swinging them into position to receive a new partner.

Jamie observed Semmes dancing with Mrs. Sheridan.
'They make a fine couple, I hope he doesn't tickle her with that damned waxed moustache' he chuckled to himself, while he waited till the dance ended to approach the Captain.
"Excuse me, sir, could I have a word? - it's most important."
"Excuse me, Mrs. Sheridan - I'll escort you to your husband - and thank you for the dance." The Captain swiftly rejoined Jamie.
"Sir, a longboat has been washed up on the beach about ten miles down the coast. It has two bodies slumped in it and as far as I can make out from a young negro boy who discovered it, the name on the boat is the *'Lamplighter'*."
"Good God," exclaimed Semmes.
"I have organised a team with transport, and we are going shortly to investigate the situation. I have kept everything quiet. Only Sir David's daughters and two of the household are involved. We are leaving shortly on horseback from the stables.
Townsend is standing by and we'll send word in advance on our findings."
"Thank you, Jamie - trust you to take control and organise things. I shall await your return but I shall go immediately and discreetly alert Sir David to the situation."

Jamie went to the anteroom, discarded his white uniform and donned a woollen jersey and black trousers and went to the stables at the rear of the mansion.Jamie was greeted by the groomsman, Crawford. "This horse responds to the name Blacky. Treat him gently and I'm sure he'll behave.Your friends are riding the ladies' gentle horses." Crawford grinned. "We also managed to find two oars, rather an unusual request, also a rifle, and lanterns."

Gaynor, driving the buggy, emerged from the stables with the four officers. Alex was riding a magnificent brown horse and Jacko looked uncomfortable on a mule. Kate came out of the gloom on a white horse. Jamie looked around. "Are we all here?"
He raised his right arm and in true western tradition (which he had read about in American books) exclaimed:
"Let's roll."

Sam, sitting in front of Jamie on the black horse, pointed the way and off they went into the dark. The dusty road was easy to follow for about eight miles and then Sam pointed out towards the right where the party could hear the surging waves along the sandy beach. Into view came the longboat.

It was wedged deep into the sand. Two negro boys were standing nearby. Jamie leapt off his horse and lifted Sam down.

'What are your friends' names, Sam?

"Daniel and Mark, sir."

('Good Biblical names,' mused Jamie.)

He was joined by Jacko and Alex and they examined the unconscious bodies in the boat.

"Hell," exclaimed Alex, "it's Kelly and Mills."

They gently lifted the bodies out of the boat on to blankets on the sandy beach and Doctor Graeme examined them in turn to ascertain if they were both breathing, which he confirmed with a sigh of relief. "Yes, they are both alive, thank goodness."

They gently laid the blanketed figures in the buggy. Jamie decided to make use of the longboat and instructed the sailors:

"Butler, Francis, get the oars, let's push the boat out, hide the name and row it round to the '*Alabama*'. Alex - ride ahead with Sam, return to the mansion and inform the Captain about the situation and request that accommodation be ready for the survivors, I'll catch you up after the beach is cleared. Take Daniel and Mark with you."

Francis waved from the boat once they had crested the waves, which Jamie acknowledged. He mounted Blacky after having seen everything was cleared from the beach and went in pursuit of the buggy.

They arrived at the stables to be greeted by Sir David and Semmes. Manservants gently removed the unconscious bodies into the back of the house, up the stairs to a room with twin beds.

The Doctor and Carruthers, ably assisted by Gaynor and Alyson, took off the men's clothes. Kate brought a bowl of hot water and washed and dried both men, assisted by Doctor MacGregor. He carried out further examinations when they were made comfortable in their separate beds. No bones were broken, they simply suffered from exhaustion and fatigue.

Hot rum was trickled down their throats and ammonia wafted from a bottle under their noses. The familiar rum had an almost immediate effect and Kelly, amidst spluttering and vomiting, was the first to open his blurry eyes and look around the company.

He was dazed and in shock. Mills came round about an hour later.

117

They were served with hot soup by the ladies and they settled down, peacefully sleeping. Everybody left the room on the advice of the Doctor and left servants in attendance in the bedroom. Kate turned to Carruthers and with a grin remarked:
"We might make the last dance. Go and put on that smart uniform. You can't escort me to the dance in that tatty old jacket." They both laughed.
"I will, if you will help me to change." They dashed to the bedroom, hand in hand.

The dance was nearing its ending when the rescue party appeared. Graeme, restored to his smart uniform, looking as though he had been dancing all night, was whispering in the smiling Gaynor's left ear.
Kate, who was waltzing with Carruthers, held tightly in his arms, mused: 'Gaynor looks so happy - she deserves it and what a catch! - a Doctor - I've only managed an engineer - just my luck, though he's a great character and I'm very fond of him, but how long will it last before he sails into the sunset?'
The Master of Ceremonies called for order.
"My Lords, ladies and gentlemen, Sir David Sullivan would like to say a few words before the last dance."
"The evening is rapidly coming to a close. I would like to say a few words of thanks. To my charming daughters for arranging the details and sending out the 150 invitations. To my staff for assisting in the catering and attending to your needs. Especially to the Captain and crew of the '*Alabama*'. We are pleased you could attend and we wish you bon voyage when you leave these shores.
Also to the Captain and officers from the '*Jason*'. You are always welcome as my guests. To my honoured guests and friends - thank you all for coming and I wish you all a safe journey home."
There was loud applause and cheering from the happy crowd.
The Master of Ceremonies, Martin, gave the final command:
"Sir David, will you please honour the company and take your partner for the last waltz."
There was a sudden rush of the younger men to find their partners. The officers from the '*Jason*' were unfortunate not to be able to partner the Sullivan sisters, as their cards had been well marked in advance.
Kate and Carruthers, following the applause as Sir David partnered Cheryl, took the floor; then Janette and Jacko, Gaynor and Graeme. Alyson was accompanied by Alex... Jamie was drinking at the bar with Owens and Butler when he was approached by a young lady with long black hair. "I know it's unusual, my name is

Gweneth, daughter of the Chief Constable. May I have the pleasure of the last waltz?"

"Certainly Miss Gweneth, but I warn you, I'm not a good modern dancer. I only enjoy Scottish dancing. I'm Jamie, by the way." "So that is why you've been here most of the evening. I've been watching you!"

Jamie assessed this nicely built young lady, with the curves in the right places. 'I wonder why she's not dancing, I suppose it's because of her father. He's worth watching - I bet he's a right bossy type. I certainly don't want to tangle with him; the brief encounter with the Captain the other day serves as a warning. I'll certainly have to watch my step.' He smiled.

He held her discreetly at arm's length. He didn't want any body contact. At any rate she was not his type. His mind was on the dance too. Gweneth waited her chance.

"Would you like to come horse riding with me tomorrow, Jamie?"

('She isn't wasting any time,' thought Jamie.)

"I'm not sure, Miss. I might be available in the afternoon, as we are having a meeting with the Captain in the morning"

"I'll meet you here about 2 pm at the stables and I'll arrange a horse for you with Gaynor." She had second thoughts. "You do ride?"

"Oh, yes, Miss, I was brought up on a farm in Scotland and we had to rely on horses for transportation, but we bred shire horses mainly for farm work."

At the conclusion of the last dance, the M.C. proclaimed a special vote of thanks to the orchestra, which the leader acknowledged. The red-coated M.C. continued:

"Ladies and gentlemen, will you please form a circle for Auld Lang Syne."

From an anteroom came the sound of bagpipes. Butler and Midshipman Owens paraded in Highland dress and the circled dancers commenced singing, "Should auld acquaintance be forgot" - the company linked hands across - "And here's a hand my trusty friend" - the Scottish bard's immortal song rang out. In conclusion the M.C's loud voice requested:

"Three cheers for Sir David Sullivan and his family."

The dancers broke up into various groups chatting away about the events of the evening. The servants brought the ladies' and gentlemen's coats and cloaks. Horse-drawn carriages trotted to the front entrance and after everybody had departed, Sir David and his special guests and friends settled in the large lounge, where servants served coffee, cocktails and wine.

The sisters and their escorts settled in a group.

"Why didn't you entertain us - Alex, Jamie, with some Scottish dancing?" enquired the youngest sister.

"Well, Janette," answered Alex, "the programme was selected by your sisters and you had a full selection of modern dancing appropriate for the guests. However we still have a few days' leave. We'll arrange another evening when we'll be in Highland dress and we will perform the sword dance, the reels and strathspeys, perhaps!" With a grin, Jamie concluded: "You'll practise like we did the modern dancing on board ship." Kate remarked: "I've got a book about Scottish dancing from one of my teachers at school. John Baker and his wife Jean demonstrated and taught us the dances. We even had a piper, grizzly old Joe Henderson. Mr. Baker also demonstrated some of the dances we did tonight, the Lancers and Quadrilles, which we always enjoyed because we had a good laugh through our mistakes."

Alyson pointed to Alex: "You got into a mess and argument in the foursome swing in the Lancers with Janette, Jacko, and myself. We were being twirled quickly around when Janette's feet left the ground and caught a seated woman behind on the chin. Most embarrassing." The company listened intently to the light-hearted conversation, racked with laughter, especially when Jacko said: "She looked very annoyed!"

Gaynor remarked after they had been served with drinks: "How about you gentlemen coming to the church service next Sunday? It's the well attended Cathedral church in Kingston."

"Good idea," said Jamie. "I'll mention it to the Captain. We will probably have a church parade. None of us have attended church since we sailed. It's an excuse to have a pipe band and drums parading from the quay, through the streets to the church. We might even find a Southern flag to fly!"

"Now that is going too far. It could bring the fight to this beautiful island," chipped in Alex.

"I'm sure the Captain will agree," said Graeme, "and he will enjoy flying the Confederate flag. It will be an eye opener for any Union sympathizers on the island."

"We have a few of them," replied Kate. "That unpleasant gent who owns the hardware stores, he's a right militant. He's always writing articles for the Kingston newspapers and holding public meetings, hoping to gain sympathy for the Union."

"I would like to meet him," said Alex. I'll hope he's a big man, for the bigger they are the harder they will fall." Everybody laughed. Graeme said with a grin:

"Now don't be like that, Alex - I'll only have to patch him up after you've given him a knock-down blow."

The conversation continued until Captain Semmes interrupted the young officers and their partners!

"Ladies, will you excuse me? Gentlemen, I've spoken to Sir David and he's agreed for us to hold a meeting in his study, say at 2 pm tomorrow, after I've spoken to Kelly and Mills. Jamie, mention it to all the other officers about the meeting tomorrow. Ladies, thank you for the able manner in which you have organized all today's proceedings. Gentlemen, I bid you goodnight," (Semmes had second thoughts, Kate remarked) "and, Jamie, I would like you to be present in the morning, say at nine o'clock when I shall be visiting Kelly and Mills."

The thought of a meeting next day quickly broke up the happy company.

Carruthers took Kate by the arm, up the marble staircase and with a long passionate kiss at Kate's bedroom door, whispered in her ear: "We have only known each other a short time, Kate, and I've grown very fond of you." He kissed her again and again to which she passionately responded. "I'll see you in the morning, my darling, until then, pleasant and happy dreams."

"I had better see how my patients are," said Graeme to Gaynor. "Perhaps you would like to come with me?"

An elderly black lady was sitting in the room where Kelly and the snoring Mills were sleeping.

"How are they, Elizabeth?" enquired Gaynor.

"They've had a good sleep. Mr. Kelly woke up and I gave him a glass of water. Mr. Mills was very restless, tossing and turning in bed, but he eventually settled down. Otherwise they have slept peacefully, except" (showing her gleaming white teeth, chuckling, gesturing) "- that chap there - snoring his head off."

Graeme gave them a brief examination, satisfying himself that they were comfortable and improving. 'No doubt,' he thought 'Semmes will want to know all the facts about how they arrived on the beach.' Finally he smiled at the servant.

"Thank you for looking after them, Elizabeth - what a lovely name, for so gracious and kind a lady. I'll see you in the morning."

Gaynor and the Doctor, walking along the corridor, embraced each other and whispered loving words to each other. They paused occasionally and he smothered her with kisses. A final kiss at Gaynor's bedroom door, then Graeme went and joined his comrades in the sailors' anteroom.

"Where's Alex?" inquired Graeme to his companions.

"Well, you know that guy after he's had a few drinks - he was last seen with Alyson. They disappeared into the garden."

"We've got a busy day tomorrow and there's the Captain's meeting. I'm hitting the hay - goodnight."

Meanwhile Alyson and Alex were fondling each other and making love on a swinging couch.

"I think, my love, it will be more comfortable in my bedroom." They lost no time, hand in hand, running to the entrance, up the stairs to Alyson's room.

Alex, feeling very tired, sat upon the bed, unlaced his shoes and kicked them off. Alyson stood over him, removed his tunic and shirt, revealing a bronzed muscular chest. She gently eased him back on to the bed. She positioned herself astride him and massaged his chest, fondling his nipples Alex lay there muttering, bemused with drink. He opened his eyes and focused on Alyson's big bosom. He slowly eased the shoulder straps of her dress down her arms, revealing large taut red nipples which he gently fondled. Alyson, breathing heavily, gently encased his hands in hers, which helped in uplifting her large breasts.

Alex's hands slowly relaxed and he lay there moaning - the nectar had taken effect. He was in a merry, semi-conscious state, with a stupid grin on his face.

'This is heavenly,' he thought. 'Where am I?' Alyson looked strangely at the unresponsive Alex.

'What's wrong with this man? Are all Scots like him, getting drunk? I should have gone for Jamie!'

She eased herself off him, stepped on to the floor, and pulled a sheet angrily over him. She took a pillow out of the clothes cupboard, placed it on the back of a chair and pulled a blanket over her naked body. She soon lapsed into sleep, hoping and dreaming for more success the next day with her new lover when sober.

The following morning both Kelly and Mills were sitting up in their beds and enjoying a hand-fed breakfast of oatmeal, served with hot milk, administered by the negro servants. There was a knock on the door and the Doctor entered. He looked surprised to see the state of his patients.

"How are you feeling? You certainly had a rough time, but I'm pleased to see you are both slowly recovering."

Graeme paused, holding Kelly's wrist, taking his pulse beat. "The captain will be along shortly and you'll be able to tell him about your recent week's adventure, since the three ships left us off the coast of Florida. You were supposed to rendezvous in Port Royal, end of January." With a smile Doctor Graeme continued: "At least you have kept that appointment." He looked at the small well-built Mills, propped up on the pillows.

"I hardly recognised you, Joe, with that long black beard."

He gestured towards the servants.

"These kind ladies have taken care of you. You are in Sir David Sullivan's mansion and you were found unconscious in the bottom of a longboat washed up on the beach about ten miles down the coast. You have to thank the young servant boy of the house, Samuel, and his two companions. That's him over there operating the ceiling fan. In the early evening they were swimming and discovered the boat, and immediately returned to the mansion and informed me of your whereabouts." He paused and washed his hands.

"When you have finished breakfast and rested, the Captain would like to hear of your adventures."

The breakfast dishes were removed and both patients were made comfortable.

Captain Semmes, informally dressed in a white shirt and black trousers, knocked discreetly on the door and entered, accompanied by Jamie.

"How pleased I am to see you - Mike - Joe. It was an anxious moment recovering your bodies, but thanks to Doctor Graeme and the Sullivan household, you appear to have made a remarkable recovery. I've brought you some special Jamaican rum and Virginian tobacco. I'm very keen to hear about your adventures since we last met off the tip of Florida."

Kelly took up the story while sipping a glass of rum.

"You will recall the three ships - the '*Lamplighter*', captained by Joe (indicating Mills who was looking and feeling comfortable, sitting up in bed), the '*Manchester*', commanded by Joseph Hardman, and myself on the '*Tonawanda*' - we headed for the delta of the Mississippi via the Florida Straights. We came across some Northern ships which we acknowledged by displaying their flag, but we didn't engage them as we were unprepared to do battle. He appeared to be still suffering the after-effects, so he paused and closed his eyes.

Mills took up the story:

"We had a meeting with the senior rescued Southern army officers. They were unanimous to return to the nearest safe port. So we decided to hug the Lousiana coastline.' Kelly interrupted -

"We were running short of supplies; after all, we had over 500 hungry soldiers' mouths to feed. I decided that the next enemy ship we sighted we would engage, and replenish our meagre stock and hopefully obtain information about the war, especially in the Galveston area." Kelly paused.

"It was windy, a rough sea, when there came a call from aloft that a barque was sighted on our port beam. We prepared for action. I commanded the soldiers with rifles to lie behind the bulwark. I signalled the '*Manchester*' and '*Lamplighter*' my intentions and told them to proceed on course and we would rendezvous late next day at a given latitude and longitude. I ordered all those not taking part in the action, below decks, so the decks appeared cleared except for a few casual seamen. The Northern flag fluttered," (he paused and chuckled in his strange mannerism) "just like you taught me, Captain, and we approached the innocent-looking barque riding the waves serenely."

The company smiled, knowing what was coming next.

"Now don't tell me," interrupted Semmes laughing, "you drew almost alongside and lowered the dam Yankee flag and displayed our colours."

"You're bloody right!" He was so excited he lay back exhausted.

He sat up and continued:

"You should have seen the look on the silly Captain's face when I jumped on board with half a dozen armed marines. I don't think he was aware there was a war on! The ship was a three-masted barque called the '*Golden Rule*'. Her Captain, Milton Charlesworth, was angry because he had been duped by the exchange of flags, but had no alternative but to surrender. Her papers showed she carried an assorted cargo and she was bound from New York to Galveston to furbish, as the Captain thought, Northern troops. We needed extra food and clothing as we had 300 hungry soldiers to feed. We cleared everything we required, transferred the Captain and his crew with their personal possessions, together with two longboats which we towed astern of the '*Tonowanda*'. The barque was put to the torch and we sailed west to rendezvous with the '*Manchester*' and '*Lamplighter*'. Kelly lay back exhausted.

Joe Mills took over the reporting: "We met at 95° longitude and 28° latitude - I remember it well as I was practising my navigation." Mills stroked his black beard and continued the past events: "A series of mishaps befell the three ships after we landed the majority of the Southern soldiers on the coast, in Louisiana, near Beaumont. They assured us there were enough troops to engage the enemy and they hoped to reach Galveston." He paused, sipped his rum, felt his beard and resumed:

"The three ships - the '*Manchester*' with Joseph Hardman in charge, Mike Kelly on the '*Tonawanda*' and myself on the '*Lamplighter*' set off to rendezvous with you in Jamaica." Mills stopped talking, eased himself in bed, took a deep breath and carried on:

124

"There was a strong off-shore wind which swept us 500 miles south into the Gulf of Mexico. While leading the way it guided us towards the Tucatan Straits. The sea was rough, huge waves swept over my ship, this was accompanied by heavy rain, and soon we ran into a hurricane." All eyes turned to Kelly who sat up in bed. He stared wide-eyed around the room.

"Then all hell let loose", he yelled, and collapsed.

Chapter 12

Mills got out of bed, put on his dressing gown and sat in a comfortable chair with a foot rest. A black servant offered him a glass of rum. He took a sip.

He was quite composed and continued:

"I don't know what happened to Hardman on the '*Manchester*', whether he survived the hurricane, but the '*Tonawanda*' lost her masts when they snapped off and shattered across the starboard side, causing the ship to list. The sea gushed into the vessel. Kelly and three seamen managed to launch a longboat and struggled through the treacherous high seas and reached the '*Lamplighter*'.

He paused and walked with faltering steps around the room. He stood in front of the seated Semmes.

"A similar fate happened to our ship, the '*Lamplighter*'. The sails were torn to ribbons and we lost control of the ship. We couldn't combat the storm and we took in water. The bilge pumps were useless against the torrents of water flooding down the companionways and hatches. She began to flounder and sink and then came that dreaded cry - "Every man for himself - abandon ship." Five of us managed to launch a small boat - how we did it I don't know - superhuman strength and the will to survive!" He paused, thinking about his adventures.

"We were tossed about in the heavy seas, two men were washed overboard - which left three of us including Mike," gesturing to his sleeping companion.

"The sea became calmer as if the hurricane seemed to be sweeping towards America. Suddenly a huge wave hit us on port side and the boat capsized.

The three of us struggled desperately and managed to scramble and lie flat on our stomachs, clinging to the keel. That is how we spent our first night, clinging to the keel - as the boat just drifted." He paused, breathing deeply, closed his eyes for a moment, and then resumed:

"The next day the sea was calm. The seaman, named Farrel, said he had experienced righting an upturned boat and he explained how. It was decided to have a go! We struggled for about two hours. Farrel was a powerfully built young man and eventually the boat became upright, but waterlogged. Mike and I splashed about in the water - I'm not a very good swimmer - we succeeded in pulling ourselves aboard the swamped boat and lay exhausted across the seats." Mike, who had been resting in bed, aroused himself and sat up. - He shouted, terrified: "Sharks - sharks!" - waving his arms in a hysterical state.

The Doctor eased him back into the bed. Joe continued: "I looked over the side, Farrel was swimming strongly towards us. He gripped the top side of the boat to haul himself into its safety. I was horrified and dumbfounded when I saw a shark rapidly approaching. Mike knelt down and grabbed his wrists and was about to haul him into the boat, when Farrel screamed - the look on his face -" Kelly sat up, shouted and sobbed. He held his head in his hands, the Doctor sat on the bed and laid him back on the pillow, but he wanted to continue the story. He pushed the Doctor aside to look at the assembly.

"I held on desperately, the shark must have gripped his leg, he screamed, I lost my grip - and his face - the expression - it will haunt me for ever - the agony and the pain. If I'd had a revolver I would have shot him dead. Slowly his pleading, agonizing face disappeared into the depths."

"No more now, Mike," insisted Doctor MacGregor. "I will give you something to calm you down - you must rest."

Mills seemed quite excited and wanted to continue the story: "By using our shoes and hands we slowly baled the water out of the boat. It took hours - we were exhausted and tired. The sun beat down, it was hot and unpleasant. We had no food or water. We were fortunate in finding a short mast with a sail wrapped around it, wedged under a seat. We positioned it in its socket and hoisted the sail. The rudder had survived the storm and we found the tiller secured under a seat.

Mike soon organised our direction and destination. He suggested we were roughly 20° latitude and 88° longitude and heading south by south-east, that is judging by the sun. To keep ourselves cool we doused our jackets in the sea and pulled them over our heads. There was no sign of any ships or land - only occasionally sharks, who appeared to be following us!"

He paused and rested, while the company had their glasses refilled, and then he continued:

"I relied on Mike's navigation experience - he was waiting for nightfall when he explained how we could be guided by the stars.

We drifted for days, dozing, my right hand and arm locked around the tiller- I don't remember how we came to be washed upon the beach. I can only say Providence played a big part in saving our lives and thank you all for rescuing us - God bless you all"
"That will be all, ladies and gentlemen,' Semmes stood up. "Thank God you are both alive." Turning to the black youth squatting by the wall, he said:
"You and your friends, Sam, will be rewarded. We will leave you now, Joe, have a good rest." The company withdrew from the room. He turned to Gaynor who had been listening intently - awestruck: "I feel hungry, could you please prepare a meal for us after this exciting episode." Addressing the officers, he said:
"Gentlemen, the next few days spend at your leisure, but Saturday evening I want you all back at the ship, except of course Kelly, Mills and the Doctor, to prepare for the church parade at 11 o'clock on Sunday morning at the Cathedral."
After lunch, coffee was served on the verandah. The four friends were relaxed, discussing the recent startling events. Kate offered freshly made coffee - and her sisters joined her and the conversation drifted into how to spend the next couple of days, prior to the church service next Sunday.
Gaynor arranged with Doctor Graeme to go a buggy ride to visit some relatives who lived about ten miles away on the outskirts of the old Spanish town.
Janette asked Jacko if he would like to go swimming in the shaded cove near to a waterfall, further up the coast, travelling east. He agreed, so plans were made for the following morning.
Captain Semmes, with the groomsman Crawford at the reins, left in a horse-driven buggy. He remarked he had been invited to stay overnight at the home of the Assistant Governor, with Sir Michael Kennedy and his wife.
Alyson kept glancing at Alex who was in conversation with Jamie. They were discussing affairs back home.
"The island of Lewis must be a cold and dreary place to live this time of the year," exclaimed Jamie.
"You can say that again," remarked Alex. (Alyson heard the question and leaned over, interested.)
"I lived in the north part of the island at a small hamlet called Habost at the Butt of Ness. We only had one general shop-cum-mailing office and the Presbyterian Kirk. My father was in charge of the lighthouse and also joined in rescue work with the coastguards, when the rocket signal was fired. Sadly," Alex paused and in a whisper, "he went out to sea, during a gale, - to rescue a fishing vessel in distress and - he never returned. From then on

life was hard and my mother and I moved to the mainland and lived for a while in Ullerpool on the Scottish mainland. My mother was a weaver and bought a machine and she worked long hours on the loom making rugs. The name 'Harris Tweed' for kilts, has become quite famous on mainland Britain. In fact I have one stowed away somewhere!"

"I bet your mother had legs and ankles like thick banister legs!" laughed Jamie.

"What was your early boyhood like, Jamie?" quickly interrupted Alyson - she didn't want to hear a discussion about ladies' legs.

"My folks were farmers, living near the village of Aberfeldy."

Alyson brightly added:

"I remember reading some of the poems by Robert Burns and he referred to the Birks of Aberfeldy."

('What a fountain of knowledge,' thought Alex. 'She's a right smart kid!').

"You're quite right, Alyson," remarked Jamie, "I'm familiar with the lovely colourful countryside - with its birks and bracken bens just like the the poetry of our beloved bard. He even remarked when he was viewing the Tay valley:

"This is truly the heart of Scotland.- so contrasting to the wildness and bleakness of the storm-swept Hebrides, the Ben Nevis Range, or the moorlands. Scotland is a most interesting country to visit!"

Alex continued the conversation to the interested Alyson:

"The whole family had to go with handcarts, or, if you were wealthy, horse and cart. The youngsters carried baskets and we travelled to the moorlands in the summer months when the weather was good to dig up the peat and store it inside or near to the house. The snow could be six or ten feet high - you had to stock up with enough food - it was like living in the Arctic - and you had to hibernate in the bleak and wearisome winter. Times were hard and tough." Alex replenished his wine.

"What was your upbringing like, Alyson?" inquired Jamie.

"As you know I have three other sisters. We lost our mother just after my youngest sister Janette was born. The four of us were brought up in Jamaica by my father. He kept enlarging the farm, growing crops, vines, fruit trees and we also breed animals. I've had a comfortable life. I was educated partly in Kingston, and in Lancashire, living with my grandparents. I work mainly assisting on the farm - or otherwise," she laughed, "I live a life of luxury."

'Life was rough in rural Scotland," Jamie was serious. "The only thing we did as youngsters was schooling, study, reading books, or working on the farm. It was a break to go to the Kirk three times on Sunday - that was something we looked forward to, as my brothers and sisters would dress in our best clothes, sit in the family pew and listen to the boring voice of the Minister. He would pray for nearly an hour and the sermon would be longer and also during the service, sing six psalms." He said with a chuckle, "That's why I'm so well read on the Bible!"

"Let's change the subject," said Alyson. "What are you doing tomorrow, you handsome ugly brute?" - she smiled showing her white teeth. "How about a horse ride to some mysterious or unexplored part of the island?"

"Good idea, how about you, Jamie?"

"I'm not sure, I'm waiting to hear from Cheryl. We are supposed to meet up with her husband, Roland, and go treasure hunting."

Alex burst out laughing. "Now that should be exciting. Will you cut me in?"

"How about you Alyson, do you want to get rich quick?"

• • •

The long scruffy haired Roland Sheridan, in tatty trousers and shirt, was studying a rough piece of parchment. It was part of a map he had bought from an old seafarer in a tavern near the wharf, in Port Royal. He took off his glasses and cleaned them. The sea cooled his bare feet as he peered into the mouth of a cave in the rocks.

'It could be any of these caves,' he thought, 'I'll just have to start digging - hoping the cave will not flood!'

There was a fire nearby on the beach. He lit a torch and was just about to enter the cave when there was a shout from a ledge over to his right. Four people climbed down and approached him. He was surprised to see his wife Cheryl.

"Hi, Roland," said Alyson. "Haven't seen you for a while. How are you keeping? The "*Alabama*' is in the harbour and Cheryl and I have brought two of the officers. May I introduce Alex and Jamie. They are interested in buried treasure."

"Pleased to meet you." Roland was a bit off-handish. (He wondered, - 'What are they after and what is **so** important about the ship - the '*Alabama*? - Never heard of it!' He collected his scattered thoughts together.)

"You're just in time, I'm only guessing, but according to this map, there is supposed to be a pirate's buried treasure in one of these caves. I've examined numerous caves in this area and I'm just about to start in this one" (indicating).

"I have a wooden shack" (pointing over a ridge) "- over there, on a green-banked wide ledge. You can approach it from this path. You'll see my horse and mare grazing there. Tether your horses nearby and just follow this path. Bring two spades - I'm sure you all like digging for gold! For it is on the north side of the island here, in Montego Bay that it was the safe haven for buccaneers and their treasures."

The geologist, carrying a lighted fire torch led the way into the cave and the rest of the party followed. The ground rose sharply, the cave opened up.

Disturbed bats fluttered around and together with the smoke of the torches this disturbed the ladies but they stumbled along. Alex assisted Cheryl.

"How much further?" shouted Jamie. Roland ignored him.

Alyson screamed - "Snakes."

Roland turned and flung his lighted torch at the reptiles. For such a slow-thinking man he acted quickly. He drew his revolver from its holster and fired three shots. The noise was deafening, it echoed and vibrated through the large cave and dust showered down. The ladies were scared. Cheryl clung to Alex, who was taken by surprise, but enjoyed her arms around his body.

Alyson was terrified, so Roland comforted her and after a brief rest the party continued with Roland leading the way. On and on he went, thrusting his lighted torch into every nook and cranny. He stopped and they all gathered around him. He looked up into a shaft and he saw daylight.

"This is it!" he shouted, thrusting the torch into Alex's hand. He peered at the parchment. He was excited. Pointing upwards and indicating it on the map, he went on:

"Twenty footsteps from the shaft of light - over there - where it's shining. Let's start digging - you," - pointing to Alex - "here, and you, Jamie, is that your name? over there" (indicating). "I'll start digging here."

He turned to Cheryl: "How are you feeling, my dear? Do you both mind going back to the shack where you'll find some food and wine. We'll need some nourishment and it's going to be thirsty work. Take this torch and be careful, and, if can you manage, bring some wood for a fire. It will keep off all these nasty insects and snakes." He chuckled. ('Wonder what tickles him,' mused Cheryl.) Alex and Jamie began digging furiously - the thought of hidden treasure! It was beyond their wildest dreams, what a story to tell their shipmates - or - should they? The spade crunched, into the sand and gravel, the sweat poured down their faces and bodies. Alex stripped off his shirt, likewise Jamie.

Two hours went by - crunch - crunch - the ladies returned, prepared a meal and lit a fire. Work stopped and they enjoyed their refreshments.

Alex studied the map and burst out into a hysterical laugh - Roland looked annoyed - 'Stupid bugger,' he thought 'it won't be the first time I've struck it rich! I wonder what amuses him!'

Jamie continued digging. He was now four feet deep. There was a different ring as he struck something solid! Roland shouted and they all gathered and looked down the hole. Jamie began to unearth the rounded top of a box. It was four feet long by two feet wide. He removed sufficient earth - and Roland jumped down. "Let me strike the padlock a blow."

Crunch - the lock snapped off; he struggled to lift the lid, assisted by Jamie.

Eager eyes feasted on the contents, but they were disappointed to see dust-coated leather bags. With trembling hands Roland reached down and carefully opened one and it revealed - Spanish gold pieces. They trickled through his fingers and he flung some into the air.

He could not believe his eyes. "What a find, we are rich! This is worth a fortune." The rest of the party were flabbergasted and bewildered. They couldn't believe that they were looking at sparkling gold!

"Let's get them up to the shack and sort them out - and I don't know about you folk, but I need a swim in the sea while it's daylight."

"Would it be a good idea, Roland, if we were to lower a rope down the shaft, over there" - indicating, - "and haul them up," suggested Alex.

"Yes, the hole above can't be so far away from my shack. You and Jamie return to the shack - there's strong rope hanging on the wall". He looked upwards.

"I will place the lighted torch in the shaft and you will be able to see the smoke rising. Make sure the rope is long enough. Have a look around the shack for a big bucket or basket and we'll use that to haul up our gold."

Alex and Jamie hurried off, located the rope and a large basket and hastened up the hill in front of the shack and soon observed the smoke lazily rising into the hot atmosphere. They secured the rope to a stout tree, tied the the other end to the basket and lowered it into the five foot diameter shaft. A tug at the other end signified the basket had arrived at the bottom of the cave and soon the first sight of the leather bags arrived at the top of the shaft.

'They havn't seen daylight for a few years,' thought Jamie. The rest of the bags were hauled up and finally the wooden chest. Alex and Jamie lay down exhausted when Cheryl and Alyson approached. "What a haul," exclaimed the excited Alyson, "I wonder how Roland will divide it?"

'We'll soon know. Here he comes up the hill," shouted Alex.

"I'll get the mule and the horse. Will you help me, Cheryl? We'll soon get this haul to the shack." They appeared about half an hour later and the bags were loaded on to the mule and the horse. The rest were carried by the ladies and Roland, some placed inside the chest, which Jamie and Alex hauled by the side handles, down the hill to the shack.

Outside it they dusted down the bags then went in and spread the gold on to a table. Eager hands counted them out and piled them in columns of ten.

"What a fortune, thank you all for helping me." Roland was grateful and eventually made up his mind: "I'll tell you what I propose; I will take half for Cheryl and myself and you can equally divide the rest between you three."

• • •

'The Seafarers' is a popular quayside tavern frequented by stevedores, seafaring men, prostitutes, layabouts, Northern Union sympathizers and army deserters. It was a haven for worldwide gossip, illegal importing and exporting of goods and humans. The tavern's fame is well known to men of the sea and, seated in a quiet corner, John Bowen and an islander David George Garth (an unusual name of Welsh and Patagonian heredity) were in conversation. The quietly spoken local man was telling Bowen how he came to Jamaica when they were rudely interrupted by two members of the '*Alabama*' crew, Roughler and Steve Moore. They were introduced to Garth. Bowen ordered jugs of ale and they were served by a busty young dark-skinned lady. She had a low-cut flimsy blouse and a short skirt. Roughler's eyes goggled when she dropped the monies down her blouse. He caught a glimpse of one of her nipples.

The conversation between the four was about the Civil War; Garth had all the latest news. Steve Moore, a Kentuckian, was drinking heartily and raised his voice in song, joined by his comrades: "Oh! I wish I were in Dixie". The singing grew louder as local taverners added their support - "In Dixieland I'll take my stand". A heavily built scruffy-looking man, casually dressed - obviously not a seafarer - lurched over and grabbed Garth by his shirt and butted him in the face. He then produced a knife and lunged at Bowen.

Roughler crashed his glass mug on the table. It left the handle in his hand. He thrust the jagged edge into the neck of the attacker. He was covered in blood, there was yelling and shouting from the victims' supporters who quickly joined in the affray and soon all hell was let loose. Bowen was hit on the back of the head with a bottle and finished on the bar room floor. Hefty Steve picked up a stool and swung it around, crushing a few bones of his assailants. Whistles blew, denoting the police had arrived.

The barmaid thrust her way through the fighting and grabbed Roughler's arm. "This way to my house - quick - before the police arrest you."

Garth hoisted Bowen over his broad shoulders. Steve Moore made a path through the fighting, maddening crowd swinging a stool. They departed through the back door of the tavern and into a narrow dirty alleyway.

"This way to my house, I'll hide you there and attend to your friend's bleeding head."

It was a small room, sparsely furnished. Garth laid Bowen on a small, narrow bed.

"My name's Josephine. I'll get some hot water - strip off his shirt - it's covered in blood and I'll wash it later."

She brought a bowl of water and bathed the wounded Bowen's head and then bandaged it. He moaned, opened his bleary eyes. Confused, he remarked, holding his head in his hands.

"My head's hurting, what happened, where am I?" He looked around the room.

A while later Garth sat him up and Josephine assisted in donning his partially wet shirt and black jacket and putting on his woollen cap to hide his bandage.

Garth, his face swollen by being butted in the face, remarked: "Listen, I think we should get back to your ship. There's bound to be trouble with your skipper and no doubt you'll get the blame."

Bowen stood up, wobbled, sat down, then stood up again with the aid of Garth and Roughler. Josephine led the way to the wharf and they were greeted by the Bosun's Mate, Ray Tyler.

"I hear there's been trouble in the tavern, just along by the wharf," gesturing. "I hope it's not you buggers, you look as though you've been in a fight. Quick, get into the boat over there, Richardson and Schmechel will row you over to the '*Alabama*' and once on board get lost, is that understood? Don't even come up to breathe". He spotted the barmaid. "Who's the lovely wench?"

"Never mind, eyes off," laughingly shouted Roughler. "She's my girl." He put his arms around her and gave her a hug and a kiss, to which she responded.

He could feel her hot young body pressed against his chest and he was getting quiet excited, when Bowen pulled him away. Then he waved to her as he descended the steps to the longboat.

"I'll be back," he shouted and waved her a final goodbye.

On board, the party were greeted by the officer of the watch - the stern looking Mr. Freeman. He shouted:

"What have you rascals been up to? You look as though you've been in a war. You look dreadful, you horrible bunch, you call yourselves seamen? Get below and tidy yourselves up and I'll see you in the junior wardroom in half an hour."

In the seamen's quarters Bowen washed himself and put on a clean green-striped shirt.

"What are you going to tell the officer?" said Moore in his slow southern accent.

"Tell the truth, they started the fight," declared Roughler. "What about this guy Garth?"

"I think we had better take him with us to the wardroom and explain why he's on board - I don't think the Captain will be pleased!"

"Good idea. Let's go and get it over with," said the thickset groggy Bowen, combing his black curly hair.

Freeman was seated at a table with Riordan and Ollie Butler alongside.

Bowen knocked on the door. It was opened by the duty guard.

They marched in line and stood to attention and saluted.

"What's this all about? You begin."

"At ease," commanded Freeman. "Now what's this all about? You begin, Bowen."

"It was like this, sir," Bowen almost whispered.

"Speak up, man," thundered Freeman.

"Well - we -" (indicating Garth.)

"Who's he?" inquired Butler. "I haven't seen him before."

"I was chatting with him - his name is Garth - when we were attacked by a ruffian who claimed to be a Northerner," exclaimed Bowen, "and I was knocked unconscious."

The tall well-built Riordan stood up. "Gentlemen, I am representing you and will help you in presenting your case."

He had made a few notes, which he shuffled.

"So this Northerner attacked first?"

"Yes, sir," burst in Roughler, "and when he hit John, I bashed a mug on the edge of the table and thrust the jagged edge into the side of his face or neck, I'm not sure. After that the enemy seemed everywhere, fists, chair legs, bottles were used mainly - there was pandemonium and then whistles blew. The young bar wench to whom we owed our safety and Garth here," (indicating the bald young man) "he heaved the unconscious Bowen over his shoulder. The wench led the way to the back door which was behind the bar. Moore kept swinging a bar stool around, cracking many a skull. He cleared the way for us to leave the wrecked tavern and we went to the safety of the wench's house."

The bearded Moore took up the story:

"She was very helpful, she bathed Bowen's bleeding head and washed his clothes and we made our way to the wharf, boarded the longboat and we were welcomed," everybody laughed, "on board, sir, by you." He couldn't help himself, grinning lamely.

Freeman bashed the table. "Silence, this is no laughing matter. Have you any questions, Mr. Riordan?"

"So you are saying you didn't start the fight, but you only defended yourselves."

"That is correct," remarked Bowen. "In fact, we only went for a quiet drink, to relax and enjoy ourselves."

"Those troublemakers started it, sir," interrupted Roughler.

"Thank you, gentlemen." Turning to Mr. Freeman, "Those are all my questions."

"Then you are dismissed, confined to quarters and no shore leave until further orders. Let us hope nothing further develops on the mainland. Take this other wretch with you, until we decide what to do with him."

The accused seamen saluted and left the cabin.

• • •

Kelly and Mills were sitting relaxing on the mansion's veranda when Captain Semmes and Jamie trotted up riding Mexican horses. They dismounted and Crawford, the groomsman, led the horses away. The host, Sir David, offered them afternoon tea after their ride into the Blue Mountains.

"Magnificient and well trained horses, Sir David," remarked Semmes.

"Yes, I imported three mares and one stallion about six years ago and now I'm breeding them. They are specially trained to round up sheep and cattle."

A buggy drew up, the groomsman held the horses' reins, while a black frocked clergyman alighted and approached Sullivan.

"How nice to see you, Granville. Come under the awnings of the verandah, it's very hot." Sullivan seemed delighted to meet his friend in clerical outfit. "May I introduce my special guests, Captain Semmes and three of his officers - Mike Kelly, Jamie and Mills.

Gentlemen, meet the Very Reverend Granville Evans - Bishop of Kingston."

They shook hands with the medium-built, blue-eyed, black-coated churchman.

"It's very hot David, do you mind if I somewhat disrobe?"

After that the conversation was mainly about the American Civil War.

"That's interesting," remarked the Bishop. "I'm glad we've met; I would like to discuss next Sunday's service which, I understand, Captain, you and your crew will be attending. It is an unexpected pleasure," he smiled. "It's not often we have an American ship of war visiting our harbour. Is there anything special you would like during the service? - say, any favourite hymn? reading?" - he paused waiting for a reply.

Semmes said: "I'm a Roman Catholic - I would like a reading from one of the psalms - the 121st, my favourite - "I will lift up mine eyes unto the hills from whence cometh my help. I got a lot of help, support and comfort when I read this psalm."

"Would you like to read it on Sunday, Captain?" ('That's one job less,' thought the wily Evans.)

"As you wish," responded Semmes. Jamie requested:

"I also enjoyed the psalms as a youth in the Presbyterian Church of Scotland:

"Would it be possible for the choir to sing the twenty-third psalm?" He paused. "The Lord's my Shepherd - and what a conclusion - and in God's house for evermore my dwelling place shall be."

Then Kelly related how their lives - indicating Mills - had been saved by an unknown seaman named Farrel - and his tragic ending. "Could you mention him in your prayers, Bishop," said Mills quietly, "and to his memory I would like the sailors' hymn - "Eternal Father strong to save, whose arm hath bound the restless waves."

"I'm sure all these requests shall be attended to, gentlemen - did I hear Captain, that you will be parading from the wharf displaying the flag, pipers and drummers leading the way?"

Semmes smiled: "I hope nobody objects."

"No indeed, on the contrary" - Sullivan smiled, "you will be more than welcome. Why not dedicate your standard to the Cathedral?" I will receive it with pleasure," said the Reverend Granville. "In fact it will have a place of honour in the Lady Chapel" - he paused - "well that's agreed."

Another buggy arrived carrying the Acting Governor, Sir Michael Kennedy.

After greeting each other, the service arrangements, the parade and the dedication of the banner were discussed with him, which he approved - after all he was acting on the Governor's behalf and should be consulted on such matters - and fully agreed also to attend in his official capacity.

"I shall put on my number one outfit and feathered cocked hat."

Sunday 25th January 1863: Dawn broke and the sun began to shimmer over Kingston Harbour. It was going to be another hot day. On board the '*Alabama*' the marine bugler Mullard sounded the reveille. It was for an early breakfast, following which the officers assembled in groups on the main deck, briefing their various squads concerning the church parade in Kingston. The longboats rowed the crew ashore, where they lined up military style. Crowds began to gather on the quay. The three pipers tuned up, together with the two drummers, Mullard and Jaffee, both dressed in seamen's rig with straw boaters.

"Bosun, will you assemble the crew for inspection. Mr. MacPherson will accompany me in the absence of Mr Kelly," commanded Captain Semmes.

"Aye, aye, sir." Bellew acknowledged the order with a salute.

"Company, fall in." His loud voice was almost heard across the harbour.

Church bells sounded, summoning the faithful to worship.

"Captain Butler, Francis and Townsend, will you line up your troops behind the pipers and - Jamie, will you lead the parade, proudly displaying the Confederate flag. I understand you managed to attach it to a suitable flag pole!" said Semmes.

"It will be an honour, sir" replied Jamie.

While Semmes was talking to the Bosun he was suddenly interrupted by the uniformed Chief Constable.

"I have here a summons against three of your crew and a chap named Garth who I understand you are harbouring, he thrust the writ into the Captain's right hand. "The charge is murder!"

Chapter 13

"'Bosun, just to remind you" (Semmes snarled it out. He was still very angry after the Chief Constable's stand against him.) "You will be in charge of the parade. The flag will lead the way, followed by the band, then myself and the officers, the marines and finally the crew."

"Aye, aye, sir. Parade, parade, Attention. Quick march."

With the drummers' beat, the pipers picked up the rhythm and commenced playing 'Highland Laddie.' The flag unfurled and fluttered in the slight breeze as Jamie led the parade.

The gathering townspeople cheered as the men from the '*Alabama*' left the quay and the column wended its way through the narrow streets until the impressive steepled Cathedral came into view.

"Parade, halt," commanded the Bosun as they approached the cathedral steps.

The organist was playing a voluntary as the white-gauntleted Jamie, proudly gripping the Southern standard, marched slowly up the aisle followed by the Captain and officers. The Dean of the Cathedral received the flag. He grasped it firmly with both hands and raised it horizontally above his head the large colourful Confederate standard unfurled fully opened, for the crowded congregation to see. The organ ceased; everybody stood up.

"Let us bless this flag and the crew of the '*Alabama*'. May it be consecrated to the honour and glory of God and may it find a resting place within these hallowed walls." The officers stood to attention and saluted. The organist played a fanfare.

The Dean housed the flag on the left of the altar and the Captain and officers seated themselves behind the Mayor and town's dignitaries. After the opening hymn - 'O worship the King all glorious above', the Bishop gave a warm welcome to the crew of the '*Alabama*' and the congregation. There was a pause and Semmes stepped forward to the lectern, thumbed through the Bible until he found the reading for the first lesson from the Psalms 'I will lift up mine eyes unto the hills, from whence cometh my help.' The Captain continued, reciting the passage of scripture without glancing at the Bible. He had memorised it as a child as it was his favourite reading and he felt so privileged to be allowed to read it in the house of God. Jamie thought 'How well he read it and with such feeling!' Semmes concluded "Here ends the first lesson and to His name be the praise. Amen."

The choir chanted the twenty-third psalm, reminding Jamie of his choir days in Dunkeld Presbyterian Church. His mind pictured his wife, Matilda, and his two daughters worshipping in Oldham Street Chapel and how this adventure was born there, during a conversation with Mr. Freeman. Jamie glanced across to the Chief Engineer who appeared to be praying with closed eyes and bowed head.

The red-robed Dean led the prayers, remembering in a sombre voice how the lives of Mills and Kelly (who were both present, sitting with the Sullivan family) had been saved by the heroism of David Farrel - a brave and honoured seaman. Mill's eyes watered he felt emotional. The Dean continued by praying for the men of the '*Alabama*' and concluded with readings from the Prayer Book. Another hymn, 'Now thank we all our God, with hearts and hands and voices'. How very appropriate,' thought Jamie, 'and written by a German, Johann Cruger, in 1631.'

The Bishop was conducted to the pulpit by his warden, carrying his staff.

"Let the words of my mouth and the meditation of my heart, be acceptable in Thy sight, 0 Lord my strength and my Redeemer."

'Gosh this sermon is going to be read,' thought Jamie, but he grew interested as the Very Reverend Evans continued:

"Let your light so shine before men that they may see your good works and glorify your Father in Heaven, let your talents and your personality be revealed to the world."

Jacko eyed Janette in her frilly hat sitting alongside her father and sisters in the left aisle. 'It won't be long now, hurry up with the sermon, mister, and I can meet my beloved in the grounds of the Bishop's Palace.' He caught her eye and he winked at her and she smiled. 'I wonder what the old goat is up to now?' she thought. The Bishop droned on.

It was hot and there was no breeze. Eyes slowly closed and heads nodded in the congregation. On and on, until - "Finally" - and everybody suddenly became alert. "Wherever you are going in the future, and whatever your tasks, lift your head up high and let your talents be revealed to the world and be proud to be a Christian. In the name of the Father, Son and Holy Ghost. Amen."

He paused and glanced at the hymn on the board.

The Dean announced: "Let us conclude our service with the sailors' hymn. Eternal Father strong to save, whose arm hath bound the restless wave. From rock and tempest, fire and foe, protect them whereso'ere they go, Thus evermore shall rise to Thee, glad hymns of praise from land and sea."

'We will be sailing with the church's blessing,' thought Semmes - he smiled faintly - 'how ironic, let us kill the enemy with one hand and then ask for forgiveness with the other.')

The large congregation slowly dispersed. The Sullivan sisters soon located their officer partners and together with the distinguished guests made their way down a shaded lane to the Bishop's Palace. The huge ornamental iron gates were swung open by servants as the chattering crowd walked slowly up the stoney cobbled path to a large green lawn in front of the Spanish Palace. It was adorned with canopy-covered tables and chairs, bedecked with flowers.

The guests were escorted to the tables by white-shirted, short-trousered black youths. The four sisters gathered around a large ten-seater table and went into whispered conversation with their friends.

Captain Semmes drew the Assistant Governor to one side.

"Sir Michael, I have an important matter to discuss with you and I need your advice and guidance. I'm acting on behalf of President Davis, who would like to appoint a Consul on the island. The person I have in mind is Joseph Mills."

"Now that's a good idea and Joe Mills is an excellent choice, - in fact I was going to suggest the same myself, for, perhaps you might not know this but there is already a Northern Union representative with his headquarters in the old Spanish town. Leave the matter with me and I'll have a discussion with some of the island's distinguished citizens. In fact I'll commence with some who are here today. I'm sure we will arrive at a favourable decision as I must admit the majority of the islanders are on your side. In the meantime can I offer you a drink?"

"How about a real glass of local rum?"

Alyson in conversation with Alex suggested they should go to their favourite secluded beach for a picnic and swim. Carruthers and Graeme arranged to go separate ways with their partners - horse-riding in the Blue Mountains.

Jamie was sitting under an awning, relaxing, enjoying a glass of wine - it was extremely hot. A faint breeze wafted the frills of the round overhead lace cover. It bewitched Jamie, it made him drowsy, he had overeaten at the banquet and he dozed off. He was rudely awakened by the loud voice of the Chief Constable.

"It's very hot. Do you mind if I join you?" He waved his arm. A servant approached carrying a tray of red wine in crystal glass goblets. He lifted two off. "Your good health!"

Jamie raised himself and gestured to a chair and smiled.

"Be my guest."

'I wonder what he's up to?' thought Jamie. 'I suppose he'll soon get round to it.'

Whittle unfastened his collar. "I don't suppose anybody would mind if I take off this tight, hot, confounded jacket - see yours is hanging on the back of your chair!" He blurted out: "What do you think of one of your crew members, named Roughler?"

'Ah! Here it comes' thought Jamie "Why, what's he done? I heard his name mentioned as being in a fight!"

"In a fight! It was a brawl in the 'Seafarers', near the waterfront. The place was wrecked! My men had to invade the place and sort things out - a chap was killed, allegedly by your man Roughler - according to witnesses. I have mentioned it to your Captain and a writ has been issued for an arrest together with three other members of your crew."

"I must admit," said Jamie, who was taken unawares, "I haven't any details. No doubt there will be an enquiry on board."

"That's not good enough" pointed out Whittle. "You don't seem to understand - a man's been murdered."

"That's a strong allegation and charge" - Jamie was getting worked up. "It takes two or more to make a fight - and no-one can be accused until he is proved guilty. Do you mean to say Roughler is accused of murder?"

Sir Michael Kennedy and Sullivan were passing in deep conversation and they heard Jamie's loud voice exclaiming "Murder, what's this, Mr. Whittle - has someone been murdered?" Kennedy enquired - and then the Chief Constable explained in detail about the brawl in the tavern.

"Oh, let that be sorted out in a court of law," casually said Sullivan with a gesture of his hand. It seemed a trivial affair. "We have a more important and pleasant matter to discuss with you, Mr. Whittle, and to seek your advice, guidance and approval."

"Will you excuse me, gentlemen," interjected Jamie. "I see Roland Sheridan over there and I understand he's an authority on the island's history." 'What a lucky escape,' thought Jamie. 'I must alert the Captain. There's going to be trouble with this guy Whittle.'

Roland Sheridan was examining a multicoloured butterfly, its wings fluttering on a white flower.

"Oh! I'm glad I've met you, Jamie. What have you done with that bagful of Spanish gold? Is it safely hidden somewhere?" he whispered.

"Yes, it's in my room in the Sullivans' mansion and I'll be returning to the ship this evening; then it will be placed in the safety of my wooden locked chest - here is the key" (fingering it) "attached to this belt."

"I wish you luck, Jamie, and in case I don't see you again I hope when you sail away God will protect you and return you safely to your loved ones."

• • •

Semmes returned to the 'Alabama'. He felt moody and irritable. He shouted for the Bosun as he walked the deck, hands behind his back, thinking. "Summon Mr. Freeman, Riordan, Moore, Bowen, immediately to my cabin. I must get to the bottom of this affair and you attend Bellew, in case there's any trouble. He snarled out while deep in thought.

'It's that bugger, Whittle - he must be a Northern sympathizer! Anyway, I must support my crew and have them properly represented in court:"

The Bosun interrupted his thinking: "If I may suggest, sir, regarding that chap, Garth, I think it's the general feeling of the crew that you may consider to register him as a crew member - after all he saved Bowen's life."

"I had thought about it, thanks for reminding me."

Mr. Freeman and four of the crew members stood to attention in the Captain's cabin.

"At ease, gentlemen, and please find seats. It seems to be the popular feeling amongst the crew that we enlist this man Garth as a crew member."

"Aye, sir," the response was unanimous.

"Find him, Bosun, and bring him here. I think he will need our protection in this pending trial, which no doubt will be coming up in the near future."

Quickly, anticipating the reason, Garth stood in front of the Captain, who was seated at his desk. Semmes looked at the fair-skinned, blue-eyed young man.

"First of all I would like to thank you for the heroic part you played in rescuing and helping in the escape of three of my crew. Of course, as no doubt you are well aware, concerning the fight in the 'Seafarers Tavern', Semmes paused and gave his crewmen a long and hard look and then he continued "I feel I ought to compensate you for your bravery. How would you like to enlist and sail under my command on this ship?"

Garth was surprised, but he had heard rumours that this might happen. He was overjoyed.

"I would be more than pleased, Captain, and thank you for giving me the opportunity to join your Navy."

"Right then, that's settled. Pass me my Bible, Ramidois," which he handed to Garth. "You will hold it in your left hand and repeat your name and say after me. I, David George Garth, do hereby swear that I will fully support my allegiance to the Confederate Navy." After a few handshakes had been exchanged, things became more sombre.

"Now let's get down to the business concerning this forthcoming trial."

• • •

Meanwhile Chief Constable James Whittle, standing on the quayside, addressed his senior non-commissioned officer. "Sergeant, muster the men into the boat. I want to pay a visit to the '*Alabama*' and arrest four men and escort them to our cells, pending court proceedings."

"Very good, sir." The sergeant saluted.

• • •

"Have you anything further to add, Roughler?" Semmes continued collecting the facts together. Being a lawyer he knew about court proceedings, but he was a bit wary of British justice. "I would suggest, Roughler, that Mr. Riordan defends you and indeed Moore, Bowen and of course our latest recruit" Semmes smiled. "Garth." He paused, thinking of a final selection. "Mr. Riordan will get all your statements and he will defend you, because he understands British law. Are there any questions?" Just then the Bosun's whistle could be heard faintly in the background outside the cabin.

There was a knock on the Captain's door.

"Enter."

"Sir," said the officer of the watch - Lieutenant Armstrong - "the Chief Constable wishes to see you."

"Have him wait." ('Speak of the devil,' mused Semmes.) "I guess I know why he's here. You men wait in my other cabin over there and keep quiet. Bosun, you stay, there could be trouble. Ask Mr.Whittle to enter."

"Welcome aboard, Mr. Whittle, no doubt you have come on official business; we have been discussing the night in the 'Seafarers'." His voice trailed off when he was interrupted rather abruptly:

144

"Sir, let's get down to business," shouted Whittle. "I gave you a writ yesterday and I have come for the prisoners who will be lodged in the police jail until two days' time when the case will be heard."

Semmes stood up quickly and looked sternly at the Chief Constable.

"My men are ready and I can assure you they will go peacefully. I don't want them chained up - is that understood?" Semmes was sharp and snappy too.

"Right, if they are ready we will depart. You can see them any-time you like and we will look after their comforts. The men from the Northern Union living on the island are not very friendly and I don't want trouble with them, especially at the trial. They have appointed a barrister who's quite an unpleasant character and he's also a Northern sympathizer.

Whittle turned to face the stern-looking Semmes. "I'm only doing my job. The summons came from the High Court. We will now take our leave. Good-day, sir."

The 'Alabama' crew watched in silence as the prisoners, escorted by the police guards, descended the gangway to their longboat.

Sir Michael Kennedy came aboard the 'Alabama' just as the Chief Constable and his party were leaving.

"What was that all about, Captain?" was his opening question when the Deputy Governor was seated in Semmes's cabin.

"I suppose you have heard about the tavern brawl when a man was allegedly killed by one of my crew. Four men have been arrested and their trial comes up in two days' time."

"That's strange,'" Kennedy looked puzzled. "Did it take four men to kill one man?" He smiled. "Well, let us discuss a more pleasant subject."

"You are always welcome, Michael. How about some of our lovely old Spanish wine. Numerous bottles were 'rescued' from one of our enemy ships."

He poured out a full glass from a crystal glass decanter "Excellent. Your good health, Raphael." He took a sip.

"I have spoken to some of the island's distinguished and professional people regarding a Confederate Consulate. You would be surprised. Everybody was enthusiastic and in favour. Your Government are very popular with my people and we like your choice in Joe Mills and we will make him welcome. In fact one of our leading bankers, John Stewart, has offered your Government a mansion, fully furnished on a five-acre estate on reasonable terms. The Mayor suggested an old historical house situated on the far end of the waterfront as your Consular Offices.

"I am overwhelmed by your generosity and co-operation."

"I know you are pressed for time, Captain, as you are anxious to leave the island to join the war effort. I have arranged a large room in my mansion to be set up in the form of a court for the occasion and an agenda has been drawn up by the Bishop. I shall chair the proceedings - but the main installation and election of the Consul is entirely in your hands, and those who attend the ceremony will have our full support. Following the proceedings my wife will lay on a buffet luncheon - Do you think it's short notice, Raphael?" - Kennedy paused - "to have the short ceremony tomorrow morning, say at eleven o'clock'? I know you have the court case the following day" - Semmes was tongue-tied. He didn't know what to say. Finally he remarked.

'That will suit me fine" he smiled. "In fact as you can see," flourishing some papers "I have been preparing some notes regarding the swearing in and declaration of a Consular Official."

"Good" said Kennedy. "I will take my leave, I still have a lot to do to make the final arrangements, and until tomorrow at eleven I'll bid you goodbye." The officer of the watch, Lieutenant Armstrong, escorted the Deputy Governor to his barge, Captain Semmes summoned his officers and discussed the following day's agenda and ceremony. "This will be a very important event, gentlemen. We will be in number one dress, buttons polished, white uniforms and looking very smart. I have invited the Captain and officers of H.M.S. '*Jason*' and I will have to pay my respects to the Union Consul. Of course there will be the usual friendly people - the Sullivan family" Semmes smiled. "I'm sure some of you gentlemen will be interested. The Acting Governor will be in charge of proceedings, assisted by the Bishop and a High Court Judge. That will be all, gentlemen, you are dismissed."

Semmes seemed agitated and curt. "On second thoughts I have another matter to discuss regarding the trial of Roughler. Ramidios, summon Riordan, Jacko and Ian Fisher."

Semmes was shuffling through some paperwork on his desk when there was a knock on his cabin door. The duty guard, Tyler, announced "Seaman Riordan, Taylor and Fisher to see you, sir."

"Come in, gentlemen, and please be seated." He beckoned Ramidios.

"Will the portholes open any wider? It's hot and stuffy today. Also prepare drinks and cigars for the gentlemen and I'll have a glass of ale."

Ramidios extended a light to the Captain's cigar.

"Gentlemen, I qualified in maritime law only in America. We are now on British soil; you have been studying together and

146

understand British law!" He paused to have a sip of ale. "At ten o'clock on Wednesday we will be in the Crown Court where Justice John Morgan will be presiding over the alleged case of murder of this Northern brigand John Mudd, who will be represented by a Northern sympathiser lawyer and I can assure you he will be brutal in his questions to our witnesses, Bowen, Moore and of course our latest recruit - Garth. Therefore Riordan will be the defending lawyer." He laughed. "I don't know, but the court will probably rig you out with a wig and gown." Everybody laughed. "I bet it will be too small."

"You'll look funny wearing that outfit," burst out Jacko.

"Dress in civilian clothing, see the Quartermaster. He has clothing for every occasion, which he 'acquired' from enemy ships. Likewise Fisher and you, Jacko." Semmes smiled. "Are you sure you studied law, Jacko, you took too young?" The Captain laughed and scratched his brown curly hair.

"I would like you to go ashore and brief Roughler and see if you can obtain the release of Moore, Garth and Bowen. I don't know why they were arrested - they are key witnesses - and I understand there was a bar wench - see if she will testify and get a statement from her. That is all, gentlemen - good luck."

The crew members stood up, saluted and departed from the cabin.

• • •

Roughler was sitting with his head in his hands in the rough-bricked cell in the police station. It was early morning and he was moody and irritable and feeling he was being neglected by the world in general.

'I'm in a mess,' he thought. 'there does not seem any hope, everybody is against me. I haven't heard from my friends. There's Moore, Garth and that hard drinking Bowen who started the row by singing 'Dixie' in his big bass voice.' His thoughts were interrupted by the jailor.

"A lady to see you, Roughler."

The policeman opened the cell door to admit Josephine, the tavern wench, carrying a basket. It had been searched by a jailor who released it as it only contained a striped shirt, fruit and some food.

"Hi! Ernie," Josephine smiled and sat on the bunk. 'I've brought you some fruit and home made pie." She was dressed in a white blouse and a skirt. ('She looks gorgeous,' thought Roughler - his eyes widened. 'That big bosom is going to burst through that blouse- and those pointed nipples'). He took a deep breath, looked into her smiling green eyes. He held her hands.

"I'm pleased to see you, Josephine, you are very kind, I feel so lonely, everybody seems against me. You are my first visitor."

"It's nice to see you Ernie, I've brought you a clean shirt. Stand up, let's try it for size!" She draped it over his broad chest, and holding it firmly in position, she looked into his dark brown eyes. He smiled and suddenly placed his arms around her and hugged her firmly.

"You are very sweet, I'm only a poor seaman, far from my native land and in a great deal of trouble."

"Never mind, I'm your friend. I promise you I'll visit you when I can, and I'll be sitting near you in the court."

"It's nice to know I'll have a friend in the court. Please sit where I can see you."

They sat on the bunk holding hands, when the policeman appeared with a tray carrying his breakfast.

"I'm sorry, miss, you have to go. There are three visitors to see Mr. Roughler.'"

"Cheerio, Ernie." She kissed him on the side of his cheek. He smiled and gripped her hands. "Thanks for coming, I'll look forward to seeing you later."

She was about to leave when Riordan, Jacko and Fisher entered the cell.

They warmly greeted Roughler.

"Miss," said Riordan, "are you the young lady that helped and assisted Ernie and his friends away from the tavern?"

Josephine nodded. Roughler confirmed that she had saved their lives and escorted them to safety from the tavern.

"This is a very serious charge against Ernie, Josephine - would you be willing to testify at the hearing on Tuesday morning at ten o'clock?"

Her eyes seemed to tell Riordan the answer. She gave her assent by nodding.

"We also have very strong support," remarked Fisher, "from his friends Bowen, Garth and Moore, who, we understand, are in cells along the corridor. They will also be witnesses for the defence and we are going to obtain their release today pending the trial."

Josephine smiled at Roughler and left the cell. A policeman brought in chairs and the '*Alabama*' crewmen discussed in detail their approach to the trial.

About an hour later Riordan called the jailor.

"We have finished our statements. May we see the other prisoners?"

"Certainly, come this way, please bring your chairs. Bowen, Garth and Moore were sitting on their bunks, having finished their breakfast, when the cell door was opened and they were greeted by Riordan and his two companions.

"Gentlemen, we are here to take statements and satisfy ourselves that we have covered all the details for the court case." Riordan was getting into his stride. "We will also try and obtain your release."

"I should bloody well think so. It's about time," blurted Moore "We haven't even been charged. We are here under false pretences". He got really agitated.

"Calm down," gestured Riordan - "I promise you will be released within the hour. Now listen, we want to take statements - you, Jacko, take Bowen's - Fisher, you take Moore's and I'll take Garth's and on conclusion, I'll go and see the Chief Constable."

Mr. Whittle was in his office writing. There was a knock on the door. He called "Enter" and in walked the tall, well-built Riordan. He stated his business.

"Please be seated, Mr. Riordan." The Chief Constable was courteous.

"On what charge are you holding Bowen, Garth and Moore?"

Whittle frowned, he hadn't really expected this question and it puzzled him!

"They are accomplices to the charge of murder!"

"Only accomplices, they did not kill anyone. They might have smashed a few heads in, defending themselves, but that's about all and I demand their release as they are defence witnesses." There was a long pause, as they weighed each other up. Whittle was thinking, he stroked his chin.

"Very well," agreed the Chief Constable. He went to the door, "Sergeant, bring in Moore, Garth and Bowen."

('They don't half pong!' thought Riordan, when he greeted the seamen.')

"You are free to go," said Whittle. "I understand you are to be defence witnesses, therefore you will appear at the court case, and you are to be responsible to ensure that they are there, Mr. Riordan. Is that understood?"

"Thank you," Bowen addressed Riordan. "I couldn't have spent another night in that louse-infested place. I like the feel of the planks of the ship beneath my feet." Riordan nodded and added:

"We'll have a final briefing just before the trial. Please return to the ship."

Then addressing the Chief Constable "Well that concludes our business satisfactorily, Mr. Whittle. I thank you for your co-operation. Good-day, sir."

On Monday 19th January, the baronial hall in Sir Michael Kennedy's residence was arranged like a court for the Consular ceremony. It was filled with islanders, the 'Alabama' crew and the officers of H.M.S. 'Jason'.

The uniformed Deputy Governor entered and sat in a chair on a raised platform. It gave the appearance of a royal throne. The large crowd, some in uniforms, stood up and applauded him on his entry and he acknowledged it by smiling and bowing, then gestured the audience to be seated.

"I bid you all a warm welcome on this auspicious occasion and I will ask my Lord Bishop if he will open with a word of prayer."

The red-robed Bishop sat down after the prayers and one of the senior Judges, Mr. Justice Phipps, placed his notes on a lectern.

"We have convened this meeting today to witness the appointment of Mr. Joseph Mills as Consul for the Confederate States of America and I will now ask Captain Semmes if he will take over proceeding with the installing and investing him with the badge of his high office." He then sat down.

The Captain of the 'Alabama' rose and stood behind the lectern. He stroked his waxed moustache as he always did on important occasions as if to give himself confidence. He then looked around the large audience.

"We are gathered together this morning to invest Joseph Mason Mills as Consular Office of the Confederate States of America and to be the Government's representative on the Island of Jamaica."

He paused and bowed to Mills.

"Mr. Mills, will you please come forward to take your oath as Consul."

The Judge walked in front and stood facing Mills. "You will hold the Bible in your right hand as you take the oath."

"By virtue of the power vested in me as a Captain in the Confederate Navy and commissioned by Mr. Jefferson Davis, President of the Confederate States of America and by order of Mr. Stephen R. Mallory, Secretary of the Navy, I hereby elect and appoint you - Joseph Mason Mills Consular Official for the Confederate States of America. Do you wish to accept this important and high office?"

"I do," was the firm reply of Mills.

"Then you will seal it with your lips on the open Bible." The uniformed Bellew, the Bosun, stepped forward bearing a blue and grey collar with a medallion attached, resting on the Confederate flag on the cushion. He approached Semmes. The Captain lifted the collar off the cushion and placed it around the Consul's neck.

"This is your badge of office. The medallion inscribed with your state of office as Consular Official is to remind you to bear allegiance to the country you represent, and I place in your hand our beloved flag which should always be raised at dawn and lowered at sunset."

The Judge approached Semmes and handed him a scroll.

"And here is the written authority signed by myself and witnessed by the Deputy Governor and the senior Judge. May I be the first to congratulate you and wish you well as our representative."

A loud cheer rose from the audience who one by one stood up and clapped the new Consul. The Chief Constable started banging his long baton on the wooden floor to restore order. Its ring echoed around the pictured hall.

The crowd was slowly seated. With a nod from Sir Michael Kennedy, Whittle addressed Mills:

"You have advantage in your favour Consul. I understand you were born in Lancashire, England, but at an early age raised in Carolina by your American mother while your father was a sea-going engineer. You are now back on British soil, but an American citizen. It is my duty as Chief of Police, to remind you and I'm sure I don't have to tell you this, but you are to uphold the laws of the country in which you reside and you can count on me for my full support. May I also offer my congratulations on your appointment?"

The Deputy Governor stood up and looked sternly at the Chief Constable (thinking 'Trust you, Whittle, to say your little piece, you big head.')

"This concludes the ceremony of your appointment, Consul, and let me also offer my congratulations." The audience responded with loud applause.

"Ladies and gentlemen, you will find refreshments at the back of the hall."

Joe Mills was overwhelmed by his appointment and the support he received from his fellow crew members and joined his friends who drank his health.

Sir Michael Kennedy took his elbow and drew him to one side,

"Consul, I would like you to meet some of our distinguished guests and citizens."

'Congratulations, Consular, you have already met Sir David Sullivan."

"I must say, Sir David, I wouldn't be standing here today if it hadn't been for your kindness and hospitality and how your household saved my life."

151

"Nonsense, man, however I am pleased by your appointment and don't hesitate if you need my help or support."

"Your Honour," Kennedy took Joe's arm "I would like you to meet the North American Union Consul."

Mills shook hands with Bruce Eastwood, a tall, thin, bearded gentleman.

"Congratulations, Mr. Mills, on your appointment." (Joe detected a cultured New England accent.) "No doubt we shall meet in the future, but I trust we can commence as friends and not enemies. Indeed we both share something in common - foreigners in a neutral country.

"Pleased to make your acquaintance," said Mills, smiling. "I'm sure a handshake is a sign of friendship and may it continue as such, even if we don't share the same political views". Kennedy steered him quickly away "You have already met the Sullivan family, the Chief Constable - he's worth watching - and I think you have met the Sheridans - oh! - no doubt the Captain has mentioned Mr. Stewart, the banker. He has offered you his estate as residence and your Consular offices are along the far end of the wharf. There he is over there," indicating, he escorted Mills to a middle-aged man, who was talking to Mrs. Kennedy.

'Ah! - there you are, my dear, meet the new Consul and may I present Mr. John Stewart."

The Kennedys left Stewart and Mills, because they had a lot to discuss.

Sir David Sullivan invited Semmes and Mills to stay the night at his residence, which Semmes graciously accepted, as he wanted to review and discuss the court case proceedings for the following morning.

Chapter 14

The white-bricked court house is situated in a square facing spacious gardens, bedecked with colourful flowers.

The court was filled to capacity. The usher commenced by shouting for order:

"All rise. Judge John Morgan presiding."

The red-robed Judge slowly entered and took his seat as members of the public bowed.

He addressed the Clerk of the Court:

"Would you please swear in the jury."

Twelve men individually took the oath on the Bible and seated themselves in the jury box. Judge Morgan addressed the Prosecutor:

"Mr Marron will you please present the case for the Crown."

"Indeed M'Lord, but first let me introduce my learned friend for the defence, Mr. Riordan." He adjusted the gown on his back.

The Judge addressed the defence councillor. "How does your client plead, Mr. Riordan?"

"Not guilty, M'Lord."

"Very good, proceed Mr. Marron."

"Members of the jury, on January 17th, at approximately 8 pm in the evening, Brian Mudd was brutally murdered, and I'm going to prove to you that the fatal deed was done by Ernest Roughler, assisted by Stephen Moore, John Bowen and David Garth, all members of the crew of the '*Alabama*'." He adjusted his paperwork.

"It was the usual quiet scene in 'The Seafarers Tavern'. People were seated with their friends enjoying themselves, gossiping and drinking. In one corner were seated the accused who were enjoying shore leave. As the evening progressed it was only natural that things livened up. Drink loosens a man's tongue." There was laughter in the court. The Judge banged his gavel, the Clerk shouted "Silence."

"Please continue public prosecutor."

"Men began singing sea shanties, people joined in, after all 'The Seafarers' is a world-famous rendezvous for men of the sea."

"You can say that again," a voice shouted from the public gallery with a burst of applause and laughter!

"Silence in court," shouted the Clerk of the Court.

Judge Morgan banged his gavel. "I will clear the court if there is any more hilarity. This is not a laughing matter; we are trying a man for murder. Please continue and get to the point, Mr. Marron."

"The evening became bawdy, the singing grew louder, and then some of the audience joined in the singing of a Southern song called 'Dixie' which roused the peaceful Northern sympathizers. An argument developed, Roughler and his friends became aggressive and shouted and swore, which roused Brian Mudd, a quiet, inoffensive," - his voice trailed off because of sniggering and laughter from the gallery - "retired army veteran, to defend himself."

There was booing from the gallery. The Judge repeatedly banged his gavel.

Marron raised his voice: "He was struck in the face by Roughler."

The courtroom was hot even though the overhead fans worked rhythmically by black youths controlling them with ropes. The Prosecutor paused for a glass of water - the heat and the smell of body odours made the atmosphere uncomfortable. The court usher opened wide all the doors and windows.

The Prosecutor carried on opening the case.

"Fierce fighting broke out. The four crewmen who started the fight conveniently left and order was eventually restored when the police arrived. The tavern was completely wrecked. The man who was badly wounded was transported to hospital in one of his friends' coaches. Mudd's wounds were fatal; as a result he died during the night without regaining consciousness. After numerous enquiries by a police investigation, interrogating witnesses at the scene of the fighting, the police were able to piece together a description of the man involved and it was the accused - Ernest Roughler."

"I would like to call my first witness, M'Lord" Marron mopped his brow and took a long swig of water.

"Call Charles Wright. Call Charles Wright" it re-echoed down the court and a tall, thin man slouched in and entered the stand.

"Hold the Bible in your right hand and repeat the following on the card - Do you solemnly swear to tell the truth, the whole truth and nothing but the truth, so help you God."

"I do." Wright confirmed in a shaky North American accent.

The Prosecutor addressed the witness.

"Is your name Charles Wright?'

"Yes."

"On Saturday evening, January 17th, where were you?"

"I was having a drink in 'The Seafarers Tavern' with some friends."

"Did anything unusual happen?"

"Unusual?" sniggered Wright. "A crowd in the corner became noisy and argumentive, they began singing bawdy sea shanties. One man stood up, that man there," pointing to Bowen. "He commenced by singing a southern American song called 'Dixie' which I found very offensive."

"Thank you, Mr. Wright, your witness."

Riordan stood up, stretched himself to his six foot three inches, took a deep breath and asked the question:

"Where were you born, Mr. Wright?"

There was a slight pause and he thought I wonder what he's hinting at!

"I was born on a farm near Chambersburg"

"Ah! that is in Pennsylvania."

Riordan paused and adjusted his wig ('Bloody uncomfortable this wig and this small gown') pulling it over his shoulders.

"Were you ever in the army, Mr. Wright?" There was a long pause, he felt guilty and before he could answer Riordan butted in:

"Have you ever heard of Bull Run in Virginia, Mr. Wright?"

A shuffle of the feet and what appeared a nod of the head.

"Is it a fact, Mr. Wright, that you were a non-commissioned officer fighting for the Union?"

No answer.

"I will repeat the question."

"There's no need, Mr. Riordan," interposed the Judge. He looked sternly at Wright. "Remember, Mr. Wright, you are under oath, and answer the question."

"Yes, I was a corporal in the 7th Virginia Infantry."

"How long were you a soldier?"

"One year."

"Were you wounded, or discharged?"

There was a long silence.

"Speak up, man, I can't hear you and I'm sure the jury can't! Were you wounded?"

"No, I left the army."

Riordan was getting near the truth. "You left the army. Did you run away? Are you saying you are an army deserter, Mr. Wright?" Riordan seemed annoyed and repeated the question in a loud voice.

No reply.

"Speak up, Mr. Wright," demanded the Judge. "Yes or no?"

In a whisper, because he seemed ashamed, "Yes".

"And how long have you been on the Island of Jamaica?"

"About one year."

"And have you had any regular work?" No answer.
"You are a Union army deserter, who hangs around the wharf front, a vagrant - a principal witness for the Crown, just a trouble maker. Those are all my questions, M'Lord."
The portly Mr. Marron stood up. Being a resident on the island a number of years and practising law, he seemed in a confident mood. His accent was dubious, if anything he had a slight Irish lilt. "Call Mr. John Underhill."
A mean-looking, shifty-eyed, unshaven man walked in and took up a position in the witness box. He repeated the oath in a thick Kentucky accent.
"Your name is John Underhill and before my learned friend asks you, I understand by your accent you were born in Kentucky."
"Yes, sir," Underhill smiled.
"And you are not an army deserter, but a seaman serving with a North American shipping company. What happened in 'The Seafarers' on the night of 17th January?"
"My ship had berthed on the morning of that date and together with some of my mates I spent the day in the tavern enjoying a yarn, a smoke and the best Virginian rum. A fight developed and that's one thing I enjoy so I got stuck into the Southern rabble."
"Who started the fight?"
Underhill was getting really worked up.
"Those beggars over there," pointing to the accused and his friends.
"It was a good scrap - give them their due, but they should not bring those Southern songs to upset the residents on this lovely island!"
"Thank you Mr. Underhill."
Riordan was already on his feet, before Marron had sat down.
"Tell me, Mr. Underhill - how many glasses of rum had you consumed during the day?"
"As many as I could drink". There was hearty laughter by his supporters.
The Judge banged his gavel.
"That's not what I asked - one hundred glasses, five, seventy - surely you have some idea?"
"About twenty-five, I reckon."
"You said you enjoyed a fight - indeed" - Riordan smiled - "so do I, being a seaman." He stroked his chin. ('This damn small gown, I'm sure it makes me look silly,' he thought.) He looked at his notes.
"You don't mind on whose side you fight?"
"I should bloody well think so!" Underthill was getting excited. I'm a Northerner and those damned Southerners came looking for trouble."

"Thank you, that will be all." Riordan looked at his notes and remarked:

"I have no further questions, M'Lord."

Marron stood up. "M'Lor, I would like to call Mr. Merner to the witness box."

There were mutterings as the smartly-dressed, well-known shopkeeper entered the box and took the oath.

The Prosecutor for the Crown addressed him:

"Mr. Merner, you are held in respect in this town, also a well-known local shopkeeper. How long have you been living on the island?"

Merner replied in a New York/Irish accent: "I came here in 1858 and married a local girl. We set up in business and it has prospered over the years."

Marron looked at his papers before asking the next question.

"You visited 'The Seafarers' on the evening of January 17th with your friends for a drink, hoping to enjoy their company. Please continue and describe what happened."

"Well, there appeared to be a lot of noise and singing, mainly songs of the deep South. I suppose this was natural as they were crewmen from the '*Alabama*'." They were joined by a number of other people for the song 'Dixie'.

This roused the anger of one of my friends, Brian Mudd, who walked towards that man there" - pointing to Bowen, "who was leading the singing in a loud bass voice. He tried to reason with him and asked him if he would refrain from singing that song."

There were shouts from the public gallery and the Clerk called for silence.

Marron continued "Did he attack Bowen?"

"Mudd only waved his walking stick in the air, he is a quiet, rather a gentle man, not at all aggressive, but that man there," (pointing to Moore) "he started the fight, he is to blame. If he hadn't thrown that glass of ale in Mudd's face he would have been alive today. They attacked us!"

"Thank you, Mr. Merner. Those are all my questions from the Crown, M'Lord."

"Does the Defence Counsel wish to question this witness?"

"Yes, M'Lord," He addressed the smirking Merner; "Mr. Merner, I'm pleased to hear that the people respect you and you came to this island five years ago; you have a prosperous business and you own the local newspaper. You have done quite well and I congratulate you. Listening to and printing gossip is your business, and naturally, living near dockland, above the shop, you have first-hand knowledge of the war in the States." (Riordan was thinking 'Must change my attack, I bet he's a Yankee spy').

He smiled as he asked the question: "Like your friends, do you enjoy a fight?"

"Not really, I wouldn't describe myself as a person looking for trouble, I'm just a quiet businessman."

"You just like pushing people and urging them on, like you did Mr. Mudd, when you were directly behind him, when he attacked Bowen."

"That's not true, I was angry when Bowen and his mates attacked us."

"They attacked you? I heard you mention, you were directly behind the deceased, when he hit Bowen on the side of the head. So you are not a fighting man?" Riordan ended abruptly. "No further questions, M'Lord."

It was the turn of the defence to call their witnesses.

"Call John Bowen to the stand."

After Bowen had taken the oath and repeated his name, Riordan asked him this first question.

"Will you tell the members of the jury what happened on the Saturday evening of the 17th January?"

"I was having a drink with my friends and enjoying singing songs of our homeland when that bugger there," pointing to Merner, "came over with Mudd and he" again pointing, "backed him up, looking for a fight."

"Would you say they were drunk?"

"Well, they lurched across the room, Mudd had a heavy cane in his left hand and something gleaming, shining, like a knife in his right hand. He had a crazed look on his face. He struck me a violent blow on the side of my head and I don't recall any more, except being carried over somebody's shoulder down an alleyway. I came to on a bed, in that young lady's house" (pointing to Josephine).

"Did you have any weapons on your person?"

"No, why should I? We were just enjoying each other's company."

Riordan asked his final question: "So Mudd came over backed by Merner, Wright and Underhill looking for a fight. You were taken completely by surprise and knocked unconscious for no reason except singing?"

"That is correct."

"No further questions, your witness, Mr. Marron."

"That is not quite correct, is it, Mr. Bowen, you threw some ale into Mr. Mudd's face?"

"That's a lie, I'm not a trouble maker. I don't remember much about the evening. They started it, Mudd, Wright, that drunken lout, Underhill and that so-called gentleman over there," pointing to Merner.

"So you didn't witness the deadly blow the accused gave to the murdered man?"

"No."

"Thank you, that will be all."

Riordan stood up. "Call Steven Moore." His heavy bass voice echoed down the room.

The well-built, casually dressed Moore walked to the witness box and took his oath, swearing on the Bible.

"Mr. Moore, describe the fight scene" quickly asked Riordan.

"Four of us were seated in a semi-circle enjoying a drink and a merry song, other people around joined in. From nowhere Mudd and his cronies lurched towards us, shouting and cursing. Mudd was waving a club in his left hand and something that gleamed in his right hand. I think it could have been a knife! He struck Bowen a glancing blow on the side of his head."

"Let me stop you there. You are sure Mudd had the club in his left hand and Roughler had the glass mug of ale in his left hand?"

"Yes, I'm certain, now I come to think of it they both appeared to be left-handed."

"Both left-handed," Riordan repeated in a loud voice. "Where was Roughler seated?"

"On my left."

"Please continue, what happened when Mudd struck Bowen on the head?"

"He fell to the floor. Roughler quickly stood up. I remember he crashed the glass mug on the edge of the hard table, leaving the handle in his left hand with a jagged edge. After Mudd had struck Bowen on the head, he turned his attention to Roughler and he gripped the knife in his right hand and swung round in an arc as though to strike Roughler in the body. Roughler counter-attacked by cracking down with his right hand on Mudd's forearm, at the same time he crashed the jagged edge of the glass into Mudd's neck. He screamed and there was blood everywhere, and Mudd fell to the floor holding his neck. Merner and his cronies backed off."

Riordan raised his right hand, indicating: "I will stop you there Mr. Moore."

"M'Lord, I have two valuable pieces of evidence for your attention, which I have just received and would like M'Lord to see."

Jacko, who was seated behind Riordan, handed him two wrapped articles.

A long wooden-handled knife and part of a glass mug were exhibited and passed to the jury.

159

Riordan addressed the twelve seated men.

"You will notice, members of the jury, that the knife, exhibit one, has two letters carved on it - B.M. - and the glass, exhibit two, if you look closely, has a dark stain down the jagged edge."

Before the foreman of the jury could examine the two exhibits after the Judge, Marron leapt to his feet.

"Excuse me, M'Lord, may I see these two objects? I have been taken completely by surprise and I was unaware of such evidence!" (they were handed to him by the smirking Riordan, who thought 'That will teach you, and be prepared for further surprises!')

The two exhibits were examined by the jury, handed back to the clerk and placed on a table in front of the Judge.

"M'Lord, I would like to call Josephine. I didn't get her surname, everybody seems to know this popular wench by her Christian name." There was cheering and laughter in the Court. Even the Judge smiled and thought: 'You can say that again and the way she dresses, I've seen her dress a bit lower!'

"Miss Josephine, what is your full name? and can you tell the jury what happened on the Saturday evening in 'The Seafarers' You can take your time and think carefully."

"It was the usual Saturday night," (she was nervous and shaking) "then suddenly everybody was fighting; jugs, furniture, bottles were flung around. I could see two men lying on the floor. There was shouting, cursing, swearing and fists flying. I made my way to one of the men lying on the floor, who was that gentleman over there!" - pointing to Bowen. "There was blood on his head, in fact there was blood everywhere. With the help of those two gentlemen" - pointing to Roughler and Garth "We managed to get him on his feet." She smiled at Ernie.

"Excuse me, Josephine. Why did you go to the aid of those particular gentlemen?"

"Well, sir, they gave me a generous tip" (gently heaving up her left bosom). There were roars of laughter and the Judge kept banging his gavel and yelling! "Order in the court"

"Please continue."

"Garth and I hoisted Bowen across Mr. Roughler's broad shoulders and carried him out with the assistance of that gentleman there," pointing to Steve Moore, "who used a stool to bash in a few heads to make a pathway for us to leave the tavern. We went to my house where I tended the wound in Bowen's head."

"Please tell the members of the jury where you went after the departure of the seamen and what did you find? Will you please speak up, Miss Josephine."

160

Riordan was getting into his stride. ('Quite a change from bawling from the mast head "Ship ahoy!'" he thought.)

"I returned to 'The Seafarers' tavern to the place where Bowen lay amongst the blood. While I was cleaning up the mess and straightening up the furniture, I noticed something that aroused my curiosity - it was a handle off one of the bar-room mugs - the jagged edge was covered in blood, and then I kicked against a wooden-handled knife. I wrapped them in a scarf. At the first opportunity I visited the '*Alabama*' and gave them to that gentleman there," pointing to Jacko, who together with Fisher were Riordan's support team.

"That will be all, Miss Josephine. Your witness, Mr. Marron."

"No questions, your Honour."

"Call David Garth."

"How long have you been living on the island, Mr. Garth?" was Riordan's first question to the fair-haired, tall, but slim, youth.

"About five years."

"And where were you born and raised'?"

"In Patagonia. I was raised by my Welsh and Spanish-speaking mother. My English father was Chief Engineer on a paddle steamer. I received a good education and I was apprentice to a Doctor. About six years ago my father died in a sea disaster and shortly after that my mother died of a broken heart. I came to this beautiful island where I'm assisting a Doctor, Charles Gregory."

"Tell us what happened on the night of January 17th?'"

"I was having a drink with Bowen, a most interesting character who was telling me about his adventures on the high seas and the way they fought against the North American ships and how many they had sunk. We were joined by two of his friends, Steve Moore and Ernie. I certainly enjoyed their company. Moore produced a bottle of ship's rum - now that takes some beating and I soon burst forth into song - those lovely old Welsh songs my mother taught me. Then John with his deep bass voice and people around the room joined in the harmony. I didn't know any of the American songs, especially about 'Dixieland', but these national songs seemed to arouse the curiosity of some of the drinkers as two chaps came lurching over and told Bowen to shut up. One - the deceased - took a swipe at Bowen, knocking him to the ground. Roughler sprang to his assistance and thrust a jagged piece of glass mug into Mudd's neck, at the same time warding off his swinging right hand which gripped a knife. We were guided out of the tavern by that young lady there" - pointing to Josephine.

"She ain't a lady," a voice from the gallery called out, there was hearty laughter.

"Silence in court," shouted Judge Morgan, banging his gavel. "I will not have this behaviour in my court. Throw that man dressed in the stripe shirt and woolly hat, out of my court."

The Judge was very angry and annoyed and after a scuffle the person in the gallery who was a Northern sympathizer was escorted out of the building.

"That is all for the time being, Mr. Garth."

Riordan turned to the prosecuting counsel.

"Your witness, Mr. Marron."

"Mr Garth, it's interesting hearing about your life story and that you have good a tenor voice. Is it not true that when Mr. Mudd advanced towards you, you threw a jug of ale in his face?"

"No," shouted Garth "that's a lie!"

"And you struck Mr. Merner on the jaw?"

"No, that's not true."   Garth was getting angry, which pleased Mr. Marron.

"And that you engaged Mr. Wright in a fight?"

"No! - no! - no! - all lies."

"You are under oath, Garth, tell us the truth. You enjoy hurting people, you also threw a stool and smashed a lovely picture mirror." Marron was shouting: "In other words, Garth, you are a very aggressive and brutal man!" Marron sat down. No reply from Garth, he was getting upset!

Riordan was quickly on his feet.

"Mr. Garth, is it true, prior to coming to this island you lived in Patagonia and you were studying to be a Doctor as you previously stated?"

"Yes, in fact I'm still studying medicine today!" Riordan carried on: "Therefore you wouldn't want to kill or maim anybody, would you?"

Garth shook his head in a negative fashion.

"You mentioned before that the deceased, Mr. Mudd, had a knife in his right hand and was aiming for Roughler's body by taking a swing with his right hand?"

'Yes, I'm positive."

"And what did he have in his left hand?"

"A hard wooden rod about two feet long." Riordan asked: "Can you identify the knife."

"Yes, it's lying on the table over there," pointing, "next to that piece of mug"

"Have you examined the jagged edge of the glass mug?"

"Yes."

"What were your findings?"

"Stained with blood!"

162

Marron quickly stood up. "Objection, your Honour, these findings are from defence witnesses!"

The Judge banged his gavel. "Objection overruled"

Riordan took control - "Will you please stand down, Mr. Garth. I now call Doctor Charles Gregory." The long grey-bearded Doctor took the stand. He held the Bible in his right hand and stroked his beard with his left hand while he took the oath.

"Doctor Gregory, are you a local man?"

"Yes, I was born and bred on the island, but I studied and practised medicine for a while in New Orleans." Riordan asked the Clerk of the Court if he would pass the mug to the Doctor.

"Do you recognize this piece of evidence as being part of a glass mug?"

"I examined it carefully. It bore evidence of blood and skin. In fact I examined the deceased's body, being the local coroner, and the jagged edge of the glass was consistent with the wound on Brian Mudd's neck where his main artery was severed. Also, and this is important, the blood and skin on the glass was identical in length to the wound."

"Thank you, Doctor. Mr. Marron, your witness."

"No questions, your Honour."

Riordan sat down and drank some cool refreshing water, feeling satisfied he had achieved an advantage over his opponents.

The Judge banged his gavel. "Gentlemen, before we proceed, I think we shall call it a day, it is hot and uncomfortable. The court will convene at 10am tomorrow."

Riordan was gathering his papers together, chatting to Fisher and Jacko when their Captain and Jamie joined them. Semmes remarked:

"Congratulations, Mr. Riordan, that was a very good presentation and attack on this beggar Merner. He's the one we've got to crack. I've been thinking, let us find out more about this lout. I have an idea, but it will require your help. You, Jamie and Fisher, move around the town, listen to local gossip in shops, dockland, taverns - find out all you can about Merner and his Northern supporters and give your information to Riordan before tomorrow morning. In the meantime I'm going to Joe Mills's new residence, located in a valley leading up to the Blue Mountains. I'm going on horseback with Bowen and Moore and staying the night. Riordan and Garth are staying on board ship. He will be your contact and we will meet at nine o'clock tomorrow morning. So I bid you good-day, gentlemen."

The casually dressed Jamie and Fisher left the court and went to 'The Seafarers' tavern for a drink and meal and listened to the local chatter about the day's events. Dockland buzzed with the court case. Jamie caught the attention of Roy Crawford, the Sullivans' groomsman. He came over and accepted a drink of ale.

The conversation naturally drifted to the day's court proceedings. "It is interesting listening to people sitting around you gossiping. I was in - I was nearly going to say" Crawford laughed, "the rogues' gallery. In this town we have a number of Northern supporters as you are probably aware, mainly down-and-outs, army deserters and drifters. They are troublemakers and everybody points a finger at Merner who operates under the guise of a local general storekeeper. He is the ringleader. Do you know he owns one of the local newspapers, which has a large distribution around the town? He is, as far as the locals know, a New Yorker of Irish emigrant descent. Not a pleasant man to have dealings with. Unfortunately Sir David Sullivan has to do business with him regarding reins and saddles for horses. I have to collect the equipment at his shop. There are always some dubious characters in his shop and he has a large warehouse at the back where he employs these men."

"Would his warehouse be worth a visit, Roy, say after dark?"

"I'm sure it can. What had you in mind?"

Jamie continued. "Well, he seems such an unpopular man. A gentleman outside and a rogue on the inside! - it would be interesting to see his goods in the warehouse."

"I have an idea," said Crawford. "The tavern remains open until the early hours of the morning - or," he laughed, "until the last customer is thrown out. Say we meet here after midnight and discuss our plan of campaign."

"You should be on the '*Alabama*', Roy," remarked the laughing Fisher. "it's guys like you our Captain is looking for!"

"Oh! I'm quite happy on the island, but there's nothing like a bit of excitement!"

Just after midnight the three men met at the tavern and to the onlookers they were friends enjoying each other's company, with a laugh and conversing with each other. Little did the onlookers know the plot they were hatching.

Crawford, acting the slightly intoxicated groomsman (he was well known at the tavern) left at 1 am and outside sat on some empty crates.

Jamie had his last mouthful of ale, stood up, sat down, stood up again and hiccupped as they left the tavern, laughing and joking. Fisher supported him. They disappeared into the darkness. in the direction where Crawford had told them to rendezvous.

"Over here," indicated Crawford, "and we must act silently and quickly."

They moved cautiously through the narrow streets leading from the wharf, until they came to the back fence of Merner's warehouse - "He had dogs in the grounds, but I've checked and the last one died, so it should be quite safe to get over the fence into his premises," whispered Roy, "I've brought the necessary tools for breaking in." remarked Fisher.

"Right, then let's get going, you lead the way."

Fisher soon opened the double doors of the warehouse, by picking the lock.

Jamie produced a lantern, lighted it and led the way passing boxes, bales of cotton, bundles of clothing, tools and farming implements.

Fisher stopped by a long oblong box covered by clothes, which he removed.

"This might be interesting," he said as he prized open the lid to reveal, wrapped in straw, twelve rifles and twenty-five revolvers.

"These are the latest repeating carbines and revolvers. I wonder where they are bound for?" Jamie had also been busy - searching. "Look over here," he exclaimed - I've found some dynamite, enough to blow up the town! We've found what we came for, this is vital information to give to Riordan. I'm taking a rifle and a stick of dynamite as evidence, and let's get the hell out of here, make sure we leave everything as we found it, especially the box which had the rifle in it!"

They made their way back to the wharf - Crawford to another tavern where he usually stayed the night. Jacko and Ian returned to the 'Alabama', where they were greeted by the Officer of the watch, Lieutenant Armstrong. Jamie roused Riordan out of his bunk and told him of their findings and produced the rifle and a stick of dynamite as evidence.

"Good." He got dressed. "I'm going ashore to see the Chief Constable, I would like you to accompany me, sir, and bring those two articles with you."

Returning to the wharf at Kingston, Jamie viewed the ghost-like ships in the harbour. They looked eerie on this humid, moonlit night.

The gig boat was manned by Ray Tyler, the Bosun's Mate, and two seamen.

One young man attracted the attention of Jamie.

"You're very slightly built to be manning the oars, what's your name?"

"Paul Harris, sir," he replied. "I come from Fort Jackson in Louisiana."

Jamie laughed. "Rowing will build up your muscles, also climbing up the rigging, and one day you'll be as well built as Mr. Riordan." The two men wandered through the narrow streets until they stood outside the court house in the elegant square. It was quiet, not even a breath of wind and nobody around, everything was so peaceful.

"That's Mr. Whittle's house over there in the corner," pointing to a Victorian-styled house. He had to bang hard on the knocker of the glass-panelled door.

Several minutes passed - a half-dressed butler answered the door. "I'm sorry to bother you at this early hour" said Jamie, "but it's important that we see Mr. Whittle."

"What's this? What's this?" The Chief Constable in his long white nightdress looked quite puzzled and angry that anybody could have disturbed his sleep, to visit him in the early hours of the morning. ('Must be important') he thought as he descended the wide mahogany staircase and confronted Jamie and Riordan on the doorstep.

"We are sorry to be calling at such an early hour, Mr. Whittle." Jamie was apologetic. "Something important has arisen regarding the court case, concerning one of the witnesses for the crown - William Merner."

"Oh! ah, - yes! please come into the library, gentlemen."

"Did you know he has guns and dynamite in his warehouse? and here is the evidence!" said Jamie, unrolling the American Spencer rifle out of a piece of canvas on to the carpet and Riordan very carefully unwrapped from a special pouch, the stick of dynamite.

"This is a serious matter. Only the police issue firearms to the public with a licence and I can assure you I keep tight control on this matter. I suppose," he said with a wry smirk, "you entered his premises illegally," but he laughed. "You can be charged - it is an offence, you have broken the law - however I will overlook it in this case." And the next minute he looked serious again. He paused and rubbed his eyes.

'Tomorrow morning about ten o'clock I will raid the Merner shop and warehouse. I will make sure Merner is not there, but in the court. I will immediately arrest his staff and before midday I will come to the court and give you a list of my findings."

He thought for a moment. "I've never liked the scoundrel - and I'm sure you - Mr. Riordan - you will prove he's an unreliable witness. Thank you for calling and giving me this vital news and I will see you in the court in the morning."

Chapter 15

Ten o'clock Wednesday 21st January 1863, the second day in the hot, stuffiness of the courtroom, mixed with the aroma of the ladies perfume, the smell of drink on bad breath and unwashed bodies would have made breathing unbearable but for the four overhead fans, which were worked rhythmically by black youths pulling the ropes, and the windows opened wide.

Counsel were in position. Riordan was eager to commence, he was going to call on Merner. He shuffled his notes together and thought 'I'm going to name and expose this Northern trash, as he calls himself to the world; that would be something to print!'

"Everybody rise." - the Clerk of the court's big determined voice echoed strongly around the croweded courtroom. The Judge staggered into his seat.

('Gosh, the Judge looks as though he's had a bad night' thought Jacko, who was seated behind the Defence Counsel.)

At the back of the court the Chief Constable conferred with Jamie about the morning's raid on the Merner shop and warehouse and the arrest of five men.

He handed Jamie a leather bag containing a rifle, revolver and a stick of dynamite. Riordan addressed the Judge:

"M'Lord, would you excuse me while I discuss with my colleagues an urgent matter that has arisen.

Merner raised his eyebrows - he seemed surprised. He looked at the Defence Counsel's table, wondering what was in the leather bag'.

Riordan looked at Jacko and in a quiet voice remarked:

"I invite Counsel for the prosecution to recall the witness, Merner, as I have further questions to put to him." He nodded and smiled at Captain Semmes who was seated next to Mills, the Kennedys and the Sullivan family. The Clerk to the Court announced:

"Recall Mr. William Merner to the witness box."

Merner stood with a smirk on his face while the Judge reminded him he was still under oath. The Defence Counsel was looking forward to the next question.

"Mr. Merner, did I hear it mentioned that being a resident on the island, you are a British subject, in fact that you obey the laws of the country in which you reside?"

The well-built Merner was taken completely off-guard with the question. He drew in a deep breath which whistled through his teeth and gave Riordan a hard look before replying:

"I'm not exactly a British subject, in fact I have filled in the necessary forms, this was about two years ago, but I haven't received a reply from the authorities, but I can assure you I'm a law-abiding citizen."

"I'm pleased to hear you are a law-abiding citizen. Then why have you firearms on your premises?"

"I don't know what you are talking about!" He snarled out the words!

Riordan produced a rifle, revolver and sticks of dynamite from the leather bag and displayed them on the long table in front of the Judge. There were gasps from the audience. Riordan continued: "You know it's against the law to store, import or export firearms?" Merner was about to reply when the Chief Constable rushed forward, his face livid and addressed the Judge:

"M'Lord, this morning, the police raided the Merner shop and warehouse and these weapons you see before you, I confiscated and I arrested five men. There's enough dynamite to blow up Kingston and we found other things as well, here is a list, M'Lord."

The court buzzed with the latest news, men stood up and shouted abusively at Merner and his cronies. He was still in the witness stand. Men started shaking their fists and threatening him. He gripped the front of the stand, his knuckles white, he swayed slightly, his face ashen, bewildered, frightened. The Judge stood up, banged the gavel several times and the Clerk of the Court eventually restored order.

"Mr. Whittle, you are not entitled to address us by suddenly coming forward, but under the circumstances, I will note your findings, bearing witness to the integrity of the Crown witnesses. All be seated and we will carry on with the case. Please continue, Mr, Riordan."

"So, Mr. Merner, to whom do you owe your allegiance? - and to what cause, is it to the Northern Union Government of America or to the British Sovereignty? - I put it to you Mr. Merner - you are a spy for the North American Government and when you were in the 'Seafarers' on the night of the 17th of January you incited your fellow colleagues, Underhill and Wright, to go and attack the seamen from the '*Alabama*' who were enjoying a peaceful evening."

Merner was stunned and speechless; he didn't reply.

Defence Counsel pulled his gown up over his shoulders and said to the somewhat bewildered Judge "Those are all my questions, M'Lord."

He sat down and sipped some warm water; his colleagues seated behind patted him on the back and congratulated him. The atmosphere was hot and humid: the Judge looked at the clock on the wall, banged his gavel and said:

"We will now break for lunch, and resume at two o'clock."

"All rise."

The Chief Constable approached Riordan; they shook hands.

"Well, that has certainly cracked this case, Mr. Whittle, and thank you for coming forward."

"I've had my eyes on this fellow Merner for some time, he's not a very popular man."

"How would it be, Mr. Whittle,' Riordan grinned, "if we took him and his cronies on a sea voyage, when we leave. I'm sure they would enjoy a holiday!"

Whittle burst out laughing. "I haven't heard that! What a good idea! and I could arrange for a few more to join them on the holiday." He patted Riordan on the shoulder. "Let's have some lunch, I know just the eating place."

When the Court assembled again, the Judge entered, looked around the court, confused, bewildered, and sat down. The overhead fans were working quicker than usual. The people in the court were excited, wondering what was going to happen next, they were soon to hear the Defence spokesman.

Riordan stood up, gripped his gown in both bands and pulled it into position on his shoulders "M'Lord, may I commence my evidence for the defence?"

"Certainly Mr. Riordan, proceed."

"Gentlemen of the jury, you can picture the peaceful scene at 'The Seafarers' on the fatal Saturday evening. Here we have four seamen drinking, laughing, enjoying themselves, singing away - and they were not the only ones - other locals were joining in. Suddenly they were attacked by a man rushing towards them wielding a club in one hand and a knife in the other hand."

Riordan picked up the rifle in his left hand, holding it by the barrel and twirling it above his head and the wooden-handled knife in his right hand and charged towards the centre of the jury box, yelling, and brandishing the rifle he suddenly stopped and smiled at the jury.

"Now that took you by surprise, didn't it! That's exactly what happened on that quiet Saturday evening when everybody was so relaxed enjoying themselves. He placed the rifle and the knife on the table.

169

"And who were the attackers? Well we have the North American, Brian Mudd. Unfortunately we can't question him - yes - a Unionist sympathiser. Mr. Merner has already testified under oath - and what has been revealed about his character? - He is a rogue, scoundrel and in my submission, a spy for the Yankees. Mudd, Wright and a Yankee seaman he employed and arranged an army to do his dirty work for him by causing trouble and consequently - the death of Mr. Mudd." He paused, thinking. 'This damned gown! Anyway it won't be long now') pulling it up. "The accused, Roughler, is a quiet and God-fearing man, who, when Bowen was struck on the head and he saw the arched hand of Mudd wielding a knife - well the only thing he could do was to defend himself by warding off the knife aimed at his chest, at the same time picking up a glass jug and with a quick action crashing it on the edge of the hard oaken table and thrusting it into Mudd's neck. Unfortunately it severed his artery, which Roughler very much regrets. His actions were hasty but then he acted on the spur of the moment. It might have been the other way around! Roughler could have been lying on the bar-room floor knifed to death!" He paused, took a few steps forward alongside the jury box and continued addressing the twelve men:

"So I put it to you, members of the jury, that the unarmed accused was only defending himself against an organised attack, which if it had been successful, would have left four seamen lying on the bar-room floor and not one Northern sympathizer. I plead not guilty for my client, he is entirely innocent of the charge of murder."

Riordan sat down and took a swig of lukewarm water hoping his final speech swayed the jury.

Mr. Marron, the Prosecutor, stood up and looked at the members of the jury. 'Twelve just men and true, I wonder,' he thought.
"Members of the jury, you have heard the words of my learned friend, defending his client as a quiet, God-fearing man. Yet he knew how to defend himself. The scene is not like that at all! The accused saw Mudd approach Bowen with a stick at his left side, this assisted him walking as he had a lame leg - a wound from the war. He has been described as an army deserter; that is not so, he was discharged because of his wound. He settled peacefully on the island. He went to the tavern to enjoy a drink with his friends. Mr. Merner, you all know him and have bought his goods. He is also a peaceful man who enjoyed serving in his shop and meeting people, not a rogue and gunrunner as my learned friend put it. These quiet inoffensive gentlemen were aroused by the singing of

Confederate songs which caused Mr. Mudd to approach the singing seamen. He shouted at them to cease singing songs from the South of America and sing English songs which everybody knew, when suddenly that man," pointing to Garth, "discharged a jug of ale in his face, which caused Mudd to retaliate by striking Bowen on the head.

Roughler, the accused, knew what he was doing, and the damage that a jagged piece of glass would do in the area of the neck - yes. he murdered Mudd, no doubt about that, and I leave it to you members of the jury to return a verdict of - Guilty."

The Judge banged on his gavel so as to attract attention to his summing up.

"Gentlemen of the jury, you have heard the evidence for and against the accused, Ernest Roughler. Did he murder Mr Mudd? Or was he just defending himself? That is for you to decide, but let me remind you about the evidence given by the Crown and Defence witnesses." He paused, took a sip of water. "It has been highlighted that the Crown witnesses were Northern sympathizers and we have heard from the crewmen of the *'Alabama'* who are fighting for the Confederate States. In other words they have brought their war and their problems to this peaceful island." He mopped his brow with a handkerchief.

"Was it murder or self-defence, that is for you to decide, but before I conclude my summing up: you have heard the evidence the Chief Constable has revealed about one of the so-called gentlemen - living under the guise of an innocent shopkeeper, and his cronies, who go out for a quiet drink in the tavern armed with weapons - all pre-arranged or not. That is the question - which leaves you with the evidence you have to decide on; what I originally stated is the case for the Crown - murder or, for the opposition, self-defence, and not guilty.

The jury will now adjourn to consider their verdict."

"All rise."

The twelve jury men had already appointed their foreman, a quiet middle-aged man, wearing a black suit and tie - Mr. Arthur Batho. Cool drinks were brought into the hot stuffy room as the men sat on chairs around a long table.

"Gentlemen," (Batho was seated at the top end of the table). "We've heard the Judge and the lawyers summing up this murder case. It seems strange to me that a bloody war is going on in America; a Confederate ship comes into the harbour and the crew comes ashore to enjoy themselves in one of our most popular taverns. Next minute there is a fight. A man is killed, people injured and the place wrecked. Who's going to pay for that damage? As the Judge remarked, they have brought their war to this island."

A narrow-eyed, shifty-looking man put his hand up. The foreman acknowledged him. "I say Roughler's as guilty as hell" he shouted. The jury men were startled! "He deliberately attacked Brian Mudd, the deceased, God rest his soul." (He crossed himself) "and killed him. He was a friendly, quiet man and he had no enemies, but enjoyed drinking with his friends."

"Were you one of his friends? What is your name, please?

"My name is Martin, I'm known as Mart. No, I was not one of Mudd's friends, but he was well-known in the town."

"I don't think so," another juror interjected. A bearded man, looking every inch a sea-dog, raised his hand: "I've visited neutral ports, being British, my mates have accompanied me to many a drinking bar. The '*Alabama*' crewmen were quite right and honest when they said they didn't have any weapons. To me a seaman is a man of discipline and integrity and when he has shore leave he just wants to relax and enjoy himself in good company and that is just what Roughler and his friends were doing when they were attacked by a man intent on causing grievous bodily harm, wielding a stick and a knife." He paused wondering what to say next, then he blurted out "Are you a Northern sympathizer, Mr. Martin?"

Mart was taken aback! "No - no," he stammered He didn't seem convincing.

The bearded gentleman continued, after he had apparently exposed Martin: "In my opinion Roughler defended himself against the knife thrust, aimed at his body, picked up the only thing handy, a glass mug, crashed it on to a hard-topped table and used it as a weapon to counter-attack the knife. I say Roughler is innocent on the charge of murder, but I think he should stand the cost of damage to the tavern."

"Hear, hear."

"Are you proposing that?" asked Mr. Batho.

"I am."

"Can I have a seconder?"

"Yes," a mild-looking man replied, who kept coughing into a handkerchief.

"Must have T.B," thought Batho. "All in favour of the proposition?"

"Aye, aye, aye." They put their hands up, except Martin. Everybody wanted to get away from the steamy, unventilated, hot room.

"I wish to abstain - is that the correct word?" he shouted.

"Then we are unanimous that Roughler is not guilty of the charge of murder but should meet the costs of damages to the furnishings in the tavern."

"What about his opponents helping with the costs?" asked the mild-looking man.

"I can't see the Judge agreeing to that; after all, Roughler is the man on trial."

"Well, that's settled. I'll let the Clerk know that we have reached a decision."

Light refreshments were laid on for the lawyers and their representatives in an adjacent room, next to the Judge's Chambers. Riordan was rearranging his paperwork. Jacko and Fisher were chatting quietly about the morning's proceedings. Marron separated himself from the 'Alabama' men and was smoking a pipe whilst reading a book. Coffee was served by black ladies. The smiling Fisher said in a hushed voice: "I hope the twelve jurymen are honest and trustworthy!"

Jacko laughed sarcastically. "From my little experience of court life, they looked a queer lot to me! And the way they were dressed; I don't think we have a chance!"

"If there are any Northern sympathizers in the twelve, we've had it!" chipped in Fisher. "Anyway, we'll wait and see."

Judge Morgan knocked on the door and entered.

"Is everything satisfactory, gentlemen?"

"Yes thank you," Riordan replied.

"May I thank you, M'Lord - the refreshments were excellent," Marron responded between puffing on his pipe.

"I appreciate it. Was it your first time in a law court?" - addressing the crewmen of the 'Alabama'. "I congratulate you on your presentation, Mr. Riordan, and the way you conducted yourself in court. I apologise for the noisy public behaviour. Mr. Marron and I," he paused, "are well used to court proceedings, although I must admit, our job is easy, there's little crime, thanks to our Chief of Police's aggressive manner. Did you know he was a Captain in the army? People fear him and he certainly maintains law and order on this peaceful island. I hear movements from the jury room."

There was a knock on the door, the Court Clerk entered and addressed the Judge:

"M'Lord, the jury have reached a verdict."

"Good, let the court convene, gentlemen, will you please take your seats."

In the crowded, noisy court, the Clerk exclaimed in a loud voice: "All rise, Judge Morgan presiding."

Jacko chuckled and thought: "The Clerk of the Court must have said that hundreds of times in his sleep."

The Judge addressed Mr. Batho, the foreman of the jury.

"Have you reached a verdict on which you are all agreed?"

"We have, your honour."

"The prisoner will rise." The commanding voice of the Clerk made some of the people in the court shudder - especially Josephine - here was a moment of truth. She looked across at the white-faced Roughler and prayed.

"What is your vedict?"

There was a deathly hush, all eyes focused on Batho.

"We find the accused, Ernest Roughler" - there was a silence, all ears alert to the decision, then Batho repeated himself very quickly: "We find the accused not guilty of murder." There was a loud cheering and clapping. It took several minutes before order was restored and everybody was seated. The Judge loudly banged his gavel.

"Have you finished your findings?" said the judge, addressing Batho. "There is one more thing, your Honour. We have a proviso for your attention and decision" - everybody in the court knew what was coming next - "that the prisoner pays the costs of the damage incurred at 'The Seafarers' tavern."

The Judge banged his gavel - 'I hope for the last time today, I've had enough,' he thought.

"Thank you, members of the jury. Mr. Roughler, you have heard the verdict of this court and I support the recommendation that you pay for the damages to the tavern."

Roughler was overwhelmed with the verdict. Josephine rushed across the court and put her arms around his neck and kissed and hugged him. She cried.

Fisher and Jacko congratulated Riordan. The crew members gathered around him to acclaim his victory.

Mr. Marron approached the Defence Counsellor.

" I must congratulate you, Mr. Riordan, you outfoxed me with your hidden evidence. You certainly did your homework, ably supported by your team. I understand your ship will be sailing in the next few days. For your first trial in a court of law you have certainly done extremely well." They shook hands. "I'm sure the law will be a more rewarding occupation than shouting 'ship ahoy' from aloft." Everybody within hearing distance laughed, even Semmes and Sir Michael Kennedy.

The Captain drew the Governor to one side.

"A word in your ear, Michael. Could you arrange to attend a meeting at our new Consulate to discuss his staff? I would like to be guided on the number of people and their status. I realise we are foreigners in a neutral country and I haven't experienced appointing such an office before - say, at four o'clock this afternoon? You see I haven't much time left as we will be leaving the day after tomorrow." "Certainly," responded Sir Michael. "I

174

would also suggest that you also invite the Judge, Mr. Whittle and Sir David Sullivan. I will arrange for them to be present - in fact I can see some of them now over there."

Captain Semmes mustered a few of his officers around him:

"Gentlemen, Mr. Mills has kindly invited us to his residence for lunch for a farewell get-together. I've also arranged with Joe to hold a meeting at four o'clock with Sir Michael on the important matter of staffing the Consular office and residence. In the meantime if you have any ideas or suggestions, please let me know before the meeting. Sir Michael has arranged two buggies to be outside the court house at one o'clock to convey you to the Consulate."

The officers gathered together in a small room off the court to discuss the four o'clock meeting.

"Might I suggest, Jamie," commenced Riordan "that we envisage the estate and the number of people and their jobs. First of all the people who will be employed in the house - the butler, cook and maids, outside, groomsman, stable hands, gardeners - and a patrolling army guard should be included."

Eventually Jamie was able to report. "Well, I've enough information, let's go and see if the buggies are outside, as it's nearly one o'clock and I'm famished."

Sir Michael and the Sullivans had supplied Mills with some staff and provisions to prepare the meal for the hungry men from the 'Alabama.' The Consular residence was a stone-built mansion with pillars on either side of the porchway. It was situated on the gentle slopes of the Blue Mountains on 200 acres of fertile grazing land, about ten miles from the old Spanish town. Ornamental iron gates signified the entrance to the estate. The gravel roadway leading to the mansion was shaded with wide-leaved tropical trees with a variety of coloured flowers.

Jamie, Josephine and Roughler in the second buggy were pleasantly surprised by the grandeur of the palatial dwelling that was going to be the home of Joe Mills and his staff. He greeted the party on the steps and escorted Captain Semmes into a long ante room. They hadn't been seated long, having been offered cocktails, when the Kennedy's butler, Douthwaite, announced that lunch was ready.

Mr. Mills, being the host, sat at the head of the table and on either side, Captain Semmes and Sir Michael Kennedy.

"By the way, Mr. Mills, I hope you don't mind but I've invited the banker, Mr. John Stewart, in case there are any questions regarding the house."

Sir David Sullivan, sitting between Alex and Carruthers, opened the conversation with: "I suppose you will be sailing in a few days' time?"

"Yes," replied Carruthers; he laughed. "There's a damned war on! And the Captain is preparing the vessel for sea, so I suppose it will be in the next couple of days." He paused and looked sideways at Sullivan.

"I know what you're going to say, Carruthers," Sir David quietly remarked. "Kate has told me all I need to know about you - which," he smiled, "is favourable. You have to make your mind up - whether to stay on the island and settle down, or go to war. It's up to you. No doubt a very hard decision to make," his eyes twinkled, "as I know you are both very much in love."

Alex, sitting on the other side, couldn't help but hear the gist of the conversation, and thought: "Hard luck, Alyson, I'm a married man and the sooner I leave the better; I don't think we are matched, anyway."

Jamie, sitting next to Francis, remarked: "What do you think, Alan? Have you any ideas who would like to stay on as part of the Consular staff?"

"I'm sure there must be some members of the crew who would like to settle on the island. I definitely want to sail - the sooner the better. I don't think we are very popular here after the court case, but some of our young officers certainly made an impression in the Sullivan household!" He smiled and then continued: "Now, come to think of it, I heard Roughler say he would like to settle here and I think I know why - it's that young bar wench Josephine, and I don't blame him!"

At the conclusion of the popular lobster and fish meal, with white wine, Semmes stood up. "Gentlemen, let us drink a toast on our own ground to our President Davis and the Confederation Government."

He sat down, cigars were passed round and lit.

"Our second toast, to the new Confederate Consul."

There was hearty response and the company applauded.

The butler entered and announced: "Your Excellency, coffee is served in the lounge." Douthwaite was a tall, thin man, rather dour, and of swarthy complexion, a native of the island, of London parentage.

They were comfortably seated, wined, the Virginian cigar tips glowed red. Not all smoked cigars - Francis and Townsend preferred their pipes. The air was thick with smoke - Douthwaite opened the windows. All waited to hear what was coming next:

"Gentlemen," Semmes settled all thoughts and doubts, "we are assembled here because I would like to hear your views and suggestions regarding staffing the Consulate."

Jamie quickly responded. 'Well, perhaps I might suggest a name, Captain, - Ernest Roughler."

"Don't be ridiculous." Whittle almost spat the words out; he seemed annoyed. "That would be preposterous - I would have a war on my hands"

Sir Michael intervened before he could finish his sentence: "You were in court, James, he was proved not guilty and I think he should be given the opportunity if he wants to."

Jamie was firm: "Gentlemen, I know Roughler, he's a man of integrity - a good tradesman, who would be more than welcome, I'm sure, with his skills and personality, besides which he is rather attracted" - he paused and smiled - "to a certain wench."

Mills confirmed: "He would be very welcome on my staff, and his young lady."

"That's settled," said Semmes, "Any other suggestions?"

There was a silence, which was interrupted by the butler, who had knocked discreetly on the door: "Sir, there is a further delegation from the crew."

"Have them enter, Douthwaite, and please seat them, and offer drinks and cigars."

Fifteen men entered and were seated. All eyes focused on Andrew Seeley, their spokesman.

"Seeley addressed the new Consul: "We would like to join your staff, sir."

"I'm pleased. Can we sort out your trades and allocate jobs?'

He paused. "Mr. Roughler, would you please take some notes, you will find writing paper in the third drawer down, in that desk. Generally these are the jobs: the butler - Douthwaite is only on loan from Sir Michael - he's willing to stay on to train somebody for the job. Anybody any ideas?"

"Yes, sir, I would like to volunteer for the job," replied Bowen. Whittle was quick to remark: "Now he's another suspect connected with the court case."

"Ridiculous," scoffed Semmes, "he was a witness for the defence. Were you present in court, Mr. Whittle?" The Captain was getting rattled, and so Jamie quickly jumped in to save any embarrassment:

"And who's going up aloft to relieve Riordan, if Bowen accepts the job?"

"Not me! - not me! - not me! - cries all around. Everybody laughed. "Mind you, it's up to John, don't forget you are all volunteers!"

"I would like the job, sir."

177

"Right, that's settled. Douthwaite - will you please fix up Mr. Bowen with his room," said Mills with a smile, "and give him some training."

"Thank you, sir," replied Bowen. "You will not regret your choice."

"Dare I ask if there is a cook in your party, Mr. Morris?" said Mills with a smile.

"Sir, we have the very man. I must admit Eric Dunbar from Tennessee has been one of our assistant cooks. He's a rather shy person, who hates violence and fighting."

"Good," replied Mills. "Douthwaite, I see you have returned, will you please introduce Eric Dunbar to the kitchen and afterwards will you find him a room."

"Sir," a seaman leapt to his feet "I would like to try my hand at cooking! It's better than shovelling coal."

"What's your name?"

"Jack Winters, sir!"

"Very well, catch up with Douthwaite." Mills was so far satisfied.

"Groomsmen, stable hands, somebody to handle horses, say four men?"

Adams quickly stood up, as though waiting for this job, and he was followed by three other men.

"Rob Adams, sir."

"You seem very keen. Take your mates - I think you will find Crawford down by the stables."

"I would like a scholar next, perhaps a qualified professional man, to be my secretary," said the Consul thoughtfully.

Everybody laughed

"You must be joking!" came a voice from the crew.

A smartly-dressed seaman stood up, clean-shaven, curly brown hair, dark penetrating brown eyes - "May I introduce myself?" - a quiet, cultured voice - "My name is John Thornhill, I'm a teacher by profession, until I was hoodwinked" - he smiled - "to join this rabble." (Hearty laughter.)

"Just the man to take notes. Come over here and take over from Ernest, as I know he wants to join his lady-love." He looked around. "Finally, we want soldiers to guard the Consulate, down by the wharf and also a security guard in my residence. Is this in order, Sir Michael? Mr. Whittle? I have to be guided by you"

"Certainly," said Kennedy. "I noticed the Spanish Embassy has guards."

"That is so," exclaimed the Chief of Police. Except they have no authority outside the confines of your land, because this property has been leased to you by law. Is this not so, Judge Morgan?"

The Judge seemed to be dozing.

"Whatever you say, whatever you say," repeating himself in a bemused tone.

"Will you introduce who is left, Mr. Seeley."

"Well, besides myself, we have - Tudor, Speakman, Moore, Joynson, Forrest and Reeves."

"Good, you look a fine body of men. You're a well-built and fit man, Mr. Moore, and you certainly handled yourself in the tavern, I think." Mills turned towards Semmes: "Can we give him the rank of Lieutenant in the Confederate Army, Captain?"

"I'm sure that can be arranged," said Semmes.

"If you don't mind me suggesting," butted in Whittle, "I was a Captain in the army and I do all my own recruiting, so it's quite in order for a sea captain to carry out this command!"

"Thank you, Mr.Whittle."

Semmes looked at the men standing to attention.

"You, Reeves, I understand you were a regular soldier in the British army? I'm sure I have the authority to give you the rank of sergeant."

Reeves clicked his heels - he was a stocky well-built man.

"Thank you, sir, I served in a Welsh regiment in India, sir."

"Well, you will find the climate will suit you out here," chipped in the laughing Sir David Sullivan.

Semmes paused for a moment, thinking.

"Of course, you will be dressed in the grey uniform of the Confederacy and be armed while on duty and allow no-one to enter the Consulate until he has been security-cleared - is that understood?"

"I think that is a bit drastic, Captain," said the smiling Kennedy. "Of course they can have rifles, but I would suggest no bullets, after all we are a very peaceful community."

"Ha, ha, I would agree with that." Whittle laughed.

"Lieutenant Moore, take your men back to the ship and see the Quartermaster for your uniforms, weapons and blank bullets."

Everybody present laughed.

Sir David Sullivan looked at his watch. "Gentlemen, you will have to excuse me, as I have a few arrangements to make regarding this evening and I trust I will see you all later."

"There is one more person I haven't settled for a job, that is Roughler," said Mills. "I would like him to be my personal bodyguard and I understand his young lady might like a job." He smiled. "She could be my housekeeper. Well, Captain Semmes, gentlemen, I'm quite happy with my team and thank you for your help and guidance."

179

"Before we depart, gentlemen," Semmes stood up and addressed Sir Michael Kennedy: "Perhaps you can give me some guidance. I'm giving Mr. Mills the rank of Captain in the Navy and naturally he will be outfitted accordingly, but I'm sure you might have some idea, Michael, how a Consul dresses?"

"Indeed, judging by other Consuls on the island, when they have attended State functions, they usually have a uniform of sorts, plenty of medals and a wide-brimmed hat, bedecked with feathers. There's a very good tailor named Sam Cohen; I'll introduce Joe to him sometime in the near future."

"One last thing, Michael," said Semmes. "I'll deposit a large sum of money with the banker, Mr. Stewart, which will take care of Joe's expenses."

The Captain looked around the assembled officers and addressed them: "I think that is all, gentlemen, it's been a satisfactory meeting. Those who are not staying will be reporting back to the ship as the day after tomorrow we will be leaving the island."

"In that case, Raphael," butted in Sullivan, "can I invite you and your officers to a farewell dinner tomorrow evening. I'll expect you at 7.30."

Chapter 16

Ernie Roughler came out of the meeting and met his friend Josephine who was waiting patiently outside seated in a buggy. He joined her and held her hands.

He was overjoyed. "Josephine, we are going to be together for the rest of our lives. We have been offered a job at the Consulate, you as housekeeper and me as the personal bodyguard to Mr. Mills."

She came close to him and put her arms around his neck and kissed him passionately.

"Why are you doing this for me, Ernie? I'm known as the whore of the waterfront!"

"Don't ever say that again," he interrupted her. "To me, you rescued us in the tavern. I might not be around today - if you get into a brawl in those places it's fatal and I have to thank you for saving my life and - I'm in love with you. Think of our future, the past is forgotten, let's start a new life."

He carried on - excited.

"How about getting married? Captain Semmes has the authority and I'm sure he will oblige us - say, on the ship, before it sails."

She kissed him again and again, clinging closely to him, murmuring:

"That's the nicest thing anybody has ever said to me and I love you for it, and I would be very happy to be Mrs. Roughler." She smiled and kissed him.

"Here's the Captain coming down the steps." He jumped out of the buggy. "I'll ask him now!"

"Excuse me, sir, I know I'm no longer a crew member, but a bodyguard to Mr. Mills - and," he held out his hand to the approaching Josephine which she grasped "she has been offered a job as housekeeper and I was wondering, sir" - he seemed very nervous, took a deep breath and blurted out: "Would you marry us - on board ship?"

Semmes looked bewildered, he had a lot on his mind - he was speechless. He paused, stroked his waxed moustache with his left hand, which he did when he was lost for words - thinking. He pulled himself together and, smiling, remarked "I'd be delighted -

when? - we've only got tomorrow and we're putting the final provisions on board. Say, about ten o'clock - incidentally, go and tell Mr. Mills the good news."

The Consul was in the lounge. Ernie knocked on the open door. "Please come in." Mills held the door open and the happy couple stood meekly facing him.

"Sir, Captain Semmes has agreed to marry us tomorrow at ten o'clock on board the *Alabama*." The overjoyed Roughler gabbled the sentence quickly.

Captain Mills was delighted with the news for the happy pair. He summoned his new butler: "Will you show my personal bodyguard and his future bride to the best room in the house. We are all going to a wedding! Tomorrow morning lay out my best naval uniform and inform the rest of our staff they are very welcome to attend the marriage of Josephine and Ernest at ten o'clock on board the 'Alabama'. Alert the cook to prepare a special reception for the happy pair after they are wed - say, for about one hundred guests. He'll have to work all night probably and get all hands to assist."

"Very good, sir."

The couple were about to leave the room, when Mills continued: "Who is the best man and have you got a ring?"

"Gee, I hadn't thought of that - I think it might be Steve Moore - after all he got us away safely" - Mills interrupted quickly: "A good choice," and with a smile: "I'll supply the ring - I'll sell it to you for one penny." They all laughed and the couple left, following Bowen to their newly-acquired bedroom.

• • •

Mr. Freeman was having an early breakfast on the Friday morning in the officers' mess. He was joined by Carruthers, Alex and Jamie. "Tomorrow we sail at midday and say farewell to Jamaica. I know you have been busy servicing the engines and boilers; made sure the coal bunkers are full, the drinking water system is working correctly, and I thank you for the efficient way you have done your duty. At the same time," he paused and with a slight smile remarked, "at the same time enjoying shore leave. Oh! I've heard the gossip from time to time." He paused to fill and light his pipe. "At ten o'clock, you may not have heard, we are going to have a wedding on board conducted by the Captain."

"That's unusual," said Carruthers. He looked around the company. "It's not one of us, is it? Don't tell me."

There was a burst of laughter.

"No, it's Ernie Roughler and Josephine and we are expected to attend in full dress." He looked slyly at the three engineers. "Don't worry, I understand the Sullivan family are attending."

• • •

Roughler returned to the ship to prepare for the following morning's happy event. Josephine spent the night at the Consulate.

Lady Kennedy arrived early the following morning, bearing a white dress and matching shoes for the bride. Flowers and a bouquet arrived and - another surprise - the Sullivan sisters in various colourful dresses and hats bedecked with flowers. They had worked hard, late into the night, preparing for the wedding. "I'm amazed," said Josephine, "with all the help, friendship, support and - look at this dress!" - holding it up. "Why are you girls all dressed up?" - she looked surprised.

Kate spoke quickly: "With your permission, Josephine, we would like to take part at your wedding by escorting you as bridesmaids," and with a chuckle, "and it will also be a chance to meet our sailor friends!"

Josephine was overwhelmed, she was speechless and felt very emotional.

"You are all very kind."

"Come on, let's get dressed." Alyson combed and did Josephine's hair while Gaynor arranged the bride's dressing. When fully dressed she looked at herself in the mirror.

There was a knock on the door; Janette opened it.

"May I come in?" It was Mr. Mills dressed in his officer's uniform. "Could I have the honour," addressing Josephine, "of being your escort and giving you away?"

Josephine just smiled and nodded.

"I think we are all ready now, Mr. Mills."

"Right, the coaches are ready to escort us to the Alabama."

Josephine smiled as she took Joe Mills' arm and they descended the wide staircase, along the hall and they emerged through the doors and on to the verandah - down another flight of stone stairs to where the lackey had opened the door of the coach. There was a loud cheer from the household staff. A black lady offered Josephine a bouquet of red flowers. She thanked her and stepped into the coach assisted by the uniformed lackey, who was 'on loan' from the Kennedy's estate. Everybody was there to give the bride a good send-off. With a loud cheer she was waved on her way.

As the coach wended its way through the narrow streets making its way to the wharf, people came out of their houses as though they knew what to expect and waved and wished the bride every happiness. Josephine waved back and smiled as people blew kisses. The jetty hove into view and the Consular and the bride were astonished to be greeted by a large crowd who waved and clapped their hands. A guard of honour was laid on by Captain Semmes. The First Lieutenant, Mike Kelly, approached and held out his hand to assist Josephine to alight from the carriage. She took Captain Mills' arm as they walked through a guard of honour to the steps leading to the boat that would row them across to the '*Alabama*'.

Ships of all nations were being loaded and unloaded, flags and buntings adorned most of the masts. The whole harbour had been alerted that Josephine was at last getting hitched and wondered who was the lucky man! The seaman standing at the rails and bulwarks waved and shouted as the Captain's boat was slowly rowed towards the '*Alabama*'. Josephine was very excited and Mills kept pointing to various ships. "Look, there's the British fleet." (The ships' crews were waving their hats.)
"There's Captain Dunlop on the '*Jason*', the one with the telescope, give him a wave." Josephine stood up, and nearly lost her balance. However she gave the men on the '*Jason*' a special wave. (After all some had been more than her friend!)
Many a sailor and officer she had entertained. She blushed slightly, dreaming of the happy times she had been embraced and had been rewarded.
The boat bumped alongside the '*Alabama*'. "Ship oars." The Bosun's whistle signified the wedding party had arrived. The crew of the '*Alabama*' were standing to attention with the officers lined up in their white naval uniforms or military grey. The seamen clothed in black wide-bottomed trousers, multicoloured shirts and wide-brimmed straw hats bedecked with ribbons. Josephine was greeted with a loud cheer as the Consul, Captain Mills, helped her step on to the deck. Mullard was playing a wedding march on his concertina.
Captain Semmes stepped forward and saluted the couple and said: "It is indeed a pleasure, Josephine, to welcome you aboard the '*Alabama*' on this special occasion. I'm also pleased, Joe, to see you looking very smart in your new Captain's uniform and I understand you are giving the bride away."
Roughler was dressed in his seaman's uniform, complete with boater and ribbons attached. (He asked the Captain's permission to wear it for his wedding.) He smiled and stepped forward and took Josephine's hand. Steve Moore, the best man, stood alongside

his friend Roughler, while the chief bridesmaid, Gaynor, stood by. Josephine and her sisters stood at the back. Captain Semmes was handed his Prayer Book by the Midshipman, Owens. He thumbed through it until he found the marriage ceremony at the back of the book.

"Doff hats," commanded The Bosun.

"By virtue of the power vested in me as Captain of the '*Alabama*' we are gathered together on this day - Wednesday 23rd January 1863 to join together this couple in marriage."

He opened the Prayer Book and held it in his right hand, while his left stroked his moustache, a nervous twitch for important occasions.

"Who giveth this woman away?"

"I do," replied Mills.

He addressed Roughler: "Do you, Ernest Roughler, take Josephine as your lawful wedded wife, to have and to hold, for better for worse, in sickness and in health, from this time forth, for as long as you both shall live?"

"I do," answered the new Consular's personal bodyguard in a firm voice.

"Do you, Josephine, take this man Ernest to be your lawful wedded husband, to have and to hold, for better or for worse, in sickness and in health, from this time forth, for so long as you both shall live?"

"I do." answered Josephine in a quiet, demure voice.

"Have you the ring?" - turning to the best man.

Steve Moore placed the ring in the Prayer Book.

The Captain asked Roughler to repeat after him, indicating to pick up the ring:

"With this ring I thee wed...."

Ernie placed the ring on the smiling Josephine's left third finger.

"I now pronounce you both man and wife."

They kissed each other passionately - the crew threw their caps into the air and gave a loud cheer.

The piper, Ollie, played a stirring marching tune.

Semmes kissed the bride on the cheek and shook hands and congratulated Ernie. Also Mills, the Sullivan family and the Kennedys congratulated the happy couple. The crew lined up, all anxious to kiss the bride! Gifts were given to the newly-married couple.

Jamie and Alex offered them some of their treasure cove. The Captain ushered the couple away to his cabin to sign the log-book and it was witnessed by Mills, Moore and Gaynor. Drinks were handed round by the Captain's steward.

Sunset Over Cherbourg

Semmes handled his glass, twirling it around and around in his fingers, thinking, wondering what to say to toast the bride and groom. Suddenly he expressed himself:

"May I wish you both every happiness in the future. I'm sure you will both settle down on this lovely island in your new jobs and at the start of your new life together. I shall miss you, Ernie, but I'm sure you will soon adapt yourself and serve the Consul as faithfully and diligently as you have served the Confederate Navy. Ladies and gentlemen, let us raise our glasses and drink a bumper toast to the happy couple."

The company had now swelled to the officers, Kennedys and Sullivans who joined in their congratulations by toasting the bride and groom. Ramidios handed the Captain a small box with a rounded cover.

"I would like you to accept this gift on behalf of the crew and myself and I would like to thank you, Joe, for giving away this charming young lady."

"May I propose a toast?" - Mills raised his glass. "To the bridesmaids, and especially Lady Kennedy for the able manner she arranged the bride's dress and bouquet. Gentlemen, the toast is the ladies."

It was the bridegroom's turn.

"Ladies and gentlemen. On behalf of my wife and I, may I thank you all for the lovely gifts, and a special vote of thanks to the Captain who has sent us on our way rejoicing, for the way he has performed the ceremony. I shall miss my many friends on this ship and I wish you every success in your future adventures; and may the Good Lord protect you all and land you safely with those you love!"

The gossip and congratulations continued for a short time.

Semmes drew Mills to one side.

"Joe, I wish you every success as Consul for the Confederacy. The islanders are sympathetic and friendly to our cause and there are two gentlemen - Sir Michael and Sir David - who regard you favourably and I'm sure you could always rely on their support. I would like you to establish yourself on the island - get to know people, listen to local gossip about the war, and read the newspapers. If you come across any deserters or sympathizers, house them and find them jobs. Entertain - that is how you will become popular - visit Confederate ships if they visit the harbour and give them any assistance. You have ample funds in the bank to maintain the Consulate and employ your staff. Write to me frequently - I shall look forward to hearing from you. You never know - our paths might again cross in the future. I will definitely

186

be visiting Cape Town and the Azores and if this our final farewell, once again," he shook his hand, "good luck to you and your staff." Before everybody departed, Joe Mills addressed the assembly "Ladies and gentlemen, I would like you all, and with your permission, Captain, any crew members who would like to visit my new home; you are most welcome."

He turned to Carruthers with a smile. "I understand you and your friends have been invited to the Sullivan residence for 7-30. I can assure you, I will ensure that you and your friends will be transported on time. I understand the Sullivans and the Kennedys have their own carriages. I will see you later, Carruthers."

"You look lovely in that red dress, Gaynor," chaffed MacGregor. "Shall we go ashore and head for the Mills' residence?"

"Jolly good idea, Mac." Gaynor smiled (and thought: 'Must make the most of the rest of the day, it will be fond farewells tomorrow.') "Will you please excuse me for a few moments, while I change out of this hot uniform into something more comfortable?"

The Doctor joined Alex, in their sleeping quarters, who was partly changed.

"Who's going ashore, Alex?"

"Jamie, Jacko and I understand all the officers, except of course Mr. Freeman. He would sooner read a book. He's the duty officer until we sail. I understand the Mills' residence is open to all the crew!"

A standby crew was left aboard ship. Most of the crew walked the five miles to the Consulate. The macadamed surfaced road with overhanging palm trees shaded the crewmen from the intense sun's rays.

Janette and Jacko rode to the mansion on horseback. Gaynor used one of the family's buggies to escort MacGregor, while Kate and Carruthers enjoyed each other's company walking hand in hand off the beaten track, stopping now and again to embrace and kiss each other.

'I'm going to miss you, 'enry," she laughed, knowing the nickname annoyed him, but he laughed, because he realised that they had to make the most of the remaining few hours together and he loved her so much. They kissed and hugged and then they made their way, partly through the undergowth, to the Consul's house.

At the Mills residence Jamie was in conversation with archeologist Roland. They discussed the buried treasure they had recently uncovered. "How much do you value the Spanish gold pieces, Roland?" enquired Jamie.

"It's hard to say as the price fluctuates, however not by much! Gold is always the best way of investing. The bank gives you good security, probably you'll get more in England. By the way I've slipped Mr. Mills a few gold pieces, which he appreciates. He seems to be a popular person and I'm sure he will receive lots of local support." "It's very kind of you, Roland." Jamie paused, reflecting. "We've only got one more day and we'll be sailing into the sunset, God knows where. I personally have enjoyed the island and its people, I'll probably come back some day and bring my family."

Roland put his hand into a bag he was carrying and withdrew a small leather pouch. On opening it, he produced a large pearl. "I discovered this by Montego Bay. I often come by them."

Jamie's eyes opened wide ('Good job they were alone' he thought, looking around furtively) and before he could say anything, Roland blurted out: "Please accept this gift for your wife, as a token of our friendship, and when you visit this island again we'll go treasure-hunting, for after all it was you who discovered our treasure."

They shook hands. "Thank you," said Jamie. "It's been a pleasure knowing you and please convey my regards to your wife, Cheryl, and your parents."

Jamie wandered off. Joe Mills, who was in conversation with Captain Semmes about his appointment to the Consul, beckoned Jamie over.

'You have a good support team, Joe, I wish sometimes I was part of it," said Jamie, smiling.

'Now, now, I want you aboard ship, my lad," exclaimed Semmes. The thinking Consul remarked: "I'm pleased, I can always employ local labour."

Semmes continued: "Make sure the staff are security cleared to your satisfaction and if they are going to do confidential work, they should sign our Secrets Act, holding allegiance to the Confederate Government. That should apply to all your staff and make them all renew their allegiance to our cause. It might be a good idea if you had a legal man on your staff - no," he laughed, "you can't have Riordan, but I think Unsworth would like to live on the island."

"Excellent choice, I'll drink to that!"remarked Joe Mills.

Mr. and Mrs. Ernest Roughler were sorting out their belongings in their new home. They had been given two large rooms by the Consul - one a lounge with a settee, chairs and a mahogany table and the other a furnished bedroom.

Josephine had collected some of her clothing from the little cottage she owned near 'The Seafarers' tavern.

"I can't believe this is happening to me, Ernie!" She put her arms around his neck and kissed him passionately.

"We are going to have a wonderful future together, my darling," murmured Ernie. "It's like being in fairyland. The job I've landed on this emerald island, instead of peeling potatoes, climbing the rigging to unfurl the sails, shovelling coal into the furnaces - we had a thousand and one jobs. Everybody had to know each other's job. There's one thing my love I'm a jack, retired, of all trades - and to be working for Mr. Mills - he's such a gentleman! And your job, running the household working under John Bowen - he'll never make a butler" - Ernie laughed. "He's more of a bodyguard like myself. We'll learn to ride, own horses and a buggy with beautiful laced fringes on top - I'm sure you will provide them - and we'll visit all parts of the island. In fact you and I are starting a new life." He smothered her with kisses and started to remove her flimsy blouse.

"Not now, my darling, later. I've such a lot to do." She pushed him to arm's length and smiled.

"Wasn't it nice of the Quartermaster to give me these suits - look at the silk lapels on this one" - fingering the collar and lapels. "Some wealthy person must have worn it on one of our enemy's ships." He hung up the three suits in a wardrobe.

"Let's get dressed for I want you to meet more of my shipmates and it will be for the last time, God knows when we shall meet again."

After light refreshments in the garden of his estate, Mills shook hands with some of his visitors as they departed at various intervals for their farewell dinner and party at the Sullivans' residence.

Kate and Carruthers were exhausted after the long walk from the wharf. Joe Mills warmly greeted them and took Kate's arm. 'Our 'Enry' followed as they made their way to the assortment of fruits, fish, fowl and meats served on a long table by black servants in the long entrance hall. It was bedecked with large old oil paintings, some were portraits of the banker, the Stewart family, his ancestors and watercolours of the island scenery, Carruthers, munching a turkey leg, was gazing at a painting of a lovely sandy cove. In the corner faintly written was 'Near Montego Bay', initialled "K.S."

Alyson came alongside.

"Hello, Kate, having a good time?" She looked at the watercolour painting. "The times, you, I and Janette - when she was old enough - went swimming, just there," pointing to the sandy, silvery beach. "It hasn't changed and the way the huge, high breakers come crashing down upon us. We have a beautiful, colourful, and in some areas, unexplored parts, which I don't think even Roland Sheridan has visited and he knows the island fairly well! Can't we entice you to stay and settle down here, - Henry?"

189

"I might one day," Carruthers caught Kate's eye. He winked at her and they both smiled.

"What about your friend, Jamie, he's such a quiet man?"

"He can't wait to return to England, to his family. At any rate in a week's time we will be on the ocean, scanning the sea for enemy ships, because that is the job we are being paid for."

"You sound so serious, Henry," said Alyson. "Let us all go on the verandah and have a drink."

Rob Adams, the groomsman, had his furnished bedroom above the stables and the stable hands also shared rooms in the same building. Out in the yard he was fondling and stroking the head of a grey gelding horse when he was joined by Vaughan and Kingston, two of his assistants.

"You have been specially chosen because you love animals. Familiarize yourselves with these magnificient beasts. Each one has its own habits and it's up to you to handle them gently and train them correctly. I'm going with Mr.Crawford to view and buy one buggy and a broken-down carriage. We'll set up a small workshop in that building over there," pointing to a long building. "I understand it was used for housing the Stewarts' carriages: see if you can fit it out as a workshop and if you give me a list of the tools you might require I'll see Mr. Mills about the monies. You, Mervyn, have had some experience as a blacksmith shoeing horses. I'm sure you'll be in demand. Thomas, having been brought up on a Welsh farm, will know all about cattle, sheep and horses."

Vaughan laughed. 'You've missed out goats, which are very popular on this island, also hens - yes, I'm quite happy to look after the farm animals.

"By the way, make sure the horses get daily exercises, and I must buy some more saddles," mused Adams. He paused. "That's the longest speech I've ever made." He laughed. 'You'll become good horsemen in time. Anyway it's better than climbing the mast!"

After visiting the Mills' residence and bidding the Consul farewell, Janette and Jacko rode on horseback to visit her ancestral home. They followed a path through banana trees and plantations. A gushing waterfall came into view with a sparkling blue lagoon.

"How about a swim, Jacko?" Janette quickly leapt off her horse, tethered it to a tree, undressed and followed by Jacko she dived naked into the clear blue water. They swam around, frolicking, Janette ducking Jacko several times. Underwater they kissed, surfaced, took deep breaths, dived and embraced each other and continued with their underwater love making. They staggered out of the water, Jacko giving a helping hand. They flopped on to a sandy patch and enjoyed the warmth of the sun as it dried their naked bodies.

Sir Michael Kennedy's coach took Jamie, Semmes and four officers to the Sullivans' residence, while the crewmen made their own way down to the busy Kingston wharf, walking, chatting, laughing in groups. They all assembled and seated themselves in the partly renovated 'Seafarers' tavern, where they were warmly greeted by the taverners who made them welcome for their last night ashore. They had been severely warned by the Bosun to behave themselves and act like gentlemen and to keep in mind they were in a neutral and friendly country.

Gaynor enjoyed the various foods and filled her plate with delicacies, some of which she had prepared. She was joined by Joe Mills and she addressed him:

"I understand you will need about three extra maids. I'm sure we can find you some nice, friendly, young ladies!"

"Thank you, Gaynor you and your family are going to be my closest friends. Ah! there's the Police Chief, I must have a few words - and I see Doctor MacGregor is about to gather you into his arms and whisk you away! I had better say my farewell to Graeme as I don't think we shall meet again."

The Doctor strode up - smiling. "May I congratulate you, Joe, on your new appointment. I want to ask a favour - will you keep an eye on Gaynor while I'm away and promise me you will not marry her yourself, as someday I shall return."

"I promise." They all laughed. I've come to say goodbye, or should it be au revoir until we meet again." They solemnly shook hands. "Will you excuse me, I know you two will want to be together, I see Ken Unsworth talking to the Law. I would like to make his acquaintance, as he's going to be my new legal representative."

The tables were prepared in the long hall to receive Sir David's guests. He stood at the top of the steps leading to the entrance to his home. He was chatting to Captain Semmes, Jamie, Francis and Townsend, who were sampling his finest Jamaican wine. Alan Francis was explaining about what life was like in the part of Wales where he was born.

"I was brought up on a farm situated in a valley in the Snowdonian range. The summers were hot, but when winter set in, with the snow and ice, we experienced hard times trying to rear animals, especially sheep, who tended to wander onto the high ground. During the snowy season they buried themselves and my father and brothers tried to locate them by prodding through holes in the snow, with rods. These holes would be caused through their breathing and sometimes we would be lucky and then we would dig them out and with the aid of sheepdogs lead them to the shelter on the lower regions."

Townsend observed: 'I've seen these intelligent sheepdogs perform. They respond to a whistle."

"I know," laughed Francis, "like this - he put two fingers in his mouth and a loud whistle shrilled out. People on the lawn looked up wondering what was the matter. Sir David quickly took advantage and beckoned everybody indoors.

Francis continued his conversation to the interested Captain Semmes and his two fellow officers as they walked into the mansion.

"I was educated at the village school, at the same time working long hours on the farm. The village only consisted of a general store, chapel and school. I passed an exam and left home to be boarded at Bangor university and what I really enjoyed was rowing in the Menai Straits, where I can assure you the currents are quite treacherous. While on holiday, staying with relatives in Liverpool, I visited the docks and was enjoying a drink in Rigby's tavern in Dale Street when some rowdy seamen came in and drank a few glasses of beer. An argument developed and then a fight. I'm a strong chap, I gripped a sweaty seaman around the chest, and was hugging the life out of him when I was hit on the head from behind and I must have been unconscious several hours. When I came to, I was lying on the Woodside stage, with my back propped against a large coil of thick rope."

"I heard similar experiences from a few of the crew members," said Townsend. He laughed - "Well you don't regret it, do you Alan? It's better than farming."

"The only regret I have," said Francis, "I suppose my folks must think I just ran away to sea!" His four fellow officers ribbed him, when they were greeted with a shout from Jamie as he ascended the ship's ladder, stepped on to the deck and walked over and joined them.

• • •

Janette and Jacko came trotting up, mounted on two magnificent stallions.

They were greeted by the groomsman, Crawford, who gathered the reins of both horses and took them to the stables. Janette ran up the steps, hugged and kissed her father on the cheek and looked at Semmes.

"Hi, Captain! how much longer have I got Jacko for?"

"He has to be aboard by midnight, so you've got about six hours. Tell your sisters if you see them and their boyfriends - tomorrow at four o'clock we sail, with or without them." He laughed.

The Sullivan sisters occupied a round table where they were accompanied by their Navy friends. The conversation drifted from one topic to another, realising the sands of time were running out.

Alex was feeling sad, he was really fond of Alyson and he was well aware of her feelings towards him. He had a family and responsibilities back home in Liverpool.

"Why are you looking so glum?" said the smiling Alyson. She whispered in his ear. "I know you only have a few hours left, let us make the most of it! How about coming up to my room for a cuddle and I'll leave you with some very happy memories to take away when you are sailing. Perhaps when you are standing on the deck and looking into distant horizons and the rolling crested waves, you will think of me."

He focused his eyes on her ample, heaving bosom which was partly exposed by her low-cut blouse. His searching eyes widened. So Alyson leaned further over towards him, never taking her eyes off his. She breathed heavily and clasping his hands tightly, whispered, coming closer:

"What are you thinking my love? Would you like to feel and kiss my bosom, it's nice and hot and waiting for your cool lips?" She took his hand as though to press it to her left breast when she noticed Gaynor looking at her. She shook her head and pointed upstairs. Alyson took the hint, winking, realising other people were looking and observing. They excused themselves and went to her bedroom.

Alyson, arms outstretched above her head, clinging to the draped curtains, was gazing through the window into the rolling landscape of the estate. Her room was situated on the third floor of this rambling old Spanish mansion, which her father had christened 'Calderstones Park' having read about a similar park in Liverpool.

She turned her head slightly to notice Alex had discarded his shirt and removed the broad belt, lowered his wide trousers, which he flicked off with his right leg. He stood only in his small pants. Alyson smiled and thought: "His black hairy chest looks like the front door mat - bless him! - he looks ready for action, I'm sure I'm going to enjoy the short time we have together.'

She gripped the curtains tightly as he approached her from behind. He eased the blouse above her head, throwing it to the floor. His groping fingers soon located her ample bosom, her nipples hardened as he handled, squeezed and lifted her heavy breasts in his large hands. She unbuttoned her skirt and it fell to her ankles and was kicked on one side. He discarded his pants and they were both naked.

He eased her slowly away from the window to the left, shuffling behind her as they faced a long wide mirror attached to the wall. She slipped her hands over his guiding them to her soft white stomach. Her breathing was light and quick.

He looked, fascinated, over her left shoulder into the mirror, her nipples were hardened and stood proud like two large cherries.

"My darling" - he eased the hair over her left ear and kissed her neck, she cringed with joy - "I'm taking this one brief happy moment away with me. I'll always remember your beautiful sunburned body." He pressed her very close to him, her right hand went behind her back and she gripped his manhood, sucked in her breath and softly murmured. He turned her slowly round and bent and kissed her stomach, then her lips, and then her soft breasts and nipples.

"Let's go to bed and have intercourse together, my love."

Chapter 17

During the evening of Friday 23rd January at the Sullivan residence, the Chief Constable drew Semmes to one side and put a proposition to him:

"I'm glad Roughler was found not guilty and I'm sure together with Josephine he is going to start a new and successful life on this beautiful island. I also like your choice of the new Consul, Joe Mills, and I will give him and his household every assistance and guidance. In return, Captain Semmes - could you do me a favour? Would you take off my hands Merner, Wright and Underhill and dump them somewhere in the ocean?"

Semmes laughed - "Now that would be too good a death for those scoundrels - leave them to me - I'll get rid of them! Perhaps we might be able to train them as seamen! Or maybe they will start a new life in Africa!" The Captain smoothed his moustache. "What about all those rifles, ammunition and explosives in the warehouse?"

Whittle smiled and remarked: "That's a deal, you are very welcome to them, I'll arrange for the munitions to be transported and shipped to the *'Alabama'*.

At midnight the Sullivan residence was empty except for fond memories of the young officers from the *'Alabama'*. The sisters were resigned that their lovers were sailing away. Alyson summed it up by remarking: "There are the officers on the *'Jason'* - it will be interesting to see how they compare and perform."

In the early hours of Saturday morning down on the wharf where the *'Alabama's'* gig boat was tied up, attended by seamen MacGuiness and Leeson, a curtained carriage drew up. Two uniformed policemen jumped out dragging with them the three Northern sympathizers, who were bound, gagged and masked. They were hustled down the steps and into the boat. The oarsmen with sweeping, strong strokes nosed the gig across the dark harbour towards the *'Alabama'*.

Merner was struggling with his hands which were tied behind his back, when he was successful; quietly and unnoticed he struggled free. He quickly stood up and dived over the side, much to the surprise of the rest of the boat's occupants. Being dark it was impossible to observe him in the water as he held his breath and dived beneath the surface. The light boat began to wobble.

Leeson yelled: "Sharks! Quickly, let's head for the '*Alabama*', and the oarsmen put all their strength into pulling on the oars.

The night air was rent by the agonizing cry of Merner's voice, the screaming, as he was being torn to pieces by the sharks. Eventually it died away as he disappeared beneath the surface. The shocked MacGuinuess boarded the '*Alabama*' first. The night duty officer was surprised when the two bound and masked figures of Wright and Underhill were marshalled on to the ship's deck by their guards. An explanation was given about the agonizing death of Merner, while the two prisoners were dispatched below deck to the ship's prison.

A longboat slipped alongside the '*Alabama*', and the sergeant of police boarded and confronted the officer of the watch.

"Mr. Lawson, as agreed by your Captain and the Chief Constable, we have brought all the weapons and ammunition from Merner's warehouse."

"I'll arrange for it to be brought aboard. Perhaps you would like an early breakfast? Mr. Tyler, will you escort the sergeant and his men to your mess and arrange a meal. Also detail men to have the weapons, ammunition and gunpowder transported into the ammunition and magazine lockers."

Dawn 5am, Saturday 24th January 1863 - a notable day when the '*Alabama*' comes to life. In the engineer officers' mess, Mr. Freeman, Alex, Jamie and Carruthers were enjoying fish, oysters, meats and fresh fruits for breakfast, served by the Chief Steward. The gossip was about the future events. Then the Chief Engineer gave his orders:

"Mr. Carruthers, will you alert the firemen and attend to the boilers. The bunkers are overflowing with coal, but we shall only use the engines to clear the harbour and then we shall look to the sails." He paused to drink a mug of coffee, and then he lit his pipe.

He then addressed Alex: "Will you arrange to raise the funnel then examine the propeller which is already housed out of the water. Make sure the guides are well greased and lower and raise it several times to make sure it is in good working order. Also attend to the drinking water system and examine the fresh water tanks. Jamie," (who was drinking a mug of coffee) "You will be in charge of the main engines."

Mr. Freeman stood up. "Of course," he said sarcastically, "continue enjoying your breakfast, I'm going to join the Captain for today's orders. I'm sure you'll have a lot to talk about, your last day in Kingston Harbour!"

"Sarcastic old bugger!" blurted out Alex, after Freeman had shut the mess door. "I don't know about you, I've got a thick head from last night - I must have drunk too much wine. What a grand farewell party!"

"And the rest," laughingly declared Jamie. "What about your love life?"

Carruthers butted in before there was a flare-up. "The islanders have given us a wonderful time over these past few days - putting up with us foreigners!"

He laughed, showing his flashing white teeth. "That is what we are - foreigners! We might still be British subjects, I suppose that is why the islanders tolerated some of us, and then a chap gets killed! That certainly didn't enhance our image - but" - he smiled - "we did capture the hearts of certain young ladies!"

Captain Semmes was writing up his log, when a knock on the door announced the uniformed Chief Constable.

"I'm sorry to interrupt you, Captain Semmes - I realise you have a busy day ahead - did you receive on board the three Northern prisoners?"

"No, unfortunately we have only accommodated two. When Merner was being rowed over from the jetty, he slipped his roped bonds and mask and dived overboard."

"Bloody hell!" exclaimed Whittle. "Not in the bay. He must have been crazy! He wouldn't last five minutes in these shark-infested waters. What a terrible way to go, but good riddance, that's one less. I'm going to ask a further favour. Will you please accept six more men? They are, incidentally, from the Northern Consul, including the Ambassador, who feels his Government is not very popular on the island and I would agree with that!"

"I can accommodate six more and I will treat them with the greatest of respect and courtesy, being Government officials. Will you please arrange their transportation? Would you share a toast with me, Mr. Whittle?" handing the Chief Constable a glass of wine.

"Certainly I will drink wine with you anytime, Captain. I know we have had our differences, but I feel we have developed a lasting friendship."

"I'll certainly drink to that. Your good health." They shook hands.

"Ramidios, summon the Bosun to escort Mr. Whittle ashore." The Chief Constable saluted and departed.

197

Sir Michael Kennedy was the next visitor - which coincided with the six members from the Northern Consulate being piped aboard. Semmes received them in his cabin. Sir Michael, the Deputy Governor, introduced the Northern gentlemen: "Captain Semmes, I would like you to meet the Consul, Bruce Eastwood; his assistant, Melvin Adams; and four members of his staff, Messrs. Crotty, Grice, Burgham and McKinnon."

"My pleasure - Ramidios, will you attend to the gentlemen's drinks."

"Excellent Spanish wine, Captain." Melvin Adams raised his glass. "Your good health, thanks for having us on board - we feel we are not very welcome in Jamaica - especially after the shocking Merner affair. We are agreed we would like to return to our native land!"

Semmes smiled. "Those are my sentiments too, Mr. Adams - I wish this bloody war was over and we could all return to our loved ones," he sighed.

"You are welcome on board, but being on a Confederate ship I must remind you that you are my prisoners, however" - Grice interupted him: "We accept that." Semmes continued by raising his right hand: "I will parole you six gentlemen, also later our two other prisoners, Wright and Underhill. This means you will be treated with respect and courtesy by my crew until you decide where you would like to be put ashore! Ramidios pass me my Bible."

He fingered his most priceless possession.

"I only have the one copy of the Good Book, I would ask you to raise your right hand and each place your left hand on the Bible: "By the power vested in me as Captain of the '*Alabama*' and by command of the President of the Confederate States of America I do hereby parole you. Do you swear on your honour that you will not try to leave this ship or interfere in any way with the running of this ship or its crew?"

They each in turn said: "I do."

"Ramidios, will you please ask Mr. Kelly to attend."

"Mr. Kelly, would you please arrange quarters for Mr. Eastwood and his staff and they are to be shown every courtesy and respect as they are paroled prisoners." They departed to their new quarters.

Semmes seated himself. "Well, Michael, that matter has been attended to satisfactorily - how about some more wine?"

"Raphael," (the Deputy Governor and the '*Alabama's*' Captain addressed each other by their Christian names) "what does the future hold for you?

"God knows!" Semmes stroked his waxed moustache. "I tell you this - when this bloody war is over I might return with my family to this island paradise," he laughed. "We shall see! I must thank you for your help since we landed two weeks ago. Such a lot of events have taken place during this period, which I realise by your patience and guidance we have been safety steered through and I might add also the names of the Chief Constable and Sir David."

Michael seemed lost for words. He took a sip of wine before replying: "Your reputation preceded you and the island burst with excitement on your arrival. Today you sail away and looking around the harbour as I approached the '*Alabama*' I was overawed by the ships of all nations bedecked with bunting and flags - expressing their farewells - also some of your crew," Kennedy smiled "have left their mark on some of the islanders. I'm also pleased you successfully established a Consulate. We can at least hear about your battles and I wish you a safe journey in all your undertakings. Perhaps one day we shall meet again." Sir Michael finished his drink and stood up. They shook hands and he acknowledged the officer of the day's salute as he descended the Jacob's ladder into his manned gig boat. Semmes mustered the senior officers to his cabin.

"Gentlemen, I would like to discuss my future plans." He unrolled a large chart across his desk. "These are the Antilles Mayores, a large number of picturesque islands" - pointing - "Santo Domingo, San Juan, Antigua, Barbados, and going further south to Trinidad and Tobago. I feel sure we shall find enemy ships in these Caribbean waters. The ships from the North will be supplying materials and provisions for the islanders. Likewise in return they will trade with the Northerners. It is our duty to wipe out this trade and destroy the enemy ships. I would like you individually to discuss these future plans with the crew and ensure that they are equipped to carry out their various duties. Have a good lunch, gentlemen. We shall be sailing on the four o'clock tide."

Mr. Freeman discussed the Captain's future plans over lunch with his engineers and when the meal was concluded Jamie led his colleagues into the engine room. The firemen had already lit the boilers and black smoke bellowed out of the raised funnel.

By 3pm the engines were on stand-by and Mr. Freeman informed the Captain. Half an hour later seamen swarmed up the rigging awaiting the order to unfurl the sails. The bars were fitted into the capstan, the sailors ready to raise the anchor. Flags and bunting fluttered from the mastheads. Ray Tyler, the helmsman, stood by the double wheel and Riordan was in position on the mizzen masthead.

The Bosun's whistle had hardly died away when the uniformed Pierre Gerhardie reported to the Captain:

"Monsieur, I'm 'appy to join you and peelot me into open waiters".
'Why hasn't the bugger learned to speak proper English?' the Bosun was thinking, but Semmes smiled. "Glad to have you on board. The ship is ready for sea. The First Lieutenant will join you by the steering platform."

The tall Semmes, with his buttons polished and his rank displayed on the epaulettes on his shoulders, looked every inch a Captain as he viewed some of the crew standing to attention amidships.

"I hope you have all enjoyed the stay in Jamaica and said your farewells to this lovely island. In a short time I will be giving the order for sailing to do battle with the enemy. You will be dismissed to man the bulwarks to say your farewells to your friends who will be following us in their various boats."

The Captain looked aloft and acknowledged Riordan's salute and nodded to Kelly, the First Lieutenant, who gave the order.

"Heave up the anchor."

The seamen manned the positioned anchor bars. Mullard jumped on to the capstan and commenced playing his concertina. The crew members' chanting chorus echoed across the harbour as the excited Jamaicans realised the '*Alabama*' was departing and many a maiden's heart was broken as her lover was sailing away, perhaps never to return.

"Start main engines" - as the two anchor chains slowly rattled through the hawsepipe down the chain pipe and into the lockers. The pilot guided the '*Alabama*' towards the entrance of the harbour and the fort at Port Royal and into open waters.

The crew on the anchored British man-o'war, H.M.S. '*Jason*' gave a cheer and a gun salute, lowered the St. George flag as the '*Alabama*' steamed slowly past. Semmes acknowledged by lowering the Confederate flag fluttering proudly at the stern.

Small boats still accompanied the raider. The young engineer officers were allowed on top deck to wave their farewells to the Sullivan sisters who in return waved handkerchiefs, and many a tear was shed as their lovers departed.

The Pilot bade farewell, wishing the crew 'bon voyage' as he alighted into his boat.

At full steam ahead on this breezy day the First Lieutenant gave the order to unfurl the sails. First, the foretopsail, then the topgallant, followed by the fore-royal-sail. It seemed the seamen manning the main mast were competing against the fore mast followed by the spanker and gaff-topsail and with full sails, billowing the '*Alabama*', her stem cutting into the blue waters of the Caribbean Sea headed towards Haiti, leaving behind happy and sad memories of the crew's brief stay in Jamaica. Even the smell of the fragrant flower-scented breeze from the island gradually disappeared into the mist of time as the Confederate raider headed into a heavy swell and was assisted by a shrill and strong north-easter wind.

They passed the Spanish Rock, which looked like a tall ghost ship in the distance. Night descended rapidly as the '*Alabama*' rolled and tossed, making it uncomfortable for the 'land-lubber' sailors. Next morning the rough sea had calmed and steaming on main engines eastwards, the lookout man Riordan shouted: "Land ho!" The Haitian coastline soon bowed into view and eight hours later the '*Alabama*' unfurled her sails and banked the furnace fires as she anchored in the River Ozama.

The crew were given shore leave to visit the old city of Santo Domingo.

Semmes, standing on the main deck, looked through his telescope at the capital town when he was joined by Jamie.

"This is the old city, Jamie, that flourished in the year 1500. It has a Catholic convent, built and housed by Dominican monks. It also has a cathedral, both in ruins. I'm always interested in visiting old historical buildings. Perhaps you would like to accompany me and maybe some of your friends? We shall be here about eight hours while we stock our provisions. Have a look through the telescope while I organise the boat."

The ship's longboat landed the Captain and his party on the stony beach. Jamie mused: 'Was it on this beach that Columbus landed and introduced Catholicism to this island in 1492? or the '*Mayflower*' in 1762? - when the Puritans established their faith later on this island.' He kicked the stones thinking: 'Did these early pioneers kick and walk over these stones?' He picked up a handful. 'What tales these stones would tell.'

His thoughts were interrupted by Alex, who urged him to hurry, to catch up the party standing amidst the ruins of the ancient Spanish Cathedral.

Alex, Jamie and Carruthers were gazing at the burning lamp above the base of the high altar, situated at the eastern end of the Cathedral. Semmes came across and remarked: "I have just learned from one of the locals that this lamp was first lit by the monks when Columbus worshipped in the Cathedral." He pointed.

"Over there the monks gathered in their choir stalls behind the colonnades - the monastic timetable was routine day after day, year after year, serving twelve hours in worship and part in refreshments. They would silently parade, chanting, to the Chapter-house where the Chaplain would recite a chapter of the Rule of

Santo Domingo - the Patron Saint of the Cathedral." He paused looking around and indicating. "From the Chapter-house the monks would walk in twos through those" - pointing - "round-headed arches supported by the septagon columns into the parlour with its wooden doorway. This was the only room where the monks could openly converse with each other. The monks would silently, except for the noise of their crosses entwining with their beads, walk round the cloisters several times, probably praying or practising chants. You can see the base of the day stairs over there, where they would ascend to the rectory."

The Captain paused and produced a pipe from his pocket which he packed with tobacco and lit. He puffed away contentedly before continuing.

"Funny," thought Carruthers "I havn't seen old beeswax with a pipe before."

"The monks ate simple food and vegetables grown in their gardens. A Chaplain would ascend the stairs over there, enter the pulpit and read Latin texts while they were eating." Semmes arched his hands, signifying: "There would be a large wooden table at the head of which the Abbot would sit in a comfortable chair, while the monks sat on rough benches, with their hoods thrown back. They would eat the food and drink the home-made ale passed to them from the hole over there from the kitchen. If they had time off they would work in the fields or attend to the flower beds in the cloisters." He stopped and looked around. Alex remarked: "Not much in life, not the one I would like to choose."

Semmes continued: "When a monk died he would be buried in a common grave, just a simple service, with a small headstone and his name, Brother so-and-so. However, an Abbot or Bishop is totally different. He is buried in the Cathedral with the traditional ceremony and a requiem mass and attended by local clergy and supervised by a Bishop."

He waved his arm, indicating. "Let us go back to the quietness and tranquillity of the ruins. The Abbots would be buried in the nave, probably under those large marble slabs," indicating the polished faded preserved floor, "and the Bishops would be buried near the high altar."

"Yes, you're right, sir," Alex interrupted. "I can see faint dates and names, here is one dated 1551 - Reverend Father Dominic - I remembered some Latin I learned at school - and another one over here" - gesturing. Jamie reflected about his childhood and what he was taught by his father.

"Captain -" Jamie, who was reared on the poetry and songs of Robert Burns drew Semmes' attention.

"These ruins remind me of the Scottish poet's visit to Lincluden Abbey in which he composed a poem during an evening's visit to the ancient ruins:
"Ye holy walls, that still sublime, Resist the crumbling touch of time, How strongly still your form displays The piety of ancient days."

"As school-children we had to learn the Poet Laureate's famous and not-so-famous works. We would be given a poem each to study and learn for the following day, and pity help you if you couldn't stand up and recite some lines - you were caned!" Alex continued the quotation - "The high arched windows, painted fair Show many a saint and martyr there." And Carruthers concluded it:
"The choral hymn, that erst so clear Broke softly sweet on fancy's ear, Is drowsed amid the mournful scream, That breaks the magic of your dream! Roused by the sound, I start and see The ruin'd sad reality."

Jamie continued showing off his knowledge further: 'In the year 1100, English monasteries were built by Cistercian monks from France and dotted around England and Wales. They travelled from place to place and built flourishing monastic abbeys to the glory of God. Two ruins I have visited were Furness and Fountains Abbey and one I would I like to visit one day, if I am in the south of England, is Buckfast.' He laughed. "I don't think the life of a monk would have suited me - I prefer the smelly engine room and then breathing the pure oceanic air and feeling the salty spray on my lips."

Semmes appeared exhausted after hours of walking and sight-seeing.

"Well, gentlemen, let us return to the ship."
They made their way along the cliff edge pausing to hear the sound of the surging waves and viewing the '*Alabama*' as it rolled gently at anchor in the blue sea surrounded by various size small crafts, some of which were supplying fresh provisions for the crew.
Proceeding along the cliff, the party came across some more ruins. They were situated on higher ground, but had a commanding view of the river.
Two youths approached Semmes and in broken English and Spanish enquired: 'Excuse me, can we guide you around these old historic buildings?"
"Certainly, I've read about the history of the island, but there's nothing like the knowledge of the locals. Please lead the way."

"My name is Alfonso and my friend is Pedro. The name of these ruins is Diego's Columbus Palace. It was a purpose-built fortress on higher sound, mainly to guard and protect the community."

The highlight of the tour was inside the ruins of a dungeon, where it was explained to the curious party who saw rings attached to a wall.

"It was here," indicated Alfanso, "through these rings, that the chains were passed which bound the famous Captain Columbus." Semmes looked in awe and amazement, he felt so humble to be standing on the same spot where Columbus had been chained centuries before.

The fortress was solidly built of stone blocks and it was shaped like two courts connected by columns and surrounded by battlements. Time over the centuries, winds, storms and hurricanes, had caused the palatial building to crumble just like its history in the mists of time.

The guides then took them a tour around the ancient city of St. Domingo, on conclusion of which Semmes rewarded them and the party returned to the stony beach to be greeted by Bob Mack and his team of rowers, and then returned to the ship where it bumped gently alongside the '*Alabama*'.

Next morning, Sunday 1st February, with the provisions safely stored aboard, the Confederate raider raised the port anchor chain. The boilers fired and on main engines the '*Alabama*' steamed out of the river Ozama and into open waters. Alex's job was to raise the propeller which he organised with the help of two seamen. Carruthers ordered the firemen to bank the fires as the '*Alabama*', under full sail and a fair wind, entered the Mona Passage where several ships were sighted and the '*Alabama*' went into hot pursuit.

On board the '*Olive Jane*' bound for New York the worried Captain, Paul Denemy, standing on a hatch cover to give him height, looked through his telescope at the rapidly approaching vessel under full sail. It seemed to be heading straight for his ship. He was taken completely by surprise when a shot was fired and whistled above his head. He was confused, watching the Northern flag being lowered and the large Southern one raised to unfurl and flutter in the breeze. Crewmen gathered around him, wondering what was happening. The '*Alabama*' with its guns and grey-coated soldiers bumped alongside. Grappling irons locked the two ships together as the First Lieutenant leapt aboard and confronted the '*Olive Jane*' Captain with:

"I demand to see your papers!"

The cargo consisted of champagne, old French wines, brandies, fruit and fish.

Willing hands soon transferred the goods aboard the '*Alabama*' - all the bottles going to the Captain's cabin and stored neatly away by Ramidios. (Semmes didn't want trouble with his crew - he had a good disciplined ship!)

It was on Saturday morning the 21st February that the '*Olive Jane*', after transferring the prisoners, was torched, and in the late afternoon a similar fate ocurred to the '*Golden Eagle*'. The ship's papers showed a cargo of guano - excrements of sea birds used for fertilizing the soil. Her Captain, Oliver Keep, was furious as he was only a few miles from his destination, having travelled hundreds of miles for this fertilizer for the Northern farmers - he too had been duped by this damned Southern pirate!

Various ships, various sizes and different nationalities passed by the '*Alabama*'. Realising they were neutral ships on this popular shipping route, Semmes bade them a silent and safe farewell. However, the '*Sarah Sands*' was boarded, her papers proved neutral. Eventually a cry from aloft reported several ships sailing in convoy. They were each inspected and allowed to proceed, except for one; the '*Washington*' was released on ransom.

Jamie, Jacko and Alan Francis were chatting on the forward end when came another cry from aloft: "Ship ahoy! on the the port beam!" Jamie scanned the distance with his spy glass.

"There's more than one!" he exclaimed. "We must be in a popular sea lane for Europe. I must see if one of the English ships will deliver my mail and I'm sure some of you will want to take the same advantage!"

Jacko was looking at the chart: "We are in approximately latitude 32° and 38° longitude."

Captain Semmes joined the group. "What's this I hear, Jacko, are you studying navigation? Your best guide are the stars at night. For your information, gentlemen, why we are in these waters is because," he turned scanning the ocean, noting white sails in the distance, "approximately ten years ago an American gentleman named Malcolm studied the charts in this area very carefully, also the weather - the winds - hurricanes - and by careful calculations recommended to the Merchant Shipping Agency a route to escape - at specific times of the year - the destructive north-east trade winds. That has saved not only time, but safety for the vessels - hence" (he gestured with a sweep of his arm and smiled.) - "we are viewing the spoils of war, and we are going to be busy between here and the Cape of St. Roque in Brazil."

• • •

It was dawn on the 1st March, when from aloft came the familiar cry from Riordan, observing through his telescope: "On the starboard beam a Northern ship about one mile away."
Telescopes swung in the direction of a tall white ship.

"It's a Yankee alright, sir," exclaimed the excited Carruthers.
"Action stations," shouted the First Lieutenant "Man the thirty-two-pounder, Mr. Butler."
The loud bang startled the Captain on the American-built brig, '*John A. Parks*'. He was bewildered when a shot was fired and were exchanged on the opposing ship. Captain MacBurnie snarled out: "Heave to."
The papers showed the cargo mainly as long wooden planks. The carpenter, Brennan, was delighted. It wasn't often that a captured ship's cargo filled his stores!
The Captain and thirty-one of her crew were transferred with personal belongings to the '*Alabama*' and twelve of her crew swarmed on the enemy ship and looted it. Their longboats were secured astern of the warship.
The hundreds of articles of clothing, blankets and food littering the '*Alabama's*' deck were quickly disposed of by the crew, and Semmes received the '*Parks*' chronometer, reluctantly by MacBurnie.
"Mr. Kelly,' Semmes addressed his First Lieutenant, "how many prisoners do we have on board?"
"Besides Mr. Eastwood and his Northern Consul staff, the two brigands and thirty-one off the last ship we have just torched - a total of forty."
'Good! Except Mr. Eastwood, put the rest to work after they have been paroled, which I shall do immediately, and muster them on deck."
"Aye, aye, sir."
So the thirty-one crew members of the '*John A. Parks*' were paraded. Captain addressed them as prisoners of war. He then paroled them and confined them to the forward end of the ship.

• • •

Semmes, sitting at his desk, was daydreaming. He kept looking through the cabin porthole, gazing at the horizon while trying to write in the ship's log:- '21st March 1863 - '*John A. Parks*' put to torch prior to unshipping its valuable cargo, which pleased the carpenter, also some mail - will be able to catch up on the war! Crossing the equator 24° longitude west, the weather was reasonable, slight swell. I could hear the thunder in the distance, reminding me of the trade winds, which I must avoid.'
"I can never understand which direction this damned war is heading," Alex grumbled as he unfolded a map of America. He was reading a Northern newspaper taken from the last captured ship.

He quoted: 'At two-day battle on December 31st at Stones River - pointing on the map - 'in Tennessee the total loss of missing, killed, or wounded was 25,500 Confederate troops, compared to 11, 600 Yankee soldiers. It's incredible, that was almost similar to last September at Antietam, or January 11th at Fort Hardman in Arkansas."

Jamie intervened: "Now where's that on the map? Why it's hundreds of miles difference and according to the newspaper 5,506 Southerners were killed against 977 Yankees!"

"And yet" Carruthers, also peering over Alex's shoulder, remarked, "at Fredericksburg 12,506 Northerners killed or wounded, and how can 2,000 men go missing? It's extraordinary and the Southerners certainly won that battle with the loss of 4,450."

"It's like this," Mr.Freeman observed. "It's where the Southerners have slowly gained ground, battling their way up from the South winning some and losing other battles, but their grit and determination and men enlisting on the journey, make them a dangerous force to be reckoned with."

He banged his pipe on the table, the dead tobacco ash trickled to the floor.

(This signified the end of the conversation.) "Let's get back to work, gentlemen. Let me know, Jamie, the state of the coal and, if we require any we'll ransack the next ship, because the enemy certainly abound in these waters."

The whaler schooner the 'Kingfisher' was the first to be sighted and captured, followed by the 'Morning Star'. Her papers showed her cargo was jute and linseed and certificated as the property of the British. Seeing she was sailing between an English Colony and Southampton she was released on bond.

Two days later on the 25th March, two more paddle steamers fell to the commercial raider. Mr. Freeman was pleased with the capture of these two steam vessels. It meant coal. He organised the transfer of fifty tons which was transported in the captured ship's boats using their crew as labourers.

The prisoners and their belongings were transferred to the 'Alabama' and the two ships burned.

Chapter 18

The night was calm, with a slight breeze, the moon shimmering across the slight swell. The '*Alabama*'s' bell signified a change of watch, Jamie was leaning on the ship's rail watching the waves surging past. He was dreaming of his home, when he was joined by one of the '*Golden Eagle*' prisoners.

"Ah! Captain," exclaimed Jamie, noticing the epaulettes on the shoulders, "I was day-dreaming, my thoughts back in England. Is everything satisfactory? Are you getting enough to eat? Are your quarters comfortable?"

"Yes, sir, my name is Oliver Keep," the tall young American officer answered. "It is more than I expected. We heard strange stories about your Captain, his sly and devious tricks, sailing innocently towards the Northern ships displaying our flag and how we were duped! My ship, the '*Golden Eagle*', had nearly reached her destination. We had sailed hundreds of miles, our holds bulging with guano for Boston, when - 'wham' - we were captured. Naturally I was angry, but we have been treated fairly." He paused. "There is something I must discuss with you, confidentially." Jamie was startled, wondering what to expect.

"I was born on the west coast of America in a fishing village, 600 miles south of New York. My father was Captain of a sailing ship and at an early age I followed in his footsteps. I studied navigation and went to sea as a deck officer on a schooner." He smiled. "Good training, up the mast, for a youngster."

He stopped talking, deep in thought as though to rephrase his sentences.

"I was eventually promoted to Captain in the same company as the '*Golden Eagle*' - I owe no allegiance to any flag only my ship, the '*Golden Eagle*', and the company I work for." He paused and looked curiously at Jamie. "This last voyage I visited the island of Puerto Rico in the Bahamas for provisions. I went ashore and in a tavern concluding my business, I overheard the name '*Alabama*' mentioned. I became interested and started asking questions. Do you remember a Southern paddle steamer ship named '*San Augusta*'? Her Captain was David Wakefield. "I vaguely remember it," said the thoughtful Jamie, asking himself, 'I wonder what he's thinking, I wish he'd get round to it.'

"Well, his ship visited this island and while he was anchored offshore, they were paid a visit by some armed men. Fighting broke out and the crew of the 'San Augusta' were restrained, bound and rowed ashore in irons. I heard they were sold into slavery and transported to work on a plantation owned by a man named Shimmon, a really brutal man, who ill-treated his slaves."

"Thank you for coming forward, Captain," said Jamie. "I will discuss our conversation with Captain Semmes, and I'm sure we will need further information later. I'm going to turn in now as I'm on the next watch."

Sure enough Captain Semmes summoned the senior officers together with Captain Keep to his cabin.

"It has come to our notice, gentlemen, that the Captain of the 'San Augusta' together with his crew are in captivity on a plantation on this island of Puerto Rico." He pointed to the island on the map, lying on his desk.

"This information has been passed on by, and," he paused, "may I introduce Captain Keep, and thank you for coming forward and offering your help and knowledge about this island. I understand you know the approximate location of this slave colony, because that is what it seems to be, and knowing this Captain Wakefield it is my intention to invade this prison and free all the men."

Captain Keep continued: "They work in squalid conditions for this monster Shimmon who calls himself a plantation owner and apparently is feared by the locals."

Semmes sniggered. "We will see about that and hope he is around when we invade this colony and wipe it out." He took a sip of wine and lit a cigar.

Jamie and his colleagues looked intently at the map, knowing there was going to be some action.

"Now this is the plan." He looked at the eager, young officers. "I aim to capture a paddle steamer, which I hope will have plenty of provisions and coal on board; remove the prisoners and man it with a skeleton crew who will sail" - he smiled - "looking innocently like a Southern ship, as these are popular in these waters. You, Mr. Kelly, will be the temporary Captain and you, Jamie, as you seem to have experience of these raids, will be in charge of the attacking party assisted by Captain Francis and his soldiers. So select your men. We will discuss it in detail as Captain Keep has volunteered to accompany you as he knows something about the terrain and about this so-called prison run by this sinister man Shimmon. Ramidios - wine for the gentlemen and some of that fine Virginian tobacco for Captain Keep." He stopped and re-lit his dead cigar.

"The two ships will anchor in this bay to take on provisions disguised as Northern ships" - indicating on the map. "Jamie, Jacko, Captain Keep - and take Ryan 'the knife', disguise yourselves as local peasants, go ashore at night, make your way to the nearest village, bribe your way in and see if any of the locals supply provisions for this prison camp. Find out all you can, and report back and we will then work out our plan of campaign."

The next day the duty officer was alerted from aloft that a paddle steamer was about two miles distant on the starboard beam. The crew mustered for battle stations. Semmes flew the Northern flag as he approached the innocent-looking schooner.

'Just the job,' he thought, looking through his telescope.

The Northern flag was replaced, two blank shots were fired at what turned out to be a Northern cargo ship bound for Europe, her cargo consisting of wines, sugar, salt, bananas, coconuts and ample provisions for her crew.

Her officers and crew were 'escorted' on to the 'Alabama' and bunked below decks.The skeleton crew headed by the First Lieutenant took over accompanied by the soldiers. The 'Alabama', together with the newly captured ship, the 'Eaglet', a four-masted paddle steamer, sailed towards the island and anchored in a sandy bay.

At dusk the dim lights of the town of San Juan twinkled about five miles away along the coast. It was quiet and peaceful that night. The only sound was the boat grinding on the sandy beach as Ryan, with a bag on his shoulder, silently leapt out and made his way along a pathway between the palm and coconut trees. After half an hour he returned and gave a quiet whistle, three times, the signal for Jamie, Jacko and Keep to join him. They were dressed in dark green shirts and brown trousers to blend with the terrain. Tyler, the Bosun's Mate, had been instructed to return to the 'Eaglet' and report back at dawn.

The four made their way along a well marked pathway, surrounded by dense undergrowth and tall trees. They soon got accustomed to the weird noises of the night creatures as the machete-hacking Ryan led the way. He would stop now and again to notch a mark on the bark of a tree to signify the return trail back to the beach.

The undergrowth cleared. The hazy moon filtered through the clouds to reveal a wider path, almost a roadway, and ahead a 'T' junction. Jamie pointed:

"Look at those tracks, it might be a roadway leading to a village or perhaps to the settlement." He smacked the palm of his hand on his neck. "Damn these insects. Good job we smeared ourselves with that rancid grease from the engine room. You never know what to expect on these islands."

The pathway continued for about one mile and then opened out and a wooden shack came into view.

"Go and reconnoitre, Ryan," commanded Jamie. He left his bag and quickly scrambled along the pathway and when he reached the shack he slid along its wooden side and eased himself up to an opening of a window. He parted the dirty torn curtains. He slightly smiled as he observed a number of men and women sleeping in groups on the wooden floor. The loud snoring indicated they were contented and sleeping peacefully.

He moved further down the wide gravelled pathway until he came to a number of shacks which formed a village. Continuing out of the cluster of huts he was surprised to hear in the distance the gentle surging of waves. He hurried on and came across a large stone building at the end of which was a long wide jetty.

Ryan had seen enough. He retraced his steps and on the outskirts of the wooden shacks he was suddenly attacked by a huge snarling dog with sharp teeth. It leapt at the unprepared Ryan who was knocked to the ground. They rolled over, the beast clawing at his chest. He managed to grip the dog by its throat. He released his right hand, got astride the animal and gave it a hefty punch on the side of its head, knocking it unconscious. He was shaken, his shirt was torn and blood-stained. He scrambled to his feet and staggered back towards his companions and fell to the ground.

Have you been fighting again, Ryan?" remarked Jacko. "What a mess, look at your chest." Oliver Keep lifted him up to a sitting position.

"I was attacked by a mad dog, I didn't kill it, I left it unconscious in the bushes. Killing it would have given the game away."

"Good thinking," Jamie, chuckled, producing a small flask, "here, have a swig of this tonic."

Ryan related the outline of the village and jetty.

Jamie looked at his watch. It was 1am. "How are you feeling, Ryan?"

"I'm all right."

"Good, we'll continue along this roadway. Captain, what you have described could be right. We might find the plantation settlement at the other end of this road," (indicating to the right of the 'T' junction.) They walked silently for about two miles, apart from cursing and muttering as they were stung by insects. A watery moon revealed the way, the only sound being the hum of the night creatures in the undergrowth on either side of the road as they moved quickly along.

The roadway widened, shacks loomed ahead on either side of the road. Jamie raised his hand. "We will wait here on the outskirts. You go ahead, Jacko, and reconnoitre. We'll be in those bushes over there."

Off went the speedy and silently moving Jacko. Shacks gave way to stone buildings. He came across another junction and turned left. After about half a mile he stopped and saw a movement of what appeared to be a uniformed soldier in the distance in front of the huge wooden gates of a stockade. 'This must be it,' he thought. 'I'll skirt around, must be alert to guards, don't want to arouse any suspicions by being careless!' He went to his right, the tall wooden stockade continued for about one mile - he'd seen enough, and so he made his way back, carefully avoiding the sentry.

He was greeted by a worried Jamie. "You've been away a long time." He looked at his watch; it was 4-30am. "Let's get away from this goddam hell hole and back to the ship for a bath and some clean clothes."

•   •   •

At 10am on Friday 27th March, Semmes closed his log book and looked at his senior officers.

"Thank you for your report, gentlemen." He looked keenly at the tall, thin Captain Keep, wondering if he could trust him. He then made a decision knowing that the Captain helped and revealed the whereabouts and exposed the position of the penal settlement.

"This is the plan. We will prepare for an invasion on this plantation if that is what this bugger Shimmon calls his business - it seems an armed fortress to me if it is guarded. First of all we have to innocently enter this stockade and I would suggest Jamie and Ryan, who seems to have made a quick recovery, should procure," he laughed, "- you know what to do - obtain a cart and donkey, dress as the locals, see the Quartermaster. Load it with plenty of fruit and cautiously enter the fort. You'll have to watch the language, perhaps it might be a good idea to take a local peasant with you, having well bribed him with gold pieces." He smiled. "It works wonders. When inside the compound make a contact with Wakefield and tell him our intentions and plans which will take place early on Sunday morning, which I hope may be a day of rest. We should be organised by then. Go to it, gentlemen, pick your teams, I wish you luck and a safe return."

In the dark on Saturday evening, four longboats grated on to the beach on this picturesque island bedecked with palm trees and fragrant flowers in the undergrowth. The forty crewmen and soldiers pulled the boats ashore. Ryan, Jamie and Keep led the way in the darkness, along the marked pathway, now and again lit up by the moon penetrating. the undergrowth from behind the clouds. They came to the main road. Jamie gave the order to Captain Francis: "Take your men and proceed to the right to the stockade. Jacko will lead the way; disperse in the undergrowth until the dawn when hopefully you see us sitting on a cart innocently approaching the fort. We will then discuss our plans for raiding the fort."

Jamie, Ryan and Keep made their way to the first shack. It was 3am. Suddenly a door opened, the three men froze. A middle-aged man appeared.

He was yawning and scratching his thick black hair. He made his way into the undergrowth to urinate.

"That seems reasonable," thought Jamie; he whispered to Ryan: "We will have a word with him on the way back."

The bewildered man shook with fright when Ryan presented a knife at his throat. Keep spoke in Spanish for several minutes. Ryan released his hold as the man seemed to relax and nodded his head several times.

"Show him some gold pieces, Jamie. His name is Rodrigo, of Spanish descent, and he's willing to help us."

The man's eyes bulged, he'd never seen so much gold. Keep continued the conversation with Rodrigo explaining the purpose of the raid and whether he could supply a donkey and cart loaded with provisions and accompany them to the stockade. He kept nodding his head and his face lit up when Jamie gave him two more pieces of gold.

So it was agreed, he would meet them in one hour and drive them to the fortress.

Just before dawn on the Sunday morning, Captain Francis and his forty armed men lay low in the undergrowth on either side of the road. From out of the gloom came the soft clobber of a donkey's hooves as the cart appeared with Jamie sitting alongside the driver and Ryan and Keep on the side with their feet dangling. They were dressed in peasants' clothes and had their faces darkened.

Francis approached Jamie from the undergrowth. Jamie gave instructions:

"We are going down to the fort. I might add that the local natives have no love for Shimmon and his men. So Rodrigo will be our passport for entry.

Hopefully if everything goes to plan, once we are inside I'll make contact with Wakefield. Ryan, incidentally is buried under the fruit and once inside the stockade will disappear and make himself inconspicuous near the prisoner's hut. Captain, meet Rodrigo.

He will return here and report to you. Find someone who can speak Spanish." Francis smiled. "That's no problem."

Jamie looked around. "I must hurry, it's getting light. Cover all the guards first; when you hear three shots from inside come hell for leather. After you have dealt with the guards outside, Ryan and myself will make sure the gates are opened and then it's up to you. Have you a spare pistol, Alan?" He thrust it into his belt and pulled his shirt over it. He jumped up alongside the driver who cracked his whip and the donkey moved slowly towards the fortress, his ears angrily twitching. It was daylight when they approached the gates of the stockade. As the guard approached, Rodrigo pulled up the donkey and spring he spoke in quick Spanish. He then produced a bottle of wine and presented it to the guard. He went to the wide, thick door and it was eventually opened when he banged on it with his rifle butt. They drove inside and stopped near a hut where gaunt faces suddenly appeared at an open window. Their sunken eyes told their story - this was the prisoners' hut. Jamie looked around and realised the camp was still asleep. He assisted the spluttering, smelly Ryan from under the fruit and he immediately disappeared under the raised hut.

"Where is Wakefield?" remarked Jamie to the faces at the window. One of the thin-faced men replied in a croaky voice: "He's in the next hut," waving a shaky hand in its direction.

"I'm an officer from the '*Alabama*' and we are here to arrange your escape. Carefully rouse everybody and be prepared to move out and attack the guards, when you hear three shots. There's a man under your hut, assist him through the floorboards and he will organise you."

"Move the cart," Jamie indicated to Rodrigo.

An armed guard appeared from a stone-built building; Rodrigo waved to him.

He slouched over and inspected the fruit. Jamie quickly smiled and offered him a bunch of bananas and Rodrigo reached under his seat and produced a large fish. The guard was satisfied and retreated and entered the guard house. Rodrigo flicked his whip and the cart moved to the next hut. Jamie began by calling softly through the tatty curtained window: "Wakefield!" He paused, then again - "Wakefield, this is urgent!"

"I'm Wakefield," answered the bearded Captain. "I'm Lieutenant Jamie MacPherson from the '*Alabama*' which is anchored six miles from here. We are here to release you from this hell-hole. When three shots are fired the stockade will be invaded by Southern troops. Do what you can in taking care of the guards. I'm going to move this cart and block the entrance to the guard house. We

don't want to take any prisoners - get the idea? Pass the word around. One of our crew is organising the men in the other hut."
"I don't know what to say," muttered Wakefield, "it's unbelievable - to get our freedom after all this time, there's certainly some reckoning to be done against this beast Shimmon." Jamie cut him short.
"Well, good luck, Captain, you will be safely berthed on a ship this evening."
He indicated to Rodrigo to move the cart and back it on to the guard house door.

In the meantime Ryan crawled on his stomach and when he was in the centre of the hut he began to bang on the floorboards to attract attention. He was rewarded, a hole appeared above him, he ducked his head and shut his eyes as he was showered with dust and a hand reached down. More boards were released and he pulled himself up and sat on the opening and eventually stood up and looked around. He couldn't believe what he saw - the skeleton-like figures, tattily clothed, mostly bearded, who had been in captivity for years. "We've come to liberate you. There's soldiers from the '*Alabama*' waiting outside the stockade, waiting to charge in, when they hear three shots fired. Those who are able, will you assist me by taking care of the guards that are on duty?" He opened his bag. "Here's some knives and coshes, we don't want any prisoners, is that understood? My job is to open the gates when the signal is given. Where's Shimmon?" - McPhie pointed. "In that house, along the road."

Ryan opened the shack door. The stockade was quiet except for three moaning men chained to a whipping stake. The gates were about 100 yards away. Two guards were on duty. They were relaxed, one smoking a cigar, his rifle leaning on the gate. Ryan moved along the side of the shack, followed by six prisoners awaiting their final opportunity;silently they rushed the two surprised guards and knocked them lifeless to the ground.

Jamie standing by the cart watched the action and immediately fired three shots as Ryan opened the gates and Captain Francis and his troops came rushing into the compound. The guards were surprised on opening the guardroom door to be greeted by a cart full of provisions - Francis and his soldiers immediately started shooting into the half-dressed guards as they came rushing around the cart, causing fatal casualties. The prisoners had gone crazy. They grabbed what weapons they could and rushed to the guard house after the firing ceased and engaged their enemy in hand-to-hand fighting. They might have been undernourished and weak, but they fought, very determined to seek revenge. They were a frenzied and wild bunch and the cry was "No prisoners!" Soon a quietness swept through the fortress, punctuated by the screaming and moaning of the dying.

Now they only had to account for Shimmon. Fifteen of the released men, led by McPhie, ran out of the compound along the road shouting, in a frenzy. They knew only too well where the notorious owner of the fortress lived. It is hard to believe that during this period Shimmon, sitting on his verandah, enjoying a cigar, was looking at his financial statements. He sniggered and thought: 'I reckon I'll be able to retire in six months. I will travel to America and try and find my wife in New Orleans, I wonder is she's still alive after eight years - at anyrate things are looking good. I had better go to the plantation.' He threw the end of his cigar away, stood up and yawned, strode from the verandah down the wide path leading to the main road to the plantation. By now the mid-morning sun beat down, the strange noises of insect and animal life he was accustomed to, suggested that everything was looking so peaceful and colourful after heavy rainfall. Then suddenly he was startled by shouting and clattering of weapons, and then a crowd of slaves rushing towards him, brandishing rifles, knives and pieces of wood, and screaming abuse as they realised who he was. He turned round hoping to run back to the house, but was greeted by his forewarned, aggressive-looking servants. He stopped, bewildered, frightened, looking around when he was grabbed and bound.

"Hang him, hang him," yelled the men. A rope appeared (from one of the servants as though he knew the outcome). Shimmon was dragged to the nearest tree, with a noose about his neck. The crowd were angry. Shimmon's slack mouth was dribbling saliva, he was shaken, bewildered, moaning, knowing his fate.

McPhie fired a shot to restore some kind of order. He shouted, while the slaves began spitting in Shimmon's face. "String the bastard up and good riddance," a man shouted. In no time the rope was thrown over a branch and Shimmon's legs were kicking their last protest. Eventually McPhie and his men returned to the compound. A crowd had gathered around the whipping posts where three men had been chained. Their shackles had been released and they were sitting as comfortably as possible propped against the posts and had been given water.

Captain Wakefield addressed Jamie: "There's a released officer here you might recognise, I've heard him mumble '*Alabama*'." Jamie gently raised the face and looked into the sunken, bleary brown eyes of - "Yes - it can't be - Joe Hardman."

All the Lieutenant managed was to grip his arm and simply murmur: "Jamie, Jamie lad - thank God you've come," his voice trailing away as he seemed to fall unconscious after the pain and endurance he had suffered. Jamie couldn't believe it. He called Rodrigo and gestured to him to bring the donkey and cart over. The two other skinny figures, their clothes hanging in tatters, were also gently laid on the cart alongside Hardman and escorted back to the beach and rowed to the '*Alabama*'.

Jamie stood on a cart in the centre of the stockade and was joined by Captain Wakefield. He addressed the assembly, men dressed in the grey of the South, seamen some still clutching rifles and belaying pins - a dangerous looking bunch.

"This looks like the end of the battle. Are all your men accounted for - Captain Wakefield and Francis?"

"Yes, sir, and ready to move out," answered Francis.

"Good, then this is what I would suggest, unless anybody has any objections.

We move the enemy bodies to the wooden huts and burn them, leaving no trace.

"Sir," - a tall skinny man held up his hand and in an American accent continued - "perhaps some of us might like to stay on the plantation and rebuild it and work the sugar and tobacco business, perhaps with some of the local people."

"That's a good suggestion. What is your name?"

"Bob Calder, sir, I was a bosun's mate on the '*Augusta*' - and I'm sure I would get some support from my mates, as we are well used to the working conditions we have been through and I'm sure we could make a living without slave labour and by treating people decently and humanely." The men cheered.

Jamie addressed Captain Wakefield and the men gathered around. "Let us evacuate this wretched place. Look around and see if there is any transport for the weak men. I would suggest to the men who are staying on to reside in Shimmon's house and on his estate employ some of the local labour to get them started, especially Rodrigo. He was the man who co-operated to make this raid successful." Again everybody cheered. "I think that's all. Let's get the hell out of here - let's go, men!"

The crackling of the burnt dry huts could be heard as the slow procession left the stockade fortress. The memories of the freed men who had toiled on the plantation, undernourished, beaten and ill treated, was bitter. One or two heads turned to watch the black flames of the funeral pyre rising and partially darkening out the sun. Most were bewildered, but all knew their thoughts were buried in the smoke. They were on the road to freedom.

The four longboats were ready at the water's edge. The Bosun's Mate had been forewarned that the escaped men were on their way from the fortress.

There was a shout as Captain Francis emerged from the undergrowth with a ragged-clothed man slung across his shoulders. Eager hands rushed forward to assist the weak men into the boats, which were soon loaded, when the last two, Jamie and Keep, emerged from the trees. They ran down to the beach and scrambled into the last boat.

Lieutenant Kelly, standing on the bridge of the 'Eaglet', turned to the Midshipman. "Mr. Owens, be prepared to receive the released men. The weak and the disabled are to be berthed in bunks. Doctor MacGregor and his staff are available to attend to any who are wounded and sick. When they have been housed the longboats will return to the 'Alabama', then signal Captain Semmes that we are ready for sailing and alert the Bosun to stand by."

"Aye, aye, sir." Young Owens was pleased he had been temporarily 'loaned' to the 'Eaglet' under Kelly as he was learning so much about seamanship from this exceptionally experienced officer.

• • •

Aboard the 'Alabama', Semmes was relieved when he saw the longboats despatching the men aboard the 'Eaglet'. Jamie climbed aboard the Southern raider, saluted the Captain and reported. - "Mission completed satisfactorily, sir and we have a very happy surprise for you. We rescued Lieutenant Hardman who was a prisoner in that bloody fortress. It's a long story and no doubt he will, in time, relate his adventures."

"Thank you, Lieutenant, you deserve a well-earned rest. I'll see you later in my cabin for a full report to enter into my log."

"Very good, sir," Jamie went below and collapsed on his bunk while 'Alabama' raised her anchor and together with the 'Eaglet' left the bay, both crews viewing what appeared to be a beautiful and peaceful island.

Semmes entered into his log: 'Successful raid on the bloody prison encampment on the island of Puerto Rico. The prisoners released - the fortress destroyed and partially burned - some approved men wanted to stay on and run the plantation. The Governor and guards eliminated. A new Governor elected name, Rodrigo De Santos, who assisted us in the raid. Captain Wakefield, his crew and the rest of the released men manning the captured.

Northern paddle steamer which is trailing the 'Alabama' as we cross the equator and proceed south west towards Brazil. Pleased to see the return of Lieutenant Hardman after his ordeal of being shipwrecked and imprisoned. Position this Friday 3rd April 1863 - 2° - 11' longitude, 26° - 02' latitude.'

The '*Alabama*', with sails billowing, sailed majestically along, ever on the lookout for the enemy. Three more ships were captured, the crew of the '*Eaglet*' ransacking and looting them, to replenish her stores and provisions.

Then they were put to the torch. The prisoners berthed on the '*Eaglet*', Captain Semmes, standing on the bridge, flexing his muscles and breathing deeply, was feeling happy; his plans were working satisfactorily. Joseph Hardman joined him.

"Pleased to see you have been restored to your former self, Lieutenant. When was the last time you were on board this ship?" Hardman stroked his bristly chin, reflecting. 'It must have been last October, when you elected me Captain of the '*Lamplighter*'. We sailed in convoy the '*Alabama*' leading the way, if you remember, followed by the '*Tonawanda*' and the '*Manchester*'. There was the raid on Dover. We took a number of Southern soldiers on board. We broke our formation and sailed into the Mexican gulf, hugging the coastline looking for a suitable place to land the released soldiers, which we eventually found near Charleston. With a skeleton crew and some twenty soldiers I headed for Jamaica, where according to your orders the three ships were going to rendezvous at the end of January."

"Yes, that was the plan," mused Semmes. "We were alarmed when the two ships didn't turn up - no doubt you heard Mr. Kelly's adventures and Mills'. It was a wonder the three of you survived. However, please continue."

"We survived a storm. The '*Lamplighter*' was a sturdy barque. We lost our sails, I couldn't furl them in time, with the small number of seamen. We helplessly drifted for a while, until a Northern gunboat, '*Montcalm*' approached and boarded us. We were taken prisoners. They sank the '*Lamplighter*', shots penetrating below the waterline and she slowly sank. We were ruthlessly interrogated by our captors, who showed no mercy. They detected our Southern accent. Some of the crew cracked and in no time our true identity was revealed. Then they really worked us over, beat us and starved us." Hardman paused, slightly overcome, he took a deep breath and continued - he faintly smiled "I suppose that is why I look so skinny."

"Oh, you will soon put that on," jovially remarked Semmes. "Run up and down the rigging, that will soon give you an appetite."

Still thoughtful, Hardman ignored the remark and continued with his story:

"One day our luck changed. A ship was sighted, the '*Augusta*' - a British ship."

"I'm beginning to understand now," interrupted Semmes.

"We were transferred. Captain Wakefield was annoyed and angry, the way we had been mistreated. We were given the very best treatment. Unfortunately there was no Doctor on board. We were made welcome and assured we would be taken care of, until we arrived at our destination in Kingston. We were approaching Jamaica, skirting Santo Domingo via the Mona passage. A storm arose and we grounded on a beach near Puerto Rico."

Semmes confined the conversation: "I am beginning to get the picture now, Lieutenant. You've had a very rough time, but I'm pleased to see you can resume normal duties."

On the 4th April a shout from aloft "Sail ho!" from Riordan - brig the '*Louisa Hatch*', her cargo a large haul of 800 tons of coal, was transported by every available boat to the '*Alabama*' and '*Eaglet*', the prisoners in their boats also taking part. When the transportation was completed the prisoners with their personal possessions were taken aboard the '*Alabama*' and their longboats secured astern.

Captain Semmes wrote in his log-book 'Torched the '*Kate Cory*', '*Lafette*' and the 16th whaler the '*Nye*'. The smell of oil was nauseating, with a number of barrels left on board - she was a beautiful sight blazing away. Experiencing April showers - looking forward to the hot dry sun.

Latitude 5° - 45' - sailing along the highway of Brazil - 26° - 4' longitude.

Captured the '*Doncaster Prince*', sailing from New York to Shanghai. Cargo - more coal! - transferred on aboard, together with her Captain - Walter Rogers - and his wife, twenty-five crew and some passengers. We now have 110 prisoners on board.

On the 3rd May the weather was fine - the '*Union Jack*' was captured with women and children on board and within two hours the '*Sea Lark*' from New York. An interesting prisoner was the Rev. Ian Mathieson from Albany, a New Englander, who was travelling to Foo Chow in China to take the post of Northern Consul.'

Semmes paused and smiled - must make a mental note - send him in the opposite direction and have a Southern Consul installed instead.'

After the torching of the '*Union Jack*' and '*Sea Lark*', the '*Alabama*' and '*Eaglet*' had 140 prisoners between them, so Semmes decided to head for the Brazilian coastline and disembark them at the nearest port, all but the parson!

Chapter 19

On the 3rd May 1863 the '*Union Jack*' was the forty-seventh ship to be captured, looted and burned.

Semmes decided to head for Bahia in Brazil to give 'Jack' some shore leave.

The harbour teamed with national shipping. Bahia was a well-known commercial town and Brazil offered the world her richest produce and minerals. The women and children were put ashore together with the paroled prisoners, only the parson remained on board the anchored '*Alabama*'.

The Captain was rowed ashore to visit the Governor and most of the crew to visit the wharf's tavern to indulge in the 'luxuries' of shore leave.

The uniformed Jamie was in conversation with the parson, both seated on the horse block, enjoying the brilliant sunshine, with a gentle breeze wafting from the Brazilian coastline.

"I understand you were baptised into the Presbyterian church in Scotland, Lieutenant?"

The relaxed Jamie, who was the duty officer, was whittling the shape of a ship from a piece of wood. He replied: "Indeed, I was born on a farm near Dunkeld and christened in the local chapel. We were a large family, five brothers and one sister. I was named after my father and I reckon I was his favourite son, but I left the life of the farm and started work at the age of fourteen working as a boilermaker on the Forth Bridge - I returned to the farm and worked for a while, mainly maintaining the farm machinery. I met my childhood sweetheart, Matilda, and we were married in the local chapel. It was a happy occasion; my brother William was best man." Jamie paused he had a choking sensation in his throat. He stood up and went to the ship's rail. He was overcome with emotion; he began to sob and held his head in his hands. 'What have I done with my life?' he thought, 'what a mess I've made of my life. Why am I confessing to this parson? But he seems a most understanding person.' But they were startled with a shout from the approaching gig boat which was returning from the Bahia wharf.

221

The Governor's aide-de-camp, Midshipman Willis, came aboard, and saluted the senior officer.

"Sir, I was an escort to Captain Semmes in the Governor's residence when he quietly slipped me a note which he said was very urgent and to take immediate action. I came as soon as I could." He handed over the small piece of paper.

"Thank you, Mr. Willis." Jamie moved away to the ship's rail, wondering what to expect in the Captain's note, which he opened and read the following:

'I have heard some disturbing news from ashore. The scheming Northerners have a secret plan to try and board and take over the '*Alabama*'. Alert Captain Butler and his marines and be prepared. I have contacted Captain Francis who is ashore and he will be available somewhere near the ship in the harbour to support you with his armed soldiers. If this attempted surprise coup should take place, fire three shots and our troops will come to your support.' Jamie walked swiftly towards the petty officers and firmly got things moving: "Bosun, we can expect trouble. Summon Captain Butler and Mr. Taylor and tell them to report to me immediately."

"Aye, aye, sir." Captain Butler reported to Jamie. "Captain, we've received a note from Captain Semmes; he's heard rumours that our ship could be boarded by Northerners. I want you to deploy your men around the ship, hugging the bulwarks."

Bellew scampered back to Jamie's side: "Bosun, place your men in the rigging with binoculars and have everybody alerted if three shots are fired. Then relax until dusk and then take up positions until you hear the signal."

Sure enough only the gentle lapping of the water against the ship's side could be heard as evening descended. In the distance the lights of Bahia twinkled together with the numerous ship's lights dotted around the harbour.

It was quiet and peaceful when a harsh whisper conveyed the approach of muffled oars: suddenly the noise of a boat grating the ship alerted Butler, who was crouched beneath the bulwarks with his men. There was a muffled clang-clang as grappling irons locked on the bulwarks. A woollen-capped head appeared, and an enemy's eyes took in the scene on the dark deck. Butler leapt to his feet and the crunch of a rifle butt cracking a skull was the signal for Jamie to fire three shots. Thirty men swarmed over the side on to the deck of the '*Alabama*'. The grey-coated marines engaged the enemy in hand-to-hand fighting. A dark-clothed man with a knife leapt at Jamie and they crashed to the ground and rolled around on the deck. The man bestrode Jamie, raised his knife in his right hand to strike him in the throat, when the Bosun swung his belaying pin at the enemy's head, kicked the body to one side and assisted Jamie to his feet. Then a seaman in a striped shirt swung a broadsword at Jamie. Jacko emerged and shot the man in the head with his revolver. Even so, the '*Alabama*' crew were being overwhelmed in numbers. So Jamie managed to climb the rigging and fired the distress signal for Captain Francis and his marines, who were expected to be somewhere near the '*Alabama*', to come immediately.

Men were shouting and screaming, shots were fired. The deck was littered with the wounded and the dead, when Francis with a sword in one hand and a revolver in the other went tearing into the enemy. His reinforcements quickly overwhelmed the Northerners. They dropped their weapons and raised their hands above their heads and surrendered. A quietness descended except for the moaning of the wounded, and order was restored. Jamie was grateful that the Bosun had saved his life and he thanked him. He then ordered Bellew to throw the enemy over the side and let them swim for it - or perhaps they had their own boats in the area and could be rescued.

Jacko came across the deck and asked Jamie if he was all right, to which he replied: "Thanks for coming to my rescue." It was understood, without sentiment. He then ordered him: "Arrange for the deck to be washed down and tidied up. Then go below and dress up in your uniform and we will go ashore and inform the Captain about what has happened - who, I hope, is with the Governor."

• • •

The small, fat Dominic Palazzio was the Governor of Bahia. He was seated comfortably opposite to Captain Semmes. They were both enjoying the finest Brazilian wine, served by a long-haired teenaged girl, dressed in a white low-cut blouse and short skirt. The Governor smiled, winked at her with his beady eye and patted her bottom. He spoke in a strange mixture of Argentinian Spanish. He had a waxed moustache almost the same length as the Captain's. He burst out laughing, stood up and pointed to their moustaches, indicating their length and proposed a toast. Semmes smiled, stroked his moustache and clicked glasses. A little later, when the maid had brought the Governor his papers, the Captain assessed him. 'Must be loco,' he thought, 'wonder what the bugger is up to rustling that damned newspaper!' It had Spanish headlines which he translated! The Governor's attitude changed!

'The Southern privateer has sunk Brazilian ships carrying coal to Britain!'

Palazzio stood up, his face full of rage. He slapped the table, pointing to the headlines and confronted the Captain ('The friendship and hospitality has disappeared,' thought Semmes. 'I wonder if I'm going to finish up in a filthy dungeon cell?'), and it seemed likely as the Governor clapped his hands, two armed guards came in, seized the Captain and marched him off, through the town, being dragged until they came to a stone and brick building and Semmes was flung into a cell and the iron doors clanged and were locked.

After a while Semmes gripped the iron bars of the open window and looked out, thinking, 'Must get a message to the ship.'

A small boy slowly passed the high barred window. Semmes whistled, the lad stopped and looked up. The Captain flicked a coin which the lad retrieved from the dust, examined it and looked up at the window, wide-eyed at Semmes, whose hands were gripping the bars. In his garbled Spanish he asked: "Can you get a message to the ship in the harbour - the '*Alabama*'?" (indicating the shape of a ship and pointing to the harbour!) There was a long pause. "Perhaps you have seen the sailors in the town?"

"Si, senor." the boy's face lit up and he smiled as Semmes tossed him another coin.

"Tell one of the crew and bring him to this window." He showed the boy another gold piece; he got the message - an extra reward! Semmes settled down, squatting in the dusty, smelly dungeon, which hummed with insects. Hours drifted by - it went quiet, the heat and the stench made him drowsy; but as it went dark quickly, there was a noise outside and when a voice whispered through the window - "Captain? It's Jamie with Jacko" - Semmes hoisted himself against the bars. "Listen carefully, Jamie, - we'll have to be diplomatic and bribe our way out of this situation. In the morning, go smartly dressed in a Northern uniform, and see the Governor and explain that you are from a Northern visiting ship in the harbour. Tell him there's a price on my head and that he is entitled to the reward. Give him fifty gold pieces for my release as you want to take me up North to be hanged. That should settle this matter. If he is hesitant give him more, anything to get me out of this hell-hole. I'll rot in here if nobody will release me!"

"Aye, aye, sir! And I've brought food and wine, and first thing in the morning I'll carry out your instructions. You will soon be released, one way or another! You can be sure of that!"

• • •

Next morning the Governor, puffing contented on a cigar was sitting in a leather chair, his feet on the polished table. He had just completed a hearty breakfast and between smoking and belching he was amusing himself in fondling the nipples of the dark-haired servant girl. There was a knock on the door.

"A tatty, uniformed guard, in a gruff accent announced: "The Captain of a North American ship - the '*Albatros*' to pay his compliments."

Governor Palazzio quickly stood up, brushed the girl aside, and waved his arm for her to depart. He then buttoned up his tight ill-fitting uniform. Jamie and Jacko in Northern naval uniforms, swords clanking at their sides, marched in, stood in front of the Governor's desk and smartly saluted.

Palazzio took a deep breath, gave a flick of his right hand to indicate a salute and settled back in his plush chair.

James addressed him in his best Spanish accent, having had lessons from the steward, Ramidios.

"Sir, I understand you are holding a certain privateer, attached to the Confederate States - a Captain Semmes, I understand, from the Warship '*Alabama*' which lies in the harbour?"

The Governor stood up, waved his arms, flicking the cigar ash anywhere on the thick carpet. Smiling, he showed his yellow teeth and inhaling deeply, remarked hopefully:

"Ha! ha! you have come to discuss the release of a prisoner - what price?"

Jamie nodded knowingly and smiled back, then he opened a small leather bag and counted out coins on the Governor's desk.

Palazzio's eyes boggled - he had never seen so much gold. He scooped it towards him and counted it himself - aye - fifteen pieces! ('This prisoner must be important.' His cunning beady eyes narrowed: 'I'll ask for more!')

He waved his arm in a gesture, sniggering, indicating it wasn't enough.

Jamie emptied the contents of the bag on to the table - another ten gold pieces; some rolled on to the floor which the Governor quickly retrieved. He then snatched the bag from Jamie's hand and commenced refilling it with the gold. He nodded, repeatedly signifying he was satisfied with the deal and then clapped his hands - his guard appeared.

"Go fetch the new prisoner from the jail. In the meantime, gentlemen, would you like a glass of wine?' Palazzio clapped his hands again and from the ante-room appeared the dark-haired maiden bearing an ornate tray of glasses and a bottle of wine. (This distracted the officers - Jacko's eyes boggled!)

'Must be his mistress,' thought Jacko. 'I wouldn't mind getting my hand down that blouse and up that skirt!' He was offered a glass of wine, he smiled and winked at her. He received a faint smile in return. All this masked the loud knocking on the door. Semmes was thrust roughly through it and staggered into the room, acting like a drunken man. ('Must be the wine,' thought Jamie. 'Look at his drooping moustache and torn uniform!'). Semmes, his hands tied, and head down, drooping, stood in front of the Governor's desk.

"Is this the man?" asked Palazzio.

Jamie stepped forward, clutched a handful of his Captain's hair, looked him in the eye and winked, then gave him, what seemed to be, a vicious slap across his face.

"Yes, this is the scoundrel that has sunk so many of our ships."

The Governor stood up and for reasons only he knew, left the room. Jamie and Jacko exchanged puzzled glances, wondering what to expect. Returning, Palazzio paused then waved his arms, scowling, and snarled: "Get him out of my sight!"

"Lieutenant Taylor," commanded Jamie in his best Northern accent, "call our guard and escort the stinking prisoner back to the ship. If he gives any trouble, you know how to deal with him." Jamie turned and saluted, and for good measure the Governor offered him a cigar! Ryan and Gow, dressed as Northern soldiers, bundled Semmes through the door and out of the building, passing the somewhat surprised but inactive Brazilian guards. Semmes pretended to stumble down the steps and he was manhandled into the waiting carriage, where to their surprise, huddled, in the corner of the carriage, was a young girl, her head and face partially covered.

The white horse was whipped and the coach lurched forward. Jacko produced a knife and cut the rope binding the Captain. Jamie offered him a tot of rum. He rubbed his wrists and smiled. "Goddam, look at my moustache and what a mess they made of my uniform." Then turning to the huddled and frightened figure in the corner of the carriage: 'Well, young lady, what are you doing here?"

"My name is Siebel" (speaking in French) "and I want to get away from that beast. He ill-treated and beat me, he's like a wild animal. Just before he came into the room," turning and smiling at Jacko "I overheard him say to the sergeant that once you were clear the soldiers were to kill you all - making it look like an accident while escaping!" She sat up and waved her arms. "You are heading into danger, turn back and take the left fork."

Without hesitation Semmes directed Ryan: "Get aloft, silence the driver and then take over the reins. Gow and the young lady will join you and she will direct you to a safe way to the harbour."

The carriage was lurching along when Ryan opened the door, glanced at the driver's back, and climbed on to the roof. Gow handed him his rifle, which he gripped by the barrel and methodically took a vicious swipe at the driver's head and leaned over so he caught the reins; then pushed the half-senseless driver off his seat and helped him (with his foot) into the shubbery on the side of the road. He then pulled on the reins, at the same time soothing the horse, and brought the coach to a halt. Gow helped the smiling Siebel next to Ryan and climbed up beside her.

"Geeup," clucked Ryan as he turned the coach around. They passed the partially recovered driver, who was moaning and holding his head. He staggered up to the roadside and commenced walking in the opposite direction, half turning and shaking his fist, waving and shouting.

"I wonder why he's walking in that direction?" remarked Jamie. "Are the Brazilian soldiers waiting to ambush us along that road?" He called up to Ryan: "Hurry, more speed, we could be having company." He thought: 'I might as well join them, and so he climbed on to the roof-top of the carriage and stretched out, lying on his stomach, clutching a rifle, watching through the dust created by the lurching coach. The white horse was at full gallop, foam streaming from its mouth, urged on by Ryan shouting and cracking the whip. Mounted soldiers were in hot pursuit and rapidly gaining, - Jamie was right - but they were half-blinded by the dust from the wheels. Bullets began to fly into and around the coach. Semmes lay on the floor, shielding the girl. He clutched a revolver, helpless to take part. The enemy galloped up, Jamie took aim and fired. A blue-coated Brazilian soldier swayed, dropped his rifle and toppled off his horse. Gow also fired and shot a horseman through the head, but by this time two soldiers drew alongside the lathered horse and one was about to leap on to its back when Ryan cracked the steel-tipped end of the whip across the soldier's neck. He screamed, clutching the wound, blood trickling through his fingers. It caused him to lose control and he fell off his horse. Gow shot the soldier on the left through the back and the two horsemen in the rear of the coach pulled up, realising it was useless to continue the fight so they turned around and galloped away.

Eventually Ryan pulled on the reins of the lathered white horse, bringing it to a halt. After a few minutes he leapt down from the coach and stroked and patted the sweaty beast in gratitude for a job well done. The young maiden, Siebel, conversed in French with the Captain, who was slowly recovering from his ordeal, advising him on taking a safer route back to the harbour.

227

There was a loose horse, which Gow mounted, and the carriage, with Ryan at the reins and Seibel beside to guide him, set off for the final journey to the ship.

Bosun's Mate Tyler, was standing guard on the wharf when the Captain and his party arrived. Semmes descended the wharf's stone steps to the waiting gig boat. In it was a young lad and Tyler explained his presence.

The boy said in broken Spanish: "Remember me, Senor? you gave me this" (showing him a gold piece) "to deliver a message which I gave to that man" (pointing to Jamie). Jacko came forward and explained to the Captain:

"He's right - Jamie and I were standing by that bollard when young Emanuel came and delivered your message."

"I understand, I am in your debt, young man" said Semmes. "How would you like to become a sailor? You look strong enough to climb the rigging."

The youth was speechless, but he obviously didn't need any more encouragement as Jamie gestured to follow him. Semmes turned round to look towards the coach and noticed Seibel seated in the driver's seat. He smiled and beckoned her down. She immediately jumped down, ran over and gripped his arm, her eyes pleading. He helped her down the steps to the gig boat, which got quickly under way to the distant '*Alabama*' lying at anchor in the harbour.

Semmes was greeted on board by the familiar sound of the Bosun's whistle; it was music in his ears!

"Welcome on board, sir, all hands have reported back to the ship. The vessel is provisioned, manned, steam on the main engine, awaiting your command!"

Mr. Kelly, we have two special guests on board - will you please arrange berths for young Emanuel and Seibel - bearing in mind she's a young lady and is to be treated with respect at all times."

"Aye, aye, sir." Kelly saluted and addressed the Bosun:

"Weigh up anchor, man the main braces and full steam on engines. 'Jack' quickly got to work, Mullard jumped on to the capstan and with his concertina led the sea shanties. The wind caught the unfurling sails. The '*Alabama*' bade farewell to Bahia and headed south to Rio de Janeiro. Captain Semmes wrote in his log: '25th May 1863 - Glad to be back on board ship to taste the smell of the briny after the Bahia misadventure! Boarded the '*Gilderslieve*' and '*Justina*' which I ransomned. During the night chased, ransacked and torched the '*Jabez Snow*' - carrying coal, replenished our bunkers. After another ten hours boarded and burned the '*Amazon*'. Then an English brig hove to and we transferred some prisoners and letters for home for a few of the crew.'

Mr. Freeman, seated in the officers' mess, was reading various captured newspapers.

"This is interesting and amusing, Jamie - it's headline news from Britain - 'Damage to Yankee commerce - danger from pirates.' He threw the newspaper on the mess table in disgust. "That's a laugh - I'm a pirate, am I? - Ha! - ha! I'll show the next ship we ransack who's a pirate!" (A prophetic remark as then came "Sail ho!" from aloft.) Captain Cyril Cobley of the Northern clipper 'Talisman' viewed the rapidly approaching warship on his port beam through his binoculars. He, too, had heard and read about the 'pirate' ship. Now it was reality, with its big guns amidships and smaller canons on the bulwarks. He was startled even more when a shell screamed through the masts tearing the canvas.

"Alter sails and heave to," he bawled to the First Mate. He had certain military cargo on board which would be valuable to the enemy.

"Mr. Smith," (addressing the first mate) "get the barrels of gunpowder on the blind side of the deck, puncture them and heave them over the starboard side pronto. It will be something less for the enemy." (There were guns and engine machinery for the gunboats in Shanghai in disguise well below deck, and just maybe they would be overlooked.)

Captain Francis, Carruthers and an escort were the first to board the 'Talisman' - Carruthers saluted Cobley: "This ship is now the property of the Confederate Government and you, Captain, and your crew, are prisoners. I demand to see your papers."

Cobley went to his cabin, opened his desk drawer and gave Carruthers the ship's papers. It showed the vessel shipping imperishable provisions to Shanghai. (No mention of the guns and machinery - Cobley had been alerted to keep it a secret until it reached its destination.)

Carruthers and the 'Talisman's' Captain went on deck. "We are going to burn your ship, Captain, and you and your crew will be safely escorted on to the 'Alabama'. Take your personal belongings with you and use your boats as they will be hitched astern of the warship, for your use when we sight land."

As the enemy crew were leaving, one of the last off - a small, thin man - addressed Francis in a Southern drawl: "I was born in the Southern States and I owe no allegiance to any flag." (He spat out a stream of tobacco juice and continued.) "I wouldn't put a match to this ship if I were you." Carruthers ushered the rest of the crew away out of ear-shot. The man had his full attention. "Just before you arrived on board the scene, we were busy heaving penetrated barrels of gunpowder over the side, out of your view -

and there's some still left on board! There could be one almighty explosion - also there are guns, ships' machinery, secretly hidden away below decks." Francis and Carruthers exchanged glances. The Captain nodded then made his decision. "Thanks for your information. What is your name?" - "Tickell, sir, - Roy Tickell." He jetted another stream of tobacco on to the deck, Captain Francis showed his authority and roughly ordered Tickell into the ship's boat while the boarding party prepared to set fire to the '*Talisman*'. Jamie came aboard and he confronted Francis: "Before you start looting and burning this ship, sir, there's something you ought to know. Her Captain has been devious and underhanded - and his papers are not in order!. A Southern sympathizer informs me there's gunpowder, ammunition, 6 twelve-pounder rifled brass guns, boilers, also valves and pipes for a gunboat in Shanghai - hidden in the holds."

"Hell, that would have been dangerous if we had torched the vessel." Tyler, Hedgecock" - Jamie informed them of what was below decks. "Take some men, search out these items and transfer everything to the '*Alabama*' and inform me on completion."

Jamie went into the Captain's cabin. All his personal belongings had been removed. He rummaged around in the cupboards and saw six volumes of Shakespeare's literature which he placed in a bag, together with a brass chronometer and double binoculars, which he fingered and focused with interest - seeing one for the first time. He also picked up some jewelry out of a drawer, which he pocketed. 'Come in handy some day,' he mused. 'What's this letter?' - it was from an army General advising Cobley if he saw an enemy ship to attack and destroy it using the twelve-pounders. On reaching Chinese waters if the cargo was still intact it was to be sold or bartered with the 'Taiplings' to help in their rebellion against China. 'The Captain will be interested in this letter,' which he pocketed.

Francis reported on deck that all materials and provisions had been transferred to the '*Alabama*' and the '*Talisman*' was ready for torching.

"Carry on, Captain," ordered Jamie. He climbed over the side, down the rope ladder and joined the gig boat. Once on board he approached Semmes, saluted and presented him with the Captain's letter.

"You know, Jamie, I think we'll eventually head for the China Seas and give these 'Taiplings' a little of their own medicine." He laughed and pocketed the letter.

Jamie was officer of the watch. "What's our latitude, Bosun?" - "Twenty-two degrees, sir." - "What does this climate remind you of, Stewart?" - addressing the young Midshipman.

"Back home, sir - typical Southern weather. I can picture the homesteaders from the South converging either on horseback, carriages, waggons or even walking to our farm for the harvest. We would enjoy feasting, drinking with home-made potent ale, followed by folk dancing led by old Hamish on his fiddle. It would go on until the dawn when all the grub and ale had been consumed and everybody tired out following the country dancing."

They were joined by Jacko - "My watch Jamie - the Captain wants to see you together with the senior officers. I have heard," tapping his nose - "that we might be going to the Indian Oceon and then on to China - so far away from home!"

"Gentlemen," Semmes addressed his senior officers, "this is the future plan of campaign" - pointing to a chart. "We will sail to South Africa to link up with the '*Agrippina*' and re-provision our supplies and ammunition, sail the east coast of Africa through the Mozambique channel, across the Arabian sea and re-fuel etc. on the southern tip of India, on to Sumatra and Singapore, ever-alert to destroy enemy shipping. That will be all, gentlemen, resume your duties."

Jamie was emerging from the Captain's hatch when from aloft came: "On the starboard beam a small fast barque!" The Northern flag was hoisted. Battle stations. The eager crew were soon at their stations. Jack loved a fight. The twelve-pounder gun was manned by Midshipman Owens assisted by the latest hand - Emanuel.

"Stand by to fire and exchange our flags," shouted Kelly. A blank shot halted the vessel, which hove to and reefed her sails. She was boarded by Lieutenant Armstrong. It turned out to be the 350-ton small barque, '*Conrad*'. It was boarded and the crew transferred to the '*Alabama*' and the prisoners were locked up below deck, guarded by Schmechel and a marine.

"Gentlemen" - Semmes gathered his crew amidships on the '*Alabama*' - "I plan to convert this vessel, the '*Conrad*', into a cruiser and appoint Lieutenant Hornby Lowe as Captain, assisted by Midshipman Owens as First Lieutenant.

(Stewart couldn't believe his ears.) "I want twelve volunteers of various trades.

First though we must appoint a Bosun. - how about you, Denemy? You are big enough and have a powerful voice." Before Paul could reply, Semmes butted in: "That's what I like, eager volunteers, that's settled. I'll leave the rest to you, Mr. Lowe, to pick the rest of your crew and perhaps there might be some from the *'Conrad'* who would like to continue? Of course they will have to be paroled and show allegiance to the Southern flag.

Her cargo unfortunately is wool, bound for New York. You will be provisioned and armed and the name to be changed from *'Conrad'* to" - there was a pause - "and some of you will know about the town on the banks of the Black Warrior River in *Alabama* - called - yes, Owens, you should know, yes! - the *'Tuscaloosa'*."

The weather the following day was idyllic for the commissioning of the new warship. Both crews in number one dress were assembled on their respective ships, standing to attention. Captain Semmes, smartly dressed, with his sword at his side, his buttons polished, stood facing the main mast. The neck of a bottle of best French champagne was secured by a thin rope to the mast. Semmes held the bottle, at the same time looking up at the masthead. "I name this warship - *'Tuscaloosa'* - the newest addition to the Confederate Navy and may God bless all who sail in her, and bring her safely to port after each voyage." The Confederate flag was raised and fluttered proudly in the light breeze. Lieutenant Owens fired a twelve pounder gun. Bellew, the Bosun, shouted: "Three cheers for the *'Tuscaloosa'*." Hats were flung into the air. The crews continued cheering. The health of the crew and the newly baptised ship was toasted with the extra rum served up by permission of both Captains.

Semmes shook hands with the new Captain, wished him luck and saluted. The two Confederate warships slowly drifted apart, both unfurled their sails, and to the singing of 'Dixie' they set off due east, hoping to rendezvous in South Africa.

•   •   •

A British paddle schooner was sighted and boarded by Lieutenant Kelly. She was returning to Rio de Janeiro because her engines needed an overhaul. Sixty-five prisoners were transferred together with their personal belongings, and their longboats. The temperature grew cold, the weather stormy; provisions were running low, also coal for the boilers. Seven neutral ships were overhauled, boarded and food was bought at a price.

On the 31st July a tall ship appeared on the horizon. The *'Alabama'* went in full flight and when she was captured and boarded, the *'Anna F. Schmidt'* proved the answer to the low-provisioned raider. She was freshly out of the Port of Janeiro. Being a paddle steamer her bunkers were full and her own crew assisted in removing the coal from one ship to the other. The paymaster, Unsworth, and

Crichton, the storekeeper, were overjoyed at seeing the vast amount of merchandise - mainly suits and woollen clothing, boots and shoes, ample food for the cook, crockery, lamps and oil. She was stripped naked and looted by eager hands. The prisoners were transferred across to the '*Alabama*' and the '*Schmidt*' torched. The Confederate raider continued on course to South Africa.
Chapter 20

Lieutenant Kelly, officer of the watch, was standing on the bridge, viewing through his night binoculars a large clipper about nine miles away. He alerted the Captain and ordered full steam ahead. The '*Alabama*' responded magnificently and the clipper soon came within firing distance. A blank shot was fired from the twelve pounder gun which whistled across her bows. Semmes was amazed when they were riding the waves almost alongside each other. He noticed and counted five gun portholes. He scowled and snarled at Kelly:
"Find out the name of the ship. It's certainly not a Northerner as we would be at battle stations engaging a formidable enemy."
Kelly picked up his trumpet: "What is your name and destination?"
"We are a British man-o'-war named '*Diomede*'. And who are you?"
"The '*Alabama*' - the Confederate raider."
Light-hearted conversation took place between the two crews - waving and cheering. They each separated and both disappeared into the night.

• • •

The temperature was very hot, the sea calm on Independence Day - 4th July. Semmes decided to hold celebrations with lashings of grog all round - why not? - his dedicated crew deserved it! Charlie Mullard sat upon the capstan with his concertina with Jaffee on drums. Ollie Butler blew on his pipes, it didn't matter that they were not the same pitch - jolly 'Jack' did not know the difference after a few jugs of ale. The singing and dancing went on till dusk, until their allocation of drink had been consumed, then they fell around the deck, bemused, drunk, or sleeping. Jamie, standing on the bridge, was officer of the watch, with Tyler at the helm. They kept the vessel on course, at the same time smiling or laughing at the antics of the crew, Jamie's foot rhythmically beating time to the pipes. He was joined by the smiling Captain who viewed the scene, with bodies strewn all over the deck, and remarked:
"After all we've been through, the officers and men deserve some relaxation, that is why, when we reach port, Jack can go ashore

and enjoy himself. Look at that fellow Ryan, propped up against the mast. He can ride a horse, handy with a knife, despatched some of the enemy with his gentle garrotte touch. He was the first to go into action - how he jumped on the whale lying alongside the *'Ocmulgee'* and bashed a chap's head in with the butt of his rifle - a great fighter. Glad he's on our side."

"Captain," - butted in Jamie, "Look at the smile of contentment on Fishwick's face. I'll never forget his charge at Galveston. Being a horse wrangler in Texas, he hurriedly trained ten men to stay on horses for the charge through the Northern camp outside the town and routed the enemy. And how Schmechel saved my life, when I was about to leave this life by being stabbed to death, lying defenseless on the ground."

Next morning it rained heavily and soon cleared the littered bodies on the deck. The *'Alabama'* plodded slowly along. That night another victim was despatched to a watery grave - the *'Express'*, all the way from South Africa, carrying a cargo of guano to New York was torched.

The *'Alabama'* sailed 900 miles across the Atlantic between 30° - 33° latitude, stormy weather, hurricanes, then a sudden change with hardly a ripple on the sea's face causing the sails to sag and droop, as though resting for the next exchanging of the elements. Jamie was talking to Grinham and Oliver Kee, who remarked: "We must be getting near land, look! - a seagull circling round the ship with its mate."

There was a buzz of excitement amongst the crew. Ryan remarked to his friend Gow. "Shore leave in South Africa - remember the Cayman islands and those lovely busty wenches." McPhie who was passing said "Show me the busty wenches: wish I could fill my hands full of them now." Gow remarked: "It won't be long now, I reckon this time tomorrow we'll be dropping anchor in Saldanha Bay. Knowing our canny Captain, he'll send scouts to reconnoitre Cape Town down the coast." McPhie butted in. " First, I suppose we'll have to patch the old girl up. Our ship has taken a fearful battering crossing the Atlantic and he'll probably beach her at high water."

It was early morning 30th July.

"Land ho!" shouted the excited Riordan. All hands crowded the main deck, to view about a mile away Saldanha Bay.

"What a beautiful, peaceful haven," exclaimed Carruthers. "Those craggy high rocks certainly give protection to the bay, and how picturesque those plants, trees and flowers."

"Look at those farmhouses. How could they live and survive in this barren rocky place," said Jacko.

There were no ships in the harbour as they approached. It was estimated by the First Lieutenant that it was high water, so it was decided to beach the '*Alabama*' on a part of the sandy beach to carry out as much underwater repair work as possible and then to refloat it on the next tide.

"Unfurl sails, Bosun. Proceed on main engines at a slow speed and we will beach her," - pointing "straight ahead." Jamie was leaning on the bulwarks admiring the picturesque scenery, when the Captain approached. "Jamie, will you organise a party to go inland to hunt game to replenish our larder. There's cows, sheep, rabbits, deer and ostriches. Be cautious, there's some ferocious wild beasts out there, including lions - so go armed and employ local huntsmen and," he lifted the telescope to his right eye and pointed, "I see a horse and wagon by the jetty. Hire them," he laughed, "I don't have to tell you how, you're experienced in these matters."

Kelly addressed Jacko "I want you to go fishing, so get organised."
"Lieutenant Armstrong, I would like you to organise a party to repair the ship and put that chap Brennan, the carpenter, in charge. He knows his job and will choose the right tradesmen."
Semmes summoned the Paymaster, Mr. Unsworth, to his cabin.
"I want you to go ashore and take a couple of men with you, I would suggest soldiers out of uniform. Hire or buy some saddle horses and proceed down the coast" - pointing on a chart on his desk to the '*Alabama's*' position in Saldanha Bay and drawing his finger in the direction along the coast to Cape Town. "I want you to contact the Governor. Tell him about the ship being in the Bay and arrange an appointment in two days' time for me to visit him officially. Find out all you can about the Governor and see if he's hospitable towards us and report back as soon as you can."
Unsworth saluted and departed.
Jamie mustered his team, including Alex, Ryan and the cook, Gillie, the expert meat slicer. They were rowed ashore to the jetty. Jamie flashed a gold piece and hired a horse and wagon; Ryan climbed into the driver's seat and with the crack of the whip they moved slowly along the beach to an opening in the rocky precipice.
"We'll have to find a guide," said Jamie. "We'll try the first farmhouse."
Johanne Hoffman, a Boer farmer, with grey sideburns and long beard, was saddling a horse in front of his barn, when the wagon driven by Ryan approached.
'They don't look like my countrymen, the way they are dressed - and that man with the rifle on his shoulder; I must take care,' he thought.

Jamie raised his right hand in friendship and, smiling, said in English, hoping the farmer would understand. "Good-day, my friend, I wonder if you could help me. I am an officer off the '*Alabama*' which is beached in SaIdanha Bay. My friends and I would like to shoot some game, hence the rifles. Would you like to accompany us by acting as a guide?"

Hoffman gazed with interest at Jamie's rifle. Jamie handed it to him and he looked at it with admiration, trying the breach and looking along the sights. He hadn't seen a modern repeating rifle before. He looked at Jamie and spoke in a mixture of Dutch and English: "Would you and your friends like to join my wife and I for a meal? Have you had your lunch?"

Jamie was relieved; he sighed - and thought: 'It must be my Scottish accent - thank goodness he's friendly.' - "Thank you, we would be pleased to join you."

The men from the '*Alabama*' didn't need much persuading in following Mr. Hoffman into the house. He introduced his wife, Ena, a small, well-built Dutch lady with a rugged complexion. She gestured where they should sit on forms around a long rough-cut table. The farmer clasped his hands and pronounced a blessing. The meal consisted of beef, potatoes and vegetables. Following a delicious meal concluding with fruit, the men sat around. Jamie offered the host a Virginian cigar and in return the crew members were invited to sample South Africa's finest wines.

Hoffman was pleased he had been approached to go hunting and announced they could start immediately and two horses were offered Jamie and Alex.

"I will be stopping at my brother Joseph's farm. He's an experienced hunter and I'm sure he'll be pleased to accompany us." For the next two miles the terrain was rough, giving way to a sweeping valley, where the brother's white-bricked farm was situated. Johanne warmly greeted his taller elder brother. They laughed and spoke in Dutch. Joseph hurriedly went indoors, threw some clothes into a bag and clutching a rifle went to the stables emerging leading a saddled, black gelding horse. 'What a magnificent animal,' thought Jamie. 'I wonder if I'll get a ride!' The party led by the two brothers led the way and left the farmhouse. The coarse grassland was replaced by luscious pasture land.

Large herds of sheep, cows, bullocks and small herds of horses grazed in this picturesque valley. It reminded Jamie of his own native land, just like the family farm. Leaving the valley the ground grew rough, and rocks strewn with trees replaced cultivation. The road ended. It was decided to leave the wagon. Ryan and Gillie rode double, minus saddle and with rifles slung over their shoulders. The party set off into the rough hinterland. Joseph carried a rope.

Johanne, leading the way into a clearing, suddenly raised his right hand and everybody stopped.

"There is a movement ahead, possibly a wild pig or boar - or be prepared in case it's a lurking mountain lion which will be poised, silently, in a tree or on a rock, ready to pounce."

A big pig was about one hundred feet away from the lead horse ridden by Johanne. The wild animal charged, passing alongside the horse, which had taken fright and nearly unseated its rider. Joseph, his brother, being an experienced huntsman, carried a spear. He charged after the pig and embedded the sharp-edged point into the beast's back. It screeched and rolled over. Joseph leapt off his horse and thrust a long knife into the pig's neck, killing it instantly. Gillie, the cook, was overjoyed as he jumped off his companion's horse. 'Our first kill," he exclaimed as he withdrew the spear from the pig and handed it back to Joseph. Suddenly the quietness was shattered by the roar of a mountain lion which leapt from a rock. It landed on Gillie's back and bowled him to the ground. They rolled over, the lion tearing at Gillie's leg. Everybody was completely surprised by the attack. Jamie withdrew his revolver, leapt off his frightened horse, ran over, gripped the struggling lion with his left hand on the back of the neck and shot it through the head. It snorted, blood gushing from its mouth and the dead beast rolled off the injured Gillie. Johanne took command as he tied a strong rope around the dead pig and the lion.

"We will make a litter for your friend and go back to the wagon and proceed in another direction."

Jacko, who had a knowledge of medicine, bandaged up Gillie's leg by tearing strips from his shirt. The party set off with an uncomfortable Gillie roped on a litter which consisted of two long branches attached to either side of a horse's saddle. They arrived at the wagon and Jacko and the strong Ryan tenderly lifted their injured friend on to soft brushes and leaves. Joseph led the way through the hilly countryside. There was a stream about half a mile away and Joseph raised his hand and everybody froze. Three deer were drinking from the sparkling flowing water. One stopped and twitched its ears. 'Must have smelt us,' thought Jamie. Ryan handed Johanne his repeating rifle who indicated by signs to take one animal each. The huntsman gave the signal to fire. A shattering volley echoed across the stream and down the valley. The horses snorted and reared, frightened. One ran off, but was quickly retrieved by Joseph. The deer were instantly killed, the huntsmen and officers being deadly shots. One fell dead into the stream, its blood trickling and trailing into the waters. The party quickly went into action, anxious to get Gillie to a Doctor. "We will return to the farm and by the time we arrive there, Joseph will have brought the Doctor from a neighbouring farm."

Ena Hoffman was awaiting the party. Darkness had suddenly descended, when the wagon drew in front of the farmhouse. The Dutch Doctor had arrived and Gillie was gently lifted into the house on to a bed and was given a sedative consisting of a glass of 'strong' rum from the flask which Jamie always carried.

The loaded wagon was unhitched and pushed into a barn and the party went indoors for a well-earned meal. Drinks were supplied by the host, who remarked:

"It's too late to return to the ship. A dangerous journey at night and you would be eaten alive by scavenging animals. I would suggest you bed down tonight and I will escort you back in the early morning. It will also enable your friend to have a restful night. The Doctor will renew the bandages first thing in the morning. Fortunately his injury isn't serious. In a month's time he will have fully recovered."

"We are very grateful to you and your wife, Ena, and we accept your hospitality."

The crowing of a cock at dawn aroused the crew members. Johanne had been up early and had hitched up the wagon and saddled the horses and added a dead sheep and some beef in a salted barrel. His wife had prepared breakfast consisting of sizzling beef and chunks of hot bread straight from the oven. Plates with large chunks of cheese and a variety of fruits were spread over the long wooden table. She banged a spoon on the back of a pan, a world-wide familiar sound. Gillie was sitting up in bed, when Ena served him some hot venison soup.

Following the breakfast the officers bade farewell to Ena. Jamie left five gold pieces on the mantelpiece above the fireplace, unknown to the farmer or his wife. He embraced the stockily built Dutch lady and thanked her for their friendship and hospitality. Gillie was gently laid on a rug in the wagon and as Ryan steered the horse through the farm gate Ena walked alongside and stopped and waved. The party followed Johanne who was riding alongside and conversing with his brother. The road was rough and stony and after about three miles they climbed the brow of a hill and there in the bay the '*Alabama*' rolled gently at anchor.

Gillie was gently lifted from the wagon, and carried down the steps to the waiting boat. Jamie and his friends thanked and bade

farewell to Johanne and Joseph, who presented him with a large, bulky parcel. Johanne smiled and said:
"A little reminder of your adventures on the hinterland!" They shook hands and the brothers wished the crew members bon voyage. As the loaded boat left the wharf, Jamie turned and waved to Johanne who was standing alongside his brother.
Captain Semmes summoned his officers into his cabin.
"Good morning, gentlemen, I would like to hear your reports, and would you make notes, Mr. Unsworth, for my log."
Lieutenant Armstrong was the first to speak: "The ship has been repaired generally, sir, except for repairs to the copper strips under the keel - this would have to be a dry dock job. Otherwise the vessel is sound, leaks have been repaired and the sails have been patched up. The guns are cleaned and ready for action."
"My report on the main engines is not so good," said Mr. Freeman. "I will need to replace two valves. I might be lucky if we capture a paddle steamer and if they have similar bore valves."
 Semmes smiled. "We'll see what we can do for you, Chief."
 Jamie continued: "We had an accident while out hunting. Gillie, the cook, was attacked by a small mountain lion and he's damaged his leg. His condition is satisfactory. We have enough fresh meats, and I understand fish, to last us several weeks. Incidentally, Captain, the huntsman presented me with a parting gift - the carcass of the dead lion, which the cooks are curing. It will make a carpet rug for your cabin." - 'What a creep,' - thought Carruthers.
"Thank you, gentlemen, everything seems ship-shape and we are ready for action." Semmes twirled his moustache - a nervous and agitated sign, when thinking. "This is my future plan. I've had an invitation to visit the Governor and we are sailing to the Cape of Good Hope for a few days. I want you to alert the crew to visit the taverns and find out any information regarding the war and any movements of enemy shipping in the area. I'll be visiting the Governor. Mr. Carruthers, Taylor and Jamie will be accompanying me in number one dress. That is all; full steam ahead to the Cape."
Lieutenant Eric Boyle and Midshipman Connolly were on leave in Cape Town from Her Majesty's Britannic Navy when they heard the exciting news that the 'Alabama' would be visiting Table Bay. They made their way out of town along the cliff edge accompanied by hundreds of people all with one aim - to find the highest advantage point. Some were walking, others on horseback, up the steep climb known as the Hill of the Lions. The oxcarts, cabs and horse-drawn wagons found the gradient too steep, so they resumed on foot. Eric offered his wide naval binoculars to his friend. "I think that is the 'Alabama' in the distance, but if you look a bit to

the right there's another ship racing under full sail almost parallel" Connolly butted in, lowering the glasses;
"That's rather unusual to be under full sail racing towards the shore, you would think they would reduce sail." They soon knew the answer. The quietness on this idyllic August day was shattered by the loud boom of a gun from the '*Alabama*' which aroused the hundreds of birds nestling in the cliffs. It also startled the people assembled on the hill.
Connolly was excited - "I see what has happened. It is definitely the '*Alabama*' by her Southern flag and a Northern flag is fluttering from the barque."
"Give me the glasses - the Raider is circling its prey - a boat has been lowered from the '*Alabama*' with soldiers with rifles and they are rounding up the crew." Connolly snatched the binoculars "Let me have a look. You are right. They must be a prize crew. That is how Captain Semmes captures and burns his enemies' ships, brilliant strategy - but wait, the Yankee is now turning around and heading out to the ocean and the '*Alabama*' is heading into the bay.
Shall we go down to the jetty, meet and converse with some of the crew?"

Captain Semmes, his buttons shining in the blazing sunshine, his left hand on the hilt of his sword, stepped ashore on the quay in Cape Town. He was accompanied by Carruthers, Jacko and Jamie. They were greeted by a large, cheering, Dutch crowd who had journeyed many miles when they heard the famous Confederate raider was visiting the bay.
A police officer stepped forward, confronting Semmes. He saluted. "I understand you have an appointment with the Deputy Governor?" His hand stroked his black beard before continuing, at the same time admiring the Captain's twirled, waxed, moustache. "The Governor is out of town, but His Excellency, Sir Reginald Gooding will be pleased to see you and I have asked to escort you to his residence. Would you prefer to travel on horseback or coach?"
"I would enjoy the coach ride, accompanied by Carruthers, but the other two officers I'm sure would enjoy horseback."
The dusty roadway leading to the Governor's mansion was bedecked with a variety of trees and colourful flowers in full bloom.
Ascending the mansion's steps, the crewmen were greeted by Sir Reginald and his wife who escorted them through the ornamental hallway and into a large lounge in which were seated

six gentlemen. Some were drinking wine, others coffee and the air held the tang of pipe and cigar tobacco.

"What a lovely aroma!' thought Semmes, looking suspiciously around the room. "I wonder why everybody looks so serious and hostile?"

The Police Chief, who already knew the officers' names, introduced them to the company: "Captain Semmes, you've already met the Deputy Governor. May I now introduce you to the North American Consul, and this is Mr. Cecil Roberts, a reporter from the local newspaper - I'm sure perhaps later you would like a private interview with him." The police officer continued. - "Joseph Hannah, Green Point Lighthousekeeper, our Customs Officer - Mr. Reginald Griffiths, The Signal Officer from the Telegraph Station - Mr. Roy Boot, and Captain Derek Arnold of Her Majesty's Britannic Navy."

"Please be seated, gentlemen, and what would you like to drink Captain, and your fellow officers?" said Sir Reginald.

Semmes smiled. "I'm sure we would like some of your delicious home-made wine." He fingered his moustache and thought; 'I don't like the look of some of these fancy dressed men. There seems to be something sinister about this meeting.'

After the tobacco and wine had been served by the butler, everybody seemed to be eyeing each other up, until the Deputy Governor spoke up: "I have gathered everybody together gentlemen, you might say under false pretences. Captain Semmes, you have been charged with a serious legal allegation by the Northern American Consul and you have been invited to this meeting to defend yourself. The charge is, violating the neutrality laws of this country by capturing a Northern ship, the 'Sea Bride' in territorial waters."

'That's rather interesting,' thought Semmes. 'At last we are getting round to the reason for our visit to this friendly meeting in an underhanded sort of way!'

"The Northern Consul will address the meeting."

'Looks like a court case against heavy odds,' thought Semmes, 'and he looks a shifty-eyed sort of bugger.'

Mr. Appleton was a stocky, well-built, middle-aged man. He flicked the ash off his cigar and in a sneering Yankee accent, snarled, addressing the bewildered Semme; "How dare you attack an innocent Northern ship and sink it? You should be had up for treason by the British Government and I demand of you," pointing a finger at the Deputy Governor, "to arrest that brigand and his crew and clap them in jail and confiscate their ship."

"Rather harsh words, Mr. Appleton!" Sir Reginald seemed annoyed at the outburst, "but you must constrain yourself. This is not a public court. I'm just trying to sort out the facts before I make a decision. I'm sorry to hear one of your ships was sunk in neutral waters. Were you a witness to the sinking off Robben Island?" There was a long pause and before Appleton could reply, Mr. Roy Boote intervened: "I am the watchkeeper at the Lions Rump Telegraph station. I sighted the '*Sea Bride*' and signalled her to display her flag, which she did, displaying a Northern flag. The Southern raider swiftly approached Robben Island displaying a British flag! It suddenly fired a shot at the '*Sea Bride*' at the same time exchanging the flag for a Confederate one. She then launched her boats and boarded the helpless Southern ship. It then turned round and headed out to sea after the boats returned to the '*Alabama*'. This so-called battle all took place about four miles from the coast."

The reporter, Cecil Roberts, was writing furiously when he suddenly stopped and asked:"Can anybody explain to me the distance of the limits of the neutrality laws?"

"Yes" two people spoke in unison - "It's a league." - "Thank you, gentlemen, that is three miles, is it not?" - "Yes," replied the lighthousekeeper, "I watched the battle through my telescope. It was five miles off the mainland."

"Ridiculous, I have first-hand knowledge. It was only two and a half miles," thundered Appleton.

"Who are your witnesses, Consular?" inquired Semmes - "Surely not your countrymen on board the '*Sea Bride*' - have you contacted them? They should know the distance!"

"I saw the smoke of the '*Alabama*' and when the gun was fired, the distance was about five and a half miles," butted in the Customs Officer. "I was standing at Point Green. The '*Sea Bride*', after it was boarded, came within two miles of the shore, then turned round and went off to sea."

"There, I told you" Appleton leapt to his feet - "it came within the league! What further proof do you want, Governor?"

"I don't think you are quite correct - two miles off the beach, you said, Mr Hannah," the uniformed British Captain, Derek Arnold, spoke softly. "I witnessed the capture of the '*Sea Bride*' by the Confederate raider as I was on board my own ship, the '*Audacious*', sailing nearby and it was well outside the neutral limits - I would say about twelve miles out. That is what I logged in my book and was witnessed by most of my crew, who couldn't believe the devious and cunning way the flags were exchanged. I must try that myself sometime!" Everybody in the room sniggered, except Appleton.

"Well, that settles everything" said Sir Reginald Gooding.

"I strongly protest!" shouted Appleton. "That man there," pointing to Semmes, "should be jailed with his crew and the ship sunk, or confiscated." The angry Confederate Captain stood up. "Mr. Appleton," referring to the Northern Consular, "If you ever put to sea I'll hound you and string you up on the yard-arm, and that's a promise."

"The enquiry is closed," said Sir Reginald. "Feel free, gentlemen, to taste our delicious home-made wine - and, Captain Semmes, I command you - after you have provisioned your ship - leave South Africa. Good day to you, sir."

Semmes put his glass down, put on his peaked hat, stroked his moustache, half-sniggered, saluted and left the room with his officers. "I'd like to get my hands on that scoundrel, Appleton," said Carruthers. "Be patient," said Semmes smiling, "you might one day."

The 'Alabama' crewmen returned to their ship to be greeted on board by hundreds of the local people who had besieged the warship, excited about being on board this famous raider. The crew were in a merry mood, trying to escort the locals around and explaining in blurry tones about the rigging, guns, and the engine room.

In the Captain's cabin, the steward with the help of the newly appointed cabin girl, Siebel, were busy arranging in vases the bunches of flowers strewn around the cabin, when in burst Semmes - his eyes opened wide. "This is not all, señor," blurted out Ramidios. "I don't know where to arrange the amount of fruit and other gifts the visitors have brought on board."

"Very well, carry on both of you, I'm glad to see you working, Siebel, I don't know what to do with you." She looked at him with wide pitiful eyes and spoke in French "Please don't send me back to Bahia, monsieur," she smiled. "Why not marry me to one of your handsome officers - say, Jacko, and put us ashore. I would be very happy living in South Africa with him - he's the only friend I have in the world!"

Semmes stroked his moustache at this unexpected news. He sniggered and thought "Trust Jacko, the handsome bugger! - why not me?" - he smiled - "I'll think about it, carry on with your work, and clean up this mess, I've a lot to do." He looked around, the smell of the flowers overwhelmed him - as well as the noise on deck! "Down to business!

Ramidios, ask Mr. Kelly to attend, also the Bosun."

"Gentlemen, we are not very popular with the local dignitaries and we have to leave these shores immediately, naturally with the 'Sea Bride' trailing behind. At the meeting this morning, certain people, especially the Northern Consular, requested in strong terms that we should all be jailed and our beloved vessel confiscated. I'll show the bugger!" He went red in the face and smacked the desk with his right fist, causing the vases to wobble. "And yet I can't understand it, how the local people have shown their friendship and kindness by visiting us." He turned to Kelly. "Is the ship provisioned and ready for sea, Lieutenant? Good, well, I'll leave it to you, gentlemen, to clear the ship in a quiet and friendly manner and we'll sail on the evening tide. Do we need a pilot?"

"No sir, we are over a league from the shore!"

Jacko was standing by the main mast, describing the sails and the masts to a small crowd of the local interested farmers, some of whom had never been on board a ship. He noticed Siebel on the fringe of the crowd listening intently.

Their eyes met and she smiled and raised her right hand to her mouth and blew him a kiss, which Jacko acknowledged.

"Would some of you younger, strong men like to climb the rigging with the help and guidance of some of our crew?" While six men rushed towards the rigging, Jacko made his way towards Siebel and kissed her warmly on the lips.

She wrapped her arms around his neck and smothered him with kisses. His right hand squeezed her warm left breast. She became very passionate and Jacko thought; 'She's a great lover, this French wench, the sort I would like to settle down with. We would have the rest of our lives to get to know each other. It would be nice to go and work on the farm where Jamie found that friendly hunter and his wife, until we found a place of our own.' Jacko, stirred, took her hand and led her to the empty aft and speaking in a mixture of English and French. said "Listen, my love, I'd love to be with you always, but I must have a word with the Captain, because I am duty-bound, being an officer in the Confederate Navy, and I would like to get away from this war!" She grabbed his arm. "Let's go now, I have work to do in his cabin and I'll be present while you talk to the Captain." Ramidios suddenly appeared on the deck requesting Jacko to report to the Captain.

"Lieutenant," Captain Semmes addressed the young officer "I'm looking for a reliable person to represent our country in South Africa; if you like, an unofficial Consular. The job would consist of listening and noting anything relating to the war. I might add the war news is not good. In other words I'm looking for a spy in the town and you will be well rewarded. I propose to go to China via the Indian Ocean and will be returning via this route. Also write and keep in touch with Joe Mills in Kingston." Semmes stopped and smiled. "I also understand there's a certain young lady would like to join you. Think it over, discuss it with Siebel and let me know your decisions."

There was a knock on the door. It was Jamie with the Hoffmans. "I'm pleased to meet you, Mr. and Mrs. Hoffman." Semmes shook hands with Johanne and kissed Ena's hand. "Jamie has told me all about your adventures in the Hinterland and I thank you for the care and attention given to our cook. I am pleased to say he's improved satisfactorily and is in fact back on duty. Also I would like to thank you for your gifts of meat, fruit and wines." Semmes gathered his thoughts and addressed Mr. Hoffman "I would like to speak frankly. - I am leaving one of my officers in Cape Town, looking after our interests - if you like, an unofficial Consular or" - he laughed "a spy, if you like."

Hoffman smiled "And you would like me to help by offering him our hospitality." - 'Gosh, he's quick-thinking.' - "Thank you, Mr. Hoffman - could you offer him work on your farm as I know you are situated near to the town. Also would you consider offering a job to young Siebel here?" - indicating the smiling, handsome, Brazilian maiden. "You see," he paused and smiled, stroked his moustache and continued, "she assisted in saving my life in Bahia and she would like to accompany and be a companion to Jacko - who will be our representative ashore." Ena Hoffman, who had been listening intently, walked across the cabin and offered her hands to Siebel, which she accepted, and looked into buxom Ena's friendly eyes. Ena put her arms around her and said "I would be pleased to take her to my home."

"Well, that's settled," said Semmes, turning to Jacko: "Lieutenant, will you collect your personal belongings, see the Quartermaster and ask him to outfit you with some good wearable clothing. Say your fond farewells to your friends and report back here."

The party left the cabin and assembled near the companion-way. Jacko confronted Captain Semmes: "Did the Quartermaster provide you with some fancy clothing, befitting our Ambassador ashore?" "Yes, sir."

Jacko was overwhelmed. "Well, here's another gift" handing him a brown leather pouch containing gold pieces. "Perhaps when we return in a few months' time you might be happily married - and settled down." Semmes shook his hand. Jacko thanked him, saluted for the last time, and made his way to the main deck where he joined Siebel. Jacko's friends had gathered around as the news of his departure quickly spread around the ship. Jamie looked into his friend's eyes. Words didn't come easy for Jacko's hasty and sudden departure. They solemnly shook hands and wished each other luck.

245

Siebel put her arms around Jacko's neck and kissed him. They were showered with gifts from the crew members who were cheering and wishing the young couple every happiness. The crew lined up to kiss Siebel, (something 'Jack' enjoyed), then her handsome, happy lover tore her away from the clutching, groping hands of his mates. As they were being slowly rowed away from the ship, they waved farewell and were greeted by loud cheering from the men from the '*Alabama*' as they moved towards the wharf to start a new life with the Hoffmans in a strange land.

"I'll miss Jacko," said Jamie to Carruthers, "as I introduced him to this ship and we served in many adventures together." - "Aye, but we'll see him on the return journey."

Captain Semmes was writing in his log. 'Due to adverse publicity regarding the capture of the '*Sea Bride*' we are sailing to Simonstown Bay to complete our repairs.'

There was a knock on the cabin door. It was Jamie, the officer of the watch. "Sir, we've just received a message from the signalman at the Telegragh Station to say there's a fierce storm brewing up and to take precautions. It has also been confirmed from the British warship, lying on our port beam."

"Very good, Lieutenant, alert the crew, take the necessary precautions regarding the masts and let go another anchor. Make sure all materials and guns, etc are secured and the ship battened down to weather the storm.

One good thing - most of the men are ashore, so they will be safely housed."

"Sir, we've just taken on board a spare anchor and chain from the lightermen who are cruising around the harbour attending to and providing for the needs of ships in trouble."

The storm lasted three days. Huge waves which seemed to commence a few miles out to sea descended with great fury from the south-west, battering the ships in the harbour and hitting the wharf and landings with tremendous force, cascading and flooding the buildings and warehouses dotted along the sea front in Cape Town.

The '*Alabama*' was three quarters of a mile from the town and weathered the fierce and ferocious gale and heavy rain. One barque, lying too close to the town, was swept along the bay on to some rocks, and wrecked.

The next day the weather was calm and the sun beat down.

Semmes summoned Jamie: "Will you go ashore and round up the crew as we will be leaving the bay in the morning, and while ashore arrange for a Pilot. Also ensure we have enough provisions to take us to Simonstown Bay as we have to purchase some engine parts in the British naval dockyard. I also hear from Chief the fresh water condenser needs attention." "Very good, sir."

It was a fine morning on the 9th August when the Pilot stepped aboard and saluted the First Lieutenant. The '*Alabama*' up-anchored and with the Southern flag proudly fluttering in the light breeze steamed out of Cape Town Bay.

Chapter 21

Eighteen sea Captains had the same idea, anchoring from the storm in Simonstown Bay; eight being British ships of Her Majesty's Britannic Navy.

Donald Hughes, a British Naval Pilot, had received a signal from his station that the *'Alabama'* had been sighted. He sailed in the direction of the outer harbour to board the Confederate raider to guide it safely into the safe haven.

Captain Semmes wrote in his log; 'The Northern brig *'Martha Wenzel'*, her cargo containing rice, being six miles within British territorial waters, was released, to the astonishment of her Yankee Captain!'

There was a knock on the cabin door. He noticed the speed of the ship had decreased to about four knots.

"Sir, the Pilot is on board."

Semmes immediately went on deck and introduced himself to Mr. Hughes and remarked to him when they were anchored: "I've never been surrounded by so many warships!" - he sniggered . "I trust they are all British and not damned Yankees as by tomorrow morning we could be blown out of the water!"

The Pilot smiled. "Have no fear, Captain, I can assure you that your vessel is quite safe in the bay - in fact I can see a Naval boat approaching." He shaded his eyes from the glaring September sunshine.

"It's the British Admiral himself from the *'Wyvern'*. By the way, Captain Semmes, I piloted one of your warships - the *'Tuscaloosa'* - into the Bay a few days ago and there she is" - pointing "lying at anchor near H.M.S. *'Scorpion'*". "Thank you Mr. Hughes" Semmes was pleased the other Southern Raider under the command of Hornby Lowe had survived the recent severe storm.

He beckoned the First Lieutenant, "Mr. Kelly, a British Admiral is approaching. Turn out the guard of honour, we shall certainly give him a warm welcome."

A tall bearded naval man, accompanied by his officers, was piped aboard the Southern warship. He confronted Semmes and saluted - which was smartly returned. "Waldrop Wishart, sir, of Her

Majesty's Britannic Navy, and may I introduce Captain Howard
Woods of H.M.S. 'Scorpion' and my fellow officers."
Semmes shook his hand.

"Welcome aboard, Admiral, please come to my cool cabin, and
partake of some of the Jamaican wine. You must be thirsty. The
temperature is high - what we would expect in this part of your
lovely country." He gestured to Jamie - "Escort and attend to
Captain Woods and his fellow officers." "What a lovely scented
smell, Captain Semmes." Even Jamie was overwhelmed; Howard
Woods commenced sneezing. Ramidios served the guests with
wine and cigars when they were seated. The Admiral opened the
conversation: "Delicious wine, and I must congratulate you,
Captain Semmes, on your victories at sea. How many is it - forty-
odd of your enemy ships sunk? amazing - I have followed your
career with interest, but I must say," with a laugh and another sip
of wine, it was only what I've read in Northern newspapers and
local gossip from other Northern ships. You are the terror of the
seas, sir, and I'll drink to that". The cabin rang with cheering and
toasting Captain Semmes.
   "I might add," butted in Captain Woods, "what I've heard is the
way you duplicate flags. The Yankees are confused and scared
about displaying flags."
   There was a knock on the cabin door, which Jamie answered.
"Sir," addressing Semmes, "His Excellency, Sir Reginald Gooding."
"Good heavens, I didn't expect we would meet again. Show him
in." The red-uniformed Mayor stepped into the cabin, doffed his
feathered hat and greeted Captain Semmes with a firm handshake.
   "Don't be alarmed, Captain, I haven't come to arrest you. I know
I commanded you to leave these shores." He smiled. "That was for
the benefit of the Northern gentlemen present. I have the greatest
respect for you, sir, and you are welcome anytime. In fact I have
arranged a banquet and dance for you and your crew for tomorrow
evening. I can assure you, sir, that bugger - pardon me swearing -
Appleton will not be invited."

   Semmes was astonished at the sudden and strange turn of
events. "Would you like some of our fine Jamaican wine, Sir
Reginald?"
"Excellent, may I propose a toast to you and your ship, the
'*Alabama*'." Glasses clicked. Semmes raised his glass in the Mayor's
direction.
   "My officers and myself would be pleased to attend the banquet
and thank you for inviting us."

"Splendid, I'll have carriages awaiting you at, say, seven o'clock tomorrow evening. You'll be most welcome, and of course the Admiral, and your Officers."

He laughed - "I'll have to arrange for some lovely young ladies to be present - but that shouldn't be difficult, they'll be flocking when they hear who will be coming!"

The Mayor stood up. "Thank you for your hospitality, Captain; I must take my leave. There are numerous arrangements to be made for tomorrow night."

The Admiral and Captain Woods, together with some of the visiting officers, stayed for lunch, ably served by the chefs and Ramidios.

Semmes faced his senior officers after the distinguished guests had departed.

"It always surprises me how well we are received. I suppose we are the underdogs in this war - well, we lose some battles and gain others - it's hard to tell. Look at our losses - Antietam - 25,890; Stones River - 25,565; the seige at Vicksburg - 31,279; Gettysburg - 31,625. Total loss 115,100 as against the enemy's 6,000 losses. Discussing with the Admiral, the turning point was Gettysburg, with General Pickett's charge - the 46th Southern Brigade's cavalry took part in that famous charge on July 3rd. Two regiments out of the Virginia Military Institute - raw recruits - survived out of thirteen. The total loss at Gettysburg - 55,000 - what a loss of life! There's one thing - we have never lost a civilian prisoner on any ship! Well, let's finish on a happier note, we have been invited to a banquet and dance at the Mayor's residence tomorrow evening and naturally I'm looking for volunteers to man the ship."

"I would like to be the first." Mr. Freeman stepped forward. "Parties are not for me, I'd sooner stay on board. Anyway I have to stay on board as I'm having problems with the fresh water condenser."

"I'll assist you, Chief," said Alex. "I'll be a watchkeeper," volunteered the Bosun, "and I'll ensure the ship is manned for the next three days."

"Well, that's settled," said Semmes. "Mr Kelly, arrange for shore leave for the men."

Jamie, chatting in the Engineers' mess to Carruthers, laughed and remarked: "I suppose you will be the first ashore to get your huge hands on some young maiden's bosom?'

'Well, do you blame me? The Sullivan girls took some beating in Jamaica! and we havn't got Jacko, he's got his hands full!" They both laughed. "I'll miss him," said Jamie. "I introduced him to the ship, I hope he's present."

The Mayor's residence was situated on a large estate, between Cape Town and Simonstown. Drinks were being served by black servants in the luxurious large banqueting hall.

Captain Semmes, smartly dressed in white uniform, buttons shining, epaulettes showing his rank, wearing a mauve sash, was greeted by Sir Geoffrey Tym and his tall, slim wife. They were served with white wine. Jamie and Carruthers drifted and introduced themselves to two British Naval officers.

"We watched the capture of the '*Sea Bride*' through a telescope on the Hill of Lions yesterday morning," remarked the smiling Lieutenant Eric Boyle. "Heard the sound of canon fire and saw how you boarded the ship."

Lieutenant Norman Connolly butted in: "Are all your battles so easy?"

"I would say we trick the enemy," said Jamie. "We have sunk fifty-five enemy ships and had one actual naval battle against the '*Hatteras*'. I'm not telling you how we did it - that's our secret." They all laughed. "You might go and copy us when you go to war!"

"I don't think so," Lieutenant Connolly suddenly butted in. "We belong to the Naval Attache, liaising with the Governor."

The conversation ceased when dinner was announced. Four young ladies descended on the naval officers. "We have been requested to escort you to the table," remarked a well-built young lady with flaming red hair. She linked Jamie's arm and together with the other three officers seated themselves opposite the Mayor and his wife. "My name is Margaret, you have already met my father, the Admiral of the Fleet, but I don't think you've met my mother, Christine."

Jamie stood up and formally shook hands with the handsome lady. The light-hearted conversation between the Mayor and those seated opposite was about the war, the background of Jamie and Carruthers and farm life in Scotland and Birkenhead. On the table was cooked every known local bird, meats and fish and the finest South African wines, supplied free by the local Boer farmers.

"I'm full," said Jamie. He laughed. "An excellent meal, thank you for inviting us. I'll be putting on weight and I won't be able to climb the mast in quick time under the command of the Bosun." He smiled. "Do you know, if you are slow, he'll come after you and tan your hide with his thick knotted rope, irrespective of rank. Even the Captain has experienced the wrath of the Bosun. It keeps you fit and healthy!"

"Perhaps you would like to see the gardens, James," said the smiling Margaret on the conclusion of the meal. The gentle breeze wafting from the Hinterland intermingled with the aroma of the sweet

251

scented flowers. She held Jamie's hand. (She was feeling romantic, he thought just the opposite.)
"I like your Irish accent," she said. "What kind of flowers do they grow in Ireland?"

"Shamrock - actually, I was born in Scotland and we grow the thistle, which is our national flower - well, it's not a flower, if you fell on it you would feel uncomfortable." He laughed, being reminded of his childhood. "In the woodlands in Perthshire where I lived as a boy, you could picture the woods and the meadows - they would be paved in a lovely carpet of primroses."
'You sound poetical and romantic. Do you like poetry? - Let's go to the summer house - there, by the lake, there's nobody around" - pointing - "and you can recite to me some of your lovely Scottish poems!"
They sat on a bench side by side, she turned and looked into his brown smiling eyes and thought: 'He's a handsome lad in that white uniform, I wonder if he's married I suppose he is and with a family, but still I don't want to know I'd like to hear him recite.'
"We have a river called the Afton in Scotland and Robert Burns would sit upon the banks and write his poetry. He had a sweetheart named Mary and one line goes like this:- 'My Mary's asleep by thy murmuring stream, flow gently sweet Afton, disturb not her dream.'
- Another line; - "There oft, as mild evening weeps over the lea. The sweet scented Birk shades my Mary and me.'
"You recited that beautifully, Jamie! Will you make love to me?"
She smiled, stood up and placed both arms around Jamie's neck and kissed him passionately on the lips. She was breathing quickly, smothering his face with kisses. He responded, the last time he had made love was to his wife in Liverpool many months ago. Being in the arms of a passionate lady made him respond - he fumbled clumsily with her low-cut blouse, his groping right hand soon fondled her big left breast. She breathed heavily, her bosom rising, nearly bursting through her blouse. His finger tips found her nipple which felt like a small strawberry. He squeezed it gently. Her mouth opened. She sighed and moaned, tossing her long red hair behind her back. She was in dreamland, never having experienced anything like it before. She gently thrust him away and said in a whisper. "There's a small room through that door with a soft couch. Come, my love."
She opened the door into an octagon-shaped room with a skylight which the moon penetrated, lighting up the three cane chairs and a large cushioned couch.

"Let me undress you" said the smiling Margaret. The tanned, muscular Jamie stood almost naked before her. She slipped off her blouse and the long blue skirt followed. Jamie knelt down and wrapped his arms around her buttocks, burying his head in her soft, warm stomach, which he smothered with kisses. His lips soon found her ripe, red nipple which he sucked into his mouth. Her hands gripped the back of his head, her groping finger tips slowly moved down his back and rested between his muscular buttocks. He smothered her with kisses on both breasts from one nipple to the other and then on her ruby red lips. He smiled and looked into her blue dreamy eyes. He lifted her into his strong arms and gently laid her on the couch. She raised her arms above her head and ruffled her long red hair. Jamie stood and admired her lovely rounded figure, as the moon flittered across her body. Her eyes followed his as she cupped her breasts, offering her hard, long nipples for his touch and kisses which he eagerly obliged by lowering himself until his mouth was poised, to envelope the offered ripe sexual fruit. 'Gosh, I have never experienced anything like this,' thought Jamie. 'She must have made love before, many times.' He paused in his thinking and smiled. 'I bet with sailors!'

They looked into each other's eyes. She was moaning: "Kiss me, kiss me on my breasts!" waiting for his warm, sensuous mouth, to smother her with his kisses. She was sighing - when suddenly there was a distant booming of a gun from the harbour. Jamie was quickly alerted. There was danger. He listened in case there was any more gunfire. He sat on the edge of the couch, and quickly dressed. A bewildered Margaret wondered what was happening.

"Come, my love, get dressed, we'll continue some other time in the future. I have to go and contact Captain Semmes."

He embraced her and gave her a kiss. Then hand in hand they ran across the lawn, along a flower-decked gravelled path to the steps of the pillared mansion, to be greeted by Carruthers, who had also heard the gunfire.

"What do you reckon it is, Jamie?"

"Don't know, we'll have to investigate. I'll go and see the Captain. Margaret, can you arrange two saddled horses for us, and perhaps you would like to show us the way to the harbour?"

The distance of two miles in the darkness was quickly covered by the horsemen with Margaret leading the way. They were met by a Midshipman at the jetty who had rowed ashore in a gig boat, accompanied by two seamen.

"Sir, there's trouble out there in the harbour! It's a Northern ship and she's firing at the '*Alabama*'. Mr. Freeman manned a long boat with two soldiers. We last saw him rowing across towards the enemy ship."

253

Tyler, the Bosun's Mate, was standing nearby. Jamie addressed him: "Take a couple of men and round up as many the crew of you can find and get them aboard the '*Alabama*'. We will row over and see what's happening and I'll despatch the longboats to pick you up and when on board make sure the men are armed to go and attack the foe."

Jamie and Carruthers rowed silently towards the '*Alabama*' and as they drew nearer they observed another ship about a quarter of a mile away with activity on the deck. On board the raider, Jamie commanded Captain Francis:

"Will you order six armed men and yourself to accompany me. Carruthers, round up as many men as you can as a back-up party and follow us immediately, approaching the aft end of the vessel on the port side."

The '*Alabama's*' starboard boat was lowered into the water and the oarsmen set off, ordered by Jamie to take a wide berth and approach the enemy ship from the stern end. There was a flash of rifle fire which gave Jamie the direction. Francis ordered the six armed soldiers to be ready to combat the enemy when they bumped astern of the Northern ship. The party silently boarded the dimly lit after-deck and were amazed to see two bound figures lying huddled on the deck and Mr. Freeman bound with his face to the main mast. His back was stripped to the waist, a heftily built man was passing the leather strands of a whip through his left hand. He suddenly whirled it behind him and was poised to strike his first lash of the whip when Jamie, who had moved up silently behind him, yelled: "Drop it, or you're a dead man!" Francis leapt forward and butted him with his rifle. Freeman and his accomplices were cut loose. He bundled his clothes under his arm.

The astonished enemy crew cowed as more Southern soldiers boarded their ship and surrounded them. Jamie still assumed command.

"Take all the enemy crew back to the '*Alabama*' and lock them up. Will you remain on board, Captain Francis, until tomorrow morning when I'm sure Captain Semmes will arrange a skeleton crew to take over."

The prisoners were locked in the '*Alabama's*' cells awaiting instructions for their punishment.

It was after midnight when Jamie and Carruthers were rowed ashore to find a worried Margaret waiting for them in a tavern. The trio mounted and galloped to the Mayor's mansion where the dance was in full swing.

Margaret gripped Jamie's arm. "Come, let's see how well you dance!"

"You will have to excuse me, I'll have to report to the Captain, but I'll leave you in the capable hands of my friend, 'Enry. I'm sure you'll find him a far better dancer than myself and I'll join you later." He thought, 'That's a lucky break, I'm sure 'Enry will entertain her, far better than myself. The funny expression on his face when I called him by his first name!' He laughed and excused himself.

Captain Semmes was in conversation with Sir Geoffrey Tym and Admiral Wishart when Jamie approached. Semmes greeted him with: "Let me introduce you to the Mayor and an Admiral of the British Fleet."

Following handshakes and light conversation, Jamie asked the Captain if he could see him for a moment. He related the evening's adventures. Semmes was concerned and thanked him for his prompt action.

"I think we'll wait till morning then I'll discuss the matter with the Mayor and the Admiral and seek their advice. Perhaps we'll convene a meeting here in the morning in the Mayor's house as I'm staying for a couple of days. You go and enjoy yourself, everything seems to be under control and I'm sure Mr. Kelly will arrange to man the enemy ship and interview the prisoners. When we all return to the ship in a few days' time we will make our decisions. I'll arrange for you and Carruthers to stay a few days and enjoy this lovely country."

Jamie returned to the dance and the Mayor's wife requested a dance before he could be whisked away by a long black-haired young maiden.

"I feel honoured to be dancing with you, Lady Tym." She smiled and asked:

"Do you know any of the latest European dances?"

"No, but I know a few Scottish reels."

"We must try them sometime, but you dance the waltz divinely."

Jamie caught Margaret's eye, who was snuggled into Carruthers' arms. She smiled and winked.

"She looks happy and contented," thought Jamie. "Our 'Enry must be giving her everything she desires."

Following the waltz, Jamie made his way to the punch bowl. Drinks were being served by white-gloved black youths, immaculately dressed in white shirts and shorts. He was enjoying the drink, gazing round the dance floor when his arm was accidentally nudged by the long black-haired young lady.

"I beg your pardon," said Jamie, "I'm so clumsy." She had smiling blue eyes. "How do you like your drink, I prepared it myself this afternoon?"

255

"Delicious." Jamie smiled back. "May I introduce myself, I'm Jamie from the '*Alabama*', and may I have the pleasure of the next dance?"

She smiled. "My name's Lucy, my father is the Admiral. The next dance is one of the latest polkas, introduced by the British Naval officers."

"I'll be delighted, but you might have to guide and instruct me as I don't know many of your latest modern dances."

They danced well together which Jamie enjoyed. She was smaller than her tall handsome partner.

Following the dance they chattered away, learning about each other.

"How would you like to go horse riding tomorrow?" She offered him another drink from the punch bowl. I'll show you some of our lovely coastline, where the Indian Ocean sweeps along miles of our golden sands."

"That sounds exciting - and perhaps we can go for a swim?"

"Say, ten o'clock, and I'll arrange for some picnic meals."

Following the last waltz, Jamie bade an abrupt good night to Lucy, explaining he had had hardly any sleep and retired to a front bedroom in the three-floored Mayor's mansion.

Following a large breakfast Jamie borrowed riding breeches from his host. Right on time, Lucy, her long black hair pleated behind her back, dressed in riding attire, leading two horses' appeared at the bottom of the mansion's steps. She waved to Jamie as he appeared.

'He looks fit,' she mused. 'I wonder if he is a good lover! We'll soon find out when I get him on the beach.'

She offered him the reins of a black stallion.

"A magnificent beast. Is he gentle? I'm not likely to be thrown, am I?"

She burst out laughing. "I can assure you he is well broken in. It is my father's favourite horse. South Africa is not my home. The family move to wherever my father is stationed. We'll proceed to the coast, which is about two miles away; I'm sure you will find our country picturesque and interesting."

The horses trotted side by side. She was curious and wanted to know about the birth and history of the '*Alabama*' and how Jamie joined it. They were soon galloping along the hard silvery sand. The horses seem to love being awash by the incoming tide with its big breakers. Mile after mile they trotted.

"Race you, Jamie?" Off they went; she was an experienced horse-woman and left Jamie behind. When he caught her up, they rested against a rock. "Would you like to try some of our famous South African wine? I reckon it's one of the finest and tastiest in the world!" - handing him a glass.

'It is certainly delicious," conceded Jamie. He took his time sipping the drink, wondering what she had in mind - he was soon to find out, when she turned over and nestled in his arms. He looked down at her smiling eyes; her white teeth gleamed when she smiled. He stroked her long black hair which she had released from the tied ribbon. "How old are you, Lucy?" she laughed.

"I suppose you are not a day older than thirty-two! I'm ten years younger, - does that bother you?" He smiled and thought: "Why not? She's lovely!"

"No." He leaned over her and kissed her red lips. She wrapped her arms round the back of his neck and smothered him with kisses.

They were startled by the sound of six pounding horses galloping towards them along the sand in the distance. Lucy was quick to learn there was danger.

"They are brigands from the hills, I can tell from the way their rifles are slung over their shoulders and the way they dress. Let us get out of here and head inland to the nearest farm." They mounted. - "Follow me - no doubt they have seen us, we'll have to hurry."

They galloped off along the shore. Lucy indicated with her left hand a path and the sandy beach gave way to vegetation and then trees. They sped along the path. They could hear shouting as the six horsemen were in hot pursuit and they were drawing nearer. A bullet whistled over Jamie's head! He realised they were in great danger and he feared for the safety of Lucy. The vegetation and trees gave way to lush meadow land where cows and bullocks were peacefully grazing. The herd gave way as the young couple galloped swiftly through them. The tranquillity of the countryside was shattered with the noise of rifle fire as the hostile enemy charged in and out of the frightened herd. In the distance Jamie noticed the smoke rising from a log cabin.

Peter Schippers and his buxom wife Nancie were enjoying an afternoon rest when they were startled to hear gunfire about half a mile away. His first reaction was that somebody was running off his herd. He removed his long rifle from its wall hook, shouted to his wife to get more ammunition and hurried outside to be greeted by two horsemen charging towards him. He quickly summed up the seriousness and recognized the pursuers and when he was shot at, he returned the fire.

Jamie and Lucy leapt off their horses and ran into the cabin followed by the farmer and his wife. Schippers threw his rifle to Jamie and shouted: "Fire through that open window. Hello! Lucy, see that box of cartridges on that shelf ?" Pointing, he went on:

"Pass them to your friend, while I get my spare rifle and I will fire through the other window. Nancie, get my pistol and bullets by the bed and give them to him," indicating Jamie.

Lucy, who already knew the Schippers, introduced Jamie. The southern hemisphere darkness suddenly descended; there was a lull in the firing.

'The enemy must be digging in and preparing for a long wait,' thought Jamie.

"Can we get help?" asked Jamie.

Peter was quick to reply: "Yes, I have an idea that we used in the past. There's the Muller farmhouse down the valley. You'll probably know the place, Lucy? Hans has four sons. He will come immediately. Lucy, I'm glad you're dressed for riding." He smiled, admiring her breeches. "I will help you through the back window. Here is a bridle. At the bottom of the field you will find Jenny, she's a gentle mare. Call her name here, give her this apple and she'll be friendly, but you'll have to ride bareback. I'm sure you can manage that!" Dusk descended.

He stopped by the open rear window and pointed: "The Muller farm is in that direction. You will have to cross another field with animals grazing and then across a shallow, narrow river. When you sight the white farmhouse, start shouting his name - Muller! - Muller! - to attract his attention and I'm sure after you have explained the danger we are in, he will come immediately with his sons - and good luck, Lucy. In the meantime we will hold them off. I don't like the silence. The only thing I fear is that they might try and fire the thatched roof and we will be doomed!"

Jamie butted in: "I've an idea, I'll go out the back with Lucy and come in front of the house, making a wide circle, and engage the six men from the rear. I'm sure you can be alert. I see you have two old rifles. One you fire and one which Nancie loads. Be careful and only fire at the flashes in the dark as they will be firing at the open windows. Alternate your windows with rapid firing." Peter smiled. "You have a lilting Scottish brogue and a name to go with it. You would make a fine minister in the chapel, and no doubt you have been in such a similar situation!" They all smiled.

Jamie went through the rear window and then assisted Lucy. He squeezed her hand and kissed her.

"Take great care, Jamie, I want to continue our romance in the near future."

Jamie had more important things on his mind. He made a wide circle crawling silently through the undergrowth until he guessed he was behind his scattered assailants, keeping the silhouette of the farm and outbuildings in view. He lay flat on his stomach, sizing up the situation. Half an hour passed, a twig snapped a few yards in front. He crawled silently forward, his right hand gripping the revolver. There was a well-built man kneeling down, his rifle at his shoulder, sighting one of the open windows. The brigand was startled to feel the barrel of a gun behind his right ear. He trembled.

"Lower the rifle gently to the ground," whispered Jamie. The black-bearded, wide-eyed man knelt on the ground. Jamie gripped the revolver by the barrel and hit him a vicious blow on the side of the head with the butt end and he sprawled senseless, face down on the ground.

'One less,' thought Jamie. 'Good job I have brown breeches and a dark shirt. Where are these other beggars? I'll try over to the right.' He saw the figure of a man standing, puffing on his pipe, his rifle lying on the ground. He appeared to be gripping and squeezing some twigs and leaves together in a ball. 'Must be preparing to fire the farm roof!' thought Jamie. He picked up a four-foot long branch and gripping it firmly, he took a vicious swipe at the man, missing his head, but crunched his right collar bone. Jamie gave the man a further blow on the back of his head and he lay lifeless at his feet. There was a yell as another brigand charged from the undergrowth with a pointed rifle.

Jamie shot him in the chest. He screamed, clutching the wound, blood oozing through his fingers.

From the darkness the fourth man charged Jamie, swinging his rifle by the barrel. It grazed his arm as he fired the revolver, which whistled above the ruffian's head. They both rolled over on the ground, struggling to get the upper hand. The big mountain man lay astride Jamie and proceded to fist him in the face.

Schippers ceased firing his rifle when he heard the sound of the revolver, knowing Jamie had located the enemy. He went through the back window running, crouching, into the familiar undergrowth. He immediately came behind a figure kneeling and raining blows with his clenched fist. He was about to fist Jamie again when Peter gave him a vicious butt on the base of his neck and the man rolled over. Peter helped Jamie to his feet. "Are you all right?" he whispered. Jamie felt the lump on the back of his blooded head and gently fingered his aching jaw.

"Must find the empty revolver. There are two brigands left, somewhere over to our right. They must have heard the noise, but are keeping quiet. Probably scared or wondering what to do. You go over there, Peter," indicating. Jamie crawled round on his stomach through the shrubbery and flower beds. Two men side by

259

side with their backs towards him, were gesturing in the direction of the farmhouse. Jamie rose and rushed towards them, wrapping his arms around their necks, and jerked their heads together, at the same time yelling for Peter. The three men fell to the ground. Peter heard the shout and came running, delivering a stunning blow on one of the brigands' head with his rifle. The other stunned man received a similar fatal blow in the upper part of his back. Jamie staggered to his feet. "Well done, Peter - for a farmer!" he laughed, feeling his bruised mouth and knuckles. "I have been trained by experts for this type of combat - we'll have to enlist you."

They sat on the ground, both exhausted. Peter lit his pipe and was about to address Jamie, when there was clattering of hooves and men shouting. "That must be my neighbour Hans and his sons, trust them to arrive when it's all over, thanks to you, Jamie." They went in the direction of the farmhouse, there to be greeted by Lucy, who flung her arms around Jamie and hugged him. Likewise Nancie who embraced Peter. Hans was introduced. Jamie's wound was attended to.

"Let's go inside and drink some ale, we need it!" Jamie with his head bandaged felt more comfortable after his ordeal. Peter was discussing with Hans how to dispose of the six dead bodies. Hans and his sons searched the area for the dead brigands, flung them on to a borrowed oxen-driven cart and amid handshakes and farewells disappeared into the night.

Next morning after a sound sleep the farmer and his wife were finishing their breakfast.

"Are you fit enough to travel, Jamie?" asked the anxious farmer. "I'm all right, thanks to your kind attention. I would like to get back to the mansion and I'm sure Lucy will guide us to the Mayor's house." Nancie smiled.

"You'll have that lump for a few days" - looking at Jamie's bandaged head. When Jamie and Lucy arrived at the mansion, the friendly greeting turned to alarm when they saw the white bandage. They were ushered into the lounge and given hot beverages. Jamie related their experiences and Lucy backed him up by remarking on the brave way he tackled the brigands from their rear, single-handed. Jamie smiled. "Peter Schippers saved my life, when I was being strangled."

Captain Semmes asked Sir Geoffrey: "Do you get many raids on the farms?"

"Both the Mullers and Schippers have been raided, their animals driven off - in fact Peter and Nancie lost one son and two farmhands in a raid by the brigands, who attack without any warning, mainly during the night. No doubt Peter quickly realised and recognised the danger when he heard the gunfire and saw two horsemen, yelling and charging towards the farmhouse."The Deputy Governor stared into his glass before continuing: "Our troops make numerous raids into the hills, searching for these mountain men. They are a law unto themselves - tough ill-bred lot, mainly Boers, who think the British are trying to take over their land. When we catch the beggars, we hang them."

"Can I give you some advice, and I'm sure Jamie will support me," butted in Semmes. "Why not fight them in a manner somewhat similar to their methods? Instead of wearing the traditional soldiers' British red uniform so that their lookouts can see you for miles around, why not disguise yourselves? Why not dress as mountain men? We have experienced raids on the enemy!"

The excited Jamie butted in: "Excuse me, sir. Do you remember the way we dressed for the freeing of our countrymen up the Delaware River?"

Semmes laughed. "Yes, you were a Northern officer attacking the stockade with a dozen 'blue' soldiers and that, gentlemen, resulted in the freeing of twelve hundred Southern soldiers, the majority we landed near Galveston."

"Good idea, I'll think about that," remarked Tyms. "In fact, Admiral, we might borrow a dozen of your marines. Perhaps Jamie would like to join us and lead the troops?"

"No," remarked Semmes sternly, "but we might be able to spare you a couple of volunteers!"

"Might I suggest Oliver Keep and Gringham, sir? They showed an interest in living in South Africa and they accompanied me on the raid."

"Good idea, I'll arrange their transfer and give them the latest repeating rifles and ammunition." Captain Semmes continued: "I'm sorry, ladies and gentlemen, but last night I received my latest sailing orders and we must leave the bay as soon as possible." He smiled. "After all, we have a war to fight!"

Everybody was taken by surprise at the sudden announcement. Lucy's eyes flooded. She looked and smiled at the bandaged Jamie. He returned the smile, but was glad in a way, though he had fallen for the young and attractive young lady. He was pleased for the chance to return to active service.

"Let's have our final toast, ladies and gentlemen, charge the glasses, steward, with our finest wine - to the Captain and crew of the '*Alabama*'. May we wish you every success and may you be safely returned to your loved ones, wherever they may be."

Semmes thanked everybody for their hospitality and after handshakes and kisses for the ladies, the Captain and Jamie departed.

Chapter 22

It was Monday morning 21st September 1863; Captain Semmes mustered his senior officers to his cabin.

"Gentlemen, I have received my orders, delivered by my secret agent in Cape Town from the Secretary of State, Mr. Malloy. We will be leaving tomorrow evening, proceeding due south, following the 40° latitude across the Indian Ocean to Singapore. The 'Tuscaloosa' left two days ago, as you are aware. Captain Lowe was ordered to provision his man-o'-war and cross the Atlantic Ocean to South America; of course, engaging and sinking enemy ships. The manned 'Sea Bride' will do likewise. Both these vessels will rendezvous in Cape Town to meet us, when we return. We now have that damned Yankee ship which fired on us the other day. I cannot do much about this paddle steamer, as according to the Admiral, it is in neutral waters."

Jamie butted in: "May I suggest, sir - as we have all the enemy crew on board our ship, why not man it with a skeleton crew and continue acting as a Northern ship and meet us at Cape Town when we return?"

Semmes stroked his waxed moustache. "Good idea. Can you arrange that, Mr. Kelly, without taking our senior officers?"

The First Lieutenant smiled. "I have a very experienced Master mariner, who recently joined us."

He looked around the faces in the cabin. Somebody sniggered. "He's - a Liverpool man - Captain Derek Arnold, together with Engineer Mackinson, and I'll have to 'borrow' one of the mates, Wallace Davies, and a soldier, Sergeant Darrach; and the rest will be volunteers."

Captain Semmes continued: "I was rather alarmed that during our visit to these shores, fifteen men have deserted us, and these will have to be replaced. Jamie, select some of your tough hands and go ashore and don't come back empty-handed, and bring enough to man this damned ship alongside."

"Very good, sir, I'll go immediately."

On the main deck, Jamie summoned the Bosun.

"Will you arrange for Captain Francis and six men, including

263

yourself, Ryan and Schmechel to go ashore; we are going man-hunting to enlist twenty men to replace the deserters. We might even find some of these louts - and 'persuade' them to return," he sniggered.

The oarsmen pulled the longboats away from the '*Alabama*'.

"We'll visit the taverns on the outskirts, Bosun, it will not be noticed getting them out of the back door without any trouble. Schmechel, will you arrange a horse and cart for transporting them back to the wharf in the dark to the boat."

Back on board the '*Alabama*', Semmes was wining and dining Admiral Wishart and officers from the various British ships in his cabin and relating his battles and adventures. He concluded with his future plans for leaving the harbour, but not their destination.

"I know you'll have the Pilot on board, Captain, to steer you safely out of this treacherous bay, but I would be honoured to proceed forward and escort you as it is not often we've been visited by such a distinguished Naval Commander - it will be a sight with the full moon. The fleet will be alerted to acknowledge and salute you. You say you've sunk fifty ships, Captain? It's more than my entire fleet could achieve." Everybody laughed. "I give you a toast, Captain Semmes." The British officers stood up. The Admiral raised his glass. "To the '*Alabama*' and its crew - may you continue to be successful in your future ventures."

The party settled down, the wine flowed, everybody seemed in a boisterous and happy mood. Semmes smiled and looked at his wine glass. "Must be the Jamaican wine," he thought.

"Do you know, Captain," Wishart was in great form, "there is another famous troopship built in the same shipyard as the '*Alabama*' that lies buried along our coastline. It is the paddle steamer '*Birkenhead*' of Her Majesty's Britannic Navy. She struck a partially submerged rock on February 26th twelve years ago. It carried troops going to reinforce the army engaged in the Zulu War.

The story of the heroism, bravery and discipline which attended the sinking - as the soldiers stood to attention 'Putting women and children first' - has become a chapter in history. Only 180 people survived." Lieutenant Boyle took up the story: "Do you know who made the most successful escape?" - a pause.

"The horses, the way they thrashed the water, heading for the shore, escaping the sharks. I understand that years later, they were running in wild herds over the plains."

Lieutenant Connolly who had been listening intently, continued: "Aye, that is not all - you haven't mentioned the most important thing hidden in the ship's safe and still lying submerged, - 300,000

264

golden sovereigns." There was a gasp from some of the '*Alabama's*' officers who hadn't heard the story before.

"Actually," continued Connolly, "one of the men who escaped was an Ensign, named Lucas, who is now residing as the Chief Magistrate of Durban. He claimed the money was for the purpose of financing the Zulu War and partly to pay the troops fighting it." His eager friend butted in: "Do you remember, Norman, we met another survivor - Corporal O'Neil, who said that for some time after the loss of the '*Birkenhead*', British soldiers were paid in Mexican dollars!" The bearded Admiral took command. He jabbed his smoking pipe at the company and remarked: "There was an attempt by a diver nine years ago, a chap named Adams. His team could only salvage a few personal possessions - so you see, gentlemen" - he laughed - "perhaps if you return to these waters and do some diving, you might become very rich. The wooden troopship '*Birkenhead*' was named after the town in which she was built as you may well surmise. She was launched by Mrs. Laird in January 1846. It will become one of history's most famous wrecks, but also one of the most valuable. The greatest danger for any diver is the sharks and the ever-changing currents." Admiral Wishart drained his glass, placed it on a tray, held by the steward. "Well, gentlemen, it has been a most enjoyable evening and we thank you for your hospitality. Your wine was delicious and we wish you bon voyage." He stood up, shook hands and saluted the Captain of the '*Alabama*'. It was approaching midnight and after all the visitors had departed, the drinking and singing by the crew continued into the night and gradually died down when the wine and grog ceased to flow. There was bumping alongside the ship's side as the longboats returned, followed by shouting and swearing as the 'volunteers' boarded, in some cases to their new home! The '*Alabama*' settled in repose to await the dawn and the final day in Simonstown.

Early morning after breakfast Jamie reported to the Captain he had been successful in rounding up twenty-five new crew members, mostly with sore heads, following resistance to the 'press gang.' The Governor and his wife were early visitors together with Margaret and Lucy, who were entertained on board by Jamie and Carruthers. Lucy was introduced to the Captain, who remarked: "I've heard all about your adventures, Miss Lucy." He kissed her hand and smiled. "If you ever want to join us you'll be most welcome." She departed. The afternoon was spent by all hands getting the ship ready for sea.

Towards midnight with the Pilot on board she quietly slipped anchor. The Admiral in his flagship signalled he would lead the way. As the '*Alabama*' slowly steamed out of the bay, her crew lined the bulwarks and rigging to say a silent farewell by waving, doffing their hats to the ships of Her Majesty's Navy. Once well clear of the bay, the '*Wyvern*' sent a boat to pick up the Pilot. Donald Hughes saluted Captain Semmes, bade him a successful and safe voyage and climbed over the bulwarks into the longboat and disappeared into the darkness, shouting and waving farewell to the white faces lining the side of the '*Alabama*', as she gently wallowed in the white, speckled waves of the Indian Ocean. The seamen climbed the rigging to unfurl the sails, chanting sea shanties to the accompaniment of Mullard's concertina. The billowing white sails filled as the '*Alabama's*' streamlined bow plunged into the ocean - her destination Singapore.

As the Southern raider voyaged south-east, the weather grew rough with heavy seas and rain. The acting ship's Mate on the double wheel was joined by Jamie. Ian Fisher was an experienced navigator. Night descended quickly in late September in the Southern hemisphere. Jamie gazed into the starlit sky; the recent stormy weather gave way to a peaceful and calm night.

"Do you still study the stars, Fisher?" The Mate pointed upward and named the stars. "They are always there in the Heavens to guide us safely to our destination." Jamie listened intently and took the wheel on the next watch.

"We are nearing the 40° latitude, sir, and the Captain has ordered that we maintain this steady course due east."

"Thank you, Fisher. I'll take the next watch." - "Very good, sir."

It was bright and breezy on Sunday morning the 11th October. Jamie was chatting to Captain Francis about his adventures in Simonstown. "Wish I'd been there, I would have soon routed the beggars out. Still, you did well, Jamie, for a seaman. They both laughed, Jamie thought highly of Francis and valued his friendship. They were interrupted by the screeching of a seagull telling the crew they were near to land! A few hours later there was a cry from aloft - "Land ahoy!' Granite barren rocks suddenly loomed out of the ocean. Shaded eyes viewed the huge craggy mountains making two small islands.

"It's the St. Paul's Islands," shouted the First Lieutenant.

"We have covered, according to the charts, half our journey to the Far East, but unfortunately we can't land. The high, sheer cliffs drop into very deep waters, making it impossible for us to land a boat. What would we find if we did land?" He swept the landscape with his telescope. "It appears to be uninhabited, no vegetation, only hundreds of birds, who probably use the islands when they are migrating or breeding."

The Captain stepped on to the bridge and addressed the assembled crew: "You could not have described the scene better, Mr. Kelly. They are just barren, uninhabitable rocks in the middle of no-where - however we will stay in this area - perhaps a whaler or schooner might be sighted. In the last 1500 miles there's been no excitement only occasionally sighting an English ship. We have suffered hardship. The sea has been rough, gale force at times, which has caused the ship to leak badly, so the first break in the weather I want all hands to repair the damages. Will you see to that, Mr. Kelly?" snarled the Captain.
The crew had worked hard, the carpenters had examined the planks and rectified any leaks and the seamen repaired the tattered sails! At 25° latitude, 19° longitude the '*Alabama*' crossed the Tropic of Capricorn.
As there was nothing to celebrate the Captain ordered double grog all round and the crew burst forth, ably assisted by Mullard with his concertina, and Unsworth on his pipes.
The '*Alabama*' plunged her sleek bow into the deep blue waters sailing at an average of 150 miles a day. Occasionally ships were sighted and boarded, their papers examined for contraband Northern goods. Semmes bade their Captains a friendly farewell and a safe journey. Captain Semmes guided his ship easterly. There was a cry from Riordan, the lookout man, that land was sighted north by north-east.
"Jamie," summoned the Captain, "bring my charts of this area. You will find them in the top drawer in my cabinet." The off-duty officers gathered around the Captain who pointed with his finger on the ordnance map which was on the gun room skylight.
"We have come up on the 100° longitude line from the 40° latitude line here," indicating. "The small islands we will be sighting are on the port beam, the Cocos: and on the starboard side, Christmas Island." Semmes glanced around his officers and he stroked his moustache. "We must take every precaution sailing through the narrow Sunda Straight, between Sumatra and Java. Regular soundings must be taken, especially going through the narrows. Keep alert, there are pirates in these waters. Have watchkeepers around the bulwarks, and armed soldiers up the rigging. Riordan has already been warned. He is a very alert young man and at the first sign of any danger sound battle stations. Make no mistake, I have been warned about these pirates. They suddenly attack in hundreds. Probably dart out from the small islands, primitively armed - some might have rifles. Be armed when on deck and drill and position your men, be on guard day and night. That is all, gentlemen." He began muttering under his breath: "Pirates and these cursed Northerners!"

'Must be cracking,' thought Jamie. He went below to the engineers' cabin and took his revolver from his drawer and examined it to see if it was fully loaded, and then stuffed a fistful of bullets in his side pocket.

As dawn broke on Friday the 6th November, Jamie, being officer of the watch, was hailed from aloft that there was a barque on the starboard beam, three miles away. The '*Alabama*' gave chase and as it drew nearer, Captain Armstrong's team fired a shot over the bows of a ship displaying the Northern flag. Her papers showed her to be the '*Amanda*'. She was bound for New Zealand.

Semmes noted in his log: 'Since our last torching thirty-two days ago, the '*Amanda*' was boarded, ransacked and burned and her crew taken prisoner. Now proceeding through the Sunda Straits. Provisions running low.'

The weather was bright and breezy as the '*Alabama*' cruised between small islands. Jamie, leaning on the port bulwark, was focusing his binoculars on the waves hitting a sandy beach when he was joined by Sergeant Briggs, Doctor MacGregor and Iain Grinham.

"What a picturesque sight," observed Briggs. "All these lovely islands, bedecked with flowers, coconuts and palm trees - it's paradise!"

"I see some naked natives splashing in the water," said the excited young Doctor. "Loan me your glasses, Jamie, and let me feast my eyes on the human form."

Sure enough brown-skinned maidens splashed, laughing and shouting in a merry mood in shallow waters. More sailors appeared and began shouting and waving. Suddenly the natives froze, then ran from the sea into their thatched huts which littered the beach.

The swift-flowing strait narrowed to about three-quarters of a mile between the islands. The First Lieutenant ordered three sailors either side of the ship to measure, record and shout out the depth. Passing safely through the narrow sound, the '*Alabama*' leapt under full sail, her propeller hoisted, and plowed into the China Seas. It was raining heavily when a cry from Riordan indicated a Northern ship racing parallel, two miles away.

Semmes ordered the helmsman to close in and both vessels raced ahead as though there was a winning post in the distance.

"Fire a shot across her bows," shouted Semmes as the '*Alabama's*' Northern flag was lowered and replaced.

Captain Forshaw of the '*Winged Racer*' viewed with astonishment the lowering of his Country's colours only to be exchanged with his enemy's flag. "Reduce speed," - he snarled at his First Mate. Sailors swarmed into the rigging and unfurled the sails and the

schooner lost interest in the race - despite her apt name '*Racer*'!
Forshaw was transferred to the deck of the '*Alabama*' and faced up
to Captain Semmes.
"What a sneaky way, Captain - why didn't you just sink my ship?.
You don't have to use underhanded tricks to beat your enemy -
you are well armed and you have a strong military force!"
"We are at war, Mister" Semmes was furious, he disliked being
called names. 'A sneak - that is one thing I'm certainly not!' he
thought. "You have a fine ship, sir," Semmes remarked tartly. "You
are a good navigator and you certainly handled it well, but you lost
the race and have to face the consequences. I'll grant you this:
return to your ship and man your boats with provisions and your
personal possessions and sail to one of those islands," pointing.
"I'm sure you'll find shelter and safety, Captain."
Captain Kenneth Forshaw gave Semmes a smart salute and climbed
over the side into his gig boat and returned to the '*Winged Racer*'.
That evening the sky glowed a deep red as the burning ship -'*The
Racer*' - lived up to her name as she disappeared swiftly into the
deep with dignity.
Next morning the red tip of the sun rising in the east sent a dull
red glow across the shimmering sea. The carpenter's mate who
was the forward look-out man, viewed the small islands through
his binoculars. He was joined by the officer of the watch.
"What do you make of the smoke rising above that hilly island
over there, sir?" remarked Grinham to Jamie, pointing his glasses
north-east.
Jamie focused on the black smoke which coloured the sky
intermingling with the sun's rays. "It's strange," remarked Jamie.
"Change course, Bosun, 10 north-east, we'll skirt round the island
and investigate."
Half an hour later Jamie observed a ship flying the British ensign
with smoke billowing from the aft end. The sea was littered with
sampans and small boats and the occasional gunfire could be
heard. Jamie quickly realised the desperate situation of Her
Majesty's vessels. "Sound battle stations, Bosun!"
The clanging of the warning bell and the shouting and bustling of
the crew roused the Captain, who was asleep in a chair. He hurried
on deck, clutching his telescope and trying at the same time to
button up his uniform.
"What is it?" addressing Jamie.
"There's a British Naval ship being attacked by what appears to
be pirates, sir, and as you can see," pointing "they are boarding
the vessel which also seems to be holed on the water line. There
was a spout of water on the port side. Jamie observed through his
binoculars a puff of smoke on the hillside.

"We are being fired at from the slope of the hill over there." Jamie pointed.

"Man the Blakely, Captain Butler, and engage the enemy on that island," bawled Semmes. He quickly sized up the situation. "Captain Francis, man the rigging with soldiers and when we come within range, commence firing. Jamie, we will be approaching the vessel on her starboard side. Shackle to her with grappling irons. Be prepared to man the ship with marines to fight these damn pirates. We will show them the art of piracy!" He swept the British warship's deck with his telescope. "I see the pirates have cutlasses and short broadswords. Order fixed bayonets and use your sword, Jamie lad - you'll find it most useful and your revolver in your left hand. Good luck!"

When Jamie landed on the deck by jumping from the '*Alabama's*' bulwarks he was greeted with fierce fighting. There seemed to be swarms of half-naked dark-skinned natives, weaving and slashing in a frenzy, using their broadswords. He immediately engaged a raggedly dressed Chinaman who weaved his cutlass in a sweeping ark. Jamie lunged his sword forward into the man's stomach and as he withdrew his bloodstained sword he half turned and shot another man in the head who was charging towards him. There was shouting, rifle and revolver firing, and a dull thud as the rifle butted against a skull.

Suddenly there was a deathly hush, the battle was over. Black smoke trickled through the engine room's ventilator. Dead bodies littered the blood-spattered deck. The British Midshipman started yelling and shouting as he pushed his way passed the '*Alabama*' soldiers towards the main mast. He was horrified to see his tall Captain impaled by a spear through his body to the mast! His head hung down, blood trickling from his mouth, his lifeless eyes open as though asking a question. His left hand gripped an empty revolver while his right a bloodstained-tipped sword. Captain Silas Locke of Her Majesty's Ship '*Chester*' had fought bravely against heavy odds. Bosun Bellew gently eased the bloodstained spear from the dead captain's chest and, with the help of Jamie, laid him on the deck.

The British Midshipman pushed everybody aside and kneeling down looked into his Captain's lifeless staring eyes for a moment, then he gently closed them. He stood up, faced Jamie, and - trembling with shock - muttered:

"I'm Midshipman Alastair Goldrein, sir, of Her Majesty's warship '*Chester*'". He became emotional, his head bowed. "I'm Jamie, from the "*Alabama*' - come and sit down over here." Grinham offered the slim young man a flask.

"Here, have a swig of our finest rum, it will cheer you up!" Goldrein took a long swig and started sputtering and coughing.
"I'm glad you came to our rescue, Jamie. We were a skeleton crew taking the ship into Singapore, which is fifty miles in that direction" - pointing. "The ship was going into the dockyard for an overhaul. We were passing this hilly island when we heard the sound of gunfire. Next minute a shell hit us just above the waterline and just penetrated the engine room. I was on the wheel and turned the ship stern first to the island and ordered full steam ahead." Jamie butted in: - "Good thinking, a smaller target!" - "We seemed to be escaping from the shooting, probably out of range, when suddenly from the numerous islands appeared a large number of boats of various shapes and sizes, and surrounded us. Bullets hit us from all directions causing casualties. The Captain immediately ordered battle stations." He paused, feeling emotional. "He was a great and experienced navigator - what a way to die!"
The Captain's bloodstained body had been covered. Goldrein gazed at the congealed blood on the deck and the numerous dead bodies, mainly pirates.
There was a stench because of the overhead sun. The calm sea was littered with debris, flotsam and dead bodies, which were slowly disappearing because of the sharks. There seemed to be hundreds of fins!
Jamie had an idea - "Throw all the enemy dead bodies overboard. I'll go and alert our Captain, come with me, Middy. The Bosun's Mate was standing by awaiting orders. "Tyler, man the wheel, Captain Francis, man the rigging and bulwarks with soldiers. You there," gesturing, "what's your name?" - "Archibald, sir."
"You look tall and agile. Take my telescope and go aloft. Watch for signals and messages from the '*Alabama*'.
The '*Alabama*' was hauled to standing by. A boat was lowered, and plowed through the churning sea. Carruthers was in charge accompanied by Oliver Keep and Schmechel on the oars.
"Where have you been, Carruthers?" Jamie addressed his friend. "The excitement is all over, you're in time to bury the dead!" Carruthers sniggered, but pleased to see his shipmate was safe. "Orders from the Captain: you are to return immediately. He wants to sail out of these dangerous waters. Is this ship able to sail under its own power?" Jamie looked around. "I haven't had a damage report yet. There is a hole aft on the port side; any carpenters present?" Brennan stepped forward. "Right, try and plug up the hole. Carruthers, take charge of the engine room, I see the fire must be dying out. I think the vessel will have to be towed, at any rate that is up to Captain Semmes. Francis, you will be in

charge and await orders from the '*Alabama*'. Come, Ally."
Semmes greeted Jamie. "Well, you seem to have had some excitement. Who is this bloodstained young man?"

"Midshipman Alastair Goldrein, sir, from Her Majesty's Britannic ship '*Chester*', and I might add, he's shown heroic bravery under heavy odds and is to be recommended for taking command, following the tragic killing of Captain Locke."

"How old are you, boy?" Goldrein saluted.

"Seventeen, sir."

"Hey, there!" Semmes called in a loud voice. He was addressing Ryan. "This gentleman has shown extreme bravery against the enemy, you know all about that! Take him below and find him a bunk in the officers' mess. Scrub him down, and present him to the Quartermaster for an appropriate uniform applicable for a British officer." Semmes began strolling the deck, smoothing his wax moustache. "That young man will make a Captain one day. He shows initiative and has a commanding personality. I wonder if that was his first battle? What a baptism."

"Mr. Kelly, summon the senior officers." Three gathered around awaiting the Captain's orders.

"Gentlemen, we will take the '*Chester*' in tow. They have just signalled they can't use main engines and she's still taking in water. When we get near Singapore we will find some quiet sandy cove and beach her where the natives are friendly! You will attend to that matter, Second Lieutenant."

"Very good, sir." Jamie saluted.

Semmes continued: "We will then proceed to our destination, taking the '*Chester*'s' dead with us, to hand over to the British Naval authorities."

It was the 18th December. The '*Alabama*' towed the '*Chester*' about forty miles. Semmes sent the cutter ahead with Jamie in charge to search for a secluded sandy beach, to ground the stricken British ship.

The shipping lanes approaching Singapore were busy with ships from all over the world, mainly Dutch and French - no Yankee ships! They thought it was better to be a live coward than a dead hero!

Jamie reported back a quiet, secluded beach, where the natives were friendly, to which the two ships approached, the '*Alabama*' leading the way, towing the '*Chester*'. Within a quarter of a mile the towing ropes were released, the '*Alabama*' steamed to starboard and the '*Chester*' slowly glided into a sandy cove and ran aground. Multicoloured birds screeched overhead as though giving a welcome to the stricken ship!

There were six survivors from the '*Chester*' besides the Midshipman. These were transferred to the "*Alabama*'.
On the 20th December the '*Alabama*' weaved its way slowly through the many small islands. Goldie named them to Jamie as they ran amidships to view through binoculars each island that had its own strange physical identities.
"Look, Jamie," lowering the binoculars and pointing, "this island is fertile, with banana, orange and palm trees. As you get nearer to Singapore the Malayan natives are curious but friendly. Look at the flock of parrots!" - Jamie located the beautiful red, blue and green plumages of the large flock as they flew above the trees, then one by one they slowly perched themselves on the branches, screeching away, and communicating with each other.
He laughed and said to Goldie: "I have only seen talking parrots in cages as nearly always would be brought home by seamen at home in Liverpool. They were presents, but there are shops who specialise in breeding the birds and also canaries are very popular. In fact I sometimes think a good speaking bird is more intelligent than some humans I know." They both burst out laughing.
The gentle and friendly Malayans came alongside bargaining for provisions, tools and in return offering fruit, meats and vegetables.
Singapore was about five miles distant when the First Lieutenant signalled they required a Pilot.
Jon Knotzle, a French Pilot, standing on the battlements of the tower at Point Pulau, observed through his telescope a masted man-o'-war in the narrow entrance between Singapore Island and Ubin. Turning to a trainee Pilot he remarked: "Now there is a ship with very fine lines, Monsieur, and look at those guns and the white starred flag. I wonder what nationality that ship is. I am curious. You'll accompany me and you will learn how to steer a ship of this size through these treacherous rocky straits."
Jamie, leaning on the starboard rail near the gangway, saw a small boat approach, flying what he thought was a pilot flag. She came alongside and the uniformed Pilot and his assistant presented themselves aboard the '*Alabama*'.
"Monsieur, my name is Knotzle - the Pilot, to escort you safely through the dangerous Johore Strait, to the dockyard."
Jamie saluted."Welcome aboard, Monsieur, why are these dangerous waters?"
The pilot stroked his pointed black beard. "There are razor-sharp, shaped rocks, just beneath the surface, which could slash the woodwork - there's been many a wooden vessel sunk in these waters."

Jamie smirked. "For your information, Monsieur, the name of our ship is the '*Alabama*', a Confederate raider. Hence our country's flag. The bottom of our ship is sheathed with copper plates, but we are in need of repair. Have you any suggestions where these repairs can be carried out?"

"Yes, there is a Naval dock which will suit the size of your ship." Captain Semmes approached. Jamie introduced the Pilot and explained about the dockyard.

"Mr. Kelly," shouted Semmes, "steam ahead to the dock, guided by Monsieur Knotzle. Proceed cautiously, these waters are treacherous. Take regular soundings, but I've been assured the Pilot is experienced regarding a safe passageway - but don't take any chances."

"Thank you, Monsieur Captain, I will guide you safely to the dock entrance, but you will have to go and negotiate terms with the British Naval authorities."

The '*Alabama*' steamed slowly down the straits, escorted by numerous small boats. Soundings were regularly shouted out which the Pilot noted and once clear of the narrows, the waters opened out to reveal the bustling and noisy docks. There were ships, sampans and boats of various sizes plying their wares, and merchants, all adding to this popular and growing port. Naval ships were at anchor, all flying the St. George flag. The British sailors watched with curiosity as the '*Alabama*', with its white flag and stars signifying the Confederate flag of the Southern States , steamed amongst them.

The fleet and the port soon buzzed with excitement when they learned about the identity of the raider.

Chapter 23

Captain Semmes commanded Jamie: "Go ashore with the British Midshipman and contact the Dockmaster or whoever is in charge of the dockyard. Goldrein no doubt will contact his superiors and possibly it might help us in the ship docking."
As the cutter approached the Naval dockyard, Midshipman Goldrein, who decided to wear his bloodstained white uniform, as advised by Captain Semmes pointed:
"Head for those steps, Jamie. I know my way around this Naval establishment, I did my initial training at the Naval School."
    Jamie smiled and thought: 'He's got grit and determination, this youngster, but that name! - must call him Goldie!' "Tyler, draw up and tie alongside those steps. Hang around, I'll be a while contacting the Dockmaster." He turned to the Midshipman and smiled. "Do you mind if I call you Goldie?" They both laughed. "I'll escort you, Jamie, to the Admiral, who is the senior officer in the dockyard. I know where his wardroom is, but I have never had the pleasure of visiting him!"
    They were met at the top of the steps by an armed British Naval seaman. Seeing Jamie in his light grey uniform and noting his epaulettes, he presented arms with a loud slap on his rifle butt, which Jamie acknowledged by saluting.
"I have business with the Dockyard Admiral. Will you please arrange an escort."
The armed seaman alerted the officer of the watch, who saluted Jamie and remarked: "Please follow me, sir."

Admiral Sir Samuel Burns, after the formal introduction, remarked: "How is Captain Semmes? His fame has spread to the four corners of the globe!"
    "He's very well, Admiral, but he has asked, because the '*Alabama*' is in urgent need of repair, if we could dock the vessel in your largest dock?"
    "What is its length?"
    "Two hundred and fourteen feet by thirty-one feet beam; and depth eighteen feet."

"That will be number seven dock." Sir Samuel called in his aide. "Is number seven dock available to dock the '*Alabama*?'"

"Yes, sir," after consulting a chart.

"Then make all the necessary arrangements."

Jamie was relieved. He did not know what attitude the British authorities would take.

"Thank you, sir."

Jamie continued by relating the epic battle against the pirates and how the brave Captain of the '*Chester*' had lost his life.

"May I add, sir, I would like to introduce Midshipman Goldrein, who showed conspicuous bravery against very heavy odds. We have beached the '*Chester*' in some sandy cove about ten miles away and left a handful of men on board. The natives seem friendly and I will be sending you a full report. We have brought back the crew including the dead. Goldrein, I am proud to say, fought bravely and heroically in keeping the pirates at bay."

"I was wondering who the bloodstained figure was, I thought he was one of your crew! Please be seated, gentlemen. It was ungallant of me, you must be worn out.'

He poured drinks from a decanter and offered Jamie a cigar. The Admiral addressed his aide: "Commander, take care of this brave young man," indicating Goldie. "House him in the officers' quarters and present him to the Quartermaster. Write a report and I'll see you later, young man."

The aide said: "Please follow me."

Before leaving the room the Midshipman saluted.

The Admiral thanked Jamie for his presentation and report and concluded by asking Jamie to pass on a message to Captain Semmes requesting his presence the following morning at ten o'clock.

The '*Alabama*' settled on the blocks in the dock and the crew were given shore leave. Jamie had a relaxed sleep and was woken at breakfast-time next morning by the cook, Eric Dunbar.

"I have a special Malayan dish for you, Carruthers has been and really enjoyed it. He said you are meeting an Admiral at ten o'clock. You had better hurry, sir. We have been overwhelmed with provisions from the local natives, so I'll be able to cook some special dishes for you and your friends."

• • •

Drinks were being served in the Admiral's wardroom. Semmes, together with the officers, were relating the '*Alabama's*' adventures,

particularly in routing the pirates who attacked H.M.S. 'Chester'. Alastair Goldrein, dressed in a white Midshipman's uniform, invited Jamie to meet his family on the other side of Singapore Island, just outside the city.
The following morning Goldie was standing on the quay with two saddled horses.
Jamie strode up the gangway to meet the Midshipman.
"I'm glad you have brought a holstered revolver, Jamie."
He addressed his new friend, who was dressed in riding breeches and a brown shirt.
"We shall be riding through some rough rocky country with all kinds of dangerous wild animals and snakes. Even bats have been known to attack humans, so be ever alert. As you can see," he slapped the leather long bag housing a rifle, "I never travel without my trusty repeating rifle."
Jamie hadn't mounted a horse for many weeks, but he soon became accustomed to the magnificent black stallion he was riding as the two naval officers left the dockyard. They passed groups of the crew on shore leave, hurrying through the dockyard to find the nearest tavern and drinking dens scattered along dockland. Many a wench would make them welcome and attend to their personal needs, leaving them penniless and pie-eyed.
Crossing the rocky terrain, Goldie cautioned Jamie about the unexpected reptiles and snakes they might encounter. "The horses are usually alert to the dangers and smell danger, but there is always the snake lying in wait to frighten a horse and then at his leisure attack a helpless rider." The horsemen jogged along chatting and laughing. They entered a rocky ravine and then emerged into a valley. A rough grey-dressed man standing on a rock fired a shot from his rifle, which caused Jamie's horse to rear and threw him to the ground. He rolled over and drew his revolver from the holster and pointed it in the direction of the man, who was about to fire again.
Jamie squeezed the trigger three times. The man clutched his chest, but then a further loud burst of gunfire caused the man to stagger and he fell and rolled off the rock. Jamie ran across the stony ground, his revolver at the ready.
He was amazed to see the bloodstained grey belted dress of a Malayan, gazing with sightless brown eyes. He was joined by Goldie, who rolled the dead body over. He was about to make a comment when he was interrupted by six mounted black-uniformed soldiers who galloped up, surrounded them and pointed their guns at the naval officers. They were addressed by their leader:
"I'm Lieutenant MacDuffy of the Singapore Police. We were rounding that bend," pointing, "when we saw this creature firing

277

and you were being ambushed. So naturally we fired back. There could be more in the area.

Sergeant, take two men and scout around." "Thank you, Lieutenant, for coming to our assistance. I'm the Second Lieutenant from the '*Alabama*', which has just anchored off the dockyard. May I introduce Midshipman Goldrein of Her Majesty's Navy. We are on our way to meet his family."

"I know the Judge. We are going in that direction. Perhaps we can escort you part of the way."

The two naval officers continued their journey without incident.

The Judge, seated comfortably nursing a glass of wine, was reading a brief concerning a murder trial, when there was a knock on the library door.

The Malayan servant announced: "Sir, your son has arrived with a visitor."

They were made most welcome by his parents. Ruth, Alastair's younger sister, who had been horse-riding, arrived in time for the evening meal. Jamie was bewitched when he met the slim, blue-eyed young lady. For the rest of the evening, he enjoyed her company, walking in the multicoloured flower gardens which surrounded the Tudor-styled British-built mansion.

"Look at these wild flowers Jamie!"

Her cultured English dialect sounded like music in his ears. Gently handling with her two fingers the large red-petalled flower, she remarked: "Our Malayan servant brought it back from a visit to his homeland; how quickly it has grown. Our grounds extend towards those small rocky mountains."

She extended her long slender arm, pointing. "And if you look closely, you can see a waterfall, which falls into a beautiful lake." She suddenly had an idea! "In the morning I'll take you there and we'll go for a swim."

Jamie reflected: 'She is certainly moving fast.' He held her hands and gently kissed her and remarked: "I'll certainly look forward to our date, say ten o'clock." "I'll have the same horse which you rode from town." Jamie laughed: "You won't be inviting your brother, will you?" She smiled. "No, he'll be looking up his girlfriend."

They arrived at the waterfall. While Jamie neatly folded his white shirt and placed it on top of his shoes and socks, the quick, sun-tanned Ruth ran past, laughing and dived into the lake. Jamie drew in a long deep breath as he watched her swimming, her long black hair streaming down her back. He dived in off a rock and, being a strong swimmer, quickly caught her up and swam with a gentle motion alongside her. Ruth laughed and ducked him under the water.

He caught her leg and pulled her with him. They embraced and Jamie gave her a long kiss on her closed lips. She pointed up, indicating to surface. Jamie thought as they lay in each other's arms on a thick rug: 'This must be the life for me.' Jamie leaned over the smiling Ruth, who lay stretched out, her arms above her head. He gave her a long passionate kiss. Ruth moaned, she had never been loved and caressed like this before. 'Trust a sailor, who has been to sea for a long time!' Both their mouths opened and Jamie's tongue found the young maiden's. She smiled, a happy smile of contentment, and they both relaxed, enjoying the sun's rays. She gave him a long lingering kiss and suddenly remarked: "How about another swim in the warm waters, before we return to my home?"

They trotted alongside each other, laughing and chatting away as lovers do. He occasionally leaned over and kissed her.

'I feel mean, and guilty,' thought Jamie, 'not disclosing I'm married. Well, here am I, hundreds of miles away from home! Will I see her again? - live today - die tomorrow - let's enjoy ourselves.'

They arrived at the Judge's country home. After the evening meal, Jamie related his adventures to an eager audience late into the night. Alastair wanted to know about the daring raids and how Jamie could adapt himself from an engineer, to navigator - to soldier.

Next morning, Tyler, the Second Mate, accompanied by Leeson, arrived on horseback with a written message from Captain Semmes - he had informed him of his whereabouts. Jamie excused himself and opened the letter, which read: 'Report to me at the Governor's residence and bring the Midshipman.'

Ruth decided to accompany the party back to the dockyard. It was an opportunity to meet the Governor's daughter, Donna. Led by Alastair, with Ruth and Jamie bringing up the rear, they trotted without any incident and arrived at the Governor's mansion, which was situated about two miles from the dockyard.

The Governor, Sir Clive Williams, the Admiral and Semmes welcomed Jamie and Goldie. They were assembled in the spacious, flower-decked lounge.

Drinks were served and cigars lit. The Captain addressed Jamie: "We've been discussing the tragic death and burial details of Captain Locke. It has been decided, as the coffin is resting in the Royal Naval Chapel, which is near the dry dock berthing the '*Alabama*', that we should take part in the parade which will pass through the dockyard. The cemetery is situated about a mile away. It has also been agreed that pipes and drums will precede the hearse and the crew will parade behind the hearse, which will be a sailor-drawn gun carriage. Will you please convey these orders to the First Lieutenant as I have been invited to spend the night in the mansion and I shall return about eight o'clock tomorrow morning to take part in the procession? I expect all those taking part to be assembled on the quay at nine-thirty. At the same time I expect the ship to be well guarded."

Jamie saluted. "Very good, sir."

"By the way, Jamie, take the Midshipman with you." Semmes turned to Alastair Goldrein. "I have been privileged to tell you the good news, young man. For your heroism and bravery the Admiral has rewarded you with a full commission in the British Navy and you are to accompany us as far as South Africa. You will then continue your journey on to England to attend the Naval School at Greenwich."

They all stood up. Semmes shook Alastair's hand and wished him luck. The Admiral butted in: "Gentlemen, I think it will be fitting if we drink a toast to the Midshipman who helped save one of Her Majesty's ships."

● ● ●

It was Friday 18th December and the '*Alabama's*' crew had been mustered early for the parade to the cemetery for the burial of Captain Silas Locke. The gun carriage to carry the coffin arrived at ten o'clock and backed to the entrance of the adjacent Naval Chapel. The black-uniformed Jamie unfurled the Confederate flag and positioned himself in front of the pipers and drummers, the crew and grey-uniformed soldiers at the rear. The tall moustachioed Semmes, also in black uniform, buttons polished, sword at his side, looked immaculate as he strode and took his position behind his country's standard. The strains of the pipes - played by the British Pipe Major Doig - signified the flag-draped coffin carried by six Britannic seamen had left the Naval Chapel following the short service. The Captain's sword and cap nestled amongst the flowers on the flagged coffin.

The parade was ordered to stand to attention by the First Lieutenant as the coffin was lifted on to the gun carriage.

In slow time the procession from the chapel was led by the lone piper followed by the '*Alabama's*' pipes and drums. The British Standard-bearer marched alongside Jamie, and the Admiral beside Captain Semmes. At the sound of the Bosun's whistle the '*Alabama's*' flag was lowered to half-mast as the parade marched slowly through the dockyard. The route was lined with workmen and Navy personnel, most with bowed heads, paying their last respects to a brave Naval Captain who had fought nobly for his country. The procession moved slowly through the silent cosmopolitan crowd. There was a large crowd, mainly uniformed, already gathered at the cemetery. The coffin was placed alongside the grave and the relatives of the deceased, and friends, also positioned themselves, together with the Bishop of Singapore, who was also the honorary Naval Chaplain and who stood at the foot of the grave and conducted the service. As the coffin was slowly being lowered into the grave, the lone piper in the distance played the lament. A volley from the guard of honour signified the Captain was finally laid to rest. The British flag was neatly folded and handed to the bereaved widow and the Captain's sword handed to his son.

Following the burial service the '*Alabama*' crew returned to the ship. Semmes summoned the officers to his cabin.

"Gentlemen, the Governor has invited us to a garden party, followed by an evening banquet. Sunday evening we will be undocking, as the dock is required for the bold British frigate the '*Chester*,' which is on its way back from the Johore Straits, manned of course by some of our own crew. We have completed what underwater repairs we can; unfortunately we have used our spare copper plates, and as we can't obtain any in this area we will try in India.

We will then return to South Africa to rendezvous with the '*Tuscaloosa*', hoping it will be able to provide us with provisions and coal and maybe copper plating. In the meantime prepare the ship for sea, and" - with a smile and snigger - "enjoy your shore leave."

• • •

The Governor's lawn was crowded with all the local dignitaries. As the coaches and horsemen from the '*Alabama*' arrived at the mansion steps, the crowd surged forward, all eager to meet the crew from the notorious raider.

Semmes and his officers were greeted by the Governor, Sir Clive Williams, the Admiral, and Judge Goldrein. Jamie rode up on the borrowed black horse. He was embraced by Ruth, dressed in a long, low-cut blue dress, her long black hair draped over her partly exposed ample bosom. She linked the white-uniformed Jamie's arm and they ascended the stone steps, through the large ornamental doors and into the music room where afternoon tea was served by a Malayan servant. There was a knock on the door and Ruth's friend entered.

"Look who I've found."

It was her brother Alastair.

'That's spoiled things,' thought Ruth. 'Here I was, thinking I could have another session with old hot-pants over there? and look who turns up. Alastair isn't at all diplomatic. Must get rid of him smartly, otherwise he is going to ruin my day.'

"How nice to see you both." She greeted Alastair with a kiss! "Would you like to join us for tea? This, if you don't know, Jamie, is an old English custom - everything stops for tea at four o'clock."

Alastair was excited when he explained to his sister and Donna about his future, starting in the Confederate Navy.

When tea was finished and the servants had taken away the dishes, Ruth remarked: "By the way, Alastair, father said he wanted to see you, I think it is about the news you have been telling us about."

Alastair took the hint and he and Donna departed. 'Now I've got you to myself.' Ruth smiled as she walked over and locked the door. She went to the harpsichord and lifted the lid and began to play. Her long tapering fingers danced up and down on the keyboard.

"Do you know this song, Jamie?" Her silvery soprano voice trilled as she sang. "It came from England, it is a 'Largo' and composed by George Frederick Handel."

Jamie stood behind her and hummed the popular song. He looked over her shoulder and parted the long black hair and kissed her on the neck. She slightly cringed with excitement, but continued playing and singing. She suddenly stopped playing, her eyes swooning, her mouth open, she gave Jamie a long kiss and searched for his tongue. They kissed and cuddled for about an hour on the couch, when their love-making was disturbed by the ringing of a bell in the hall. Ruth sat up and smoothed her hair.

"That is the Governor's call to assemble on the lawn for the banquet."

The Governor, Sir Clive Williams, and his wife, Lorna, were seated next to the Admiral and his wife. Judge Goldrein stood up when his daughter arrived and offered her and Jamie their seats at the end of the long canopied table which faced the assembled guests.

"Gosh, it's hot. I see others have draped their jackets on the back of their seats, that's better."

"Is it always so hot?" He wiped his brow. "In Scotland, where I was born, the snow would be twelve inches high this time of the year." Ruth laughed. "What's snow, Jamie? Tell us more about the composer, Handel."

Jamie took a sip of wine. "He composed in four weeks an oratorio which he called 'The Messiah'. I remember an Irish seaman telling me it was first performed in Dublin with a large choir and orchestra and I think, if I can recall, George Frederick Handel conducted the performance. It became very popular as it was taken from various verses from the Bible, mainly of course about the Messiah."

Ruth who had been listening intently remarked: 'When I play the 'Largo' next time I'll recall our conversation and perhaps some day I'll be able to buy the Oratorio. Come, Jamie, I would like to introduce you to some of my friends."

They joined the first canopied white table and were invited to drink some fine imported Spanish wine.

"Jamie, may I introduce you to Jonathan Wakely." "I feel honoured to shake hands with an officer from the '*Alabama*'. I heard how you rescued my friend Alastair and the horrific ending of the '*Chester's*' Captain."

Jamie acknowledged the appreciative remarks by adding: "Indeed the battle was almost ending when we boarded the frigate, we only had to sort out a few of the pirates, if that is who they were - it was Alastair who was the hero. He fought bravely against heavy odds."

Jonathan laughed. "I've heard a different story. I'm a Subaltern attached to the Governor's staff." Jamie thought: 'A typical British army cadet trained at the London Barracks.' He smiled.

Jonathan continued: "I was originally with the Bengal Lancers in India. Life was costly on the border; I heard about this quiet British possession, applied, and here I am."

Jamie regarded the khaki-uniformed young officer, complete with holster, and thought: 'If it's so peaceful, why is he wearing a gun?'

The party was joined by Donna on 'Enry's arm. They were chatting and laughing. Things seemed so quiet and jolly, when Jamie noticed a long-robed, belted, bearded man, wearing a turban, emerge in the distance, walking quickly up the path which divided the tables. He was heading for the long table where the Governor and his party were seated. He was about ten feet from Jamie, when he noticed something shining in his right hand, which was partially hidden under his baggy robe.

Jamie quickly sized up the situation. He approached the Subaltern and withdrew his revolver as the white-robed figure rushed past him, shouting and screaming. He was waving a short broadsword, charging towards the Governor. Jamie rapidly fired five shots into the back of the running man. He didn't even falter, but carried on running.

The frightened Governor stood up. The white-robed man yelled loudly, raised the sword above his head and it was about to descend, to split open the Governor's head, when Jamie fired the last shot into the back of the villain's head. The sword fell out of his hand, on to the Governor's right shoulder, narrowly missing his head and ear.

Jamie rushed forward and dragged the dead bloodstained body off the table.

A khaki-uniformed officer leaned over the body, a revolver in his right hand. He gave Jamie a strange look and expressed his emotions: "I'm Captain Maudsley, the Governor's Military Attache. That was quick thinking, sizing up the situation and acting quickly. You saved the Governor's life. My grateful thanks."

The '*Alabama's*' Doctor MacGregor eased the Governor's bloodstained jacket over the wounded shoulder and ripped off his shirt.

"Hand me that bottle of whisky, Madam?" addressing the Governor's wife.

He poured it over the wound and, with a smile, said: "Have a swig. It will ease the pain."

He dabbed the wound with a handkerchief. Lorna ripped a piece from her undergarment for a bandage.

"That's better, it's not serious, it's only a flesh wound - he'll be better in a day or two."

He turned to the Admiral. "Will you please arrange for him to be transported to the comforts of the house?"

Captain Maudsley was discussing the incident with Jamie. "This man," prodding him with his foot, "a political fanatic and as you can tell, half-Malayan Chinese. He belongs to a secret society whose aim is to oust the British from this Colony. All of today's guests had been carefully examined."

Maudsley smiled. "Excluding yourselves, of course, but he easily disguised himself as a servant, as you can see by his dress! He had been trained to resist pain and torture as you can tell. Five bullets didn't stop him. It was a good job you had a sixth, otherwise we would have been looking for a new Governor! I see they are taking the Governor up to his residence. Will you please accompany me as I will have to make a written report. I see by your accent you're Scottish."

As they walked along the wide gravelled pathway leading to the large mansion, Jamie gave a brief outline of his adventures since he joined the '*Alabama*' to the interested Captain.

The bandaged Governor was sitting up in bed when Jamie, accompanied by Maudsley, visited the crowded bedroom and was introduced to Sir Clive Williams.

"I'm feeling much better. Thank you for coming and saving my life. I also understand you led the raid that saved the '*Chester*'. I heard from Captain Semmes that your ship will be leaving tomorrow, to fight your war. I wish you luck in your undertakings and may God go with you."

Ruth was waiting for Jamie with two horses.
"You were very quick to act when the Governor's life was in danger, Jamie."
He smiled.
'I don't know, Ruth. It could have been your life or anybody sitting on that top table. I understand that these fanatical people are spreading. Your life could be in danger. I would advise you and your family to leave Singapore. The '*Alabama*' will be leaving tomorrow evening - where we sail to goodness only knows. I've got to go and fight a bloody war."
The strains of the recent events had upset Jamie. He was overwrought.
"Look, Ruth, will you accompany me to the dockyard?"
"Don't leave me, Jamie, stay with me!" she pleaded.
Jamie's reply was to mount the black horse and gallop off. Ruth mounted the white and rode in hot pursuit.
The docks were crowded with Chinese, Malasians, Dutch, Spanish, Indians, all peddling their wares. The smell and the noise were overwhelming. Rickshaws, horse and bullock-drawn carts crowded the wharf leading to the Naval Dockyard. Once inside the yard, Jamie felt an air of peace. It was gratifying to hear the different dockyard noises. He dismounted and handed the reins to the guard, when Ruth charged up, leapt off her mount and flung her arms around Jamie's neck, kissing him on the mouth.
"It's no use, Ruth, I'm going away. There's no hope for our future. We live in different worlds."
Tears streamed down her face. He gently wiped them away with his fingers, kissed her and squeezed her hand, saying: "Perhaps some day we may meet again."
He quickly turned away and walked along the crowded quay towards the gangway. Water was already surging into the dock, lapping around the '*Alabama's*' keel. The deck of the ship bustled with activity, seamen up the rigging examining the sails and ropes, gunners attending to the Blakely guns.
Leeson and Ryan were polishing the brasses on the main wheel and the bridge.
The First Lieutenant was strutting up and down, keeping an eye on the provisions being carried up the gangway by the Malaysians. He was joined by Midshipman Goldrein, who smartly saluted him and inquired: "I have come to report, sir - orders from the Captain."

Kelly tapped his telescope into the palm of his hand - a nervous habit. "Very good, Middy. Get out of that ridiculous uniform into working clothes. Climb that rigging" - pointing - "and watch the seamen at work. Next job - report to Mr. Dunbar, the cook, and learn the trade" - Kelly laughed. "No doubt your first job will be peeling potatoes. Then visit the engine room. Mr. Freeman, the Chief Engineer will show you how to fire the boilers and then start up and maintain the fresh water system. That will keep you busy and I will personally watch you start up the main engines and see you lift the propeller out of the water."

Kelly tapped his peaked cap, signifying the completion of his commands.

"That will be all, Middy, go about your duties."

"Yes, sir," said Goldrein, saluting. Jamie joined the First Lieutenant.

"That's a good start, sir, sending the Middy up the mast."

They both laughed, watching the Bosun chasing Goldrein up the mast, rapping him on the behind with his knotted piece of rope. "We'll make a sailor out of him by the time we arrive in South Africa!"

• • •

Dawn, 21st December. The uniformed Jamie ascended the companionway, yawned and flexed his muscles. He relieved the officer of the watch, Captain Francis.

"It's been a quiet night, Jamie, except for some drunken crewmen returning. The weather is fair for this time of the year and we'll be sailing at midday."

Jamie returned the salute. "Thank you, Alan, go and enjoy a good fish breakfast; it was delicious, cooked and served by the British Middy."

The level of the water in the dock was slowly rising, assisted by the incoming tide. High tide was at eleven o'clock, which meant the water in the dock and the straits would be at an equal level - ideal for undocking an hour later.

Towards mid-morning the dock area and the ship were busy with the crew preparing last-minute provisions and the shipyard workers undocking the ship.

At ten o'clock the First Lieutenant commanded all hands to harbour stations and the uniformed military marshalled on deck. Crowds gathered on the dock wall. The Judge and his family soon located the Midshipman who was standing by the main wheel and waved him farewell. Ruth fluttered a white handkerchief to attract Jamie's attention, who waved and blew her a kiss.

The signal was given by the Naval Dockmaster that the dock gates had opened and the '*Alabama*' was ready for undocking. The First Lieutenant took command.

"Haul away forward, haul away aft."

Mullard, sitting astride on the capstan, commenced playing his concertina and to the lusty strains of 'Dixie', the ropes were hauled in from the quay and the sailors swarmed into the rigging awaiting the order to unfurl the sails. The Confederate raider with engines in reverse and black smoke billowing from her funnel, slowly eased her way out of the dock amidst cheering and waving from the crowded quay. The ship weaved in and out of the crowded harbour and once clear, the slight breeze filled the sails. With her Southern flag proudly fluttering at the masthead, the '*Alabama*' sailed (minus her engines) passing the numerous small islands and avoiding the numerous small boats who were affected by the wash as the ship gathered speed. Malacca was sighted on the starboard beam and the straits gradually broadened out to the widest part between Georgetown and Kuta Rajan on the northerly point of the island of Sumatra and then into the Arabian Sea.

"Two sailing ships," shouted Riordan through his trumpet on the swaying mizzen mast, "rapidly approaching dead ahead and closing."

"Action stations," snarled Jamie, who was the officer of the watch.

"Man the eight-inch Blakely gun, pointing it to starboard and the nine-inch gun to port and when the enemy target is in sight, fire across their bows. Bosun, change the colours."

'Bang' went the port gun, whistling across the Northern ship's bows. The '*Alabama*' rolled with the force of the impact, causing the eight-inch gun to fire later with a low elevation, which penetrated the enemy ship below the waterline.

Jamie was alarmed that the damaged ship was listing and he ordered:

"Man the boats and pick up survivors."

On board the '*Sonora*', Captain Higham Slater was enjoying the race towards Singapore down the Straits of Malacca against his friend Matthew McCracken, Captain of the '*Highlander*'. He thought: 'A Scotsman on a Scottish-named ship, belonging to a shipping company in Boston. His ship is lighter than mine, but I have more sails and I will win the bet!'

A ship was approaching dead ahead which Slater viewed with apprehension through his telescope.

'It's heading straight for us, as though it wants to come between us!' He was startled when the three ships were almost level to see the strange ship bore a Southern flag, and two shots were fired from midship guns. It rocked his ship with a shattering blow. Men came shouting and yelling from below decks. Fire gushed from the forward hatch - the ship was uncontrollable! The 'Sonora' was sinking.

Then came the dreaded cry "Launch the boats, abandon ship and head for that Southern ship."

On board the 'Alabama' Captain Slater lunged at the Confederate Captain in a threatening manner.

"How dare you sink my ship by gunfire? What kind of monster are you? An innocent ship going about its business and then fired on and sunk!"

Captain Semmes was annoyed. "We are at war, Mister, and you are minus two ships. I have two Yankee flags to prove it, to add to my collection of sixty." Semmes gestured to the First Lieutenant.

"Mr. Kelly, take this man out of my sight and lock him up with the rest of the prisoners." Slater started to struggle.

"Put him in irons," yelled the Captain. "That should cool him off." The 'Sonora', amidst a white foam and black smoke, disappeared into the Indian Ocean.

"Fire the 'Highlander'," shouted Kelly. Jamie went with a boarding party to take part in the operation.

'What a shame to torch such a fine schooner. I'll have a look around while the men are setting the torches.' He searched various cabins and drawers, pocketing watches, binoculars and coins. 'Ah the Captain will be interested in this,' handling a chronometer. Jamie opened a door marked 'Officers' Quarters' and was about to close it, when he heard a whimpering sound. In the dim light he observed the huddled figure of a young woman.

"What on earth are you doing here? The ship is burning and sinking, the crew have been taken off." He helped her to her feet, wrapped a blanket around her and assisted her up the companionway on to the main deck.

"Hedgecock, help this young lady into the longboat and abandon ship." The 'Sonora' was burning furiously as the longboat bumped alongside the 'Alabama'.

Jamie assisted the young lady on to the main deck. They were greeted by the astonished Semmes.

"What have we here?"

"I found her in one of the cabins, sir. Her name is Mrs. Julie Gratton, the wife of the Second Mate."

"Fetch him up, Bosun, from the prison and bring him to my cabin," thundered the Captain. "Come, my dear, we will not harm you," to the trembling lady. The Mate confronted his wife. She wrapped her arms around his neck, sobbing.

"What's the meaning of this, Gratton," rapped out Semmes. "neglecting your wife?"

Mrs. Gratton butted in: "It's not his fault - when I heard the shooting on deck, I knew there was danger and something wrong. I thought at first we had been boarded by pirates - they show no mercy. Then I smelt smoke and I was really terrified and settled down in our cabin."

The nervous Gratton remarked: "It was like this, sir, I didn't have time to find my wife, as I was forcefully moved off the ship and into a boat. I found myself on the deck of this ship and before I could protest and tell somebody, I found myself imprisoned." He hugged his wife and sobbed. "Thank God you are safe, my dear." He turned to Jamie and shook his hand and said: "Thank you for saving her life." Semmes looked at the young couple and felt compassionate.

"I'm sorry for the inconvenience you have suffered and I shall make the rest of your stay with us comfortable, then we shall transfer you to a British ship in the near future."

On Christmas Day the '*Alabama*' hove to in a calm sea. 'Grog all round' was the signal for the band to assemble on deck. Mullard commanded proceedings from his stance on the capstan. Irish and Scottish dancing commenced with lusty singing and the seamen enjoyed the special dinner. Semmes celebrated the Festive Season with his officers in his cabin. Cigars and pipes were lit and there was a choice of Jamaican, Spanish or Italian wines.

On the 15th January 1864, the '*Emma Jane*' was captured and torched off the island of Ceylon. The prisoners landed on the southern tip of India, and the '*Alabama*' sailed into the Indian Ocean.

Numerous British ships passed, were searched and their papers examined, which proved they were legal, carrying materials for the rapidly growing development of her Majesty's Britannic Empire. On and on sailed the Confederate raider, ever vigilant for the capture and sinking of her enemy. Semmes wrote in his log: 'January 31st, crossed the equator, weather hot - unbearable. 5th February, continuing down the Mozambique Channel to Africa.'

Chapter 24

Jamie leaned over the ship's rail, watching as the '*Alabama*' gently eased her way, sails unfurled, into Table Bay in the Cape of Good Hope. It was Sunday morning 20th March 1864.
The barometer was high and there was a strong breeze blowing from the south-west. The Table Mountain top presented a picturesque scene, outlined by billowing clouds as the ship settled in deeper waters. Jamie, being the officer of the watch, thought it prudent, for safety measures, to release both anchors.
Two days later the gale moderated which allowed the approach of the smaller boats laden with provisions and coal, which the firemen shovelled into the bunkers. The cook, Eric Dunbar, attended to the barges which bumped alongside, laden with fresh fruit, vegetables, meats, flour and barrels of salt. Alex, the Engineer, piped up the fresh water supplied from a lighter.
Cape Town is one of the principal ports of the world for commerce and naturally, having a passing trade, receives all the world news, particularly about the American Civil War.

• • •

Visitors thronged on to the "*Alabama*', mostly curious, some on their way to seek a new life in the rapidly growing British Empire in the Far East. The officers entertained visitors. Jamie, with his friends, were introduced to three British Naval officers who hailed from Merseyside. Naturally the conversation concerned home news.
"I'm Jamie, I live off Rodney Street, with my wife and two girls. Have you any local news?"
"Well," replied the tall, black-uniformed Lieutenant, "my name is Derek Fuller, I live in the village of Formby. I'm off to India, to a gunboat in Bombay. I must say the news headlines about Laird's Shipyard is very disturbing. I'm afraid John Laird has gone into disgrace since it was reported that the '*Alabama*' had sunk over fifty Northern ships. You must realise that a British shipyard must not build a ship, particularly a warship, for a country at war - because that would violate international rules of neutrality. Also

the cotton mills are closing down, one by one, because the ships
from the Southern States cannot supply cotton, because they can't
get through the blockades."

"This is a most remarkable and interesting ship," butted in
Lieutenant James Rudman. "I used to work in the Birkenhead
Iron Works, serving my apprenticeship as an engineer. It is true
what Derek has told you. John Laird is in real trouble as he is
also a Member of Parliament. I live opposite the old battery at
Egremont and the newspapers' headlines are mostly about the
war and this famous or" - with a chuckle - "this infamous warship;
I suppose it depends which side you support."

"I'm here for the grog and the spoils," laughingly burst in Alex.

"Same here," responded Carruthers. 'I cannot wait to get home
to sort things out, and then I'll be off to Jamaica to be united with
my Kate."

Jamie broke in: "We have certainly benefited, fighting for the
South, but I think it's for a lost cause."

Mr. Freeman approached and Jamie remarked "Sir, I would like to
introduce three British Naval officers -Lieutenants Fuller, Rudman
and Richard Logue."

"Gentlemen, my pleasure. I'm sure you would like to have a look
around our engine and boiler rooms! The Second Engineer,"
indicating Jamie, "will show you the way and explain about our
new design of propeller and how we retract the funnel to give us
further speed."

"What a well-laid out engine room," exclaimed Logue. "I understand
it was built to the latest British Naval standards. It must be
gratifying that this sturdy wooden ship has survived a twenty-
month rampage, battling through three oceans and capturing or
burning fifty-four merchant vessels and sinking one Union warship.
It is amazing! What an accomplishment, ably handled by the genius
of your Captain with hardly any loss of life!"

Jamie and his friends were a bit over-whelmed by the
compliments. Alex continued "Mr. Frank Weighill, ably supported
by Len Withers, designed this new horizontal steam engine, which
was built in Laird's shop, together with the boilers. Jamie and I
were involved almost from the beginning on building, running and
testing the engines. The boat itself is in desperate need of repair,
her seams keep bursting open and need caulking. On the keel and
on the bottom of the ship, the rolled copper needs replacing. That
is why I understand in the next couple of days we will be leaving
Table Bay and sailing back to Europe."

"Thank you for showing us around," remarked Jim Rudman. "I
only hope that when we board our respective warships in the Indian

Ocean they will be maintained and serviced as well as this one, and I am sure, speaking on behalf of myself and my comrades, we wish you well and bon voyage."

The curious visitors were ferried ashore in small boats. The '*Alabama*' was ready for sea, her coal bunkers bulging, and provisions were stowed on board, sufficient to reach the Azores.

On the morning of the 25th March, the creaky vessel steamed out of Table Bay, escorted by a fleet of small vessels. To Captain Semmes' surprise the fast Yankee steamer, '*Qung Tang*', approaching the bay, passed very close to the '*Alabama*', and as she was in territorial waters, she could not be intercepted. As the Confederate raider was now under sail, Jamie and his fellow engineers had left the engine room and lined the rail to watch as the ships silently passed each other without any sign of recognition. Both the stern flags nearly touched each other.

'What a prize,' thought Jamie, as the '*Alabama*' headed into open waters.

• • •

Later after the midday meal, consisting of thick soup and 'Irish' (different varieties of meat), made by the officers' experienced cooks - Dunbar and Gillie Fisher - the Captain came into the officers' mess, a bundle of papers under his arm. He placed them on the mess table and remarked: "Gentlemen, the news is not encouraging. The enemy have gained so much ground. We lost the vital bloody battle at Gettysburg, where, if the gallant Pickett's charge had been successful, we could have gained a decisive victory and it could have been the turning point of the war. Instead, we had to retreat with heavy losses. Vicksburg has surrended, Atlanta and Chattanooga fallen, and - due to the large enemy fleet - the entire eastern coast has been blockaded. Our finances are very low, so is the morale of our troops - it looks like the end. However, so long as we are afloat, we will play havoc with the Union's mercantile fleet, but first we must head for a European port for refurbishing and refitting." Semmes paused and took a deep breath.

"Mr. Freeman, have we enough coal on board to reach Europe?"

"Certainly, sir, in fact we have extra in the specially built bunkers."

"Well, gentlemen," said the Captain, "let us concentrate on our future and I sincerely hope that we reach a safe haven, which I hope will be St. Helena."

It was quite an uneventful sea passage. The creaky ship under full sail with a good breeze blowing from the south, eventually sighted the barren rock of St. Helena.

A longboat was despatched under the command of Bosun Bellew. Ray Tyler was on the tiller and Ryan and Hedgecock rowed the boat towards the island.

Bellew reported back on his return to the Captain, after interviewing some of the unfriendly inhabitants of the island, that no provisions were available. The '*Alabama*' upheaved anchor, steamed out of the harbour and after unfurling her topsails sailed along at a steady eight knots into the homeward bound Translantic Lane, right into the paths of the enemy, looking for provisions.

● ● ●

The '*Alabama*' passed numerous ships on their way to the Cape of Good Hope - no enemy ships, all English - until early evening on the 22nd April, when a Yankee barque appeared in Captain Semmes' telescope.

The raider immediately gave chase at thirteen knots, her canvas sails billowing in the south-westerly breeze, and the chase continued through the moonlit night.

The enemy skipper plied all his canvas, but to no avail and as the dawn broke, only one mile separated the two ships. She hoisted her Northern colours.

"Man battle stations," snarled Semmes. "Hoist our Confederate flag."

A shot was fired from the '*Alabama*' which fell just astern of the prize which turned out to be the '*Rockingham*'. She hove to and a boarding party was headed by Captain Francis. The tough Welshman presented himself to the '*Rockingham's*' Captain, who in turn handed him the ship's papers.

These were examined by the Welsh captain and they showed that her cargo was owned by the Brazilian Government and that she was bound for Dublin in Ireland.

Some stores and provisions were transferred to the "*Alabama*'. The prisoners were put in their own boats, with enough food and water. Captain Powell was given a compass and directed to St. Helena - which was about fifty miles away to the south-east.

"Man the guns and prepare to sink the enemy ship, but first, put her to the torch," ordered the agitated Semmes.

Shots were fired and directed below the '*Rockingham's*' water line. (This was to give the gunners some practice, and to make her sink faster.)

The '*Alabama*' then continued on course northbound for Europe. Two days later, on the 27th April, the look-out man, Riordan, shouted down that a ship was approaching, about three miles away. The weather was fine with a strong breeze and as she drew nearer the First Lieutenant ordered the Southern flag to be struck, and alerted Jamie to be prepared to board the enemy ship.

Captain Humphrey Birley on the '*Tycoon*', thinking of the safety of his crew and recognising the Confederate raider, ordered the Mate, Peter Williams, to lower the flag and surrender. He didn't want to go down with his ship!

A party of marines, led by the Second Lieutenant, boarded the Northern ship.

Her records showed she was bound for Boston and she had an assorted cargo, but there was nothing to signify, when Jamie examined her papers, any claim to neutral property.

The '*Tycoon*'s' Captain and crew were transferred to the '*Alabama*' and the Captain ordered his crew to help themselves to anything on board. The Quartermaster helped himself to all the clothing and bedding. Jamie ordered the Bosun's Mate, Ray Tyler, to set fire to the '*Tycoon*'. The red glow could be seen until the '*Alabama*' sailed over the horizon.

The tradition of Father Neptune was observed on the 2nd May as the warship crossed the equator. Jamie was selected after a 'unanimous' vote to be greased and dressed up like Neptune and amidst shouting and cheering he was ejected backwards into a make-up tank that was positioned on the port side amidships. Well into the night 'Jack' enjoyed himself with generous offerings of grog which added to the merriment and pleasures of the journey as the '*Alabama*' plowed her way steadily northwards. The monotony was disrupted by thunder, lightning and heavy rain, followed by calm weather.

Semmes kept to himself in his cabin. His once tall, straight figure was limp. He felt weary, fatigued and stressed. In the two years he had piloted his beloved ship and faithful crew he had strictly observed the orders of the President, which were to attack, subdue, scuttle and burn Union ships. So over twenty-four months, sailing half-way round the world he had sunk fifty-three and ransomed and sold another eleven ships.

The last batch of newspapers captured from the '*Tycoon*' was gloomy and disastrous, concerning the war. General Grant had had great victories on 1st May 1864 at Vicksburg, Chatanooga and Richmond. His opponent was Robert E. Lee. Fighting was intense and by 22nd May, Grant was again on the move, heading south-east in a flood of Union soldiers driving towards Atlanta. The future looked bleak and the South doomed. Still the '*Alabama*' sailed further north nearing her destination, but ever alert to engage the enemy.

On reaching her old rendezvous and sighting the islands of the Azores, she eased her way into Prava Bay and anchored.

"Mr. Kelly, kindly attend to the prisoners and see that they are safely despatched ashore. Check that we have enough provisions and coal to reach Europe."

"Yes, sir, I have even arranged for some livestock to be shipped on board."

"Thank you, Mr. Kelly, but I don't want to hear any news, I'm not in the mood, I think we have lost the war."

Jamie leaned on the astern rail and watched the islands disappear in the wake of the '*Alabama*'. He could not help but reminisce on the naming of the ship and how he had signed articles of war to support the Confederate cause.

Jamie was joined by Alex and Carruthers. Alex opened the conversation: "It does not seem like two years since we sailed from these islands. Remember how we struck our first blow at the enemy's whaling fleet, shortly after leaving the Azores! I was scared stiff, but didn't the Captain handle things well, with his skill and previous knowledge?"

"I would certainly agree, he is certainly a very experienced naval strategist" butted in Carruthers. "Don't forget he saw a great deal of action in the Mexican War!"

Alex closed the conversation: "Whatever you may think, we have certainly done well out of this war, when you consider how much loot we have legitimately obtained, and we can look forward to a very happy and comfortable future, especially you, Carruthers, with Kate. I don't know about you chaps, but I'm off to bed - pleasant dreams!"

To Jamie and his friends from Merseyside, they were homeward bound, knowing the ship was not welcome in England!

The '*Alabama*' battled on against huge waves that shook her from stem to stern, hugging the Portuguese and then the Spanish coast, into the unusually calm Bay of Biscay, France and then the English Channel on 10th June 1864.

The eager crew gathered on the port rail and watched as the Lizard lighthouse hove into view.

Alex, standing amidships, had a curious look on his thin gaunt face and remarked to Jamie, shouting above the noise of the wind: "Home at last, I feel so relieved." He continued stroking his stubbled chin.

"I hope to return to the Hebrides. Perhaps I'll go back to farming, I am a wealthy man like you, Jamie, thanks to the fair deal we received from the Captain - and it's been well rewarding. I'm off to dinner - coming?"

'Home,' reflected Jamie when he was alone, and with tears in his strained eyes, thought: 'How are my loved ones?' He became very emotional, buried his head in his hands and burst out crying.

A crowd of men gathered around the First Lieutenant, Mike Kelly, eagerly awaiting any news. He addressed the grouped anxious seamen gathered aft: "It is very unfortunate that we cannot dock in England. When the Birkenhead Iron Works built this so-called merchant ship in secret, giving it number 290, the company infringed Britain's neutrality and this has set up a precedent. Now the only port of call that will carry out repairs is Cherbourg, where we are heading, when the Pilot comes aboard. I know you Englishmen have a great urgency to jump overboard and swim to the safety of your native land. I don't blame you, I would do the same myself, however I must inform you that the ship is in urgent need of repair, as you no doubt are well aware, so we hope it will be received in the neutral Normandy sea port."

Jamie butted in: "Sir, will there be any chance of us visiting our families?"

"Leave that with me, Jamie, I'm sure there will be. I'll ask the Captain as the vessel will be in dry dock a few months."

It was early morning, misty, as the Channel Pilot, Maurice Derbyshire, boarded the 'Alabama'. After introducing himself to the Captain he guided the raider through the gloom. By midday the weather suddenly changed; a south-west storm was brewing which sped the ship on its way, nearer and nearer to its destination. Next morning the French coast was confirmed by the look-out man. The Channel Pilot guided the 'Alabama', hugging the French Normandy coastline, passing Le Havre, until she finally anchored in the harbour of the naval seaport of Cherbourg.

Semmes was relaxed as he conversed with the Pilot, Derbyshire, who, between drinking rum, was bubbling with questions.

"How successful have you been with your ventures in the last two years, since you left Birkenhead?" Derbyshire was amazed, as Semmes concluded:

"Sunk, ransacked, burned sixty-seven Northern ships? Most remarkable - and lost no men, sailing three oceans? I would like to shake your hand, Captain, what an achievement, and my congratulations. Wait till I tell my folks in Cornwall!" The Pilot shook the Captain's hand and saluted.

"Thank you for bringing us safely to this haven. I will arrange for you to go ashore.' Semmes summoned his steward after the Pilot had departed.

"Ramidios, ask Mr. Kelly to come to my cabin."

"Hello, Mike, well, I hope at last we have reached our goal. Take a longboat and another officer - say, Jamie, he dresses smartly; the Bosun's Mate, Alec Allan and two seamen, Hedgecock and Ryan. Make sure they are smartly dressed, also land the Pilot. I would like you to contact the Port Admiral and discuss with him about landing the last of the prisoners we have on board.

Most importantly, as you are well aware, we are in desperate need of repair and require the use and the facilities of a dry dock."

Jamie was summoned to go ashore, so, smartly dressed in number one kit, sword at side, he entered the longboat and was introduced to the Pilot by the blue-uniformed First Lieutenant. With Mate Allan on the tiller the two husky seamen rowed the boat towards the crowded jetty. Jamie could not help but reflect as they approached the landing what lovely old buildings adorned the waterfront and he admired the colourful dotted houses on the hillocks, that enveloped the town like a horseshoe.

Mike and Jamie, after the boat was safely berthed, enquired the whereabouts of the Admiral's office. Being informed they made their way along the waterfront and finally viewed the old white-washed Admiral's building, with its French naval flag fluttering in the breeze. After knocking on the large brass-handled door knob they were greeted by a smartly dressed young French Naval officer Ramon Bruchez, who welcomed them, took their swords and hats and ushered them into the Admiral's office.

"My Lord Admiral, may I present Lieutenants Kelly and MacPherson, Naval officers of the Confederate States of America," said the young French officer (whose English was most remarkable, with a thick nasal accent).

"I greet you well, I'm afraid my English is not good, however may I introduce myself. My name is Jean Berbière." He was a dapper little man in his Admiral's uniform, decorated with a row of medals pinned on his chest, no doubt, as he must have been expecting the sailors.

'What a strange podgy man,' mused Jamie. 'I bet he won those medals fighting the English! - I never did trust the Froggies!'

The Admiral continued "May I say what a remarkable adventure the '*Alabama*' and her crew have experienced in the past two years. I have read about the ship with great interest in the newspapers. It is really amazing the feats performed - sinking, burning and ransacking the Union vessels. From one seafarer to another I must congratulate you and please ask your Captain if I can be of any assistance?"

"You certainly can, sir." Kelly was quick to seize the opportunity. "May I request if we could land the prisoners?"

"That is no problem. They will be released after you have left the port. The town has buzzed with the news about your arrival, in fact it has been telegraphed to the United States Consul in Paris.

Indeed," continued the Admiral, "I think all Europe knows about this famous ship."

"There is also another serious matter, Admiral," said Mike Kelly. "The '*Alabama*' is in a very bad condition, open seams, the copper-plated bottom certainly needs replacing and repairing, her rudder and propeller need attention; in other words - is it possible for the ship to dry dock?"

"Well, regarding the docking," answered the agitated Berbière, "I regret that this is purely a naval base and the docks are controlled by the Government. If a foreign warship were to dock, permission has to be granted by the Principal Naval Overseer, Captain Mario Dvorak, and he is at present enjoying himself, sunning in Biarritz in the south until three weeks time! So will you please convey to your Captain, that you are welcome to berth at the jetty, or anchor in the harbour. Thank you for coming, it's been a pleasure meeting you. Good-day, gentlemen."

He alerted his aide-de-camp, Lieutenant Ramon Bruchez.

"Will you please escort our guests to the door and show them out."

●　●　●

The American Consul in Paris, Tom Ruxton, made contact with the U.S.S. '*Kearsarge*', a black wooden-hulled 1,150 ton Union warship. The 162-manned enemy ship under full steam sailed for Cherbourg. Captain John Winslow was a sick man and was not popular with the Union Government. He was anxious to please his superiors. So on 14th June his warship anchored off Cherbourg.

Captain Winslow sent his senior officer, Eric Steveson, ashore to communicate with the authorities, the idea being to say that he had heard about the prisoners ashore and wanted to augment his crew - however his request was refused. The officer returned to the '*Kearsarge*', which steamed further out and anchored seven miles off the breakwater.

In the meantime Captain Semmes gave most of the crew shore leave, except those engaged in provisions, coaling and preparing the ship for sea.

Mr. Freeman, Jamie, Alex and Carruthers took their personal effects, including booty and savings in trunks. Jamie had a pouchful of pearls and lodged them safely in the vaults in the local Banque d' Affaires, in Rue du Couriats, which was near the quay where the '*Alabama*' was berthed. The four friends, after a drink in the waterfront tavern, returned to the ship.

The next day Captain Semmes realized the French authorities could not supply him with shells and gunpowder - which was needed as '*Alabama*'s' supply was damp - as it would be a breach of neutrality. He decided to take action and assembled and addressed the crew from the aft deck.

"Officers, crewmen, it's only fair to inform you that the enemy ship, under the command of my old friend and former messmate, is waiting off the breakwater to do battle and I have informed him I accept the challenge, with your approval of course, and it will take place tomorrow morning."

He paused to let his challenge sink in, to the astonished crew.

Captain Semmes continued: "I have had a restless night weighing up our prospects and there are three options." He twirled his moustache.

"Firstly: we could attempt an escape and make a run for it with this worn out and weary ship, in desperate need of repair, and sail out to look for another haven."

The crew got a bit restless and talked amongst themselves.

"Secondly: we could abandon our well-loved and victorious ship, here in the harbour, as it has served its purpose."

A loud crescendo of - "No! - No! - No."

"Or, thirdly: we will go out and fight the enemy."

A mighty cheer rang out from every throat - shouting:

"Battle! - Battle! - Battle!"

Little did they realise that in the last couple of days, rumours had spread around the town that the Union warship had heavy anchor chains slung over each side and held in place by boarded wooden slats, to protect the hull. Also her guns were far superior to the '*Alabama*'s.'

Captain Semmes, with strong determination, knowing now he had the full confidence of his crew behind him, continued: "The name of our ship is well known in these waters and in all ports." A pause. "Shall our good name be tarnished by defeat?"

"Never! never!" - the crewmen, now at fever pitch and highly excited, responded lustfully, hurling their caps and hats into the air "long live the Confederacy!"

"Then let us prepare for battle,' continued Semmes.

"We have enough provisions and coal on board; I know this game old ship is loose in every joint, seams open and her copper plate bottom in really bad shape. Never-the-less, let us scrub our decks and polish the brass work, sharpen our swords and cutlasses, secure our rigging and go out in our best dress with flags flying. Tomorrow we will go forth and win the fight. Go and enjoy yourselves, triple grog all round, and then have a good night's sleep. I wish you all good luck and may God protect you."

For days Cherbourg had buzzed with the news of an impending sea battle.

Newspapers spread it across France even to the capital itself and thousands of people had also arrived for the opening of a new civic hall, adding to an excited and large crowd wondering what the morrow would bring!

An English banker and merchant, Anthony Lankshear and family from a stately home near Wigan, in England, was in the harbour aboard his Laird-built yacht '*Deerhound*'. It was within hailing distance of the '*Alabama*'. He invited the officers on board. So on the eve of the battle on the 18th June, Jamie and his colleagues assembled in the luxury lounge and met the family. He asked the owner if he could provide him with pen and paper to write a letter home. Jamie in a quiet corner of the lounge addressed a letter home to Fairview, which Mr. Lankshear assured him would be delivered.

'My dearest Matilda and loving daughters...' Jamie hardly knew where to start.

'You are ever in my thoughts and a few days ago I actually sighted my beloved homeland and prayed that I could land, but the Captain had other ideas and now I am aboard a British yacht in the Port of Cherbourg. The owner, Anthony Lankshear, who lives near Wigan has promised to deliver this letter. Tomorrow our ship is going to steam out and do battle with the U.S.S. '*Kearsarge*'.

Goodness knows what will happen! I can only pray that the Supreme Being will protect me and land me safely once more in your loving arms. If I die in battle, contact the Banque d' Affairs in Rue Du Courlats in Cherbourg. Safely stowed in the vaults is my treasure chest, which I hope will keep you in comfort for the rest of your lives. I hope it will make up for the two missing years I've been away. God bless you all and keep you safe always, I pray. Your loving husband,
Jamie.'

After the party on the '*Deerhound*' the officers returned to the '*Alabama*' by the dinghy. Back on board the crew were in great spirits and in a very merry mood. They were enjoying themselves, aided

300

by the generous 'triple' plus grog all round. For some of them must have had in mind 'for tomorrow we die!'

Jamie, Alex and Carruthers joined Mr. Freeman on the aft deck where the Merseyside lads were gathered and joined in the singing of popular English songs.

These damned young Merseyside rascals, as one American officer had described them, had never even paid a visit to the Southern States of America, but they had sworn allegiance to its flag and were prepared to risk their lives for it. They were lustily singing, led by Charlie Mullard playing his concertina, accompanied by the Irish fiddler, Gow - a made-up English tune: "Dear England, we are bound for home, Our native land, our very own, Soon we shall stand on English soil, After we have sunk the *'Kearsargee'*.

The Merseyside Irishmen took over with their lilting Irish songs and the decks were soon cleared to make way for their stiff rhythmical dancing.

Then the Scots, not to be outdone, were next. Jamie quickly strode on to the polished deck, dragging Carruthers and Alex with him. He shouted to the piper, Ollie Butler: "Give us a reel."

That was it! - the Mackays, MacKenzies, Monroes, Andersons and Doctor MacGregor, took over; yes, the clans gathered and for the next hour they danced their jigs, strathspeys and reels. Then, not to be outdone, it was the Americans who dominated the scene and they concluded with the South's 'National Anthem' - 'Dixie', in which everybody joined. The evening ended with the lone Scottish piper standing near the stern end, silhouetted against a backcloth of a lovely sunset over Cherbourg. He played stirring marches and with the soft lapping of the water against the ships side and in the stillness, concluded with the lament -'Flowers of the forest!'

The decks cleared, and the crewmen, some very intoxicated, staggered or were carried to their hammocks or bunks. One of the last to leave was Jamie.

In the tranquillity of the idyllic June night, with a slight gentle breeze fluttering the flag, he leaned on the stern end and looked north towards the English Channel.

Jamie's eyes were closed, he felt emotional, wondering what tomorrow would bring and whether he would see his homeland again. Hands clasped tightly together he prayed fervently to the Almighty: "Lord, keep me safe this night, and if it be Thy will, deliver me safely to my loved ones, or to Thine Eternal Peace! He wiped his moist eye. "May Thy blessing be on this ship, its Captain and its crew. Amen!"

Chapter 25

After a restless night's sleep, Jamie rose at dawn and after a hurried breakfast descended the steep wooden steps into the engine room, followed by Alex and Carruthers. The shirtless firemen and stokers, their sweaty bodies caked with grime, had been working since the early hours, shovelling the coal from the bunkers into the furnace and firing the boilers. Jamie examined the gauges and was satisfied there was enough steam on the main engines and thanked the men for their efforts.

Mr. Freeman, drawn and looking very serious, seemed nervous and agitated, not his usual self. Indeed who would have been, having heard the most recent news? He descended the wide steps and gathered the engineers around him.

"Let us prepare for sea, gentlemen. I've just been talking to the Captain. The news is very grim. The war is almost lost and as you are aware the Union man-o'-war, the U.S.S. 'Kearsarge' is waiting for us just beyond the breakwater and we are just about to engage her and win the battle." He paused, thinking.

"Let us turn to, man your stations, and, may I add, good luck."

"Are the engines ready, Jamie?"

"Ready, sir, in fact the firemen and stokers have been working since dawn, getting up steam." He tapped the pressure gauge.

"The correct steam pressure is on the engines."

"Very well, I'll inform the Captain."

Semmes was standing by the wheel, his head bowed, when Freeman approached. "Engines available, sir."

"Thank you, Chief."

The 'Alabama' was berthed at the quay wall, the Captain and officers were standing in a group on the main deck by the main gangway. Semmes addressed the First Lieutenant: "Is everybody on board, Mr. Kelly?"

"Yes, sir, except Midshipman Goldrein who is not permitted on board, sir, by the French authorities. Also as you are aware the Paymasters, Mr.Unsworth and Mr. Fisher, you directed ashore, to ensure the funds and payroll for the crew were kept in safe custody, which they have attended to, in the Banque d' Affaires. Actually, sir, if you look where I am pointing you will see they are standing on the quay, near that bollard."

"Thank you, Mr. Kelly."

The Sanctus bell could be heard peeling, reminding the towns-people to pause and pray as the sacraments were being blessed by the Priest. The bell attracted the silent, curious crowd, standing on the nearby cliff and milling on the quay, who thronged to see the impending battle that might take place between these two foreign ships. The news had spread quickly.

Captain Semmes, being a devout Roman Catholic, heard the muffled bell being tolled, calling the faithful to worship. He doffed his hat and knelt down, his head in his hands, and prayed to the Almighty for forgiveness for his past sins.

The officers and crew noticed his attitude of prayer and one by one followed suit, some kneeling, some with clasped hands and heads bowed, each filled with their silent thoughts and prayers.

The Captain stood up, and Jamie, who had seen what was happening, went to his bunk and retrieved his Bible from under his pillow and handed it to the Captain. He thumbed through it to a passage and with quiet reverence read from Psalm 107:

"They that go down to the sea in ships, that do business in great waters; these see the works of the Lord, and His wonders in the deep... He maketh the storm a calm, so that the waves thereof are still. Then they are glad because they are quiet; so He bringeth them unto their desired haven."

He handed the Bible back to Jamie. Following the reading the Captain continued:

"Gentlemen, shall we conclude with the prayer our Saviour taught His disciples. With bowed heads the officers and crew quietly and with reverence said the Lord's Prayer; even the crowds on the quay acknowledged the fact that a solemn act of worship was taking place by the men of the 'Alabama'.

"Very well, gentlemen," the Captain braced himself as he addressed the crew.

"Today we meet the enemy; I have despatched a challenge to Captain Winslow of the 'Kearsarge'. You will recall our last sea battle was on 5th January 1863, against the U.S.S. 'Hatteras'; that's a year and a half ago. We have been unable to repair our beloved ship, our powder has deteriorated and we have been unable to replenish our stock." He looked round the silent crew.

"We have sailed around the world and have destroyed one half of the enemy's commerce; that is quite an achievement, gentlemen. I wish to thank you and I'm sure you all feel very proud under our

303

flag of the Confederate States of America. We are now in the English Channel and to some of you, home waters.

All European eyes will be watching us and we have a good reputation to live up to, so let us uphold the flag and what it stands for - Liberty, Justice and Peace for all, whatever their race, colour. or creed. Let us not forget our ship's motto - 'God helps those who help themselves.' Go to your quarters and may God go with you." He saluted his crew - which was returned.

"Good luck, gentlemen." He turned to the First Mate and commanded "Cast off, Mr. Kelly."

At nine o'clock on this bright, beautiful Sunday morning, the *'Alabama'* slipped her moorings and eased her way from the quay watched by a silent crowd who were wondering whether they should have cheered - some waved.

Large crowds gathered on the walls and fortifications of the harbour as well as on the quay. The upper stories of houses were crowded with eager people, all wondering who would win the battle; and most were sympathetic to the underdogs - the Southern Confederates. The *'Couronne'*, a French iron-clad frigate, tacked slowly behind the *'Alabama'* as she headed out of the western entrance of the harbour, passing the Fort du Romet on the port point. Also six French pilot boats and the Birkenhead-built yacht the *'Deerhound'*. Captain Lankshear watched as the *'Alabama'* rounded the breakwater and headed towards the awaiting *'Kearsarge'* positioned seven miles to the north-west where she had dropped anchor.

It was half past ten on this idyllic June day. In the *'Alabama's'* boiler room the stokers were working furiously shovelling coal into the furnaces, urged on by Jamie, the Second Engineer, to get a good head of steam on the boilers. All hands were at quarters. The batteries were cut loose, the yards slung in chains and stoppers prepared for the swivelled heavy guns. The magazines and shell rooms were opened up. Captain Francis drilled the crew in hand loading the shells and transporting them from the gunroom to the nine-inch and Blakely guns. The scrubbed decks were sanded down and water tubs were at the ready to swill the decks. The surgery was washed down and the Doctors and their staff were prepared to carry out operations once the wounded arrived.

The smartly dressed Officers, swords at their side, and the neatly dressed crew, were standing by as the Captain addressed them from the bridge:

"The enemy is yonder and in the next hour we will be engaging the *'Kearsarge'* and I am confident we are going to show the world that we will win this decisive battle and uphold our flag." He stroked his moustache, a nervous habit!

"God bless you all, good luck - stand by battle stations."

It took three quarters of an hour for the *'Alabama'* to steam within battle distance of her enemy. The alerted *'Kearsarge'* suddenly turned and headed straight for the *'Alabama'* and then tacked on starboard bow.

Captain Townsend, in charge of the midship gunners, gave the order to fire and the hundred-pounder pivot gun went into action when the vessels were one mile apart.

"Full steam ahead, give me everything you've got," yelled Semmes, which was relayed to Mr. Freeman in the engine room.

Within five hundred yards both ship's batteries went into action and to prevent colliding, both gave 'hard to port'. From then on the action was fought around a common centre which eventually became a circle.

The officers yelled their orders above the din and the screaming of the wounded. "Bring up more shells," shouted Captain Francis, who was in charge of the Blakely guns. The sweaty gunners were stripped to the waist and coated black with the powder. Their movements were slow, not having had any regular battle drill.

In the boiler room Jamie and Alex replaced two of the exhausted stokers to shovel the coal into the hungry furnaces.

Both ships, enveloped in black smoke, circled each other in a grim cat-and-mouse game.

The spectators thronging the Cherbourg hillside could not see the two ships, but could hear the muffled sound of guns and observe the clouds of black smoke that floated over the English Channel.

Captain Semmes, standing by the mizzen mast, observed the action through his telescope. He called loudly through the trumpet above the din and shouting:

"Mr. Kelly - use solid shot. Our shots are hitting the side of the enemy ship and falling into the sea."

The Captain had not realized it, or had ignored the warning, but it was strongly rumoured around the town, that the *'Kearsarge'* had chain armour on both ship's sides which was hidden by wooden slats. Semmes thought the failure was due to defective ammunition so he alternated between shot and shell. The two ships were deep in the throes of battle about a quarter of a mile distant. After fifteen minutes of ineffectual firing, a shell from the *'Alabama'* ripped through the bulwarks of the *'Kearsarge'* and exploded on the quarter deck. Another tore through into the sternpost, violently shaking the ship's timber, but it failed to explode - due to the defective ammunition.

'Good aiming,' thought Semmes, watching through his telescope - 'must congratulate the gunners.'

This seemed to Semmes to be the turning point of the battle, and he was sensing a victory, when suddenly a shot from the *'Kearsarge's'* eleven-inch guns smashed the *'Alabama's'* steering gear. Another exploded near the aft pivot gun, killing and wounding half the gun crew. Semmes shouted and swore as a piece of shrapnel hit his right arm. He staggered with the shock of being hit, grabbing his arm, and watched the blood ooze through his jacket and onto his left hand. He leaned against the mast, stunned. Another enemy shell tore into the *'Alabama'* beneath the water line, collapsing a bunker on top of and injuring, two firemen, Finley and Williams.

The hot, steam-shrouded engine room shook when the coal bunker was hit.

'Go to the stoke hole, Alex, and see if you can be of any assistance. You can also go and help, Carruthers," yelled the sweaty and grimy Mr. Freeman.

"You go on deck, Jamie, I'll be all right on my own."

Alex and Carruthers were met with water seeping into the black-smoked stoke hole and discovered the two firemen in a semi-conscious state, lying covered in the coal-soaked water, which was now rising quite rapidly. They hoisted Finley and Williams on to the cluttered deck. The noise was deafening. Dead and wounded lay everywhere and shouting intermingled with the cries of the helpless and the wounded and with the loud banging of the guns. The firemen recovered sufficiently to replace two wounded gunners, Kirwin and Bill Armstrong, who made their way crawling across the sanded, bloody deck, to the crowded surgery, where they were attended to by the bloodsoaked-gowned, Doctor MacGregor.

Alex returned to the engine room and informed Mr. Freeman that they were losing steam pressure and that he had opened the exhaust valves. The eleven-inch shells from the *'Kearsarge'* did enormous damage, being aimed with precision on, or below, the water line.

The spanker gaff was shot away, taking with it the Confederate flag. It was immediately replaced by Bosun Bellew who climbed the mizzen mast and hoisted the Southern colours.

The enemy's sharp, quick firing, commanded by the senior officer, Lieutenant Bill Stephenson, ably supported by the Gunner's Mate, Gerald O'Toole, was kept up, and the *'Alabama's'* quarter-deck was soon littered with the dead and scattered limbs. The First

Lieutenant grabbed Jamie's arm and ordered him to throw the limbs overboard and clear the decks of the dead. Jamie felt sick performing this gruesome task, but it had to be done. With bullets whistling around him, he then swilled the decks down from the nearby water buckets.

Three shots successfully hit the '*Alabama's*' eight-inch gun which was positioned forward of the bridge structure. The first swept off three gunners, the second killed Captain Towsend, and wounded three soldiers. The third killed the Second Mate and wounded three seamen. The gun carriage was wrecked. Powerful Ray Ryan threw it overboard. The engine room began to flood slowly after a shell had penetrated the hull just below the water line. Jamie, when he heard the news dashed below and found a bewildered and shocked Mr. Freeman standing knee deep, shrouded in steam from the hissing engine. He assisted him up the wooden steps to the main deck, where he slumped against the skylight.

Jamie returned to the engine room and opened up the steam-hissing, main exhaust valve. He then made his way, wading through water and floating debris to the smoke-filled deserted boiler room and shut down the furnaces. Returning back to the deck by the main wheel, he reported to the Captain that the engine and boiler room were flooding rapidly.

"Mr. Kelly," summoned Semmes, "go below, search the ship for damages and report back to me immediately.

"Come back with me, Jamie, as you know your way around down below."

They went forward and descended into the devastation and carnage in the wardroom which was serving as an emergency surgery. The shocked Doctor Edwards was staring, mouth open in a state of shock, at what had been his operating table occupied by a seaman. It had been swept away! The water was slowly penetrating through a small hole on the port side. Jamie assisted the Doctor to the ladder, wading through the dirty water with floating objects brushing against his legs. Edwards collapsed, so Jamie hoisted him over his shoulder and carried him to the forward end of the ship and laid him down propped against the towing post.

Captain Semmes realised his ship was doomed after hearing the report from the First Lieutenant. He ordered him to head the crippled ship as best he could to the shores of France. The vessel pivoted to port, righting the ship and the thirty-two pounders were able to continue firing. The head sails were hoisted, by a very weary crew, and the helm righted itself and by hauling aft on the trysail it very slowly commenced drifting to the visible coastline. The aft thirty-two-pounder was abandoned and the gunners rushed to the pivot gun to assist the lone Captain Francis who amid the surrounding dead bodies and the moaning wounded, continued firing the thirty-two-pounder.

The ship was now lolling in the waves upright, with its stern low, and it continued heading slowly for the shore. Black smoke and hissing steam were beginning to envelop the deck through the vents. The situation looked grim and hopeless to Semmes as he gripped his wounded right arm. Kelly reported: "We are now making water fast, sir, and going down by the stern."

"Cease firing, Mr. Kelly, and prepare to abandon ship. Hoist down our colours and keep them safe, we are doomed and have lost the battle. Get the wounded into the boats and inform the enemy our condition." Kelly commanded the Bosun: "Launch the dinghy and contact the '*Kearsarge*', informing them we are sinking and abandoning the '*Alabama*' and require assistance for the wounded."

His orders were duly carried out and Jamie was handed the Confederate flag by the Bosun just before he left to negotiate with the enemy ship. He carefully folded it, tied it with rope and secured it on his back. As the dinghy, manned by Jones and Hedgecock, rowed towards the '*Kearsarge*' showing the white flag.

Semmes was alarmed when a further five shots were fired at the stricken and sinking '*Alabama*', even though she had taken down her colours, which was a sign of surrender. He looked up, bewildered, to see if the flag was still flying. He was confused, he could not believe his eyes - firing on a helpless sinking ship - and thought: 'It does not seem a charitable attitude, not what we were taught at naval college!'

On the '*Kearsarge*', Captain Winslow thought Semmes was up to his usual tricks by exchanging flags and so he decided to continue firing and those were the last five shots Semmes heard!

The dinghy returned to the '*Alabama*', but none came from the '*Kearsarge*'.

Semmes ordered the available boats from the aft deck, which was now awash. The two Doctors, Edwards and MacGregor, assisted the wounded into the boats, helped by the able-bodied seamen and headed for the "*Kearsarge*".

'Surely the enemy would show some mercy!' thought Semmes. The order was given to don lifejackets, grab spars and anything that would float and jump into the sea.

When the decks were cleared, save for the dead, Captain Semmes, holding his wounded arm, went to the wheel and read the ship's motto - 'God helps those who help themselves.' He gave a wry grin. The sea was lapping around his ankles. Jamie looked towards Mr. Freeman, who was supported by Alex and Carruthers, and with a sly grin acknowledged that so far they were still alive.

"Gentlemen," Kelly ordered, "grab whatever you can and jump into the sea and head for that nearby yacht. Do not swim for the '*Kearsarge*' - you will be taken prisoners."

Semmes was in pain and it was with difficulty that he tried to remove his naval jacket, but he was assisted by Captain Francis and Lieutenant Bill Armstrong, who removed the Captain's boots and used the laces for tying them around his neck. They then eased Semmes into the sea which was a turmoil. Some men were swimming to the safety of the boats that had come to rescue them, but the anguish of those drowning could be heard as Jamie swam towards the yacht. He noticed Dave Finley was in difficulties and went to his rescue and finally helped him into a nearby boat, with the help of Brian Leeson.

'I wonder where my friends are?' he thought. 'Ah! There's our big look-out man, swimming strongly on his back, and supporting two men who appear unconscious. Thank goodness, Alex and Carruthers between them are helping Mr. Freeman, and the Captain is also heading for the yacht. Kelly, Tyler, Briggs, Butler, Kirwin, Schmechel - I would not be around today...he saved my life!"

Francis swam alongside. "Are you all right, Jamie?" he gasped.

"I'm all right - look -" indicating towards a man who was just disappearing beneath the waves.

Francis swam and dived and came up with the spluttering fireman and at the same time Mullard swam up and between them they assisted Williams towards the yacht. All around the survivors was floating debris, flotsam, but most were heading for the safety of the friendly boats that had come to their rescue.

The '*Alabama*' was settling stern-first in the English Channel. Semmes had reached out to be pulled into the '*Deerhound*', the English yacht, when he paused to take a last look at his beloved ship and just before she disappeared all eyes turned, each man with his own thoughts as the '*Alabama*', just before she disappeared, thrust her bow proudly into the air as though bidding farewell to the men whose home she had been for two years. The Southern raider then descended rapidly to her last resting place, where she was buried safe from the Northern Yankees.

The French frigate the '*Couronne*' and the pilot boats came immediately upon the scene and commenced rescuing the men still struggling in the cold waters.

One pilot boat removed all the floating drowned bodies. They had died bravely, some supporting a strange flag, but most enjoyed the adventurous life and the spoils of war, but did not live long enough to enjoy its pleasures. Other men were rescued clinging to spars, few had time to don lifejackets. Most of the crew had learned to swim - Semmes had seen to that - except Ramidios. The faithful Captain's steward, when he heard the call to 'abandon ship', had left the Captain's side, gone to his Master's cabin and retrieved two packages. The cabin was shattered and a devastated wreck but there among the floating debris was the Captain's favourite painting of the '*Alabama*'. He was reaching out to retrieve it when the ship gave a violent shudder. Ramidios returned quickly and gave the two packages to his Captain, who in turn handed one to Jamie and the other to Captain Francis, two of his trusted crewmen, for safe keeping. The quiet man turned and unnoticed by anybody disappeared into the Channel, never to be seen again. He couldn't swim, he feared the water.

The sun was just dipping over the horizon when the last of the survivors had been rescued from amongst the flotsam of the now still and silent waters off Cherbourg. The Bosun, Ray Hedgecock and his friend Jones had managed to elude the grasping hands of the Yankees when they tried to pull them out of the water. They were lucky as they would have probably spent the rest of their lives in some jail.

Tony Lankshear, Captain of the '*Deerhound*', had taken a very dim view of the time loss and rescue attempts from the '*Kearsarge*'. He rescued as many as he could and also encouraged the French ships to do the same. He immediately headed for Southampton with forty-two rescued and grateful crew members from the '*Alabama*'. Captain Semmes after having his arm bandaged by Mrs. Lankshear, a trained nurse, was stretched out in the yacht's luxurious lounge with some of the rescued crewmen, including Alex, Jamie, Carruthers and Captain Francis. The lounge was crowded, some sitting, standing or lying on the thick carpet, wherever they could find a place in this large yacht, owned by the wealthy Lancashire cotton broker, Mr. Lankshear, a pleasant, tall and well-made man in his early fifties. A happy family man who enjoyed the company of his wife and two boys, who were on holiday on board his yacht. It was only natural the two boys, Colin and Duncan, were very excited, having been first class witnesses to the naval battle.

Tony Lankshear, in chatting to some of the crew members remarked: "We were on a leisurely holiday sailing from Cowes in the Isle of Wight when we came over just by chance to Cherbourg for extra provisions. We had heard of this famous Confederate raider, the '*Alabama*', reading all about it in our newspapers and how the Civil War was being fought, but little did we suspect on this lovely Sunday until all the people milling around the waterfront attracted our attention. It was the boys who learned and reported back to us - a battle was to take place! We were supposed to have attended the local English Church, but the lads changed all that and hence we steamed out after you, following the pilot boats and the French frigate, the '*Couronne*'. We hoved to off the breakwater and watched the one-and-a-half-hour battle. When we saw how badly the '*Alabama*' was damaged, we came to your rescue with the other hovering ships.

"Just as well you did," butted in Captain Francis. "We would not be sitting here, but on our way back to America and probably, being English, we would be executed. How grateful we are! I can only thank you very sincerely."

"What annoyed me and made me very angry," continued Lankshear, "was the fact that the '*Kearsarge*' did not seem to have any rescue intentions, until I passed within hailing distance and commanded the Captain to launch his boats and rescue the wounded and those fighting for survival in the sea. I can assure you I had no intentions of handing you over as prisoners to the '*Kearsarge*'.

When we arrive in England you will find courtesy, hospitality and safety in my homeland." He paused as though waiting for a question, but the men were too weary, most had already fallen asleep after their bitter experiences.

"If there is anything you require, please don't hesitate to ask and we wish you well, whatever the future may hold."

'Whatever the future may hold,' thought Jamie. 'My war is over, I am desperate to get away from it all, to be with my loved ones, but it is gratifying to know I will not be returning empty-handed.' He was sitting on the floor, so he put his head in his hands, silently wept and went into a restless sleep. The '*Deerhound*' landed at the quay safely in Southampton and the Captain of the '*Alabama*', before departing, thanked Tony Lankshear for rescuing forty-two men from a watery grave.

There were fond farewells, handshakes and hugging as they embraced each other - what comradeship! - each with his own thoughts and memories and the friendship and trust that had developed during the last two years.

As Jamie stood on English soil, he prayed fervently to the Almighty, thanking Him with tears welling in his eyes for returning him safety to his native land. He turned and saluted the '*Deerhound's*' St. George's flag, fluttering proudly at the stern end, ever mindful that if it was not for the '*Deerhound*' and her crew he would not be standing in dear old England.

Mr. Freeman, Jamie, Alex and Carruthers were of one mind. Just like they had been for the last two years. They had practical minds

311

like most engineers, so they went to the nearest tavern to have a drink and discuss their future, whilst the rest of the officers and crew dispersed and went their separate ways. Mr. Freeman, being the senior, immediately took command, but Jamie interrupted him before he could speak, having his own ideas.

"Might I suggest," retorted Jamie, "that I return to Cherbourg, I understand Mr. Lankshear wants to return to resume his holiday, so if he will take me I will recover our trunks and, all being well, say, in about ten days' time, we will all be united at Fairview in Toxteth and what a happy surprise, when our loved ones open our trunks! It will be like opening Pandora's box. What do you think of my idea?" The three other pals, feeling very relaxed, thought it was a good idea.

"Sounds all right to me," remarked Mr. Freeman. "But I will go with you, as I think four of those heavy trunks will be too much for one person," and with a laugh, "not that I don't trust you, Jamie lad, but you know the size of those trunks, about three feet long by two feet wide, and they are quite heavy."

"That's a good idea," chipped in Carruthers. " I'll go along with that," said Alex. "I'm sure we will all have a very happy reunion to look forward to in the near future, back in Liverpool. The four companions of two years' adventure, stretching nearly around the world, settled down for a good meal to be washed down with old English ale.

They had much to talk about, discussing their adventures, the friends they had won and lost. Then they retired to a well-earned night's rest in the comfort of comfortable beds, all with separate thoughts and dreams about the future.

Next morning Mr. Freeman and Jamie visited the '*Deerhound*' and learned from Tony Lankshear that they were departing on the mid-day tide, returning to Cherbourg, and would be happy to have them on board. In fact the boys, Colin and Duncan, were overjoyed as they would hear more about the '*Alabama's*' adventures.

They returned to the 'Fisherman's Wharf' tavern, and after final drinks with Alex and Carruthers, made their farewells with the companions of their former toils and returned to the "*Deerhound*".

The yacht cast off as scheduled. Alex and Carruthers waved their friends goodbye. The yacht, its sails fluttering in the breeze, headed down the Sound, passed the Needles off the Isle of Wight and into the English Channel.

There was a slight breeze and after dampening down the furnaces, Lankshear hoisted full sail and made good progress towards the French coast.

Mr. Freeman was keen to see the steam yacht's propulsion and descended the companionway accompanied by the Lankshear's youngest son, eleven-year-old Duncan. He began asking the 'Alabama's' Chief Engineer all kinds of questions.

"Is this engine as big as the `Alabama's'?"

"No, it is only a small engine, used only for getting this large yacht in and out of ports and for berthing and then they look to the sails."

"Were the sails bigger?"

"Could she sail faster?"

"No, the 'Alabama' had two horizontal steam engines, but I can tell you, Duncan, this engine and the ones built in the 'Alabama' were built in the same engine shop, next to each other in the Birkenhead shipyard. The boilers were also manufactured in the yard. I remember this yacht being constructed at the very end of the slipway, near the water's edge as it was obviously much smaller, and easier to launch than the larger schooners higher up on the slipway!" He paused for a moment and with a smile, tapped a pressure gauge.

"The 'Alabama' had a new design of propeller fitted, that could be lifted out of the water and housed in a small compartment, also the funnel could be lowered." He filled his pipe and lit it; the Chief was getting into full stride!

"Gosh!" said the bewildered child, "why was that, Mr. Freeman?"

"Well, it had the effect of streamlining the ship so it could sail faster and as you know, we would be looking for extra knots!" He paused to relight his pipe. "It also had an unusually large total area of sail - 14,970 square feet which includes the forward and main mast and the mizzen mast."

Duncan didn't understand a word he was saying, so he butted in:

"It must have been a fast ship?"

"Yes, it could travel at 13 knots under sail and steam."

In the meantime in the lounge, Jamie was in conversation with the sixteen-year-old son Colin, who wanted to know who started the Civil War in America? How was it progressing? Was it nearly over? Who was winning?

Mrs. Lankshear laughingly butted in:

"Hold on there, son, Jamie is very tired - go easy on the questions."

"It is no trouble. I know Colin is interested, and perhaps you and Tony might also be, seeing the yacht is in the safe hands of the helmsman, Peter Booth. Four years ago, Colin, Abraham Lincoln was elected President of the United States of America, when the country was split between slave states and free states. In the South, slaves were believed to be essential for raising cotton, the principal crop, which is considered by the way to be the principal import to England, especially Lancashire. I don't need to tell you this, being Lancastrians yourselves, and you will probably realise that is how the '*Alabama*' came to be built in Birkenhead, as Merseyside supported the South." "Indeed, we are well aware, now the mills are being closed down and people thrown out of work and are starving," butted in Lankshear in a loud voice.

"Colin, I see you have a map of the United States!" suddenly butted in Jamie.

"As you might have read, certain states broke away from the Union. On December 20th 1860, South Carolina was the first to break away, and was soon joined by Mississippi," indicating on the map. "Then Florida, Alabama - yes, our ship was named after this state - Georgia, Louisiana and later Texas. The Southern States met, and in early 1861 elected Jefferson Davis, Provisional President of the Confederate States of America." Jamie paused, thinking, and then resumed by saying, as if in a trance: "August 24th. 1862 is a date I can well remember; I swore allegiance to the Confederate flag and its constitution and it was sad to see the British colours lowered on the '*Alabama*'. "There was a silence, which was suddenly interrupted by Peter Booth shouting down the companionway hatch:

"You had all better come on deck, hurry! According to my chart, we are passing over the spot on the port beam where the '*Alabama*' sank!"

They all leaned over the rail watching silently the watery grave of the heroic ship which rested peacefully below, in the silence of the deep. Mr. Freeman doffed his hat and offered a short prayer. "Bless our brave comrades, may they rest in peace."

"Amen - Amen," was the quiet reply.

Nearer and nearer sailed the '*Deerhound*' towards Cherbourg.

She skirted around the breakwater passing the Arsenal docks, the fort on the starboard beam and headed for the wharf and finally tied up and berthed on the wharf.

Crowds soon gathered around on the quay, watching the now famous yacht with interest.

Mr. Freeman and Jamie bade the Lankshear family farewell and thanked them for their hospitality.

The two friends, now dressed in casual seamen's clothing, made their way down the gangway, pushing through the crowd, answering many questions.

Walking up the Rue du Courlets to the Banque d'Affaires they presented themselves to the Bank Manager, Monsieur Berbière, after going through the introduction formalities.

314

Mr. Freeman addressed the Bank Manager: "Sir, we are the Englishmen who deposited wooden locked identified trunks with you for safe keeping. I did mention at the time, we were naval officers, who served on the ill-fated '*Alabama*'.

"Mon Dieu, I remember you well," remarked M. Berbière.

The Chief Engineer continued: "May we now take possession and I also have letters for the same request from Mr. Carruthers and Alex Mackenzie."

"Certainly, Monsieurs, I do remember Alex very well. Although I speak and understand English," he gave a chuckle, "I could hardly understand Monsieur MacKenzie. Where do you say he was born?"

"The Outer Hebrides, those remote islands off the north-west coast of Scotland and they all speak a strange language called Gaelic and so they rarely converse in English."

"That's very interesting, and now to business."

'Thank goodness,' thought Jamie. 'A good job I didn't open my mouth, we would have been here a few days!'

The Manager summoned two of his assistants, Jaques Martini and his son, Stephano, and addressed them in French:

"Go to the vaults, open the large safe and you will see four labelled trunks - take care, they are heavy - and bring them to my office."

Turning to Mr. Freeman, the dapper M. Berbière remarked: "These are your four trunks - where would you like them depositing?"

"If you could please provide transport, we are staying overnight at the 'Wharf' tavern and we shall be returning to England as soon as we can arrange passage, and I would like to thank you and your staff, for all your help and assistance, Monsieur Berbière."

"I am only too pleased to see you have survived that terrible sea battle. I was actually standing on the cliffs amongst a large crowd and all we heard in the distance was the muffled noise of gunfire and clouds of smoke and then a deathly hush. I felt very emotional and upset, but I'm so pleased to see you alive, and may you safely return to your native land." A handshake and au revoir.

The trunks were loaded on to a cart by the strongly-built bank clerk, Stephano, ably assisted by his father, Jacques. Freeman and Jamie assisted in guiding the cart through the narrow crowded, cobbled streets and deposited them safely inside their already booked rooms in the tavern. Jamie tipped the bank clerks, thanked them and shook their hands.

The next business was arranging passage to Liverpool, which Mr. Freeman managed satisfactorily through a friend he knew, Ronald Downing, a shipping agent in the town.

Following their evening meal and drinks, Jamie left the pipe-smoking Mr. Freeman with his dreams and made his way along the sea wall, which gave way to the narrow cliff path, and passing the high-walled Fort du Romet he continued along the high cliff edge, to the Pointe et Fort de Querqueville.

It was quiet and peaceful on the balmy June evening, the only sounds seagulls squawking overhead and the surging of the sea hitting the cliffs below. Jamie was standing alone, looking towards the west.

He was reflecting and thoughtful about the past two years, hectic events, as he looked across the English Channel. He could almost see, hear and picture the last scene about nine miles out, beyond the breakwater, of the decisive battle of the warships in mortal combat, when the '*Alabama*' slowly sank, and he was plunged into the raging sea and fought for survival in the water and was surrounded by debris and flotsam and his drowned comrades; how the Supreme Being held out His hand, took a firm grip and rescued him to safety aboard the '*Deerhound's*' dinghy.

Yes, he had to thank the Almighty for his safety as he looked with tears streaming down his face, towards his native land.

HE THEN WATCHED THE SUN SET OVER THE CHERBOURG CHANNEL.